THE BRIEF
HAUNTING OF
RASPBERRY HILL

A Crabapple Yarns Mystery

Jaime Marsman

ALSO BY
JAIME MARSMAN...

A Crabapple Yarns Mystery Series:

Book One: The Knitting Fairy

THE BRIEF HAUNTING OF RASPBERRY HILL

A Crabapple Yarns Mystery

Jaime Marsman

PRAISE FOR
"THE KNITTING FAIRY"

What do you get when you combine a novice to the world of fiber working in a yarn shop with the owner, a mysterious, fairy-tale inspired character? You get Jaime Marsman's magical, whimsical story of "The Knitting Fairy" which is sure to be enjoyed by knitters everywhere. **Penny Sitler, Executive Director of The Knitting Guild Association (TKGA), tkga.com**

"Whenever an author combines stories and stitches, I smile. Jaime Marsman has done just that in her new book, 'The Knitting Fairy'. With a nod to Agatha Christie as well as fairy tales about Brownies who appear when no-one is looking to complete domestic tasks for those in need, Marsman has crafted a tale that combines mystery, fun, and knitting. Filled with phrases like, "she kitchnered Old Mrs. Harrison's toes together," "Oh, honey, let's go home and cable," and "as Louise reached into her small knitting bag, I had a distinct feeling of foreboding," knitters will find themselves laughing through each chapter, wondering who the knitting fairy could be!" **Donna Druchunas, author of six knitting books including Arctic Lace, sheeptoshawl.com**

"Amidst the characters, humour, and mystery is the fun of witnessing a non-knitter's assumptions and observations turn to affection and obsession. It made me wish to be a new knitter again!" **Sally Melville, sallymelvilleknits.com, sallymelvilleknits.blogspot.com**

"A page turning mystery with yarn shops and knitting - what else could you ask for!" **Carol Feller, Author of Contemporary Irish Knits**

A heartwarming and witty novel, guaranteed to make you smile. Molly Stevenson's new found love of yarn brings her comfort and friendship but leaves her with many unanswered questions. Appealing to the non-knitter as much as the knitaholic, this wonderful and enthralling mystery detailing the weird and wonderful goings on in Crabapple Yarns knitting store, will have you totally hooked." **UK Hand Knitting Association, ukhandknitting.com**

"It is obvious that Ms. Marsman is writing about what she knows: books, libraries and yarns. I really enjoyed following Molly's adventures in learning to knit and solving mysteries. The Knitting Fairy always keeps you guessing!" **Alissa Barton, Owner, Knitting Fairy Yarn Studio, knittingfairy.com**

"What I loved best about The Knitting Fairy is how perfectly Jaime captured that as knitters we actually fall in love with knitting. She reminded me of the butterflies, excitement, and joy of falling in love with my first skein of luxury yarn, falling in love with perfectly tensioned stitches and the euphoria of completing my first project. Not only did The Knitting Fairy remind me of why I fell in love with knitting in the first place, it made me pause (as a deadline-driven professional) to think that I still need to stop and smell the roses from time to time." **Kristin Omdahl, Author of 6 knitting books, styledbykristin.com**

The Brief Haunting of Raspberry Hill

Cover designed by Jaime Marsman

Jaime Marsman https://www.facebook.com/JaimeMarsman2/

Printed in the United States of America

First Printing: December, 2018

Thank you, God.

KNITTING

The Merriam-Webster definition:**

- To form by interlacing yarn or thread in a series of connected loops with needles
- To tie together

The definition that should be in the dictionary:

- The mystifying and magical process whereby linear fiber is twisted and reshaped by needles of varying sizes not only knitting fabric together, but hearts and minds as well resulting in lifetime friendships, a sense of self-satisfaction and personal identity.

**knit. 2012. In *Merriam-Webster.com*. Retrieved June 22, 2012, from http://www.merriam- webster.com/dictionary/knit

CHAPTER 1

Grandma Rose was a corker. At least that's what my mom always said. "Your Grandma Rose was a corker," she would say… and then her lips would get very thin and rather white. It didn't matter when I asked or how I asked…the reply would be the same… "Your Grandma Rose was a corker." And that's about all she would ever say. She never said it with a great deal of warmth either. It was almost like she would have preferred using a different word but didn't quite dare.

The only other thing I knew about Grandma Rose was that she had died when I was a baby. Yep. Died when I was a baby. You heard me, right? Died when I was a baby. Let's recap, shall we? What are the two things that I knew about Grandma Rose? Yes, you are correct… she was a corker who died when I was a baby. This was probably why it was such a shock when I got the letter yesterday informing me, in solemn and legal tones, that Rose Whittman passed away two weeks ago.

You know how sometimes people say you should be sitting when you hear bad or surprising news? I always thought that was a bit ridiculous. Like your legs would ever really give out on you just from unexpected news. Until, of course, I read the letter and my rear end and the ground met in a flurry of movement that I don't even quite remember. I had to re-read the letter twice and then check that it was addressed to me, Natalie Wolcott. Which, of course, it was. Besides letting me know that my corker of a grandmother had died, the letter also hinted at an inheritance, which I was invited to come and discuss at my convenience. No rush. I just had to be there by Thursday. The letter had arrived on Wednesday. How they even found me at all was a mystery. The letter also suggested that this might take a few days or so and to plan accordingly. Looking back, I often wonder why this never struck me as strange.

I confronted Celia about this – over the phone, of course – I never knew where Celia ever was at any given point in time… but I should have known. Celia lied about everything. Why not lie about this too? Of course, she prefers not to call it "lying" but rather an alternate viewpoint of reality.

Whatever.

Which is how she explained to me that Grandma Rose, hadn't, indeed, been "physically" dead all my life – just dead to her. Wow. That really made it all better. I'm not sure (because, as you know, the fiery red-haze of anger burns your eyes and dulls your senses) but I think it's just possible that I hung up on her. Loudly. Oh well. It wouldn't be the first time. And, I'm sure that it won't be the last – if I ever speak to her again, that is.

As a child, I had longed for a bit of family. Well… I did have some, but you don't really want to know about them (think Celia – only ten times worse). That's not the kind of family I meant. How I longed for a dear, sweet, bespectacled grandmother who sat in a rocking chair and baked cookies. Someone who would hug me and say, "Oh, you dear child…" you know… a relative like that. Not that I was a dear child, but it would have been so nice to have at least one person think that I was. I knew that those type of relatives existed, because they were on TV (a constant companion and valuable source of information). Celia loved to drag me all over the country - wherever her current "winds of inspiration" were blowing. Which, in reality, meant, "Wherever the guy she was currently interested in wanted to go." I forget how many places I have lived. But, it was not all bad, and I am now very wise and I can tell you with great authority – that the food at greasy spoons tastes the same in every city, town and village… motels all smell the same… apartments with mold and mice are always more affordable than those without and, if you get carsick easily at age 2… you'll still get carsick easily at age 32. And, no, just because you get carsick does not mean you get to sit in the front seat – unless, of course, there's no one more interesting in the car than you (I can assure you that this does not happen often).

Living in Oak Harbor had been a radically new way of life for me. I was born with a deep-seated craving for a steady home, and yet, after college, I had found it difficult sticking to one place. For more panic-stricken months and years than I want to recall, I had feared that I was doomed to remain an eternal wanderer – a miserable eternal wanderer –always wondering (with a sickening feeling of dread) if, indeed, they really had changed the sheets in the motel room (sometimes you were lucky if there even were sheets- and I've never been able to decide which was worse.) But, then…. then I had found Oak Harbor. Or maybe Oak Harbor found me. I had literally driven into the city and fallen in love. It was so quaint. And cozy. And cheerful. Strangely enough, it was a little lacking in oaks, but other than that, it was perfect. I had decided, right then and there, that I was going to live here forever and ever. Amen.

It had been a big decision, and there had been more than one internal debate on whether this was the best course of action for my life. After all, if you have been brought up to only know one way of living, it is harder than you might believe to give up this way of life – even if you think you want to.

So, this morning, as I loaded up my wee little car with my suitcase and bare essentials, I was more than a bit sorry to leave Oak Harbor– even temporarily. It was the closest thing I had ever known to a true home, and for the first time in my life, I felt like I belonged somewhere. True, I had no real friends and I still had no permanent job, but hey, living in one place for more than three weeks? This, my friend, was progress.

My landlady had seen me off. She had hugged me and told me to let her know if I should "need anything." I had almost laughed (which would have been horribly rude, of course). But what she thought she could possibly give me that would make it easier to go to the reading of a will for my grandmother whom I had never seen and thought was dead for my whole life was anyone's guess. I'm thinking a casserole wouldn't quite cut it. But, still, it was sweet of her to offer, and I know she said it with a sincere heart, so I had hugged her back and assured her that I would indeed call should I "need anything."

Then, I had gotten into my car, and with a mighty groan and quite the commotion of smoke, it had reluctantly huffed and puffed down the road. Which is currently where I was. On the road. A familiar feeling, but not a happy one at the moment. Driving reminded me of Celia. Which reminded me of my grandmother. Which left me fuming in anger.

Actually, at the moment, I preferred anger to the other emotions that were currently banging on the door of my mind for entry. So maybe it was a good thing that driving reminded me of Celia. It forced me to remain angry. As soon as I stopped being angry, I knew what would happen. Sadness would pour in like a tidal wave through the window, and I would drown. The sorrow of lost time, moments that could have been made but never would be and mind-numbing regret would pick me up in its current and drop me over the waterfall of grief. I had stuck my toe in the river last night, and it hadn't been pleasant. You probably already know this, but sorrow weighs heavy on your soul. It's suffocating and exhausting and drains every other emotion and feeling out of you. So, anger it was.

I spent the first half hour driving and fuming and re-playing the conversation with Celia over and over in my mind. I didn't realize I was talking out loud until some of the people I passed (not that I was speeding or anything) looked at me quite strangely. Huh. Perhaps one could overdo anger. It was also a bit tiring. Also, I was not entirely certain if I had the emotional stamina or the needed natural disposition to maintain anger for any length of time.

But what else could I do? The thought of my poor, little old grandmother alone for all of those years when I… but no. I wasn't going to think about that, was I?

Okay. Deep breaths. There must be another way to handle this situation without scaring the other drivers or pulling off the side of the road and crying for days.

And then it came to me.

Denial.

I love denial. I have spent a lot of time with denial in the past. Celia had, at least, taught me that art quite well. Perfect….but still not quite enough. I needed something else too. If you're going to live in denial you need to have a backup emotion in case denial goes for walkies… as it sometimes does. I pondered this for a few moments. Ah-ha… What about… curiosity? Ah, yes, the perfect dance partner to denial. You see – denial suppresses certain things while curiosity makes you think about the possibilities of other things. I had perfected this technique as a child, so perhaps denial and curiosity would be the ideal emotional state to live in now. I pondered. Yes, I think this could work. I could handle this. I would just pretend that I didn't have a "real" grandmother. I was merely going to pick up something that had been left to me. There was no sorrow in that. I didn't know the person – which was, actually, true. That made the denial even easier. It totally didn't matter who that person was. I could pretend that it was just "one of those things." Everyone in life has these things. The death of some obscure relative who has left you her diamond ring… or rocking chair… or hairbrush. It's just something you have to do, and it provides great conversation fodder for years to come. "Oh yes, I remember the time I had to go pick up Great-Aunt-Cousin-Twice-Removed Winifred's rocking chair. We still have it in the basement…the cat loves it." But I wasn't going to get a cat. Anyways, that's beside the point.

You know… a healthy dose of denial. Just like when you go to the grocery store, buy hamburger and you pretend that it didn't really use to be a cow. Yeah. Just like that. I could do that. I wouldn't think about Grandma Rose as a person, but merely a thing. An object of the past. There. "Grandma Rose." Done. I could even say her name without a hint of emotion. I tried it again. "Grandma Rose." A faceless unknown. No problem. One more time and I think I would have it. "I am on my way to the reading of Grandma Rose's will. I will take home whatever she has left me and it won't be a problem. I don't need to call my landlady. I don't need help from anyone, because there is nothing to worry about. I'll be just fine. "

As if on cue, goose bumps broke out on my arms. I rubbed them vigorously with my right hand (which wisely left one hand on the steering wheel). Oh dear. This could be a bad sign. Perhaps, I thought uneasily, it was ominous foreshadowing. Just like you read about in books. Of course, that would make me either the heroine or the ill-fated friend of the heroine who gets her head lopped off.

Were those the cold fingers of premonition sneaking up my spine? I shivered and glanced anxiously up at the sky to see if the clouds were gathering in a strange and terrifying manner. If they were, I was turning this car right around. Inheritance or no inheritance. Little ripples of doubt washed over me…perhaps I was at a fork in the road of life. If I wanted to continue as I had been, I should stop. Turn around. Ask the landlady to bake me a casserole and be done with it. This may turn out to be a really, really bad idea. Maybe going to the reading of Grandma Rose's will would change my life forever. Perhaps… I gave myself a firm mental slap. Get it together, girl. It's autumn and the temperature is falling. Just roll up the window and see if that helps. So I did. There. No more goosebumps. No cold fingers of premonition. The clouds were starting to look a little weird, though.

The drive from Oak Harbor to Springgate wasn't long at all – only about an hour and a half. And no (I know what you're thinking) the irony of how close I had been living to my dying grandmother was not lost on me… and I had to quickly chant my denial speech to myself again. Huh. As I passed a rather frazzled looking family in a minivan I could see that they were looking at me strangely. Obviously denial and curiosity don't make you look any less crazy than anger does. I filed that away for future reference.

And… I was here. Springgate. Much larger than Oak Harbor, but still, rather lovely. Main Street (why is it that founding fathers never have a more original idea than to call the main street of the city "Main Street"? I find that strange, don't you? You would think that if you had enough courage and imagination to forge a brand new city, you'd… never mind…) appeared to be the, umm… the main street. Yeah. I know that sounds a bit silly. What I mean is that many local businesses found themselves perched along Main Street. I drove as slowly as I dared and spotted a little antique store, a coffee shop, a candy store, two or three clothing stores, a department store called, "Colson's" with the somewhat cute tagline of "If Colson's doesn't have it - you don't need it," a diner… all of the necessities of life. Streets branched off of Main Street at regular intervals and peeking down them as quickly as I dared revealed even more shopping opportunities. Wow. Springgate people were all very fortunate. I glanced down the empty sidewalks. I wondered where they all were. The street was quite empty. Eerily empty. Perhaps Springgate was in financial difficulties. Perhaps it sat perched on the edge of a toxic waste dump. Perhaps it was only a pretend city that movie studios used for charming town locations. Perhaps aliens … Oh. Reality arrived on the slow bus. Perhaps most people were at work? Yep. That could be it. Daily work was still something of a new concept for me. Celia certainly hadn't believed in it. And, with the Spartan way we had lived, she usually only worked two weeks out of the month. It never ceased to amaze me how we could roll into town, Celia would park the car, hop out into the closest store/restaurant/gas station/hotel/whatever, and come back with a job. She'd work, or her version of work anyway, for a while and then either get bored or fired and we'd be off again. It was very exciting.

My appointment with the lawyer wasn't until 1:00 p.m. I had time to spare, so I retraced my route back down Main Street and pulled into a parking space in front of the diner. I wasn't quite sure where the lawyer's office was located, so I could fill up my stomach and wrangle some information all in one stop. I thought that was very clever of me.

My little car gave a great sigh of relief as I turned off the ignition. Apparently, he had not enjoyed the ride at all either. I patted the hood affectionately as I passed by. Poor thing. He was looking for a rest from the road, too.

The diner was cool but cozy on the inside. I parked myself by the counter. I knew, from experience, that this was the best place to sit if you wanted to have a little chat with the waitress. I was not wrong.

Renee turned from her duties at the coffee pot to greet me. Her name tag was old and worn… but so was she. Oops. Sorry. That wasn't very nice, was it?

"Good morning," she greeted me with a warm smile, "what can I get for you today?" Despite the coolness of the restaurant, her curly hair was damp with sweat, and she looked like she had been working for hours. She probably had. Ah. Good. Perfect. She was tired and wouldn't mind standing still for a few minutes to answer my questions.

"I would love some coffee and bacon and eggs and pancakes and hash browns please," I said with my most winning smile. What? I was hungry. Don't judge.

She returned with my coffee almost immediately. My winning smile was clearly working well for me today. "Cream and sugar?" she asked.

I nodded, and she took her time rummaging under the counter. While she did so, I was amused to note that she was appraising me. "Just passing through?" she guessed.

Huh. Sometimes I think that I'll never be able to wash the look of traveler off. "Just in town for the day," I amended. "I live in Oak Harbor." For some reason, it felt important that she knew I wasn't a homeless gypsy.

She finally put some cream on the counter, but obviously, the sugar was a little harder to catch. She kept up the search valiantly. "I've been to Oak Harbor many times. My sister lives out there." She leaned over the counter conspiratorially, "Don't you think it's a little strange that there aren't more oaks?"

I grinned at her, "I know," I said, "but it's still a pretty place to live."

"So what brings you to Springgate?" she asked, triumphantly brandishing two little packets of sugar. Rats. It looked like that was all I was going to get. I wondered if my winning smile would work to resume the search party for two more? I decided not to risk it.

"I'm here for the reading of my grandmother's will." I was really, really proud of the way my voice didn't even shake.

Her face folded up with sympathy. She patted my hand, "I'm so sorry to hear that," she said. "And she lived here in Springgate?" I nodded. "What was her name?" she asked. "Maybe I knew her." I won't deny that my heart leapt at that. What a blessing it would be if she could tell me more about Grandma

Rose… hopefully, she would have something to say other than that she was a corker. At least she couldn't say that Grandma Rose had died when I was a baby.

"Rose Whittman", I said.

And then… the weirdest thing happened. Her face shut down. Seriously. It went completely blank. The comforting patting of my hand stopped and she stepped back from the counter with a quickness I didn't think she was capable of.

"Your order will be up in a minute," she said stiffly.

"But… but…" I protested weakly. But it was too late. She was stalking off towards the kitchen with such purpose that I didn't expect to see her back anytime soon. Huh. Maybe Grandma Rose really *was* a corker. Rats. So much for information gathering. Oh well. At least I would be eating well. Or so I hoped. From the look on her face, I sincerely did hope that she wasn't heading back to the kitchen to poison my bacon.

CHAPTER 2

I was well fed and a bit weary when I arrived at the lawyer's office. It was a surprisingly modern looking building, which, for some reason, I had not anticipated. It made sense that an old lady would have an old lawyer in an old office, right?

I know. That's what I thought too.

The girl sitting behind the Scandinavian office furniture in the lobby was young and perky. She bobbed her curls happily at me and told me to have a seat. This always annoys me. If you have an appointment to meet with someone at a certain time, then they should be ready at that time and you shouldn't have to wait, right?

I know. That's what I thought too.

So instead of taking my seat in a very expensive looking waiting room chair and reading boring magazines, I smiled serenely at her and decided to explore a bit, walking past her down the hall to where I assumed the offices were. Her mouth fell open in a little "O", but my instincts were correct, she wasn't the confrontational type. Too bad for her, but she would learn.

The first door on the right was open. It was an impressive looking conference room, complete with massive mahogany table and crystal-looking water glasses. Huh. Nice and intimidating. Probably just the way that they liked it. Next to the Conference Room was a little kitchenette with one of those fancy coffee makers where you put the little thingie in the top and out comes a steaming delicious gourmet coffee drink. I love those. I was debating whether or not to help myself when a voice across the hall stopped me.

"Well, there's no way you're going to get that to work anymore. You're just going to have to try a different angle." There was a brief pause and then a low laugh, "I have some ideas, don't worry."

Now that, at least, is something I expected a lawyer to say. Just the right blend of wise and sneaky. I peeked around the doorway of the kitchenette and found myself staring unexpectedly at the man behind the voice. Wow. Nice. It would probably be too much to ask for him to be my lawyer, right?

He smiled charmingly at me, "And who might you be?" he asked, tucking a phone into his front pocket. "A spy from another office across town? I can save you some time. Are you here to gather information on a specific client list or learn our corporate secrets?"

I grinned back, "Learn your corporate secrets, of course. They're much more lucrative."

He gave a short bark of laughter, "I like your honesty." He held out his hand, "Nathaniel Goldmeyer."

"Natalie Wolcott." I shook his hand, liking the firmness of the grip... and his lovely smile. "And, actually, I was just wandering because I don't like waiting... although I was contemplating the legalities of stealing a cup of coffee when you walked in."

"A cup of coffee we can handle," he said with a twinkle, "but corporate secrets might take a bit longer." He gestured towards the machine, and happily, I began scanning the little flavor packs.

I was just contemplating my next move with the cute lawyer when the perky blond came in and ruined my day. I was really starting not to like her.

"There she is, Mr. Garvey," she said, pointing a little skinny finger at me. "I asked her to wait, but she..."

Mr. Garvey (presumably my lawyer) was, unfortunately, portly and well into the process of balding. He was smiling rather broadly as he looked between Nathaniel and me. "Now, Brenda," he said, "I think Ms. Wolcott has found something more amusing to do than read old magazines."

In spite of myself, I blushed.

"It's a good thing I was here," Nathaniel said. "She was just about to steal all of our corporate secrets and sell them to the highest bidder."

Mr. Garvey's smile grew even broader, "Well then, you must be Rosie's granddaughter," he said. "That sounds exactly like something she would have done."

Two minutes later I found myself sitting (with no coffee – it wasn't any more fun after that) at Mr. Garvey's desk. The office was warm and cozy and welcoming. Pictures of (presumably) cherubic grandchildren adorned the desk in front of me. The man sitting in the chair was beaming at me like a long-lost daughter. It was giving me heartburn.

"So, Natalie," he began, "I understand that your grandmother and your mother…" here he paused to ruffle through some papers on the desk, "…Celia…had a less than amicable relationship." He smiled kindly at me… the few strands of white hair on the top of his head waving weakly.

"Celia always told me she was dead," I said bluntly, watching the smile slip just a bit.

"Family dynamics can be difficult," he said easily, with the manner of a man who has spent a great deal of time smoothing things over, "but I am sure, had Rose not died quite so suddenly, a reconciliation would have been forthcoming."

"I seriously doubt it."

A shadow crossed his face. I was clearly not cooperating in the manner which he expected. However, what he didn't realize was that denial and curiosity had no time for sympathetic, over-smiling lawyers. At all.

"Well, my dear," he said, smiling again, "I am sure you are wondering what your grandmother has left you."

"Yes," I admitted, "I am curious as to what the item may be." See. Curious is good. And it comes in handy. I told you so.

Impossibly, his smile widened. "Well, my dear, I can't tell you what it is."

I sighed. I knew this wasn't going to be easy. After all, Grandma Rose was Celia's mother. And, apparently, she was a corker. The waitress had unwittingly corroborated this piece of evidence. "Then why I am here?"

"I can't tell you," he repeated, "because I have to show you." He stood up, pulling car keys out of his jacket pocket. "Are you ready?"

Huh. I wasn't quite so sure that I wanted to get in a car with Mr. Smiley. He jingled the keys expectantly. But, I guess, if worse came to worse, I could take him. After all, he was pretty old. And I doubted he could run fast at all.

His car was beautiful. And comfortable. And very expensive. It did not sputter or belch smoke as we glided along the road. In a strange way, it was a bit boring. After all, if you know your car is actually going to get you to your desired destination, it takes a bit of the adventure right out of it, don't you think?

We drove straight down Main Street. After we passed the last little trinket store on the corner, the road suddenly and completely changed its mind and reared up in front us in the form of an impressive, looming hill. Main Street, a half mile ago, while lovely and charming, had been flat and unassuming. Main Street, ahead of us, was dark and wild.

The trees here seemed discontent with their appointed lot in life to merely grow alongside the road. Instead, their long arms stretched menacingly out at us, twisting and bending together to form a dark canopy overhead. Even from my view out the car window (Mr. Garvey was not a fast driver by any stretch of the imagination – I think I saw a turtle pass us), I could see the wicked thorns on each branch. There had only been a slight breeze in town, but here the branches dipped and beckoned in an alarming frenzy that made me grateful, at last, for the safety of the expensive car. I knew immediately and without any hesitation that these trees hated me. And I hated them. They were out for blood. I swallowed and then did the unthinkable. I looked to the lawyer for support. He beamed sympathetically.

"It looks pretty scary, doesn't it?" He let go of the steering wheel to pat my arm reassuringly. Whoa. Dude. I didn't need *that* much comfort. "This is Raspberry Hill. Some folks around here say that it's haunted."

Wow. Nice. Thank you. That was amazingly reassuring.

There was a sudden, sharp turn in the road. And then I saw it.

13

CHAPTER 3

Yes. I saw it. They say your first impression is everything. If they are right, then my first impression should have sent me howling back down the hill. Thankfully, I have had lots of practice with internal fortitude and I beat down the desire to run with every ounce of willpower in my body. It is a good thing I stopped at that diner and had some energy from all of that food. Because, my friends, there is no other way to say this. Standing proudly and arrogantly on the top of Raspberry Hill was the biggest, ugliest, scariest looking house you have ever seen. And, this time, I am not exaggerating. To make matters worse, it definitely looked like the type of house that would be considered…well…haunted. I'm sure it was probably just my imagination, but, as if on cue, something in the third-floor window flickered. Yep. Most definitely haunted.

Built in three main sections, the central piece stood the tallest – thanks to the big round tower reaching towards the sky. Windows were everywhere – and in all shapes and sizes. There were rounded windows in the tower and square windows below. Some windows were small – just room enough to peek out – while other windows were so large you could have driven your car through them. Each wing had its own soaring gable with crazy, swirling woodwork. Little porches appeared at various levels, some seeming to come from nowhere. I was, not surprisingly, quite reluctant to leave the safety of the car, but Mr. Garvey got out with no hesitation, and I couldn't look like a baby, now could I? One had their choice of how to approach the front door, as the stairs rose either to the right or the left and met under a small gazebo-like structure above the front door that was probably supposed to mimic the tower soaring directly above it. The porch continued on along each side of the house for quite some time, ending only once it hit its respective wing. Even stranger was the color of the house. A rather startling shade of smoky blue that seemed to change hues with the shape of the house, while the trim was painted bright white.

I was speechless. A rare occurrence for me.

"Shall we go in?" Mr. Garvey asked. I don't think it was really a question, though, as he was already ascending the right-hand staircase towards the front door. Because I was not scared or intimidated, I chose the left.

He drew out a large ring of keys from his briefcase and showed me one, "This one opens the front door," he said gravely.

I guess that would explain why he was putting it into the lock...? I mean, seriously, what a strange thing to say. Like I think he'd use the back door key on the front door? I was already - just a little bit - regretting my adventure with the lawyer. I should have insisted that someone else come along – someone like Nathaniel... the door opened with a tremendous creak and a puff of stale air... or really, even Brenda would have been welcome right now.

His large hand reached through the darkness behind the door, and I re-evaluated my opinion of the over-smiling lawyer. He was quite brave to stick his hand into the inky void. He must have known where the light switch was, though, because a few seconds later, the foyer was bathed in warm, comforting light. It's amazing how something as simple as light can make you feel better... well, a little better.

Mr. Garvey entered, so I reluctantly followed as well. Huh. It was... quite pretty. The staircase that went upstairs was absolutely stunning... large, with wide steps and a graceful arc that cut through the gigantic foyer like a work of art... I instantly had a vision of me sliding down the banister as a child... or maybe it was my inner child. I don't know, but the brief flash of pain was all too real. I was grateful when Mr. Garvey began babbling nonsense about the history of the house... something about the architect and the years it took... and the moldings... blah blah blah....

Feeling a bit braver, I ventured towards the first door on the left…when all of a sudden something dark and furry and wild flew down the stairs straight towards me. It was emitting a high pitched squealing noise countered with low moans and other incomprehensible sounds.

It was terrifying.

Without conscious thought, I jumped onto the nearest piece of furniture. I do believe it was some sort of hallway table. It looked very old… it wobbled… I wobbled… but at least the…. whatever that was… (a giant rat perhaps??) couldn't reach me. I grabbed a handy wall sconce to steady myself. It was probably an antique something or other, but right now, I didn't really care. My only thought was staying away from the thing trying to eat me. However, the "thing" was not deterred by my sudden ascension of fewer than two feet. It pounced and attempted to jump up to the table next to me, but with the cautious use of my purse, I gave it a small little push (… and no matter what Mr. Garvey may have said to other people later – I was not screaming – I was merely trying to encourage the bloodthirsty giant rat to go eat someone else. For pity's sake – Mr. Garvey would have made a much better meal than I would). It circled the table around to the left and then back around to the right, watching for cracks in my defense. I tracked it steadily, pivoting my head back and forth… not knowing where the next attack would come from. It jumped… I spun, once again, to use my purse as a weapon, but… alas… I had to let go of the wall sconce to turn and all of the spinning had made me dizzy and… and…as if I were in slow motion, I felt myself falling… falling to my doom. The creature did not hesitate. It leapt upon me, attacking my hair and pulling at it in great clumps. (Alright. I'll admit it. By this time, there might have been a *little* bit of screaming). Mr. Garvey was valiantly trying to do battle with the fiend, but it only had eyes (and a mouth) for me. Until, all of a sudden, he thundered, "ABRAHAM LINCOLN!"

I jumped. The fiend jumped. The screaming stopped. The fiend became silent. We both sat on the floor, on our rear ends, and gaped at him.

He yelled again, "Abraham Lincoln!"

I whipped my head around and gasped, "Where?" I think that says a lot about my current emotional state, don't you? I mean, seriously? At that point, would it really have surprised me to see our long-dead president standing behind me waving the Gettysburg Address in the air? Nope. Well. Not much.

"Abraham Lincoln," Mr. Garvey said sternly, "you will cease that behavior immediately."

Abraham Lincoln?? The creature on the floor twitched self-consciously and then turned its head to glare at me, just as if he were saying, "She started it."

I tried rising to my feet, but a low growl from the creature helped me to reconsider.

"Abraham Lincoln," Mr. Garvey repeated, "you are being a very bad dog."

A DOG? The fiend was a DOG? I stared speechlessly at… the dog. Wow. That crazy little monster was a dog? I studied him more carefully. It certainly wasn't a very attractive little dog. It was all black, with long hair that stood up straight all over its tiny little body. Its ears were way out of proportion to its rather small head. I realized with a start that he was staring right back at me and had the distinctively unpleasant feeling that he didn't like the looks of me either. I read a book once where the author said that no matter what the situation, there was always something positive to find, and that once we found the positive we could release the negative. So, I tried to find something nice about him…he snarled. Huh. I tried harder. Ok. Maybe the little pink tongue that darted out from between the sharp pointy teeth was kinda cute. Yeah. This was not helping at all. I bet that author never was in a situation like this one.

He growled low in his throat again, and I skittered to my feet. And, again for the record, I did not run to cower behind Mr. Garvey… it was just a coincidence that the spot behind his ample bulk was the best place in the room to stand. Yes, that's it.

He turned his head to smile patronizingly at me. Normally, I would have had something to say about that, but given the events of the last 30 seconds, I felt he was entitled to one patronizing smile. "Now, my dear," he said, "there's absolutely no reason to be afraid of Abraham Lincoln. He just isn't very used to visitors."

I decided to be gracious. "Th-That's alright, Mr. Garvey," I stammered. "What a cute little dog." An outright lie.

Mr. Garvey snorted in disbelief, "Well, that just might be the first time in his life that anyone has ever called him cute, but I'm really happy to hear that you like him."

I took a cautious step out from behind my portly lawyer... Abraham Lincoln twitched an ear... I paused. An awful feeling was beginning in my stomach. Followed by an echo in my head. I really, really regretted that deep-fried breakfast right now. Sickening dread. I believe that is what they call it in books. The growing discomfort of sickening dread. "Oh. My. Word." I said slowly, face falling and stomach heaving, "That's why you brought me here, isn't it?"

A look of confusion fluttered across his face. "That's Grandma Rose's monster... I mean... dog, isn't it? I've inherited a monster, haven't I? There is no rocking chair for my cat, is there?" I could tell by the look on his face that I was correct. "I can't believe this. Denial and curiosity my foot. I should never have come here. I should have just let Grandma Rose be a figment of my imagination for the rest of my life. I mean, what kind of grandmother was she anyways? Just because I thought she was dead doesn't mean that she thought I was dead... and now she really dies and she wants me to take care of a furry, evil, mean-spirited, foul creature that wants to bite my face off? And there's no rocking chair for my cat? Well... you can just forget it. Find someone..."

Mr. Garvey was waving his hands frantically in the air in front of my face, gesturing for silence to speak. He was, clearly, one of those old-type gentlemen who doesn't interrupt ladies... even ladies who are yelling at them. Since I was out of breath and my heartbeat was pounding in my head like a drum, I decided to be gracious (yet again) and let him talk. Then I could tell him what I really thought.

"I'm so sorry, Miss Natalie," he said, with such a sincere look that I actually almost believed him, "I thought it was obvious." I stared at him trying to make it clear that the only obvious thing in this room was that I was not going to take a monster home with me. "Your grandmother didn't leave you the dog."

Oh. The room suddenly looked brighter. That Mr. Garvey. He was really such a nice man.

"She left you Raspberry Hill."

My mouth fell open. It was not ladylike… and for the second time in as many days, my legs collapsed out from under me, and I fell to the floor. Abraham Lincoln obviously saw this as a victory for him and promptly rushed forward to attack. Thankfully, Mr. Garvey's large hand scooped him up before he could reach me. I heard footsteps… a door slam… and then the most pathetic yowling, whining, yipping noise you can imagine… so I could only assume that Mr. Garvey had shut the foul beast up into some type of room. He crouched down next to me uncertainly. He looked like he wanted to say something, but didn't quite know how, so instead he settled for awkwardly patting my head a few times.

I had to clear my throat before I could speak. "So basically what you're saying is that Grandma Rose left me a haunted house?"

Oh dear. I could tell from the look on his face that not even the news that I had inherited a monstrous old house complete with a monstrous little dog was the worst news that he had for me. What next? Were there bats in the belfry? Ogres in the woods? An evil witch that lived in a cottage made from gingerbread down the hill?

I grabbed him by the lapel with one shaking, sweating hand, "Mr. Garvey," I said as evenly as I could, "I appreciate the fact that you are trying to break this to me as gently as you can, and while I appreciate that, if you don't tell me exactly what is going on here in the next two minutes, I will be out that door faster than…."

"Of course, my dear," he said hastily (clearly my grabbing of his suit coat overrode his sense of propriety in regards to interrupting ladies when they are speaking). "Let's just go into the sitting room, shall we? It will be much more comfortable in there." Somehow I doubted that but I allowed him to help me up and guide me to a room that was actually quite lovely – it had floor to ceiling windows with pretty flowered curtains and matching furniture arranged nicely in front of a massive fireplace. The coffee table had bite marks on it.

I sat on the little love seat, promptly curling my legs to the side so that Mr. Garvey would not have any doubts about where he should (not) be sitting. He took the hint very well and sat his sturdy little self down in a ladies-sized armchair covered in chintz. I tried not to smile at the picture that presented.

He pulled out some papers from the pocket inside his suit coat (have you ever wondered why they don't put those handy little pockets in women's clothing?) and his glasses out of another pocket and studied his papers for a moment before speaking. I think he was working up the nerve to speak to me. Poor man. It's too bad that I had no capacity for feeling anything besides the mind-numbing disbelief and panic currently jumping around in my heart like a crazy ballerina or I might have felt a bit sorry for him.

"Your grandmother," he began, "was always deeply troubled at the rift in your family."

I frowned at him, "Then why…."

He held up his hand, "For reasons which I do not know, she refused to contact you while she was alive." That really should not have hurt as much as it did. "However, shortly before her death, she came to me and asked me to write her a new will." He raised an eyebrow at me over his glasses when it looked like I was going to interrupt. I meekly subsided. "In this new will, she leaves you the property, house and all of its contents with the provision…" he paused. This was one dramatic lawyer, wasn't he? "With the provision that you live here and only here for one year, three months and four days. After that, you can do as you wish with the property, house and all of its provisions. Until then, everything must remain as it is… that is… you can't sell the house or furnishings, etc."

He smiled at me benignly. Obviously, I was supposed to think that this was a Great Plan. I stared at him. "You're joking, right?"

His smile fell just a bit, "No, of course not. I never joke when it comes to fulfilling my duties to my clients."

I snorted, "This is completely and totally and absolutely insane. And, it's not really even very imaginative. Did Grandma Rose read a lot of novels, because this sounds like a plot to a very badly-written one." I glanced around the room, "Is there a crazy groundskeeper or a devoted butler or someone like that whom I am supposed to fall in love with and get married so that the house and family live happily ever after?"

He actually looked puzzled, "I'm not quite sure what you mean…" he said. "There is no staff. Your Grandma Rose took care of things herself… although she would sometimes hire a girl or two to help her with the deep cleaning, and little Henry, my grandson, would do her outside maintenance. She really wasn't what you would call a social person." He was very good at totally missing the point, wasn't he? "The terms are really quite simple. You live here and you get to keep the house. You don't live here and the house goes to the historical preservation society to be used as they see fit. Although," he said with a conspiratorial wink, "I would not like to see what they would want to do with the place."

I got up so that I could pace around the room. It always feels better to pace when you're upset. I don't know why. "I can't possibly stay here," I said as reasonably as I could. "You said it yourself- this place is haunted."

"Nonsense," he said jovially, his good nature returning now that the worst of the news (I hoped!) had been delivered, "That's only what some people say in town. Truth is… not everyone in town cared for the free spirit of your Grandma Rose, and, as you know, that can lead to unkindness. This house may be a bit unconventional and large, but it is well-maintained (we did a thorough investigation) and clean (I had a cleaning crew come in), and I think if you just ponder this for a while, you'll see that this is a beautiful legacy that your grandmother has given you. Perhaps it was her way of giving you something in her death that she could not give you in her lifetime."

Huh.

What a bunch of hooey.

And then he wiggled the really big carrot, "If you do wish to sell later, I can tell you that this property would be worth quite a significant sum." He wiggled his eyebrows for emphasis, "A very significant sum."

CHAPTER 4

Since I still didn't look quite convinced, Mr. Garvey all but threatened (in the nicest, sweetest way) that should I choose not to follow Grandma Rose's last wishes (for which I would be a wicked, ungrateful granddaughter), the historical society would convert the house to a museum which would be a complete waste of valuable property (and I would be a wicked, ungrateful granddaughter) and be a major drain on the city of Springgate, who could not afford the upkeep, and… you guessed it… I would be a wicked, ungrateful granddaughter.

I really didn't want to be a wicked, ungrateful granddaughter. But, I didn't want to live in this horrible house with that horrible little dog-thing either. For a whole year. No, a year, three months and four days. That was a little weird, wasn't it?

"Why that long?" I blurted out suddenly.

He must have been talking about something else… I really wasn't listening… because his mouth opened and closed in a rather humorous manner while the gears in his brain spun to catch up. Huh. They were a lot greasier than I would have guessed because it didn't take long. "Your grandmother was a very thorough woman. She did her research and budget and figured out exactly how much money it took to live here per day, and then she left a formula in her will."

I stared at him hard. "You mean that all the money she had left goes into the formula, and however many days are funded for living here that is how many days I have to stay here?"

He bobbed his head happily, obviously glad that his little simpleton had caught on.

"Dude," I said, "that is the stupidest thing I have ever heard."

He was not amused. "It most certainly is not stupid," he blustered. "It is quite a stroke of genius."

Uh-huh. I was beginning to think that perhaps Grandma Rose had a bit of help with her "stroke of genius" plan.

"Your heat, electric, water and certain maintenance expenses are all covered by the terms of the will."

"What about food?" I asked.

"Errr.... no...." he admitted. "That is not covered."

"Oh well," I said with false cheerfulness, "It's only one year, three months and four days. It's not like I'm going to need to eat anything during that time. And, I'm sure that little monster in there can keep himself quite full eating the furniture and assorted rodents."

Mr. Garvey's face puffed up, turning quite red, "I can assure you," he sputtered, "that there are no rodents here."

I rolled my eyes, "I'm sure that's true, Mr. Garvey," I said in my most reasonable voice, "but the fact remains that I have no money for food and clothes and everyday life." My eyes bored into his, hoping to communicate what I needed to without words. Obviously, that plan was not going to work. I sighed. "I don't have any money saved," I said honestly. "You've seen my car. I live in a tiny little apartment and don't have a steady job. Even if I had a steady job, I would find it somewhat tiresome to have to drive back and forth every day."

He was a little appeased, "I completely understand your hesitation, my dear," he said, "however, the fact is that your grandmother was somewhat of a....a...." here words seemed to fail him, "...a recluse." His face lit up with relief at finding a suitable word that would not be offensive. "And she, I believe, always regretted not... err... not forming... err... not having... err..."

I hoped most of his living was not made in the courtroom. He wasn't a very good speaker.

"You mean she regretted the fact that she died old and alone?" What? I was just trying to be helpful. I certainly wasn't going to get emotionally involved in my dead grandmother's life at this point, now was I? What could possibly be the point of that? Nothing. Denial and curiosity, my friends. The only way to go.

His face flushed once more. I bet he was sure going to be glad when this day was over. "What I meant to say," he said slowly, "is that your dear grandmother regretted living so isolated and she did not want that kind of life for you. She suggested that you find a job here in Springgate to accommodate your more daily needs of food and clothing." At this point in the speech, he eyed me up and down rather critically, clearly not believing that I would need a great deal of money to maintain my wardrobe. "It wouldn't necessarily even need to be a full-time job," he said innocently.

Well, I'm sure his heart was in the right place. But I was done talking to him. I told him I would think it over. He told me he'd have someone drive my car up here. I told him I'd come and see him in the morning. He told me to have a nice night. He was still talking as I bundled him out of the door quite neatly. As soon as I heard his tires crunching in the driveway, I sank to the floor against the front door.

"I can't believe this. I have a house."

I tilted my head back to look out the window in the door... the sky was getting even more grey and overcast. It looked like it was going to storm. From someplace further in the house, there was a whine and the scratch of nails on wood, reminding me of yet another battle that needed to be fought. "I can't believe this. I have a house. And a dog." There was an ominous creaking that sounded like footsteps on the floor above me. "Naturally," I said, shivering and trying to imagine that it was only the sound of the old house settling. A streak of lightning lit up the sky. "And of course it's going to storm now," I said as the sharp crack of thunder made me jump. The pouring rain wasn't even a surprise. Yep. Right on cue. "And that's just perfect."

Three hours later and it was really dark outside. It felt much later than the afternoon hour that I knew it was. Maybe that was why I felt exhausted. The door felt reassuringly solid against my back as another boom of thunder shook the house. Yes, I was still sitting in front of the door. So what? I was tired. And I had a lot to think about. And… it was a little overwhelming to all of a sudden be alone in this huge, scary old house. Which, as I might have mentioned before, might or might not be haunted.

I hadn't heard my car come up the driveway yet, otherwise, I might have just left. It's not like I was financially, morally or otherwise obligated to stay here. I would be no worse off if I just said "No, thank you," and went back to Oak Harbor, would I? I don't know. Maybe I would be a wicked, ungrateful granddaughter.

Perhaps this was just the opportunity and the answer that I had been searching for my whole life.

Or, maybe, this was the worst idea ever.

I just couldn't decide what to do.

So there I sat.

There was a pathetic whining sound from behind the door down the hall. Bummer. I had been enjoying the quiet. I guess that little dog-thing had woken up. Seriously? What was I supposed to do with him? Alright, I admit it. I was terrified to face him again. What if he tried to bite me? He was little and quick and had big teeth. I had neither of those things. He could do some serious damage in less time than it took me to jump on the nearest coffee table. And, think about this… what if there was no coffee table handy? Perhaps I could find a way to slide food in under the door and he could just stay there for a while until I figured him out. That is, if I decided to stay here. Maybe I should just leave.

I let my head thunk against the door. The door thunked back.

OH.

MY.

WORD.

Holding my breath, I thunked my head cautiously again. This time, three loud thunks answered back. My heart seized painfully. I knew it. Raspberry Hill was haunted.

I scrambled away from the door, crawling alongside the wall. Could ghosts come through walls? I just couldn't see a ghost knocking for entrance, can you? It would probably just float right on through. Wait. Maybe it wasn't a ghost. Maybe it was another form of creature.

I gasped.

Werewolf!

Werewolf? I sneered at myself, you seriously think that? No. No, I didn't. But wasn't there some sort of thing that needed to be invited in? What was that? I bit my lip anxiously. It was too bad that I didn't have one of those smartphone things... I could look it up. Or maybe I should be running out the back door instead of thinking this through? Then again, I didn't exactly know where the back door even was. And, who knows...even at this very moment...I could be surrounded.

Then... I heard it... and suddenly...I couldn't breathe...because... it was calling my name. "Natalie..... Naaaataaaalieeeee..." it called. I shivered. It sounded so sinister. The pounding resumed. Thunder boomed. Lightning lit up the foyer and with the startling clarity of light came the startling clarity of reason.

Oh.

Someone was at the door.

And, given the fact that probably only Mr. Garvey knew I was here... it was probably Mr. Garvey. Abraham Lincoln howled forlornly, and I had a brief twinge of guilt. Alright... it wasn't guilt exactly... more like I just hoped Mr. Garvey wouldn't notice that Abraham Lincoln was still where he had left him.

Taking a deep breath, I stood up and took a few more steps away from the door (we certainly didn't want Mr. Garvey to think that we had spent the last three hours sitting in front of the door, now did we?) and switched on the light. I tried to look out of breath as I went to the door. It was a big house. Perhaps I was far away... way, way, way upstairs in the attic with the bat people and it took me a long time to get to the door, and when I did I would be out of breath. Right? Right.

Rain blew in as I opened the door. Two figures stood in the doorway, huddled against the cold and wet. The one closest to the door blinked at me in the sudden light of the foyer; he was tall with broad shoulders and short, sandy-colored hair that he wore in little spikes. Light freckles were splashed generously across his slightly upturned nose. Surprise flashed across his face when he saw me, and we stood frozen as the rain sprinkled his hair with glistening droplets. And then... his face lit up with a wide, welcome smile that showed all of his perfectly white teeth.

The door slammed in his face.

CHAPTER 5

know what you're thinking. You don't even have to say it. You're probably right. Slamming the door on someone isn't very nice. Especially since Mr. Garvey was out there too. And it was cold. And raining. But, you don't quite know all of the facts yet, so until you do, perhaps it would be better if you didn't say anything and just waited until you knew everything. Well, almost everything. I don't think I could tell you everything.

Like I was going to say, I slammed the door in his face. And then I locked it securely behind me. And then I hid. Well, not really "hid" - I couldn't think of anything else to do so I just stood to the side of the door and waited until they went away.

I thought it was a great strategy. That is until I heard the key turning in the lock.

What a little rat. He never said that he had another key. I don't think that is very professional, do you? I mean, how was I supposed to sleep soundly at night knowing that anybody could just get into the house at any time? I ask you... How was that supposed to happen? If, that is, a person could get any sleep whatsoever in a haunted house that contained a killer animal.

I was still growling to myself over the knowledge of the extra key when the door opened. Huh. Perhaps I should have moved away from my spot next to the door. It was just a little bit possible that I looked like I was hiding next to the door. That would never do.

Mr. Garvey, the rat, looked almost sympathetic as he entered the foyer. "I'm afraid we might have startled you just a bit, Natalie," he said kindly. "I'm so sorry, my dear."

I glared at him and then at the man next to him. "I can assure you," I said with such frostiness of tone that the water droplets in his sparse hair should have turned to ice, "that I was not at all scared." I refused to look at the other person, "What is HE doing here?"

Mr. Garvey beamed paternally at me, "I'm so delighted that you recognize him," he said. "I understand that it's been quite a while since you two last saw each other."

"What is HE doing here?" I repeated impatiently.

"That's just what I was going to ask," HE said. "What am I doing here?"

Mr. Garvey waved a hand at me in a shushing motion. How rude. No one shushes me. But he did, and for some reason, I shushed. He then turned his attention to the other man, "Now, I'm sure you're wondering why we drove all the way out here."

"The question did cross my mind," he admitted. "I take it I'm not here to pick up my grandmother's rocking chair, huh?"

Well. That was just weird. He thought HE was going to get the rocking chair?! He could just back off. If anyone was getting a rocking chair for the cat to sit in, it was me. Me.

Mr. Garvey started to look a bit nervous. Obviously, this conversation was a bit too close to the one he just had with me only hours before. He cleared his throat self-consciously. "Rose came to me shortly before her death and asked me to write her a new will." Mr. Garvey shot me a quick look that kept me silent, "In this new will, she leaves the property, house and all of its contents…"

I couldn't help myself. "To ME!" I yelled. "You told me she left them to ME. So what is HE doing here?"

And then do you know what Mr. Garvey did? He completely and totally ignored me. Amazingly rude, obnoxious, odious man.

"In this new will," he started again, raising his voice in case I decided to interrupt once more, "she leaves the property, house and all of its contents to

30

certain family members with the provision that you live here and here only for one year, three months and four days. After that time, whoever has fulfilled the terms of the will shall be free to do as they wish with the property, house and all of its provision. Until then, everything must remain as it is… that is… you are not allowed to sell the house or its furnishings, etc."

Good grief. Did the man have this speech memorized or something?

My cousin Jack stared at him with complete disdain. "You're joking right?"

"Of course not," Mr. Garvey said indignantly. "I would never joke about fulfilling my duties to my clients, and your Grandma Rose…"

Jack snorted derisively, "That is the stupidest plan I have ever heard. And totally lacking in imagination. Did the old lady read too many romance novels or something because this sounds like a plot to a particularly poorly written one."

I hid my snort in a fake sneeze. I might not like Cousin Jack, but it was kinda funny to be on this side of the conversation. Then again… this wasn't funny. At all. Jack had to leave.

"Excuse me, Mr. Garvey," I said as sweetly as I could, twirling my hair around my finger in a manner that I hoped looked equally sweet. "But we might have a little problem here. You see, Grandma Rose wasn't even related to Jack." Mr. Garvey blinked at me. "So Jack is not related." Another blink. "Therefore he's not a family member." And yet another one. "Jack is not related to me or Grandma Rose," I explained slowly, as my temper rose, "so he is not a family member. Therefore, he doesn't get to inherit anything." I felt like stamping my foot. "He has to leave."

Jack did a very good job at looking wounded, "Now Cousin Natalie," he said gently, "that's not very nice."

Mr. Garvey rubbed his balding head as if he was getting a headache. "Natalie," he said wearily, "your uncle adopted Jack when he married Jack's mother. That makes him family. But even if that wasn't true, Jack is named in the will as an inheritor. Therefore, he is eligible for inheriting."

"I am not living here with him," I said firmly. "He has to go."

Mr. Garvey took out a handkerchief and patted his head with it. I wish I could say that I felt sorry for him. Well, maybe if he took my miserable cousin Jack with him I could conjure up some sympathy. "I'm very sorry, Natalie," he said, "but these are the terms of your grandmother's will. If you choose not to abide by them, you will forfeit your share of the inheritance. It's really quite simple."

I looked slowly between Mr. Garvey and Jack. "Yes," I said, "it's very simple." And with that, I turned on my little heel and marched slowly down the hall.

On my way past the door where the monster was obviously stashed, I did something quite wicked.

I opened the door.

Abraham Lincoln was very, very happy to be free.

I chortled evilly to myself as I could hear Jack saying, "That's just ridiculous… what do you propose we do for food?"

The teeniest bit of guilt that I *may* have felt about loosening the beast upon them was squashed when I heard that. There was no "we." There was him. And there was me. And he was going to have to go.

It took Abraham Lincoln very little time to race down the hall back to the foyer. And then I heard what I had been waiting for, "What th-" followed by the scrape of shoes and the creaking of wood. After that there was the satisfying crash of something heavy. Abraham Lincoln was going crazy – barking and moaning and yapping and growling – and every sound in between. Jack was still yelling, although, thankfully for my delicate sensibilities, it was muffled enough by the sound of the dog and Mr. Garvey trying to catch the aforementioned dog.

I decided it was time to go explore the house. And pick out my room. Before Jack got there first. The toad.

I don't think I've ever been in a house as big as this. It was really, really, really big. Do you think it could be haunted? I mean, like *seriously haunted??* I don't think I believe in ghosts. At least, right now, I really didn't *want* to believe in ghosts – or even pretend like there was a real possibility that they existed. I do believe in God and the Holy Ghost, but that's not quite the same thing now, is it?

So, as I prowled from room to room, I talked to myself freely. Why? Because, you know, if you don't believe in ghosts then there's no reason not to talk to yourself because there's nothing there to hear you beside yourself. However, if you did believe in ghosts then you would tiptoe and be really quiet because you wouldn't want the ghosties to wake up and get you. That makes sense, right? Right.

So, you're probably wondering what this place looks like, aren't you? I'll do my best to explain, but I'm no expert on architecture or anything, so don't get mad if I don't say it just right. The door where the beast had been hiding behind led to the library (which was AMAZING – I was so coming back here soon to do some more prowling)… it had floor to ceiling bookshelves that were loaded with books. I ran a finger over a shelf experimentally and it came back coated in dusty grey… yep… that was some cleaning crew… I bet they didn't do the corners or the windows either. If I went out the north door of the library and crossed the hall, I found another sitting-type room that looked a bit more "lived in" than the other sitting room had… there were several comfy couches and a large TV and armchairs… and end tables with coasters… I could only imagine that Grandma Rose had spent a lot of time here. I backtracked to the library and down the other hallway. I think that room might have been a music room or something. At least, there was a large piano in the corner, so, therefore, it must be the music room. Congratulating myself for my brilliance I found a second set of staircases across the hall from the music room. These stairs were rather dull and practical looking, so I concluded that they were probably for the servants. To keep a house this big nice and squeaky clean probably required the use of several servants. If Jack stayed I could pretend that he was a servant, couldn't I? That might almost be fun.

I headed back down the hallway past the room which I now decided to call the "living room" (not a very grand name, perhaps, but it seemed to fit) - ah-ha! I found it. The end of the house! Ha! I knew it couldn't go on forever. I turned right and the corridor ended in a very practical looking laundry room. Perfect. Another room for Jack.

Going back the other way, next came the kitchen. It was… nice, I guess, as kitchens go. I was a bit surprised. For some reason, I had been expecting golden-colored appliances and dirty Formica. The stainless steel and gleaming marble were quite something. If one was interested in that type of thing. Which I wasn't. I decided not to explore the kitchen any further. I doubted that I would spend much time in there, and you never know… what if I found mold in the refrigerator? Then I would be all grossed out and Mr. Garvey would think that I was even weirder than what he already did. And we couldn't have that, now could we?

Past the kitchen, down the hall, I found a few rooms that I am sure had a function, but what that function was I don't know. Hey. It's not like I spent a lot of time hanging around mansions every day. Oh! A name came to me…Conservatory… that was a type of room with plants hanging everywhere, correct? Huh. I think so. Oh well. There were a lot of green things in that last room, which, now that I was in charge, were likely all doomed to die. Poor things. And maybe that other little-unfurnished room was like a servant's quarters or something. Maybe Jack could sleep there. It would be very convenient for him to be so close to the laundry room. There was some type of room under the steps too. Perhaps that is where they kept the little boy with the magical powers? Ha. Don't worry. I checked. It didn't look like anyone had been living in there. Perhaps Jack…? Ha!

The whole west side of the house was one big room. I think it was probably a ballroom once upon a time. It was huge… huge and absolutely beautiful… with a soaring ceiling and hardwood floors. I couldn't help myself and, forgetting about the ghosts for a minute, I spun across the floor with a few practice twirls. Oh! The stories this room could tell. I could almost feel them.

They whispered through the air around me. Things had happened in here. I knew it. Later. I would come back later and try to listen.

Intuition told me that if I exited the door on the other side of the room I would be back out in the foyer. So, being sneaky like a fox... I eased the door open and tiptoed across the foyer. I tried not to chortle evilly again as I heard cousin Jack say something followed by a low growl from the beast.

The staircase rose in a graceful twirl and sweep to the second floor. As I climbed the stairs, it would have been so easy to take a few moments to pretend that I was a princess or Scarlet O'Hara or... you know... some beautiful fantasy along those lines. I am sad to say, however, that I was only contemplating the odds of Jack falling to his death when he attempted to slide down the banister. The odds weren't as good as I would have liked them to be. Of course... I am only kidding.

I think I counted seven bedrooms. I won't bore you with the details... because... hey... a room with an old bed and dusty dresser gets a little dull after the 2nd or 3rd description, right? I mean, I am sure that an art historian or something like that could get a little excited about the furniture or floorboards, but... me... not so much. The sizes and shapes of each room varied, which made sense. I tried to match up the windows with my memory of the outside of the house, but that really hurt my brain, so I stopped trying. One room was obviously in the tower part of the west wing, because the room itself was rather rounded-shaped, but other than that... I couldn't really figure it out. I was getting all turned around, and the darkness outside wasn't helping anything either. It would be easier to figure out in daylight – if I was really interested, I could figure it all out tomorrow... if it ever stopped raining, that is. There was even one room in the "middle" of everything. The hallway made a perfect square right around it. The room was locked. Great. Just great. A locked room where they kept the monsters. Or the gold. Or the bodies. I also will not bother you with descriptions of the bathrooms. I don't believe that would be very polite, do you? They were clean enough, that's all you need to know.

I did find two bedrooms that interested me. The first one was clearly the master bedroom. It was absolutely enormous – almost like its own little house within the house. As you entered, there was a large sitting area to your left with an overstuffed armchair in front of a little fireplace grate. A charming bay window probably made the area very cozy in the sunshine. To your right, there was a private bath that was bigger than my living room at home, and the bedroom sleeping area was so big you could have started a football game. The bed itself looked to be a King size bed, but it was so tall that any normal person would have to use a ladder... wait a minute... as I circled the bed I saw it... yep... like I said... any normal person would have to use a ladder – or that cute little stepping stool thing that stood like a miniature staircase on the right side of the bed. I really didn't like the big beams coming from the four corners or the high foot endie-thing (I might have to do a little research on furniture soon so I don't sound like a weirdo when I describe things). I shuddered. Laying in this bed would feel overwhelming... like you were laying in your own big box... or coffin. Yuck. No thank you.

I found the second interesting room as I was trudging back down the hall, not feeling too excited about any of my sleeping options. I was contemplating the merits of dragging a mattress back down to the ballroom. It was pretty down there... and I could wait for the ghosts of the past to whisper to me... when I saw the door of the last room I had yet to explore on this floor. It was rather fancy, having two doors that opened French-style, and the trim around the door frame was carved into little flowers. Pretty. I liked it already.

I swung the doors open, not expecting much, which explains my total and complete enchantment with what I found. It was perfect. It was my room. Mine. I was obviously now in the main tower area over the front door. The little sitting area was nestled in the curve of the tower. Lovely little flowered curtains hung gracefully down the sides of the windows, coordinating perfectly with the small loveseat and rocking chair around the low rounded coffee table. Built-in bookshelves lined the walls from ceiling to floor along the wall, which looked really cute because the wall curved too. I even had my own little porch, although it might take some creative testing to verify that it would hold my weight. Back to the right was the bed, and to my eternal relief, I was so happy to see that it was not a monstrosity with high foot ends and big columns, but a large bed with a huge, fluffy down comforter that just begged to be snuggled in. I pulled the comforter and blankets back experimentally… were the sheets clean? They *looked* clean. Oh dear. Decisions. Decisions.

There was even my own little private bathroom with a claw foot tub, gleaming sink and a small wardrobe full of towels. The wallpaper had little pink and red rosebuds sprinkled all over. So sweet. I could probably live here for a little while without throwing up. Maybe. I examined the door. It just needed one thing. A lock.

Back outside again, I also found a door that led presumably up to the attic. I decided to save that for another day. And venturing back down to the main floor, there was a door that led down to the basement. There was no way that I was going down there. No way. Not in a scary thunderstorm. Maybe tomorrow. Or the day after that. Or maybe never. There was a very strong chance that a house like this would have really big spiders in its basement.

I ventured back into the main sitting room where Jack was still in deep discussion with Mr. Garvey. I wondered if Mr. Garvey was sick of him yet? Peering through the crack of the half-opened door I could see that Abraham Lincoln sat perched docilely on Mr. Garvey's knee gnawing away on what looked like a long twisted stick. I could only hope that it was something he was supposed to be eating. Now that he was nice and calm, I tried again to find something positive to say about the little monster. I studied him carefully. Nope. Nothing came to mind. Unfortunately, I had no great love for bizarrely huge ears or raggedy hair that stuck up in every direction. Let's just face it. He was quite ugly. Poor thing.

Mr. Garvey patted his head affectionately as he explained one more time to Jack how the will worked. Do you see what I mean about Jack? He really wasn't very bright. If you will recall, it only took me one time before I understood that my late grandmother was totally and completely crazy. I idly wondered if Jack was actually contemplating staying. I shuddered. Living with him for over a year? Not my idea of a good time. I barely survived the few summers we were forced to spend together. I really didn't see how this was going to work…And then I suddenly realized that without even thinking about it, I had made the decision. I was going to stay- or at least I was going to give it the best try that I possibly could. For one thing, there was just no way that Jack was going to inherit anything without me. She wasn't even his real grandmother for pity's sake.

There was a sudden stillness in the room that hadn't been there before, and so I looked up to see what was going on. Huh. Both men were staring at me. Somehow the door had glided all the way open, and I probably looked just a bit silly standing there like a little spy. And judging by the smirk on Jack's face, he thought so too.

I scowled. "What?"

Mr. Garvey was looking at me sympathetically again. I was really going to have to watch it with him - he was starting to think I was some sort of weak little woman or something. And that would just never do.

Jack's face lit up with instant rapturous joy, "Cousin Natalie," he said, "it looks like we're going to be spending a lot of time together. Isn't that great?"

You will be so proud of me. I did not walk over and kick him. Although, I wanted to. Instead, I smiled sweetly, "I really don't think you're going to last that long, Jack," I said. "So I wouldn't get too excited. There probably won't even be time for you to put superglue in my hair."

His grin widened even further, "I can't believe you still remember that," he said. "We were just a bunch of crazy kids, weren't we?"

"One of us was," I muttered. I then turned to Mr. Garvey, "Shall I see you to the door?" I asked. I needed to regain some control of this situation and establish myself as the boss. I could tell from the pleasant look on his face, that, finally, I had said the right thing. I decided to take it one step farther, "I hope you don't think I'm kicking you out or anything," I said, "but Cousin Jack and I have a lot of catching up to do and…"

He melted just like I thought he would and was soon headed towards the front door. "Wait," he said, suddenly halting his progress. I smiled what I hoped was a patient and encouraging smile, "I should tell you that Abraham Lincoln's food is on the second shelf of the pantry. He gets one scoop a day. There are several bags of t-r-e-a-t-s on that shelf as well." From the way Abraham

Lincoln's ears perked up, I think Mr. Garvey totally wasted his time spelling that one out. "Be sure to let him out when he wants to go out. Never call him anything short of Abraham Lincoln;" and here he lowered his voice conspiratorially, "he really doesn't like it." He paused to think, and I took advantage of his distracted state to practically push him towards the door. Jack trailed along like an obedient puppy while Abraham Lincoln clung soundlessly with every fiber of his being to Mr. Garvey's pant leg. I never thought I'd see the day where Jack was better behaved than anyone else. Mr. Garvey shook him off as gently as he could, and Abraham Lincoln whimpered pitifully. As I was trying to close the door in poor Mr. Garvey's face, he finally remembered what he was going to say. "And this is very important," he said seriously, "you must never let him see himself in a mirror."

This guy was seriously cracked. I heard Jack trying very hard to turn his laugh into a believable cough. "Of course not," I said gravely. "We wouldn't even think of it." I shoved the door harder. "Thank you, Mr. Garvey. Have a good night. Drive safely."

I was really quite appallingly good at shutting doors in people's faces. If only it was possible to make a living out of it.

Abraham Lincoln let out a plaintive wail and sat squarely down in front of the door. Facing the door.

"Well," Jack said cheerfully, "who wants to go find a mirror?"

I decided that the best way to handle Jack would be to completely ignore him. So I did. I began the process of locking the door, although it didn't make me feel quite as safe as it did before knowing that Mr. Garvey and who knew who else had a key.

"Uh," Jack said, "you may not want to lock it."

I spun on him. "Why? You think he's coming back? Or did you want to take Abraham Lincoln for a little walkie? Or..." I was just getting warmed up. Rats. It had only taken me about 30 seconds to completely forget my "ignore Jack" plan.

"No," Jack said with maddening calmness, "I just thought you might want to get your things out of your car before it really gets all the way dark."

I find it so annoying when someone else knows something that I don't. Don't you? Especially when they rub your nose in it. Yes, I could have paid better attention to what was going on outside, but the sudden appearance of my long-lost (but not lost enough) cousin (who wasn't even really my cousin) had, understandably, thrown me off my game a bit. There was no reply that wouldn't make me sound like an idiot, so I settled for lifting my nose a bit more up into the air and stepping outside. I stopped on the porch for a minute to peer through the rain and dark gloom at my poor little car. There was really no way I was going to get out of going out there, was there?

CHAPTER 6

It took me longer than you might imagine to perform the seemingly simple task of going out to my car and fetching my things. No… it was not because I was scared of the monsters in the dark… where do you get these ideas? It was mostly due to the inconvenience of Abraham Lincoln. It's amazing to me that so many people in this world own dogs.

I had very cautiously scooted his little furry rump aside to get out the door, but either I did not shut the door all the way behind me or Jack cracked it back open (and I think you know where my vote lies on that one), but somehow he got outside ahead of me.

Abraham Lincoln was most definitely not scared of the monsters in the woods. Or of the fur-flattening rain. Or the cracking thunder. He was a really weird dog. He put his little nose up in the air (which I think he may have already learned from me) and seemed to take great energy from the chaos around him. With a triumphant bark of victory, he charged forward towards the bushes that lined the sides of the porch.

I was petrified with fear. How could I possibly catch him? With the way those tiny legs could run - he would be in Oak Harbor in less than five minutes. There was no possible way that I was going to catch him if he chose to run. And, if he did run, he would run straight through the woods. And then I had a really big decision on my hands. Would I be brave and chase through the haunted forest after him… or would I…not? I don't know which I dreaded more – venturing in after him or telling Mr. Garvey that he had gotten away. I wonder if losing Abraham Lincoln would make us forfeit our inheritance?

Amazingly, the front door opened again and Jack emerged. I gaped at him. He smiled grimly. I shrugged, and he joined the fight. We were two enemies momentarily joining forces for the greater good of humanity. Luckily, Abraham Lincoln seemed to have a great fascination for those bushes... and I saw him watering many of them... which gave us time to mount our attack.

I will not bore you with the details of the battle with Abraham Lincoln. They were not pretty. After we had chased him back and forth, and then around the house (and it's one BIG house), down the driveway (to the point where my heart sat in my throat – positive that he was going to get away for good), Abraham Lincoln doubled back towards the house...I fell and slipped in the muddy driveway.... Jack fell and slipped in the muddy driveway... Abraham Lincoln barked and pranced with joyful abandon – head raised as he tried to catch the falling rain in his mouth... we circled around and tried again... and again...but there was just no way to catch him. I had the distinctively uneasy feeling that if anyone were watching, they'd pull out a chair and pop some popcorn. We almost had him cornered once... and I shouted to Jack over the din of the rain to block the gap... but, unfortunately, Abraham Lincoln showed a bit of teeth and Jack chickened out.

And then... when I was at my lowest – freezing, wet, shivering, emotionally depleted and physically exhausted... Abraham Lincoln did the worst thing he could possibly have done. He went back inside. By himself. We stood panting and gasping as he calmly trotted his wee self back up the stairs, onto the porch and through the door that Jack had left open. I could see him in the light of the doorway. He looked pityingly back and forth between me and Jack. Obviously... he was done... and we had provided very poor entertainment for him.

I felt like falling face-first back into the mud. Abraham Lincoln was going to be nothing but trouble.

Once I had tucked my meager belongings (after all, I had only planned on staying one night not one year three months and four days) away in the gigantic wardrobe and changed my muddy clothes, my stomach reminded me that it had not had anything to eat since the diner this morning. I wondered if

Grandma Rose had any food to eat in the kitchen...and if there was - if it was still edible or not. Tomorrow, I would have to go and try to find a job so that I could continue to feed my stomach in the manner in which it was accustomed. Which, actually, wasn't that great. Cooking has never really interested me. It was just such a boring process. You had to have all of the ingredients on hand, follow the instructions exactly... and if it was something that needed to be put in the oven... you had to remember to take it out again. It was way easier to order out. I certainly hoped that Jack didn't think that I would be cooking for him either. We were going to have to establish a few ground rules before too long.

I was shocked to find Abraham Lincoln at the top of the stairs waiting for me. "What?" I asked him. "Is it your dinner time too?" His tail thumped twice on the floor. I guess that was a yes. I suppose I would have to go find his dog food and give him one scoop. I would contemplate the t-r-e-a-t-s later if he behaved himself... which wasn't real likely, was it?

We descended the swirling staircase, and I thought about what Mr. Garvey had said about the mirrors. Was he trying to be funny or something? Now... if he had said to not feed him after midnight, then I would know he was just joking... but *don't let him see himself in a mirror?* That was just plain strange. Then again... he was a very ugly little dog... maybe it upset himself to see it too.

We were at the bottom of the steps when there was a knock at the door. I paused... grabbed by a sudden premonition which had me sitting down hard on the bottom step. Abraham Lincoln seemed to think that was a good idea because he sat down next to me. The door was knocked upon again. This time, though, I was smarter. I knew it wasn't a ghost or a werewolf. It was not here to suck out all my blood or eat me alive. No... it was much, much worse than that. Ice settled in my stomach and, like Jack Frost decorating a windowpane, the ice grew and crawled and wound its way up to clutch my heart in its frozen grip. I knew what was behind that door, and more than I have ever wanted anything in my life, I wanted that something to go away.

Jack came around the corner from wherever he had disappeared to, "Natalie," he was calling, "I think there's someone at the…" he stopped when he saw my face. "What's the matter?"

But it was too late. Already, a key was turning in the lock. The door opened slowly. And the nightmare came in.

Jack was arguing heatedly with Mr. Garvey. "This is ridiculous," he practically yelled. "She CANNOT stay here." The one thing, and only one thing, good about Jack was that he had never liked Celia either.

She stood demurely in the center of the room looking frail and unloved. So sweet… almost shy really. She wore a light blue dress (I didn't even know she owned a dress) with a pale cream sweater over it. The sweater had delicate little blue flowers embroidered around the neckline. Her hands were folded neatly and bravely in front of her and she kept her eyes on the floor as the arguing washed over her. She was always very good at drama. I gave her five minutes before she started to weep, very gently, into a handkerchief that would undoubtedly be procured by Mr. Garvey.

I was lying on the sofa. I had yet to say anything to anyone. The ice had left me numb, and, I have to say, it felt pretty good. It almost felt like I was a spectator in a really, really bad off-Broadway play. Jack kept shooting me strange looks, and I could tell that Mr. Garvey found my behavior totally inappropriate, but I couldn't find any energy in me to care. For some reason, Abraham Lincoln had jumped up and laid down by my feet. He growled low and menacingly in his throat each time Celia twitched… and the one time she had tried to say something, he had jumped to all fours and, fur standing on end, had barked and barked and barked so long and so hard that I almost fell asleep waiting for him to finish. See? Remember that author I was telling you about? The one that said you had to look for the good - that author was right… even Abraham Lincoln had his redeeming qualities. He was a great little barker. He even knew how to time it right.

Mr. Garvey held up a warning hand to Jack (by the time he was done dealing with this family he just might make a feisty trial lawyer) and, once again, went through his spiel. Jack paced angrily up and down the carpet behind him, muttering loudly (and rudely) under his breath. He had quite the vocabulary.

"I don't understand," Celia said feebly. "Do you mean I have to live here for one year, three months and four days in order to inherit…"

"She can't inherit," Jack bellowed suddenly. Mr. Garvey sighed with the air of a long-suffering man, "She never even told us her mother was alive. How can you just let her walk in here and…"

I couldn't listen to this anymore. Without a word, I stood up, brushed the dog hair off of my legs and did the bravest thing I have ever done in my life. I reached down and picked up Abraham Lincoln. Then I walked out the door.

Abraham Lincoln wiggled in my arms, shifting his little rear so that it was more securely wedged in the crook of my arm. I chanced a glance down at him and realized that he was looking up at me with as much surprise as I felt about the situation. I literally do not know what possessed me to pick up the little monster. Somehow it just felt wrong to let an innocent (well… you know what I mean) animal remain in that room any longer. Especially since I knew that if I had remained in there any longer… this house really would be haunted -- with the ghosts of several murdered family members – and maybe one sneaky lawyer.

I ventured into the kitchen with my furry companion and, setting him down on the floor, found his dog food, gave him fresh water (I did not attempt to pat him on the head – he seemed to take his dog food very seriously) and then left him there to go upstairs. I assumed that he had a spot where he liked to sleep, and I figured that he could take care of himself pretty well anyways. I then used the servant's staircase to creep upstairs to my room. I crawled into bed without even taking my clothes off, pulled the comforter over my head and cried until I ran out of tears.

Sometime later, there was a hesitant knock on my door, but I ignored it. There was no one in this house that I wanted to see. Ever. Isn't it strange how people will tell you to cry and let it "all out" and you'll "feel so much better?" It isn't true. They are lying. You don't feel better. You just feel... emptier... and more tired... and even more awful because all of the same emotions are still there, but now you've added red eyes, a pounding head and a runny nose into the mix. I lay there, huddled under the covers, listening to the sounds of the house falling asleep around me, and I wondered what I was doing here. What *was* I going to do? Night would be over all too soon and a decision had to be made. Now that Celia was here, all previous decisions were up in the air.

Should I stay?

No. I most definitely shouldn't. I didn't want to see Jack. I never wanted to see Celia. I was definitely leaving.

So... I was going then. I'd leave first thing in the morning. (Even I was not brave enough to sneak out of the spooky house in the middle of the night.) Yes, I was leaving. But.... that would leave Jack and Celia to live here together. I smirked. Good. They deserved each other. But then, if by some miracle, both of them managed to live here until the deadline, they would get to keep this house - or sell it... and I would still be living in a rotten little apartment eating noodles from the microwave. No. They couldn't win. I was definitely staying.

But... who cared if they won? I mean... it's not like I owed Grandma Rose anything. She certainly never tried to reach out to me. Who cared if her house went to the historical society? Let them have it. I was leaving.

But... if I left... didn't that mean that I was weak? I was not scared of Celia. Or of Jack. Why should I let them push me around? Why should I leave? They should leave. Not me. Yeah. I was definitely staying. Celia would never be able to do it, anyway. A whole year in one place? She'd get bored of playing the grieving daughter soon enough, and then she'd be gone. Yeah. I would stay. And they would leave. And then I would inherit this house. Just me. What I was going to do with it after that was something to think about later.

Then again… I didn't want to see Jack. And I most certainly didn't want to have to even look at Celia. A year, three months and four days (well almost three days) was a long, long, long time. I was definitely not staying.

Thankfully… at some point… I fell asleep.

Something woke me. I could tell by the moonlight streaming in through the big windows (as I had not drawn the curtains) that the night was not over yet. I longed for daylight and yet dreaded it at the same time. And still, the night dragged on, keeping all of my doubts, fears and insecurities wrapped in its cloak of darkness. There was a creaking in the hallway. I froze. There was a strange scuffing sound from above. Gracious. Was this house noisy all day and all night? Couldn't a person get a moment's worth of silence? The hallway creaked again. I comforted myself with the knowledge (garnered from a very reliable source called "television" that all old houses make noise and that there was nothing unworldly about that) until I thought I heard my doorknob shift. Rats. If the doorknob was moving, then it wasn't a ghost trying to come in… it was a human… most likely a mother-type-human. Rats. I think I would have preferred a ghost. I kept my eyes glued to the door, but no crack of light indicated that entry was imminent.

Instead, I heard something worse. A scratching noise. On the side of the bed. My bed. The scratching stopped and then resumed. Mr. Garvey had assured me that the house was rodent-free, however, how did he know that? Just because the cleaning crew told him? Ha. They were probably sitting in the living room eating snacks and watching TV all day while they were supposed to be cleaning. Remember how dusty the books were in the library? That would mean that the rats were still here in the house. Or maybe it was spiders. Did spiders make noise when they were moving around? They probably would if they were BIG enough! But what to do? I could jump out and make a run for the door, but there was a distinctively real possibility that I was surrounded. What if I stepped on one? I don't know how I could live to see daylight if I stepped on a huge, crawling, hairy spider in the dark. No. I couldn't get out of bed. But… what if they were crawling into bed with me. What if a horrible spider was, even at this minute, crawling across my pillow… any minute now I was sure to feel the tentative press of a terrible, hairy spider leg upon my forehead. Oh!

There was one more terrible scratch followed by a strange snuffling noise. My mouth was dry and my heart pounded in fear…and then… something dark leapt up at me. I had no strength to scream, and my arms were full of… of… wait a minute… I recognized that smell… and the strange little silhouette… I sighed… my arms were full of Abraham Lincoln. I pulled him back from my body, "Now how did you get in here?" I demanded. He gave a little bark. If I didn't know better, I would think that he was laughing at me. "Now, you just get out of here." Just in case he couldn't understand me (which I knew was impossible), I made a sharp gesture with my arm in the direction of the door. "Shooo." In reply, he circled around by my feet and snuggled down into the comforter. I sighed again. I could scoop him up (What? I had done it before. I could do it again. I think.) and put him outside the door, but then, being the uncooperative, ill-mannered dog that he is, he would probably bark and scratch at the door and go crazy and everyone would wake up and think that I was scared to have him in my room or something. Besides, it is just possible that spiders are afraid of dogs. "Alright," I said, "but you stay down there and don't make any noise. Don't move. Don't…" I grimaced, "don't go tinkle on the bed." He glared at me, snorted and settled back in.

It was harder than you might think to fall asleep with a dog in your bed. Have you ever tried it? I mean… what was he going to do while I was sleeping? What if he decided to crawl up the bed further and I didn't hear him and then I rolled over and squashed him? I really didn't have money for vet bills. I decided to lay very, very, very still. And, as I laid there, contemplating my life and the choices I would have to make tomorrow and the people I would have to face tomorrow, it was very odd that the gentle snore coming from the foot of the bed was strangely comforting.

CHAPTER 7

A braham Lincoln was true to his word. He remained at the foot of the bed all night. Or, at least, I think he did. I have no recollection of a smelly dog by my nose. And, he was still down there when I woke up, so I gave him the benefit of the doubt.

Being indecisive is one of my least favorite things. I hate rolling back and forth on the ship of doubt, so I made my daily decision before my feet hit the floor. I decided that today would be spent in doing two main activities. Number One: Finding a job (that shouldn't be too hard, after all, I was very skilled at a cash register and knew my way around a diner and had many other marketable skills including typing, filing and answering the phone) and Number Two: Go back to my apartment and get some more things.

What? Of course I was staying. Like I would ever let Jack and Celia boss me around. Crazy!

I marched determinedly downstairs in my last remaining clean clothes, Abraham Lincoln trotting obediently at my heels. He probably figured I was good for some breakfast. So, I headed towards the kitchen. I might be gone awhile, and who knows what he'd do to the house if I left him here hungry. I seriously doubted whether Jack or Celia would think about the feeding needs of Abraham Lincoln. To my dismay, Jack was already there. I never would have figured him for an early riser. Or, as I sniffed the air appreciatively, capable of cooking. He had several pans on the monstrous stove, and it looked like he was in the process of adding cheese to whatever was in the skillet on the left. He looked up when I entered and smiled hesitantly. Jack, just like his late father, could be extremely charming whenever he wished to be. You had to build up an immunity to it. Luckily for me, I had. Enough for two lifetimes.

"Good morning, Natalie," he said, stirring vigorously.

"Good morning, Jack," I said. "I trust you slept well?" I really didn't care how he slept, but I am not, by nature, a rude person.

"I did," he said, "but I never realized that old houses make so much noise all of the time." He was quite intent on his little stovetop fiasco and barely looked up as he was talking. I never really thought of food as taking a whole lot of concentration to cook…especially not just eggs and bacon, so I figured that he was trying to avoid eye contact. That was fine with me. I had no great desire to chit chat with him either. The less contact I had with these people, the better.

I rinsed and dried Abraham Lincoln's bowls before filling them with food and water. "Well, Mr. Garvey did tell you that this house was haunted, didn't he?" What? I was just planting a little seed of haunting fear. It couldn't hurt.

Jack turned from his fascinating stove and grinned. "No, he didn't tell me that." His grin grew wider, "But he did tell me that he told you that."

I rolled my eyes at him and prepared to leave. "Wait!" he called after me. "Wouldn't you like some breakfast?"

I eyed the pans on the stove. Yes. Yes, I would love some breakfast. I don't remember eating dinner last night, and my stomach was so empty it was rolling like a boat in a storm. "No, thank you," I said with stifling politeness. "Have a nice day."

Jack flipped a few knobs on the stove, "Natalie, wait," he said again, coming across the kitchen floor. "I made more than enough, and I'd really like to talk to you for a few minutes."

"I'm sorry Jack," I said… and that was the truth… I was sorry… I was really sorry that I was too stubborn to eat that delicious food, "but you've probably poisoned it or something, and I've got a lot of things to do today. I assume Mr. Garvey gave you your own key, so I know you can come and go as you please. I really don't see that we actually need to spend any time together at all. It's a big house. I'll stay out of your way. You stay out of mine."

I was turning to leave when Celia entered the kitchen in a cloud of perfume. "Good morning, my dear," she said, reaching towards me like she was going to hug me. I skittered backward out of her way. She did her best impression of a hurt mother bravely carrying on when her wayward daughter turns her back on her and, lip trembling slightly, turned to Jack, who was also wisely retreating a few steps. "Good morning, Jack," she said warmly. "Something certainly smells delicious."

Jack backed up all the way to the stove, "I'm sorry, Celia," he said. "You're certainly welcome to use the stove after I'm done." Wow. He was really a very gifted not-quite-liar. I was going to have to remember that.

I made a scoffing sound which had Celia glaring at me as I left the kitchen and fled the house as if all the ghouls in the world were chasing me. I have never, ever been so glad to be back in my old car as I was at that very moment. I sighed, breathing in the sweet smell of old car. This, at least, was comfortable and familiar. My car must have felt the same way too, because it started up on the first try, which was always a pleasant surprise, and wheezed its way happily back to town.

My first stop was, predictably, the diner. I needed breakfast. And a job. I said a little prayer that they would be hiring. And that Renee wasn't working. Well, at least I got breakfast. The burning fire flaring from her eyes when I sweetly inquired about the possibility of a job almost scorched my hair and burnt my bacon. I had wisely waited to inquire about the possibility of a job AFTER I had received my food. Well, such is life. I didn't really want to work there anyway. Grandma Rose was supposedly a recluse. Therefore, I concluded, not that many people in town would know her. And… if I didn't tell them who I was, how could they possibly know that she was my grandmother? Now who was the corker? I cackled gleefully to myself. I would show Renee.

Hours later I knew two things. One, I was quite confident that Springgate would be a very charming town to live in for a year, three months and four days… ahem…excuse me… it was three days now. It was really very, very

51

adorable. I loved the little shops. And the flower-lined streets. And the cute little townspeople. Summer was just beginning to yawn and blow breezes that smelled of fall and leaves and schoolbooks and warm, cozy sweaters. There was even the tiniest hint of color on a few of the trees, and the candy store on the corner was hanging a sign that promised the arrival of caramel apples very soon. The second thing I knew was that getting a job in Springgate was going to be a lot harder than I thought. Either Renee had a serious vendetta against me and had spread the word all over town that Grandma Rose was a corker and a scandalous person and that, as her granddaughter, I would probably be trouble too, or else I just looked like a terrible person who shouldn't be hired. I had a hard time believing that was true, though. Personally, I thought I had a nice, open face with not a hint of shifty eyes.

It was well past lunchtime when I trudged my way back towards my car, but there was no way - no absolute way - that I was going back into that diner. Ever again. My pace slowed. There was a suspiciously familiar-looking car parked next to mine. I paused. It couldn't be. I stared harder. It was.

She was here.

Two very nice looking people were about to enter the diner. So I held the door open for them. And used the opportunity to peek inside. The sound that came out of me might have been a little scary because the couple looked a little anxious and skedaddled inside very quickly. I had to tell myself to unlock my jaws. My teeth were starting to hurt. It was. It was her. She was inside. And she was working. At the diner. The diner that was not hiring.

I did the only thing I could. I marched right on in.

I saw Renee behind the counter and so I slid onto a barstool. "Hi, Renee," I said cheerfully.

She looked up from wrapping utensils in napkins to nod her head curtly.

"I see you hired someone today."

She nodded again.

"I thought you weren't hiring."

She shrugged. I was really starting to think that Renee wasn't very nice.

I smiled brightly. "I'm so glad you changed your mind," I said. "My mother really needed the job." Hee hee hee.

She looked up from her task and blew a strand of hair away from her eyes. I giggled gleefully to myself. This was it. Celia was about to get fired. This would be a record. Even for her.

"I know," Renee said, her face puckering up with sympathy, "it is just so sad, isn't it?"

You could almost hear my bubble bursting.

"What's so sad?" I heard myself asking.

"How her mother..." and then she stopped and pursed her lips shut. "Never mind," she said. Wow. Celia was good. Even better than I remembered. Whatever yarn she had spun had been so good that Renee had not only looked over Celia's fatal flaw of being related to Rose, but she also got her to feel sorry for her AND swore her to secrecy. I knew the vein in the middle of my forehead was bulging. I could feel it. I tried to take a few calming breaths. Bursting a vein could be ugly. And messy. And probably fatal. The only good part would be the thought of Celia having to mop it all up. I slammed the door on my way out. And then... I decided to visit my friendly lawyer.

Brenda led me straight into Mr. Garvey's office this time. The girl was learning.

Mr. Garvey tried very hard to look happy to see me. He was a perfect gentleman. He settled me nicely in the chair across from his desk, politely inquired if I would like some coffee and then sat in his most dignified pose.

"Mr. Garvey," I began, "there must be something we can do about this will."

He cocked his head and gave a small shrug, "I think I explained this to you yesterday," a small smile crossed his lips, "several times."

I sighed impatiently. "You explained things quite well," I said, "but surely you can see that this is all quite unreasonable. There is simply no way that it is going to work."

It was his turn to sigh, "I'm very sorry, my dear," he said, "but if you do not find a way to make it work, you will forfeit your rights of inheritance."

I leaned forward, "But surely you can see," I tried again (usually I have more verbal skills, but I was getting a bit desperate), "that this will is just silly. What good does it do? There's no real purpose. Let's just skip the whole 'one year, three months and four days' thing and move on." I gave him a bright smile, "What do you say?"

He leaned back and steepled his fingers. "I cannot reply as to the benefit of any of this, but I can assure you that it is perfectly legal and binding. Your grandmother was in her sound mind when she made the will, and whatever reasons she may have had, she was quite within her rights to place these criteria on your inheritance. Whether or not you choose to participate in this or not, is up to you."

I frowned. This was really not going well. He was no help at all. I decided to try a little whining. "But I can't even find a job in this town," I said as pathetically as I could, "no one here knows me, but they all seem to think I'm a horrible person."

"Now, now," Mr. Garvey said, "It's only early afternoon... you couldn't have possibly met everyone in town." His eyes twinkled, "Where did you apply?"

"Ummm..." I said, "The diner, the candy store and the toy store."

"Well that's hardly the whole town," he said. "The fact is, your biggest mistake was stopping at the diner and talking with Renee. She's never been especially partial to your Grandma Rose. Her sister owns the candy store and is best friends with the lady who owns the toy store."

"Ah," I said, "I see. I've read about small towns, but I guess I never realized that they really did work that way."

He began rummaging through the top drawer of his desk, "Actually," he said, "I am glad that you stopped by this morning. I have a friend who is in need of a new assistant." He peered over the top of his glasses at me, "You do have administrative skills, don't you?" I nodded obediently, and he produced a business card, waving it triumphantly in the air, "Let's just give Bill a call, shall we?"

CHAPTER 8

I returned to my new home slightly happier than when I had left this morning. Bill had been very obliging. I turned the ignition off, noticing that my mother had not yet returned home yet. That, at least, was a relief. Jack, it seemed, had no car of his own. I grinned to myself. It was quite a walk to town. It would be good exercise for him - if he was lucky enough to find a job, that is.

The house, itself, had not changed at all with the change in the weather. I had missed the glow of sunshine upon it, as it was now evening and grey was returning to the sky once more, but I doubted that even a warm burst of light and pretty, puffy clouds would do anything to add to the charm of the house. It was and would always be quite, quite ugly. It was one thing to inherit a building like this - what I couldn't comprehend was someone actually *building* a monstrosity like this. On purpose. Did someone really wake up one day and think, "You know, I'd like to build a three-story house with…." I sighed. Never mind. Obviously, someone did.

Studying the second floor from my seat in the car, I could see my bedroom window. I grabbed the steering wheel tighter. What was that? The curtains twitched again. Someone was in my room.

I left all of my belongings in the car and charged toward the house. Underneath the fury roaring in my ears, I was mildly surprised at my own speed. Normally, fast running and I do not belong in the same sentence. It's amazing the things you can do when the adrenaline is flowing. The stairs of the porch melted under my blazing footsteps. I reached for the door handle, half wondering what I would do if it were locked, grabbed the handle and pulled.

Hard. Much to my surprise, and dismay, the door was already in the process of opening from the inside... which completely knocked me off balance and I fell to the porch floor in a great heap of indignation.

I scowled up at Jack who was standing in the doorway with such a look of shock on his face that I... yeah... I believed it.

"Natalie!" he exclaimed, "Are you alright?" He extended a hand to help me up, but I swatted it feebly away. The adrenaline was fading fast, leaving me weak and shaky. I struggled to my feet and surveyed Jack critically. He still looked a bit shocked, as if I had frightened him as much as he had me. He was not breathing hard or sweating... nothing that indicated a mad dash down the stairs from my room. I felt a little bit sick. It hadn't been Jack in my room... I was sure it had been Jack.

"Is Celia home?" I demanded, entering the front door. Abraham Lincoln came running and barking, but I continued my angry march towards the stairs. Jack followed, looking bewildered. His hands kept coming up like he was expecting me to fall at any moment. Weird. Maybe I looked a little worse than I thought.

"No," he said, "she hasn't been home since this morning."

Shocking how fast a new situation becomes your reality, isn't it? I had just called this place home. Again. This place that I was forced to share with the two people I most disliked in the world. I might not have too many people in the world that I knew with more than a passing politeness, but, honestly, anyone else would have been preferable.

Lacking the strength to take the steps two at a time, I was forced to go upstairs at a much slower pace than I would have liked. I shot Jack suspicious glances. He looked so nice. And innocent. That was always the problem. Just when you thought maybe, just maybe, he had changed and was going to be nice, bam! That's when it got worse. True, I had not seen him for many years, but one thing I did know.... people never change. That I knew all too well.

The thought triggered the memory of our conversation in the kitchen this morning. Jack had said that Mr. Garvey had told him that he told me that the house was haunted. Whew. Complicated, but...HA! That was it! Jack was trying to make me think that the house was haunted so that I would leave. He probably had a friend (did Jack have friends?) or, more likely, a paid associate to go upstairs and stand so that when I returned home I would see the scary shadow in the window. Was it merely a coincidence that Jack happened to be opening the door at the exact minute I was flying in? I think not. I smirked to myself. We would soon see.

With this knowledge, I felt a little fortified and my strength returned just a bit as I climbed the last step. I walked quickly to my bedroom door. Jack was still making questioning noises, and I hissed for him to be quiet. I approached the door cautiously.

His freckles stood out against his skin in the pale light of the hallway lamp, "Do you think someone is in there?" he demanded, looking both ways up and down the hall. What a great actor; he really did look nervous. Perhaps he missed his calling. He should have been the one related to Celia. Jack put a hand out to stop me from touching the door. "We should call the police." He half twitched away like he was going for the phone, but stopped because he didn't really want to leave me alone. Yes, he was good.

"Give me a break, Jack," I whispered, "you didn't really think you would fool me, did you?"

"What are you talking about?" he demanded in a stage whisper back, "You're being completely irrational."

I pulled a broken toothpick from my pocket and smiled grimly, "We'll just see who the rational person is now," I said. His eyes were huge and conveyed a deep fear for my sanity.

I pushed the door open and watched the swinging motion carefully. Half of a broken toothpick fell to the ground from the 2nd little knothole in the door frame near the floor. You might never notice it if you weren't looking for it, but I was. I had put it there. Rats. That was disappointing and could only mean one thing. No one had come through this door after all. Maybe I *was* being irrational. Unless... frowning... I picked up the toothpick and compared it to mine. Rats again. A perfect fit. Same toothpick. Same hole. What were the chances of that? None. That's what the chances were.

I glanced up at Jack. He was currently staring at me in the same manner you would have stared at an alien coming down in a spaceship and asking for a grilled cheese sandwich. "Do you mean to tell me you put a toothpick in your door? On purpose?" he asked. "Why?"

"I should think the answer to that is obvious," I said coolly. "I needed to see if I had any unwanted visitors while I was out." I frowned. We'd better clear this up right now. "And tomorrow, there will be another way I will be able to tell, so you just remember that."

He leaned against the door frame, "I have absolutely no desire to go in your room."

I snorted, "Yeah, right." I flipped the light switch on and entered the room cautiously. Jack came in behind me, "See, you're in here right now."

He huffed, "That's only because you're acting like there's a mass murderer under your bed."

I paused from examining the closets to consider his words. Under the bed would be a perfect place to hide, wouldn't it? Maybe someone climbed in, miraculously, through the window... my heart quailed.

Jack rolled his eyes and dropped to his knees next to the bed. With a great flourish, he whipped up the bedskirt, "AAAAHHHHHH!" he screamed, leaping away.

I couldn't help myself. I jumped. Then I went to kick him, none too gently, as he lay on the floor laughing. "Get out!" I yelled. "And don't come back in here again. I don't care if there is a mass murderer under my bed. It would be better than having to put up with you."

He wiped his eyes and clambered to his feet, "You should have seen your face," he said. "That was a good one."

I pushed him out the door, shutting it firmly in his face. He was still laughing on the other side. I then checked the room over top to bottom. Side to side. Front to back. Nothing was out of place. This was not reassuring news. Because if it wasn't Jack...or some compatriot of Jack's... then who was up here? How did they get in? And...more importantly... were they coming back?

I put all of my humble possessions neatly into the carved armoires and matching drawers. I was a little embarrassed for them. Oh well. They were clean. They might not have been the fanciest, but I had worked hard to buy them, and they would just have to be happy with that. The same way that I did.

There was a very polite knock on my door. I considered ignoring it, but... I was the nice person in this house. It was probably going to be hard work to keep remembering that.

I walked a little bit more slowly than I usually did to the door, enjoying the feeling of the cushy carpet under my toes. Just because I was being nice didn't mean I had to be quick, did it? I had kicked off my shoes at some point during my room search. I always feel that a place cannot be a home until you can walk in it comfortably barefoot. Don't you agree? I know. Me too. I wasn't quite at the barefoot stage, as I still maintained my socks, but I was working up to it.

I gritted my teeth and opened the door. To my astonishment, Abraham Lincoln sat in front of my doorway in a perfect little sitting posture with his feet tucked up under him. He looked up as the door opened and yawned widely. I stared at him with some consternation. What was this thing? Was it really a dog? Or some sort of creature from another world? How could he possibly be capable of knocking on my door? For that matter, what did he use to knock with?

"I'm really sorry about before," he said.

The breath left my lungs in a whoosh. I felt a little dizzy as I began backing slowly away. Abraham Lincoln tilted his little head quizzically, following my retreat with his gaze.

Jack peeked his head around the corner, keeping his body out of sight, "Please don't be mad," he said. "I didn't mean to make fun of you. If you really thought someone was in your room, I should have been more helpful."

I wilted to the floor. "What are you doing?" I asked weakly.

His face scrunched up in disgust. "This sorry excuse for a dog won't let me stand in front of the door."

The room began to feel brighter, and I felt my focus returning.

He made a motion as if to move further into the room, and little lips curled back from sharp, pointy teeth. He wisely retreated. From my vantage point on the floor, it all looked rather comical, and considering the events of the last 24 hours, I didn't feel too unjustified when an (almost) hysterical little giggle bubbled up. I tried to hide it with a cough, but obviously, I didn't do a good enough job, because Jack's face morphed from friendly to concern. That was enough to restore my sanity. Never show weakness in front of your foes, my friends. Remember that.

"I've made chicken for supper," he said, watching me carefully. "Would you come down and eat some?"

I wavered. On one hand, the chicken sounded really good. On the other hand, I had no desire to spend any time with Jack. On the other hand (what? I can't have three hands?), I could consider it reconnaissance, couldn't I? On the other hand, what was the likelihood that the food was not sabotaged? I had absolutely no inclination to be sick right now. I contemplated Jack carefully when genius struck. No problem. When we sat down to eat, I would switch our plates.

CHAPTER 9

Well, the chicken was delicious. Even if I didn't get a chance to switch plates. But, I did watch carefully. Like a hawk. Both of our meals came from the same steaming dish on the stove. Nothing sinister was sprinkled over it on the journey from the stove to the table either. Unfortunately, Celia came waltzing through the door just as we began eating, bringing with her the distinct smell of a diner. Don't you wonder why places like that don't have better exhaust systems? I do too. If I ever opened a diner (which was not likely, but you never know), a crazy-good exhaust fan would be my first purchase. She promptly invited herself to join us, and after that, I had no appetite.

"Oh my dears," she gushed, flinging back her long blond hair (bottled blond, of course) away from her face, "I'm so happy to tell you that I got a job today."

Jack made a noncommittal noise as he chewed his food politely. His method of dealing with Celia seemed to be to keep food in his mouth at all times. It was rude to talk with your mouth full, wasn't it? I stubbornly stared at my plate.

She twittered nervously, "I'll be working at the diner 5 days a week. The hours will vary, but I'll put up a schedule on the refrigerator." She took a dainty bite of chicken and beamed around the table at us. "I think…" she began, but Jack cut her off.

"I got a job today too," he said. This was news, and I perked my head up interestedly. What kind of job could Jack have found? "I'll be working at a bakery."

"A bakery?" I sputtered. I couldn't help myself.

He grinned, "Yep. It's so perfect for me. I love to cook, and Ryan (that's my new boss) needs some extra help. It's not exactly full time, but I think it will be enough."

"And where is this bakery?" Celia asked. I groaned inwardly, hoping Jack would not tell her. He would regret it. She would come in every day and make such a nuisance of herself that Jack would soon be unemployed…

"It's on Roberts Alley," he said, "right across from Colson's Department store." My ears twitched at that. I wasn't about to tell either one of them that there is where I would be working. Odd that I hadn't noticed the bakery. But, then again, I had not ventured any farther down the street than Colson's, so I guess that made sense. "It's got three little stores down the road. There's the bakery, a hardware store and a yarn store."

Celia sputtered derisively, "Yarn store!" she said, lip curling, "Just what the world needs."

But my heart was soaring. A yarn store! Here in town! And Celia didn't like knitters! The next year and three months and almost 2 days were beginning to look a lot better to me. I loved yarn stores. I loved everything about them. The color, the textures, the feel, the smell… the thrill of excitement of looking at a skein of yarn and imagining what it could turn out to be. I thought of the empty needles sitting upstairs in my closet and felt a healthy glow of expectation light up my stomach. I had only been in a few yarn stores, but one of them had had a little area where you could go and sit and knit. Perhaps this one had that too! What a beautiful little haven of sanity that would be for me. I sent up a prayer of thanks and re-attacked my dinner with gusto. I even helped Jack with the dishes before saying goodnight and retreating to be by myself. I put water and food out for Abraham Lincoln, whose absence was welcome, but a little worrisome. I tried not to think about what he was up to and consoled myself with the fact that at least the door to MY bedroom was securely shut. If Jack and Celia were not that wise… well… that was their problem.

I swung by the library to see what kind of taste Grandma Rose had in books. As I examined the titles, I realized that she had been quite the little eclectic. She pretty much had a book on every topic you could think of. And, while I am sure that the migrating habits of the ruby-throated hummingbird are fascinating, and maybe someday I would want to learn how to strip and rehabilitate old furniture (especially if I was going to live here), I was beginning to think that I would have to go out and get my own books to read when I found her section of mysteries. For some reason, the mystery section was between the cookbooks and the home repair books. What her system was, I have no idea. I selected a delicious looking murder mystery and decided to retire to my room.

I was three chapters in, and snuggled very comfortably into my bed, when there was a furious pounding at my door. It was so loud and sudden that I almost fell right out of bed. I was still huffing to myself as I flung open the door. Celia and Jack were standing there. Jack had a firm grip on Celia's arm and she looked furious. What a shame.

"Is there something I can help you with?" I asked sweetly. "Or are you two out for a midnight stroll?"

I saw Jack valiantly trying to suppress a smile as Celia growled unbecomingly low in her throat.

He scratched the back of his head with his free hand and looked at the ground instead of me as he spoke, "Err... your m... Celia has had a bit of a shock and she would like for you to come to her room for a moment."

I backed up a step from the doorway. "No thank you," I said firmly, "I have no plans on leaving this room tonight. Whatever you two are up to is just going to have to wait until morning."

But Celia did have other plans. Her plan was to grab my arm in the vice-like grip that I remembered so well from childhood and drag me down the hallway towards her room. Somehow it did not surprise me at all that she had chosen the room with the tomb-like bed.

"Would you stop pulling at me?" I demanded. "I am not two years old anymore, and you have no right to drag me around this awful house in the middle of the night."

"It's hardly the middle of the night," she hissed, "And when you behave like a two-year-old, you get treated like one."

Well. That did it. I stopped right in my tracks, stopping Celia's forward momentum briefly. She pulled again, and while I might have a bruise, there was no way I was going to allow her to treat me like that. Those days were over.

Jack bobbled his head in the direction of Celia's bathroom. "I think you're going to want to see this," he said. "It's quite interesting."

Celia let go of my arm. "Interesting?" she shrieked. "So it was you, wasn't it? I should have known!"

Okay. Maybe this was something I would want to see. So, I walked over to peek in the bathroom door. I gasped and, for a moment, my knees felt weak. It was a murder scene. Blood was everywhere. Splashed over the tub. The floor was splattered... and the sink was filled with the disgusting fluid. "You have been warned. Leave now, interloper," was written in bloody handwriting across the mirror. I felt a little sick to my stomach when a voice in my ear said, "Relax. I already checked. It's just paint or something like that."

Oh. Well. That was different. I could hear Celia still ranting in the bedroom about ungrateful children and useless waste, so I turned my head fractionally to look at Jack. "I bet that freaked her out," I said quietly.

"I'm two doors down," he admitted, "and I could hear the scream."

Our eyes met, and I almost felt myself smiling at him. "Ha." I said. "But you really shouldn't have done this. You know she's never going to clean it up by herself." He stared at me in shock, "And... seriously... 'interloper'? You could have asked. I would have helped you figure something better out than that."

His mouth was hanging open. "I didn't do it," he said. "I thought maybe you did. Until, of course, I saw your face when you saw the..."

I rolled my eyes, "Don't be ridiculous," I snapped. "Of course I didn't do this." I thought for a moment, "Although I may have done it if I had thought of the idea first. You obviously have a more devious mind than I do."

"It was not me," he insisted. "I swear it wasn't." He looked quite serious. But, like I have already told you, he was very good at acting. And, it had to be him, didn't it? There wasn't anyone else left to blame. Other than Abraham Lincoln. I doubt that he was capable. Well...maybe. He *was* a strange little dog.

Celia interrupted our whisper session by pushing me further into the bathroom so that she could stand in the doorway. I had to do a quick two-step to keep myself from touching any of the disgusting red paint. "How could you do this to me?" she wailed, clasping her hands together at the bosom. "I thought I was going to have a heart attack when I saw this. I thought maybe something had happened to one of you. I thought…" she paused and wiped her eyes with a still-shaking hand. I shared an uneasy glance with Jack. She really did look quite upset. "I may have made some mistakes in the past, but…"

That was it. We were done. I couldn't let her get any farther. I plowed my way back through the doorway. "What you have done could hardly be called a 'mistake'," I growled. "I don't care who made that mess in the bathroom. And I don't care who cleans it up, as long as it isn't me. And I don't care if you don't believe me when I tell you that I didn't do it. I am going back to bed and, right now, I don't care if I ever get up again. Do you get it? I don't care. You two can play your little games, but leave me out of them."

And with that, I swept back out of Celia's room and stalked back to mine. I was a bit dismayed to see Abraham Lincoln already sleeping at the foot of my bed. "Stinking dog," I muttered. "Why are you picking on me? Why don't you go sleep with Celia or Jack?"

He lifted one eye open to glare at me.

As I was falling asleep, a thought came to me. Perhaps it hadn't been Jack at all. Maybe he was innocent. Perhaps it had been Celia. I wouldn't put it past her. She could be making a play for sympathy…or trying to get rid of a few fellow inheritors. Didn't Jack say that there was a hardware store next to the yarn store? I was buying the biggest lock that I could afford tomorrow… after I bought some new yarn, of course. It's important to keep your priorities straight.

CHAPTER 10

I stumbled out of Colson's at 11:45 a.m. trying very hard not to cry. Judging from the moisture I could feel on my face, I don't think it was working. I rubbed at the offending drop of weakness angrily. It was my own fault. When would I learn how to keep my mouth shut? I sighed. Probably never.

The only thing that would make me feel better right now was... yarn. I turned left and, sure enough, Colson's ended right where Roberts Alley began. It was a short little alley, as alleys go. Only room for the three stores that Jack had mentioned. The bakery, the hardware store and the yarn store.

In spite of my misery and acute fears for the future, I wiped my face and plastered on my nicest smile before venturing down the alley. I will admit, to you only, dear reader, that as I passed the bakery, I did a weird little run and duck... just in case Jack was inside and working. It would never do to let him know that I was.... Never mind. I also just have to say one more thing...it really, really stinks that Jack picked the bakery next to the yarn store to work at. How handy would that have been to be able to pop over for a delicious bite of something during knitting...? Stinking Jack. Stinking good smells coming out of the bakery. Stinking... everything. Then again, the yarn store could be horrible, and I wouldn't have to worry about the bakery. See? I can find the bright side of a bad situation.

The hardware store was... well... what can you say about a hardware store that hasn't already been said? I mean, I'm sure it was nice, as hardware stores go, but if you've seen one nut, you've seen them all. I wish I could make some sort of joke right now about all of the nuts in my life, but I'm just not up to it.

Why don't you think of one yourself and add it right here and save me the trouble? Alright? Thanks. I would, however, have to stop by on my way back and get the lock I had been promising myself. Even if it took my last penny, I was so seriously done with not feeling secure in my own room. Even Abraham Lincoln came and went as he pleased. And that was just wrong.

I stopped walking. I was here. The yarn store. Possibly my happy place in all of the current gloom. The sign above the door said, "Crabapple Yarn Shop." Let's hope that no one here was really crabby. I was a little bit nervous. What if this didn't work out? I so wanted it to work out. I needed this to work out. I took a big breath. It was one of the prettiest little buildings I had ever seen. That had to be a good sign, right? The brick and fieldstone were absolutely perfect, and I even loved the crooked little chimney. There was a big picture window that gave a charming and inspiring view of the store. I could tell already that this was going to be a great place for me. From my outside vantage point, I could see several people milling about the store. I gave myself my best "pull yourself together" speech (in my head, of course – we wouldn't want the knitters here to think we were weird, now would we?) and grasped the beautiful iron handle. A little bell chimed to announce my presence, but it must not have been that big of a deal, because only one head bobbed up to see the newcomer. She had shoulder-length brown hair and a sweet smile. I liked her already. I liked it here already. I spied the sitting area. Correction. I loved it here already. Honey, I was moving in.

As I wandered around the yarn store, admiring the wide variety of fibers, needles, books and accessories... I shamelessly eavesdropped on every conversation that I could. I like to think of it as reconnaissance rather than spying. It was very enlightening, regardless of what you wanted to call it. Apparently, the girl behind the counter was named "Molly", and she had only been working at Crabapple Yarns for a short time. Everyone seemed to love her, though. Carolyn was the owner. And there was also a lady named Louise who worked there. I gathered from the comments that Carolyn was the elderly lady currently helping three people at once. Molly was busy ringing up purchases as fast as her little fingers could throw yarn in a bag. Of course, though, she didn't throw it. She stacked it very neatly, and obviously had something nice to say to every person at the counter, because everyone was leaving with a big smile. People like her always mystify me just a bit.

I selected two or three books with patterns in them to take back to the big oak table with me. I had never seen these particular books, and the patterns looked inspiring. I was toying with the idea that maybe it was time to knit an Icelandic sweater. I was pretty sure that I could do it. After all, it was only knitting with two colors at once instead of one at a time. How hard could that be, right? And, according to this book (it would have to be the book that was the most expensive), there wouldn't be any seams to sew up if I knit one of these kinds of pullovers. And there were so many fun little patterns to put into the yoke. It would be really, really hard to decide which one to do. And then... once I decided which pattern to do... I would have to choose colors... and type of yarn. Sigh. I could tell that I was probably going to have to spend a lot of time here at the old yarn store. I was still giggling to myself over this terrible piece of news when another knitter flopped down in the chair across the table from me. She did not look happy. She set her knitting bag very gingerly down onto the table in front of her and rested her head on one hand.

She was obviously in great distress. I frowned to myself. What could her problem possibly be? Did she have to live in an ugly old house for one year three months and two days with her two least favorite people in the world? I think not. Did she have to put up with an ugly little killer dog that insisted on sleeping in her bed? I think not. She really probably had nothing to complain about other than a problem with her knitting. I snorted. Poor thing. I went back to studying pretty patterns and ignored her.

A little foot kicked me in the leg. Hard. I checked discretely under the table, but there was nothing there. The foot kicked me again. I sighed with the realization of what was kicking me. It was my stinking old conscience. It didn't happen very often, but when it did... it was just a bit annoying. And then I remembered that I was at this yarn store for a reason. I should be making friends instead of hiding behind a knitting book. What was I even thinking? Here was a knitter in distress, and I had the know-how to help her. Maybe. Even if I didn't...I could probably make it up. At least I could be happy knowing that I had done all that I could to help a fellow knitter in need. My conscience patted me enthusiastically on the back. See? I felt better already.

I smiled tentatively at the depressed, wilted knitter across the table. "Are you having problems with your knitting?" I asked sweetly. I thought I said it pretty good, actually. Maybe I could even make a friend or two here. The thought made me a little nervous.

She lifted her head weakly. "Gracious," she said, "you wouldn't believe it. I have such a problem."

I decided to give her my most friendly smile, "Do they help you with your problems here?"

A little animation returned to her face. "They sure do," she said. "They're really sweet about it." She paused to look around the store impatiently, "Although you should really plan your mistakes for a less busy day."

I saw my opening. Here I went. I was going to be friendly and make a friend. "Would you like me to look at it for you?" I asked. "I know a little bit about knitting."

Her face lit up and she scooted herself over to the chair next to me faster than you could say, "Purl."

"Do you really mean it?" she asked. "I would be so grateful."

"Sure," I said enthusiastically, while at the same time, really, really, really hoping that she did not have a problem that was going to take forever to fix. My conscience tapped me on the shoulder. I shrugged it away irritably.

She pulled a little piece of knitting out of her bag. It was a light, variegated lilac, about 12 inches wide, knitted in stockinette stitch, with a seed stitch border. I guessed that it was going to be some sort of children's sweater. If she thought it was going to fit her, she was sadly mistaken. I couldn't see anything tragically wrong with the little piece of knitting. Certainly nothing worth hanging your head over. Besides that, even if she had a life-shattering mistake in her knitting – how horrible would it have been to just take it out and do it over? It was twelve measly inches. People are so weird sometimes.

She wiggled it in front of my nose, "Isn't it terrible?" she asked.

I grasped the terrible piece of knitting to examine it more closely. "I'm afraid I don't see…" I began.

With a shaking finger, she pointed to the offending spot, about halfway across her knitting, and I saw it. She was right. It was terrible. The worst thing that could possibly happen to a knitter.

The horror.

Not.

I grinned to myself. This was definitely something I could help her with. I was so going to be a hero.

"Yes," I said, "I see the problem now." I pretended to study it more closely, "Hmmmmm… this…" I paused. I really didn't need another kick from my conscience. "This is just a dropped stitch."

Her jaw hit the table. "Just a dropped stitch?" she gaped. "I know it's a dropped stitch. That's not the problem. The problem is how am I going to fix it and not have a great big gaping hole in my knitting?"

I gave her another considering look. Huh. Perhaps little Miss Crankypants wasn't someone I wanted as a friend. She seemed like a real whiner. I would probably end up tying her to the chair with her own yarn if I had to actually spend any time with her. Well. That's what happens when you try to make friends. But, I guess I could still help.

"So," I said, "there are several ways to fix a problem like this. You could unknit back to the point that you dropped the stitch."

She huffed impatiently, "Do you have any idea how long that would take?" she asked.

Right. What was I thinking?

"Or you could pull your needles out and unravel back to the dropped stitch then put the stitches back on your needles."

Her indrawn breath of horror was enough answer.

"Or, you could just pick up the dropped stitch."

"If I knew how to do that," she wailed, "I would have done it already."

Wow. She really was a whiner. You know, having friends maybe wasn't as much fun as it sounded. There really was nothing wrong with enjoying the company of yourself, was there?

I sighed patiently (and as quietly as I could). "My knitting teacher told me that the first thing you should learn, after the knit stitch, is how to fix the knit stitch. She always said, 'If you can fix your knitting, you won't be afraid of your knitting.'"

The knitter sighed dramatically, "She was probably right," she admitted woefully. "I guess I should learn how to fix my mistakes and then I wouldn't panic so much when I make one. It's just that it's so hard."

I had to stop her. "It's not hard," I said firmly. "Watch me." I picked up her knitting again and pulled at the loop that was currently three rows down from where it should be. "This is the loop that should be up on your needles, right?" She nodded miserably. "And see these bars behind your loops?"

"There's three of them," she said.

"That's right," I said encouragingly, "that's because your stitch has run down three rows. Do you have a crochet hook?" When she obligingly pulled one out of her bag, I showed her how to insert the hook through the loop and then pull the bars through the loop, one at a time until it was back up to where it belonged.

I transferred my gaze to hers. She was currently looking at me with such a look of amazement, gratitude and wonder that I felt a brief glow of self-satisfaction. "Wow, thank you!" she exclaimed.

"You're very welcome," I replied. "Do you see how easy it is to do now?"

"Sure," she said happily, "you are so right. It is really easy."

You know, sometimes you just have to have tough love for someone. Or else they never learn anything. "Great," I said, "now it's your turn."

The amazement, gratitude and wonder turned to stunned incredulity tinged with righteous anger as she watched, in horror, as I pushed the stitch back off the needle and let it run back down three rows. "I can't believe you just did that," she breathed, every muscle in her body tense. "You had it all fixed and now you ruined it!"

"Oh, come on," I coached, "you've got to learn sometime."

Ten minutes later, she had successfully picked up the stitch herself. I think she may even have grasped the concept of picking up a running stitch. She should have been glowing with pride. Unfortunately, she only seemed to be glowing with anger.

She thanked me quite nicely, albeit a bit icily and left the store.

The girl behind the counter (Molly – I mentally reminded myself), came over to sit at the table with me. "That was very nicely done," she said softly. "I know Carolyn's been trying and trying to get Michelle to learn to fix her own mistakes for quite a while." She grinned ruefully, "I think it's just easier for her to come in here and have them fixed for her. Thank you."

I shrugged, "It was really nothing," I said. "I was happy to do it. I think it's important for people to learn how to take care of their own problems."

"Ah, yes," a gentle voice behind me said, "but it's even more important when someone helps you learn how to take care of your problems."

I turned to see the lady I had previously identified as Carolyn standing at my shoulder. She had such a sweet little face; I liked her immediately.

She held out a hand to me, "My name is Carolyn," she said. "It's very nice to meet you."

I shook her hand politely, "Very nice to meet you too," I said. "My name is Natalie."

Carolyn glanced at the customers still milling about the store. Apparently satisfied that they needed no help, she plunked herself down into the chair next to me. "I don't think I've seen you in here before, dear," she said. "Welcome."

"Thanks," I said happily, "I just love your store. It's so pretty and inspiring." I grinned at them both, "I feel like I want to live here."

Molly grinned back, "I know the feeling," she said, "I do live here."

I was stunned. "You live here?" I demanded. "In the store?" I pictured her making a little nest of yarn each night.

Her smile was delightfully dimpled, "No," she laughed. "Above the store."

"You are so lucky," I said, and I meant it. How wonderful to live so close to all of this lovely yarn. I bet she slept well at night.

"I know it," she said. "I love living here. It's the best place I've ever lived. You should see the apartment upstairs. It is so cozy and cheerful."

Cozy and cheerful. Instead of cold and haunted. Ok. I'll admit it. I was jealous.

"When did you move to Springgate?" Carolyn asked. "I can tell you're quite a knitter. It's hard for me to believe you've been here long and we haven't met."

"Two days," I admitted.

Carolyn laughed. "Well," she said, "that's not long. Are you staying or just visiting?"

"I thought I was just visiting," I said, "but now it looks like I'm staying." I sighed, "Maybe."

"That's great," Molly said, "I hope we see a lot of you then."

"I hope you don't charge for sitting here," I said, only half joking. "I can't afford yarn and sitting time."

Carolyn smiled, "You are welcome here anytime." She studied me for a moment and then hesitated, "Are you, by any chance, looking for a job?"

I stared at her, "Is this some kind of joke?" I asked.

"No, my dear," she said, "I'm quite serious. I saw how nicely you handled Michelle, and we could really use another helping hand around here," her brow furrowed slightly, "It would only be for a few months or so until our other employee, Louise returns, I'm afraid." I'm pretty sure my mouth was hanging open. She glanced around the store and then back at my face, "I'm sorry. Of course, you don't want a temporary job. Please forget I asked."

"No!" I all but shouted it. "Are you kidding? I would love to work here. You are a complete answer to prayer."

Carolyn tipped her head, "How so?" she asked.

"Well," I said, "I just moved here, and I was hired yesterday at Colson's, and today…" I paused. Perhaps I shouldn't tell them. After all, I could be ruining my chances at a job with my honesty. But, it was either that or be kicked again by my conscience. And, for some reason, I felt like I could trust this kind-faced, white-haired lady. And that doesn't happen every day. "I...I was....fired this morning."

Molly's eyebrows rose in surprise. "Well that certainly did not take long," she said, trying to hide a smile, "What happened?"

I was starting to like Molly more and more. Celia and Jack would have said, "What did you do?" not "What happened?" The difference was small. But it was huge.

I sighed. "Well. At first, it was just a small thing. The boss, who shall remain nameless, was having a meeting. He asked me to bring in the coffee and donuts (which, by the way, are a very unhealthy snack choice). While I was in there, he made a big deal of pointing me out to all of the head honchos who were in there. And then, he smiled really patronizingly and asked me what I thought they could do to make their small appliance sale even better. I saw the smirks going around the table, and I knew they were laughing at me. So..." I paused. How honest do you think I should be? Molly and Carolyn's faces were just the right combination of interested and amused. I decided to go for total honesty. "So I said, 'Why don't you put a sale on vacuums and make big posters that say...'"

Molly was trying to hold back her laughter, "Oh no," she said, "You didn't!"

I rolled my eyes and sighed, "Yes I did. I don't know why I did. But I did." Now, I could see how stupid I was. Why do I never see these things when they are happening?

I could see that Carolyn had not arrived at the same conclusion that Molly had, so I was forced to continue. "So I said, 'Why don't you put a sale on vacuums and make big posters that say, *Colson's Sucks.*' I thought it would be exciting and eye-catching."

Molly's face danced with shared mischief, "And they obviously didn't think the same?"

I couldn't help myself. I giggled. "Nope. One guy actually spit out his coffee."

Carolyn's smile was wide and amused, "Perhaps if they had a little more fresh thinking like yours, they wouldn't be struggling to stay in business." But then she turned serious, "And you were fired for that?"

I toyed with the book on the table, neatly evading either of their eyes. "Well," I admitted, "not specifically for that, but it was one of the reasons cited. The second reason was because when the boss came out of the meeting, he said to me, 'Ms. Wolcott, can you please go get me some lunch and pick up my suit from the cleaners?' I said, 'No. Can you?'"

I heard a choking sound and looked to see Carolyn trying very hard not to laugh. Molly didn't even try to look like she wasn't laughing. She put her head on the table and pounded her fist. "That is so funny," she said, "You are amazing. I wish I would have been brave enough to say that if I had been you."

Carolyn patted Molly's hand affectionately. "You are plenty brave, Molly," she said. "Don't ever think you aren't."

Molly shook her head, "I don't think I'm *brave* Carolyn," she said, "not like Natalie. I would never have said that to him. I may have muttered it under my breath... on my way to the dry cleaners, that is."

I grinned. "Well, it really wasn't that funny before I came in here," I admitted. "I was really feeling hopeless. I didn't know what I was going to do. I had such a hard time even finding that job. I should have just kept my mouth shut and put up with his pompous, sexist..."

It was my turn to have my hand patted by Carolyn, "Obviously, it isn't your nature to remain quiet when you feel injustice." Her smile was warm and sweet. "It is a gift... but it can also get you into trouble."

"I know," I sighed. "I'm trying to learn to control it." I raised worried eyes to Carolyn's. "I hope that doesn't change your offer."

She looked scandalized. "Of course not," she said. "I appreciate straight-forward personalities."

By the time I left, I didn't even remember how miserable I was when I came in. I was employed at a yarn shop. See? It's a good thing that I am a positive person and look on the bright side instead of dwelling on the negative. What? You just be quiet.

The only bad thing is that I forgot to stop at the hardware store. I also forgot to duck when I was going past the bakery. I didn't even realize my mistake until, two seconds after I was past the door, I heard it burst open and a loud voice yelled my name. Rats. Double rats. Happiness can be dangerous.

I turned slowly on my heel, trying to remember how happy I was. "Good afternoon, Jack," I said politely, "are you having a nice day at work?"

He wrinkled his nose, making the freckles dance, "You know, politeness just isn't your thing."

I stuck out my tongue at him. "I really don't know what you mean," I said. "I happen to be a very polite person."

He shrugged, "Why don't you come in and meet Ryan?"

Somehow I found myself inside the bakery. I wasn't quite sure how it happened, but I'm pretty sure it wouldn't have happened if I had been a little less hungry.

Ryan was a likable-looking guy with a friendly face and lots of red hair. There must be something wrong with him, though… for one thing, he was a skinny baker (what was up with that?) and…after all, anyone who hires Jack has to have a brain problem.

"Oh yeah," a little voice in my head whispered, "he hasn't gotten fired yet, has he?" Sometimes I really wish that the little voice was a real person… so that I could punch him in the nose.

They were both looking at me expectantly. I slowly realized that they were expecting some kind of answer from me. I wondered what the question was.

Ryan rolled his eyes, "Never mind, Jack," he said. "She's got the look of someone who has just come out of the yarn store down the street. I don't know what they put in the yarn at that store, but everyone comes out addicted."

Jack was eyeing me contemplatively, "Now that you mention it, she did act rather strangely when I talked about the yarn store yesterday." He grinned suddenly, "Natalie, I never knew that you were a yarnie-type person." Give me a break. He was going to be so annoying about this, wasn't he?

"Knitter, Jack," I said coldly. "They call us knitters." I put my nose in the air, "And that just shows you what you know."

Ryan smiled broadly and easily. "Yep, Jack. You were right. Your cousin is a little feisty."

My mouth fell open, and I was not speechless. I was rapidly and furiously trying to think of how to reply. Before I could, Ryan laughed, "Got you!" he said, "I was only kidding." He reached under the counter to pull something out. "Here. A peace offering. All the knitters are crazy about these. I'm not sure why. I mean, I know they're delicious, but for some reason, the knitters really, really love these."

I took the delicious smelling bag graciously, "Thank you, Ryan," I said, reaching towards my purse, but he waved his hand.

"No, my treat. I insist."

"Thank you," I smiled at him, "but I should be the one thanking you. If you hadn't given poor Jack a job, he probably would have starved on the street corner. Also…" I continued, "it gets him out of my hair for a while too."

Jack scowled. Ryan grinned.

Life was good.

CHAPTER 11

I ate the contents of the bag on my way back home. It turned out to be a cinnamon roll. I could see why the other knitters were addicted... it was beyond delicious... just the right combination of sweet and chewy with a tiny hint of... something that I couldn't identify, but I really loved. That settled it. I didn't care if Jack was there or not. The bakery was on my list of daily stops.

I paused in my chewing. Wow. That was really, really sneaky of Ryan. He knew exactly what he was doing. Sure. Give away a free cinnamon roll. It makes you look sooooo nice, but really, you're just guaranteeing future business. Sneaky. Sneaky. I wondered, briefly, if he could possibly be related somehow.

I urged my little car faster through the scary trees. I was really starting to hate these trees. I'm pretty sure that they had murderous inclinations towards me. I swear I could see their branches reaching out to me with their little thorny fingers. The thorns were horrible. It was almost a relief to make the turn and see the hideous house looming in front of me.

Abraham Lincoln sat demurely on the front porch. He barked at me as I got out of my car. I groaned. Was there never to be a moment's peace? At least he wasn't outside running through the haunted forest like a crazy dog. That was kind of odd, wasn't it? I was starting to wonder if there were two dogs that lived here. One that was well-behaved and one that was wild. I read a book like that once... where, at the end, there was a big dramatic surprise that the heroine wasn't really the heroine, but the twin of the crazy person who was pretending to be the heroine. Does that make sense? I think it might make more sense than a schizophrenic dog, don't you? Or maybe it was just a simple case of split personality.

I walked up the steps with the weirdest sense of unreality. Could it really only have been a few days ago that I walked up these steps for the first time? In a way, I felt like I had been living here forever. I opened the front door, which wasn't locked (we were going to have to write a serious memo about that one. What? It beats talking face to face, doesn't it?) and stood in the foyer. Something was wrong. I could feel it. Abraham Lincoln whined by my feet. He could feel it too. I listened carefully, trying to figure out where this feeling was coming from. And then I heard it. Raised voices in the ballroom. I froze. Someone was in my house. I froze, listening harder. It sounded like two women. I relaxed just a little. Everyone knew that burglars were usually men. It was probably just Celia arguing with someone. That would not be a new experience. I debated whether or not to go in and investigate. The sound of glass shattering had me moving without thinking.

I burst through the ballroom doors. "What do you think you are doing?" I demanded, anger already pulsing through my brain. I stopped so suddenly that Abraham Lincoln, who had been devotedly hot on my heels gave a little squeal of surprise and immediately backtracked. There was no one in the ballroom.

The room was silent. Empty.

No women engaged in confrontation.

Nothing.

I shivered in the pale coolness of the room. Okay. That was strange. And a little weird. I rubbed at my arms and looked down at Abraham Lincoln, "You heard them too, right?"

He backed slowly away from me and ran from the room. Great. Just great. Now I didn't even have the somewhat dubious comfort of a furry protector.

Outside, I heard the roar of tires coming up the driveway. I ran to the window and peered out from behind the heavy curtains. Celia was parking her car behind mine. Jack got out of the passenger side. Celia was saying something to Jack, and he laughed in reply. Something inside me twisted, and I stepped away from the window. They were coming in.

I looked around the empty ballroom once more before running out the rear door. I didn't know where I was going, but I was not staying in this house to play happy family with Jack and Celia.

I wiggled my way through the house silently and let myself out the back door. I know what you're thinking. You're thinking that I wasn't being a chicken. Such nonsense. I was merely making a swift exit in my extreme excitement and haste to go and explore the rest of the property. Thank you. That sounds very reasonable. It is also very nice of you to never again mention the fact that I thought I heard voices coming from the ballroom. I really like you.

Bummer. As soon as the door slammed shut behind me, I realized that these were *so* not the right shoes for exploring rough terrain. The grassy area around the house ended sharply into a heavily wooded area. As in… one minute there was grass… and in the next step, there were woods. And not just woods…woods with brambles. What was up with this house? The trees had thorns. The bushes had thorns. I think even the thorns had thorns. I walked a little desperately around the perimeter of the grass searching for a way into the wild woods. If I didn't hurry, someone in the house would see me lurking in the backyard. There! Ha! A wee little path leading into the woods. I took a tentative step onto it. Great. Maybe in a hundred years, they would find my bones, bleached by the sun and wind. Perhaps someone would remember me with fondness. I glanced back over my shoulder at the house staring at me with all of its shiny, windowed blind eyes and I quickly stepped further down the path out of sight.

The path wound its way delicately through the prickery woods. The woods were so dark I could barely see the sun glinting through the trees above me. For some reason, woods always freak me out. They are just too quiet. A bird twittered overhead. And too noisy at the same time. They're cold. They smell funny. And… I really hate the feeling you get when something creaks in the woods and you wonder if someone else is in the woods with you… and if they are… who they are … and what do they want… and do they want to eat you… see what I mean? Woods are no fun.

But, I was a stubborn person. Snapping sticks and long shadows weren't going to get the best of me. I plunged resolutely ahead until the path ended in a clearing. I was almost ridiculously happy to be out of the trees. I looked around the open space and was pleasantly surprised to find a little house. It obviously belonged to the big house, because it was the same color and style – just on a miniature level. I wondered if this was supposed to be a guest house or a playhouse… perhaps I could move out here…I stopped suddenly. The little house had a big problem. A problem like a recent fire, by the looks of it. Singe marks clearly showed where flames had licked up the sides with their fiery tongues. I got a little closer and sniffed the air. Judging by the smell, it was pretty recent, too. And then I froze, a sickening feeling turning my stomach to ice. Yellow police tape fell from the house in ominous shredded ribbons. I backed away, my ankle twisting a bit painfully on a stone, and I stumbled, catching myself on a very handy nearby tree. The horror of the possibility of what could have happened here was paralyzing, and for the first time, I wondered something that maybe I should have wondered about much earlier. How exactly did Grandma Rose die?

I was currently in the sitting room on the same little sofa I had plunked myself down in when speaking to Mr. Garvey. I propped my still tender ankle up on the edge of the sofa discreetly. If any pesky family members happened to pop their heads in, it would just look like I was resting lazily on the sofa after a long day of work (well, a half day of work and a half day of weirdness). I even brought a book along to complete my illusion.

But, it's not like I probably had to worry about it. Judging from the creaking coming from over my head, Celia was doing yoga in her room. And, judging from the smells coming out of the general direction of the kitchen, Jack was cooking dinner. Again. We were going to have to have a memo talk about that too. There was no need for him to feel obligated to cook dinner every day.

Especially if he thought it was going to get him out of cleaning or laundry or something like that.

I was currently working on a schedule of such trivialities along with the required weekly/monthly deposits of needed incoming cash. I'm sure it was going to be a huge hit with my lovely housemates. But someone in this house had to be realistic. It was a bit scary that that person had to be me. And, after about 20 minutes of business, I decided to reward myself with a few chapters of murder.

They had just discovered the body in the swimming pool (in my book, of course) when the doorbell rang. I waited patiently for someone to go get the door, as I certainly had no desire to talk to anyone who wasn't presently in the room. The bell rang again. And then again. With a great sigh and upheaval of my very comfortable body, I hobbled my way across the room and out to the front door.

I flung it open very dramatically, as befitting the lady of the house. I hoped that I looked intimidating. "Can I help ..." I asked... open air. Yes, my friends. I had gotten up to answer the door for no one. No one. That makes me rather angry. What a rotten trick to play on someone who just twisted their ankle. Actually, it was a rather rotten trick to play on someone with two perfectly healthy ankles. I wondered if it was Celia or Jack. It certainly wasn't a ghost. Those didn't exist, remember? You're not remembering the voices in the ballroom, are you? No. Me either.

I made my pathetic way back to the sitting room and got all comfortable again. They were just fishing the body out of the pool (which isn't really as easy as it sounds) when... surprise...surprise...you guessed it... the doorbell rang again. I sighed. Really? Perhaps it was funny once (it wasn't), but it certainly wasn't funny again. Well...someone else could just go and get it this time. This lady was done being pranked.

It rang. And rang. And rang. Jack finally came out from the direction of the kitchen. The doorbell rang on. He poked his head in the sitting room, giving me a rather annoyed look. "Perhaps you did not hear the doorbell ringing?" he inquired politely.

"Oh, I heard it," I answered, "I just prefer not to waste my time opening doors for people who aren't there."

"What are you talking about?" he asked, raising his voice to be heard over the sound of the chimes.

I smiled smugly and returned to the murder in my hand.

The doorbell stopped ringing. The door slammed. Jack's loud footsteps echoed their way back to the sitting room. "How did you know that there was no one there?" he demanded.

"Probably because there was no one there the last time the doorbell rang either."

As if on cue, the doorbell rang.

He frowned, "Must be a short in the wiring."

I looked over the top of my book innocently, "Or a ghost."

Jack rolled his eyes and marched back to the door, muttering under his breath. I heard the door slam again and giggled to myself. Then, I sobered. I put my book back down. Could it be that there really was something wrong with the wiring? That would be an easy answer, wouldn't it? Maybe it was Celia. I still hadn't forgotten the whole not-blood incident in her bathroom. Was it possible that Celia didn't want to see me any more than I wanted to see her? Could it be that she wanted to inherit this house all by herself? Could it be that she was childish enough to play silly tricks to make Jack and I leave? I considered it. Yes, she could. Or... on the other hand... it could be Jack. He was a guy. Didn't all guys have built-in electrical knowledge? I'm sure that there is a way to make a doorbell ring remotely, aren't you? Perhaps he had some type of controller in his pocket. He was working next to a hardware store, after all. I know you haven't known him for a very long time, and my opinion of him is admittedly a bit biased based on certain childhood experiences which I will not bore you with, however, I can tell you that I do know, for a fact, that he is a very good actor. And... pretty devious, too.

So which one is your money on? Oh dear. I know what you're thinking. It's amazing. It's like we are on the same wavelength or something. I can assure you, with all sincerity, that I am not secretly the villain, trying to get rid of Celia and Jack. I do applaud your imagination, though. It is very active.

Jack returned to the sitting room with a bunch of wires in his hands. He wiggled his eyebrows evilly, "I don't think we'll be having any more doorbell trouble," he said with a terrible smile.

I tried to compose myself and keep my face straight. "Good. That's very nice. Thank you, Jack."

"Yes, well, I think that…"

My dear little friends, I wish you could have seen the look on his face when he was interrupted by a very loud… knocking. It was so funny. His face turned red and a little purple vein in his forehead bulged out. The knocking continued.

Jack took a deep, calming breath. It looked like he was saying something under his breath.

"What was that, Jack?" I asked sweetly, "I couldn't quite hear you."

He took another long breath before turning his full attention to me. "If I find out that you're playing some kind of joke on me…" the threat dangled in the air between us.

I gulped loudly. "Whoa. Now that is scary. I shudder to think of what you would do…" but it was really no fun arguing with him right now with the knocking providing a counter beat to my words. "Oh bother," I said, "Just go and answer the door."

He spun on his heel and marched toward the front door, obviously expecting me to follow him. I hobbled behind him as fast as I could without looking like I was hobbling. The knocking stopped suddenly. He flung the door open. No one was there.

Jack turned to me slowly, "This is really not funny." I was starting to believe in Jack's innocence – in this matter alone, of course.

"I don't think it's funny either."

He eyed me suspiciously. "Do you think Celia would think this is funny?"

"You know," I said slowly, "I really don't know what Celia does and doesn't think is funny. I don't even know who she is."

The annoyance left his eyes for a moment and his expression softened, "She's still your mom," he said softly, "I'm sure…"

"I think you'd better stop right there, Jack," I said, feeling the storm clouds gathering above me. "You are in no position to tell me about Celia. From what I remember…"

"Please," he said, voice rising, "How many times are you going to sing that sad song of 'Jack was such a horrible child?' It's so yesterday. Grow up."

"Grow up!" I yelled at him, "I'm not the one making the doorbell ring and…"

"I am not making the doorbell ring!" he yelled back, leaning over me so that his angry, red face was in my face. It was not a pretty sight.

"Admit it! You're trying to get rid of me. You want this house all for yourself!"

"When are you going to realize that…"

A soft voice cut through our arguments. "Excuse me, folks…" someone said.

It was so unexpected that we both jumped back away from the door. I jumped back with a little squeak of surprise, while Jack managed a more manly one-step retreat.

The man in the door removed his hat and cocked his head to the side as if unsure how to proceed. Twisting his hat in his hands, he said, "I'm really sorry to disturb you."

It was then that I realized he was wearing a policeman's uniform. And he had a very nice smile. His hair was light brown and feathered out around his face most attractively. His biggest feature, however, were his eyes. They were light blue and when he smiled, little crinkles appeared in the corner of each eye.

"Oh dear," I said, "I'm so sorry, officer. We certainly didn't see you standing there." I took a step forward towards the door, forgetting about my sore ankle… and with a little gasp of pain almost fell to the floor. Jack and the police officer both reached to catch me, however, Jack was faster. His hand was strong under my arm, and he sent a glare towards the officer that had him retreating a few steps.

"I thought something was wrong with you," he said irritably. "You were sitting on that sofa so quietly."

"Really?" I sneered at him, "Is that how you know when something is wrong with me? When I'm quiet."

"Pretty much," he admitted, "How about I carry you…"

I tried wriggling out of his grasp. "No, thank you," I said, trying, without good results, to free my arm, "I am perfectly capable of walking."

Jack opened his mouth to retort when a small clearing of the throat had us looking back at the door again.

"Oops," I said sheepishly, "We forgot you were there again."

Jack looked indignant and re-adjusted his hold on me to drag me in front of the police officer. "I certainly didn't forget," he said with an unrepentant grin at the police officer, "I just had to lend a helping hand to my poor, ailing cousin before I could come and be civil."

My growl would have made Abraham Lincoln proud. Speaking of which – what kind of guard dog was he anyway? Was this not the perfect time to prove his worth and earn his kibble?

Jack extended a hand to the policeman. "My name is Jack Sherman."

"Finn O'Reilly," he replied, shaking Jack's hand, "I'm the Sherriff here in Springgate. It's very nice to meet you." He turned to me, "And your poor, ailing cousin is…."

I aimed a well-placed elbow at Jack's midsection and stepped forward to extend my own hand. "Natalie Wolcott," I said with my sweetest smile. "You'll have to forgive us for looking a little strange…"

I thought I heard Jack mutter, "Some of us can't help it."

I scowled at him and continued, "…but we've had a little bit of weirdness happening here this afternoon. The doorbell kept going off, and no one was at the door." I paused to regard our visitor with just a hint of suspicion.

He was quick and obviously knew what I was getting at. "It wasn't me," he protested. "I just got here a few minutes ago. I did try the doorbell," he admitted, "but nothing happened. That's why I knocked. And then when no one came to the door, I walked down to look through the windows."

I exchanged glances with Jack. It was anyone's guess whether or not he was telling the truth. Looking over his shoulder, I could only see a small portion of his fender, as he had parked behind my car and Celia's. That, at least, would explain why we had not seen the car in the driveway.

"What can we do for you?" Jack asked, taking control of the situation once more. Rats. I wanted to do that.

Sherriff Finn twisted his hat in his hand once more. Clearly, he was not here to bring us an apple pie in welcome. "Well," he said with a small sigh, "I actually came out to welcome you to Springgate."

O-kay.

Weird.

"And also to give you my number in case you should need it." Two business cards were suddenly in his left hand, (or maybe they had been there all along and I was just now noticing. What? With blue eyes like his, why would I be wasting time staring at his hands?) and he gave one to each of us.

Jack and I exchanged glances. For once we were in complete agreement. This guy was a little cuckoo. "This is great," I said happily, "I've been wondering who I should call to have Jack arrested."

Sherriff Finn's eyes rose into his hairline, "What?" he asked in surprise.

Jack rolled his eyes and repaid me with an elbow in my ribs, "She's joking," he said. "She thinks she's funny."

The eyebrows returned to their normal place on his face. "Right." He eyed me uncertainly. "I see."

"So you visit every new person in town and give them your business card?" I asked skeptically. "That's right neighborly of you. But, for the record, it would be much better accompanied by some sort of baked dessert."

This time, he knew I was joking, and it was so worth it to watch him smile. "I'll remember that," he said before his face turned more serious, "No, actually I had heard about you folks moving into Raspberry Hill, and I was a little concerned."

"Why?" Jack asked. "It shouldn't be so unusual for relatives to come when their grandmother dies."

"No," Finn agreed easily enough. "It isn't unusual at all. And please accept my condolences on your grandmother's death. What's unusual is Raspberry Hill. Things inevitably happen around here, as your Grandma Rose knew well enough. It could just be the novelty of the big, weird-looking house – no offense. We've been up here on calls more than a few times, and we've never been able to figure out if it's kids or vandals or…"

"A ghost?" I piped up helpfully.

He looked a bit relieved that I had said it, "I know it sounds crazy," he said, "and, to be honest, I don't really believe in ghosts, but that doesn't stop the fact from being true that your Grandma Rose had quite a bit of trouble over the years." He scratched the back of his head thoughtfully, "I just thought I'd be proactive and tell you to be on the lookout. And," he paused to look us both meaningfully in the eye, "to call me if you should think something was wrong."

Wow. He was starting to scare me a little. Jack fidgeted a bit next to me. Maybe he was nervous too. I peeked a look up at him. I couldn't believe it. He was actually trying not to laugh.

Two minutes later, he had very politely gotten rid of Sheriff Finn (which was too bad – we could have at least invited him for dinner), closed and locked the front door and finally allowed himself to hoot with laughter, which I found somewhat inappropriate.

"What is your problem, Jack?" I snapped. My ankle was starting to throb again, and so I shuffled myself back to the nice comfortable couch I had left behind, muttering irritably as I went.

"Can you believe that guy was actually trying to make us believe that this house is haunted," Jack crowed. "Man, that was too funny."

"I don't think he was trying to make us think that our house is haunted, Jack," I said. "I think he was just trying to be nice."

"Oh, Natalie," Jack said, wiping tears of laughter away from his eyes, "you've always been a sucker for blue eyes."

"You shut up," I said, settling back against the pillows and throwing an extra cushion at Jack. "You're just so warped that you don't recognize nice people." I paused to find my place back in my book, tucking Sheriff Finn's business card in the book snugly. You never know. It could come in handy. "What do you think…" but Jack was gone again. Rude. I shrugged. Oh well.

Two seconds later Jack was back. He dropped a towel filled with ice rather unceremoniously over my ankle, which was again propped up on the arm of the sofa. I stared up at him… speechless.

"Who says I'm not nice?" he drawled, leaving the room. "Dinner will be ready in half an hour." He poked his head back around the doorway, "Oh – and Natalie?" I looked up obediently. "Next time you hurt yourself, why don't you tell someone about it? You don't have to suffer all by yourself, you know."

My stare must have become a little weird because Jack colored slightly and left the room quickly.

Two minutes later I slammed my book down in disgust. Rats! I had missed a perfect opportunity. I should have asked Sherriff Finn how Grandma Rose had died. Now, I would have to go see my mean old lawyer tomorrow. Unless… I pulled Finn's business card from my book thoughtfully….unless I happened to call the Sherriff and ask to meet him tomorrow to discuss it. What? I have to do something on my lunch hour, right?

CHAPTER 12

Would it be too trite to say that working at Crabapple Yarns was a dream come true? I really don't care if it is. Because it was a dream come true. I had been working for a whole 15 minutes when I realized that I had been born to work in a yarn store. I loved the fiber. I loved the patterns. I loved Molly. I loved Carolyn. I even loved the horrible coffee that Molly made. Yes, my friends… there was a lot of love going on at Crabapple Yarns today. A lot of love. And to make it even better, for eight whole hours, I could pretend that I didn't live in a crazy old house that might be haunted with a mother and a cousin that I didn't really like. Life was good at Crabapple Yarns.

Molly seemed to prefer checking customers out, so I stayed on the sales floor (Don't you just love my retail technical talk?) to assist the customers as they came in. Carolyn floated serenely through the store. She was wearing the cutest plaid pinafore (which should have looked silly on someone her age, but somehow didn't) with a frilly white shirt underneath. Her own gleaming white hair was tucked up adorably in a wispy updo. How did she do that? I caught Molly staring at it more than once, so I don't think I was alone in wondering how someone could get their hair to do that without a fairy godmother, talking mice or a magic wand. I certainly wasn't handy with a bobby pin, so my hair usually just ran wild. Having naturally curly hair can be a blessing and a curse, but most days, it sort of arranges itself. If I was feeling particularly adventurous, I would put a barrette in.

When the customers dwindled, I put my spare time to good use, playing with (err… I mean, tidying) the yarn and fawning over (err…tidying and sorting) the patterns. For a small store, Carolyn had an amazing inventory. From cobweb-light fingering weight mohair to baby yarn to wools… she had everything that you could possibly want. Or so I thought. I literally could not believe it when this little snippy thing walked in. She had a pattern in her hand.

"Excuse me," she said, impatiently, "I need a little help over here."

"Wow. You literally just walked in the door." I said, "You've got to at least give me time to cross the room."

Behind me, I heard a wheeze-like sound that could have been a smothered laugh coming from Molly. Oops. Right. Customers are a necessary part of the business. I had to be nice. It's just that the yarn store was so much more peaceful when they weren't here.

Her mouth opened and closed like a little guppy as she stared at me with her big ol' bug eyes. I softened my comment with a very sweet smile, "What can I help you with today?" I asked politely. "Perhaps some sock yarn? We just received a new shipment yesterday." Of course, I had not been working at the time, but I saw no reason to share that little tidbit, do you?

She watched me warily…obviously not quite sure how to take me, so I smiled again. One probably could not smile too much when working in a yarn store. That part was probably going to take some practice. She looked around, probably looking for Carolyn, and when she realized I was the only cookie in the jar at the moment, she reluctantly pulled a magazine from her suitcase-sized handbag. Which brings me to another point… why do women do that? I mean, if you want to have a purse, that's fine. But is it a purse… or a piece of luggage? Do you really want something so large that you have to walk at an angle just to carry it? There. Just had to get that off my chest. I feel better now.

"I would really like to knit this sweater," she said, flipping open to a dog-eared page and pointing to a model wearing a lemon-colored sweater and holding a croquet mallet.

I bobbed my head, maintaining my friendly smile. "That's very pretty," I said. "So how can I help?"

Her eyes rolled and she looked around the store once more, searching for another soul to wait upon her. Ha. Still the only cookie in the jar. "Well," she said, with a great deal of forced patience, "I need yarn."

Wow. I never would have guessed that she needed yarn. *Look around you, honey…* I was so tempted to say, *there's yarn everywhere.*

We smiled at each other for another second or so before I realized that she wanted ME to find the yarn for her. Good grief. It's not like the store was a mile long and categorized by the ancient Babylonian yarn-organizing method using hieroglyphics and ancient runes… "That's great!" I said enthusiastically. "You've come to the right place. Why don't you take a look around and see what you like."

The magazine flopped to the table. "No," she said coldly, "I want to knit this out of this yarn."

"What yarn?"

"This yarn," she said, pointing to the model still swinging her mallet.

"Okay," I said, "I'm so sorry. I didn't realize you had a yarn in mind already." I studied the pattern in the magazine a little more closely. At least it was a yarn I recognized. Carolyn had quite a nice selection of it in the cubbies along the back wall. "Right this way, please," I said pleasantly. We walked back to the cubbies and I made a beautiful sweeping gesture with my arm, "Isn't this a lovely selection?" I asked. "Now, what color were you thinking?" I could see she was a very needy customer, so I figured I might as well stay and help her pick out a color. That would get her out of the store much faster.

She was currently staring at me like I had lost my little mind. "I want this yarn," she said, pointing to the magazine once again.

I tilted my head, trying very hard to understand. "I understand," I lied. "And this is that yarn."

"But I want this yarn."

We were definitely having a communication glitch.

"I'm afraid I don't understand," I said. "If this is that yarn, and you want this yarn… then…?"

"It's not the same color," she said, as if I was the dumbest person on earth.

I studied the color in the magazine. It was color #L05, a light lemon with a hint of frost. I studied the yarn in the cubbies and selected the yellow. It was color #L06, a light lemon... but no frost. Still, a very beautiful yarn. "This one is very close," I said, showing her the skein.

She barely looked at it, "No."

"Perhaps another color?" I asked. "This color would look great with your skin tone." (Lemon wasn't going to be doing her any favors.)

On the space right next to the yarn we were currently looking at sat some skeins of light lemon with a hint of frost. Lemon must be a popular color this year. You wouldn't think so, would you... headed into fall? Strange. Either that or Carolyn got a really good deal on it. Anyways, my heart jumped with delight. Perfect. What a little salesperson I was.

"Ah!" I said. "This is perfect. Just look at the color. It's an exact match for what you were looking for."

My delight ended where her disdain began. "It's not the right yarn," she said.

I double-checked the labels. "You're right," I admitted, "this one has 5% more silk, but it's the same silk/wool blend, the same weight and the same color."

She sighed. "Thank you very much for your assistance," she said. "But I think I would like to order the proper yarn. I'll just go see Molly at the desk."

I stared in disbelief at her retreating back. "But you're the same color," I whispered to the yarn I still held in my hand, "Practically the same yarn. The same weight. The same everything but the manufacturer."

Carolyn squeezed my shoulder, making me jump. "You'd be surprised," she said, "about how many people see something in a magazine or a book and they feel like they need to use exactly what was used for the sample. It's the same thing here at the store. If I make something as a sample, I have to order three times as much of the color I knitted the sample in, because so many people want to knit it exactly how they see it."

"But... but... that's just crazy," I sputtered.

She smiled tolerantly, her wise old face crinkling and folding with the action, "We all have our own way," she said philosophically. "I like to think that there's no right or wrong in knitting. Besides," she said, lowering her voice, "knitters are crazy." She winked, "At least that's what Molly is always telling me."

Huh. I sighed. So far, my first customer experience was a complete downer. Perhaps the *reality* of a yarn store was not quite as beautiful as the *dream* of a yarn store. Now that was a depressing thought.

After the crazy lemon lady left, I joined Molly at the counter. "So, did the little copycat get her yarn ordered?"

Molly giggled, "Yes, she did," she said. "Olivia is always very particular about her yarns."

I rolled my eyes, "Crazy."

Molly bobbed her head enthusiastically, "That's my working theory," she said.

"What's that?" I asked, "What's your theory?"

Molly reached out a hand to stroke the yarn next to her, "My theory is that knitters are crazy."

We exchanged conspiratorial grins, "You could be right," I said. "That would explain a lot."

"You know it," she said. "But it would be present-company excluded, of course."

"Of course," I said, "There's no evidence to support that we are crazy." I paused to watch Molly a few more seconds, "Unless, of course, petting yarn is considered crazy."

Her hand jumped back guiltily, "That's not crazy," she defended, "That's just a yarn store employee becoming better acquainted with the yarn."

"Of course," I said again, "That explains that too."

A little clock chimed from somewhere in the close vicinity. Molly's head shot up and her eyes widened in surprise.

"What's the matter?" I asked a bit warily... even though, of course, I knew that she wasn't crazy.

"It's time," she announced gleefully, rubbing her hands together.

I took a cautious step back, "Time for what?"

"Time for a cinnamon roll!" she said, walking backward towards the door.

"Mmmmmm!" I said, unconsciously rubbing my hands together too, "get one for me, would you?"

"You bet!" she said, her brown hair whipping around as she spun to open the door. She almost stumbled into the lady trying to come in the door. Molly laughed and held the door open for her, "Good morning, Jean," she said, "I'm just on my way to get a cinnamon roll."

Jean looked like she might be a bit of a sour-puss. I don't think many people could have resisted the happy little smile on Molly's face – but Jean did. And she did it quite well. "Have a nice time," she said frostily. "I'm sure that there will be someone in here who can assist me while you leave."

Molly's smile dimmed just a bit, "Yes," she said, "of course, Jean. Natalie would be happy to help you." And with that- she was gone. Leaving me alone with Jean. Well, Carolyn was here somewhere too. But, she was helping a customer, so that didn't count.

I put on my best customer-service smile, "And how can I help you?" I asked. I hoped that she would, at least, be more interesting to help than Olivia.

You know… there's a reason behind the saying… "Be careful what you wish for" and I think I just found it.

Ten minutes later, we were still hunting for the perfect skein of yarn for her new moebius scarf. Apparently, she had knitted one a few months ago, loved it and wanted to knit another one. But the yarn had to be absolutely perfect. Soft, but firm enough to hold it's shape. Fuzzy, but not too fuzzy. Warm, but not too warm. Something perhaps brown, but not brown-brown, more of a warm-brown…You get the idea. I was really starting to buy into Molly's "Crazy Knitter" theory.

Jean was also a crafty, nosy little knitter… as we hunted for yarn, she tried to wheedle my life story right out from under me. It was a bit amusing to watch her try, so I continued to dole out tiny little morsels of information… just enough to whet her appetite, but not enough to satisfy her curiosity. I was enjoying the challenge.

"So, you're here because your grandmother died and you inherited her house?"

She was finally putting it all together. Bummer. The fun was almost over.

I nodded and held up another skein for inspection. She shook her head. "No, too brown."

I put the skein down in disgust. Too brown. Give me a break.

"So where is her house?"

"What's that?" I asked absently, holding up another skein.

She shook her head again. "I like that brown, but the mustard undertones don't work with my skin tone."

I set the skein back down. What had I even been thinking? Mustard undertones. These people were seriously strange. I'm a knitter…shopped in yarn stores many times… and I've never been any trouble like this. Granted, there was that one time when I tipped over a big, fuzzy yarn display, but that was a total accident. Yarn stores shouldn't use stands with feet that stick out so far. But that wasn't the point. The point was that I would never have demanded this type of help from the poor knitting store employees who probably only wanted to sit and eat their cinnamon rolls in peace. My stomach growled in agreement.

"So where is the house?" She asked again.

My fingers were busy searching for the perfect brown, with no mustard undertones… "Raspberry Hill," I said absently.

The silence was almost deafening. I looked up at her again. She was staring at me strangely. Very strangely. Almost like she was… outraged. I looked at the yarn that I was currently holding in my hand. "Sorry!" I said, hastily setting it back down, "I know… it's way too mustardy." I held up my hands in a non-threatening way. She continued to stare at me. "I was just moving that yarn to get to the other one down here…"

"Raspberry Hill," she said coldly. "You must be related to Rose Whittman then."

I nodded slowly, "Yes, she was my grandmother."

She put the yarns down that she had been holding as "maybe yarns" and stepped away. She was making a big mess out of the store.

"I think I'm just going to go and see what Happy Knits has," she said.

"But... but wait..." I said helplessly, "what's the matter?" I paused to stop and think about what she said, "What's a Happy Knit?"

"I'm sorry," she said, her tone causing frost to fall from the ceiling and settle on the skeins around her. Her eyes narrowed into slits. "I don't do business with murderers," she hissed, taking a threatening step forward.

Something inside of me froze in a sickening, heart-dropping way. Clammy, cold sweat bubbled up like little geysers beneath my skin. I took a step back on my still tender ankle, but the floor betrayed me, no longer steady and reliable under my feet. It rose up with a loud swirl of color and motion.

Pain exploded behind my eyes as my forehead crashed against something on my way down, down, down. The support of the floor was a welcome relief, as I curled in on myself, one hand instinctively going to my head, feeling something hot, wet and sticky between my fingers.

High pitched voices buzzed around me. They sounded like angry bees fighting over the last flower of the summer. Hands plucked and pulled, but nothing made sense over the screaming in my face. The worst thing was that everything was so dark. I was gripped with fear. Blinding fear. Which was somewhat ironic because...I was... blind. The blow must have destroyed my vision. I was blind! Panic and pain bubbled up and overflowed, and I wiggled to get away from whoever was trying to sit me up. Didn't they understand that I was blind? I didn't have time to do stupid things like sit up.

My hand was pulled away forcibly from its protective hold over my head, and something wet and cold was pressed there instead. I heard a little whimper. It might have come from me. The cold was penetrating and welcome. Words were starting to make sense.

A warm hand was patting my cheek affectionately. "Just open your eyes Natalie dear," a soft voice said.

What did she say? Open your eyes? Huh. I thought they were open. I guess that explains the blindness then. It should have been a bigger relief than what it was, but a strange remoteness was settling on me. I couldn't quite remember how one opened one's eyes, and I really didn't care either. I was just going to lay here with the balm of coldness against my throbbing head and let things settle for a moment. I had no desire to look up and see Jean's eyes still narrowed in hatred against me. Or my grandmother.

The nauseating smell of sugar and cinnamon was making my stomach churn, so I figured that Molly must be back.

"We should get her to the Emergency Room," Carolyn was saying in a worried voice.

"Her cousin Jack works at the bakery," Molly exclaimed. "I'd better go and get him."

That was all the motivation that I needed. I tried to say, "No, please don't bother. I'll be fine," but what came out was more like "Nooooooo... guh." I gingerly opened my eyes and the first thing that I saw was Jean. Her eyes were round and she was staring at me with horrified guilt. I shut them again.

"That's a great idea, Molly," Carolyn was saying, "why don't you..."

Ok. That was enough. Just because I had taken a little tumble was no reason for everyone to freak out. For pity's sake. Couldn't a person just lie on the floor and catch her breath for one minute? The last thing I needed was for Jack to see me like this. Maybe I should crawl over to Colson's and beg for my job back. Making coffee and getting laundry might be easier than dealing with these crazy knitters.

I gathered all of the energy that I could find within me and wound it up like a ball of yarn and lurched to my feet... well... to my knees, at least. Breathing heavy, I clutched my forehead once again as the change in altitude sent more shockwaves through my head. Nausea churned in my stomach and lights danced in front of my eyes. That's strange. I don't remember Carolyn having twinkle lights on this side of the store. I focused harder on what was in front of me. The floor. Yes, it was strange because I was almost positive that she didn't have twinkle lights on the floor. I paused, two knees and one shaking hand on the floor and tried to remember why getting up was so important. The floor really wasn't that bad. Maybe I could just lie back down for one more little minute...

"Natalie!"

Oh yeah. That was why.

One large, warm hand was suddenly on my back, replacing the little trembling hands that had been alternately patting and pulling at me, while another hand came around to pull my hand away from my forehead. I heard a quick indrawn breath, and then felt the welcome coolness of the towel again. At least I hoped it was a towel and not a knitting display quickly sacrificed for my benefit. That would be terrible. Most likely it was a towel from the little kitchen. I hoped it was a clean towel. Not that Carolyn had dirty towels, but wouldn't that be gross to be holding a used towel to your bleeding head? Who knows what bacteria could be… right now… inching and crawling their way out of the towel into the bleeding hole inside my head. Oh! The horror. I could feel them right now. They were going in!

I batted feebly at the towel.

Jack re-positioned his hands on me, "What is it?" he asked, bringing his head down to make eye contact with me. Strangely enough, he looked worried. "What's wrong?"

I pushed harder at the towel, "Not clean," I managed to get out. "Ba..bact…"

He disappeared from my line of vision, but I could hear his eyes rolling, "Shut up," he said roughly, holding the towel more firmly against my head. "A few bacteria are better than bleeding yourself to death."

The light, fluttering hand that I was coming to recognize as Carolyn's rested against my upper arm, "Don't worry, my dear," she said, "it's a clean, clean towel."

Jack snorted, "Don't humor her," he said. "You'll only make it worse." And then, to me, "Do you think you can stand?"

The bacteria were having a party in the hole in my head. They were dancing and making a lot of noise, and Jack didn't even seem to care. I was staring morosely at the wood grain of the floor when all of a sudden Jack's face filled my frame of vision again. I groaned and closed my eyes.

"Want some help with her?" another male voice asked. I groaned again. It was probably Ryan. This was a worse first day than my job at Colson's had been.

How totally and completely humiliating.

I wound my yarn ball of energy up once again and lifted my head. "He doesn't need help with her," I said, as clearly as I could. "She is fine." And with the strength of a superhero, I did the most amazing feat that anyone can do after she has whacked her head and laid on the yarn store floor in humiliation while everyone else stood around, staring mercilessly – I rose to my feet. "See?" I said, sticking my chin out. And then the blackness claimed me once more. After that, there was a confusing jumble of light and noise and movement until the world became beautifully black once more.

When life came back into focus, I was lying on my back on something a little softer than Carolyn's store floor. There was a suspicious smell of antiseptic and the general odor of doctors wafting about me. Great. I was at the hospital. I tried to raise my arm, but someone was holding my hand. I cracked an eye and blinked in surprise. It was Jack. He blinked in surprise back at me, before his face lit with a soft smile, "Welcome back," he said. Someone behind me talked, and he looked up at them and nodded.

My pipes were a little rusty, so it took me a few moments to gather enough spit to talk, "Why did you take me to the hospital?" I demanded. "Am I dying?"

"Not yet," he said cheerfully, "but it was fun listening to you babble all the way over here about how you thought you were dying and that the bacteria were eating your brains… and then we had to listen to a whole diatribe about how worried you were that your brains would fall out of the hole in your head."

"That's ridiculous," I said, frustrated that I was unable to manage a frown because my forehead stubbornly refused to budge.

"I know," he said, making his eyes wide and innocent. "That's what I told you. You have to have brains in your head before they can fall out."

I tried frowning again. No luck. I looked to Jack for an explanation. He winced sympathetically, "They've numbed your forehead," he said, "because they have to put some stitches in. You cracked your head pretty good, so you also have a slight concussion."

I was about to tell him that I did not require any stitches and that a few band-aids would work just fine when the big, not-so-pretty face of what I assumed to be a doctor suddenly loomed over me. I couldn't help it. I flinched back. Not only did he surprise me, but he must have had garlic for supper last night. Eeewww. It should be against the law.

"We'll get you stitched right up, my dear," he said. "You'll be back home in no time."

GREAT. The last place I wanted to go.

"Actually," I said, "I'm headed back to work."

Dr. Stinky Breath exchanged a glance with Jack, "You will not be working the rest of the day," he said sternly, "and not tomorrow either. You need to rest and let your brain heal from the concussion."

"I don't…"

"Have a brain?" Jack supplied helpfully. "Don't worry," Jack told the doctor. "She'll be resting."

I glared at them both as best I could and rolled my head to the side to see what the pesky doctor and his nurse were up to on the table next to my bed. My stomach churned in response. I really, really wished I hadn't looked. I don't have much use for needles – unless they are knitting needles, of course. The thought of someone poking through my skin and… I took a deep breath… and tried not to think about it anymore. Which was kind of hard to do since the doctor was picking up the needle already.

"This won't hurt a bit," he promised. Why do they always say that? They're never telling the truth. Don't they think that we know what that really means? It means, "This is really going to hurt, but since I have told you it won't hurt, you will keep quiet when it does because, otherwise, we will all think you are the world's biggest wimp." I guess saying that, however, would not inspire much confidence in the patients. "It's actually a nice, simple cut and shouldn't scar a bit."

I swallowed back my reply and looked back at Jack, who squeezed my hand sympathetically. "You'd probably better leave now," I said. "You don't want to see this." I jumped a little at the touch of a cold, gloved hand on my face.

"Oh, I don't mind," Jack said with a smile. "I'm just going to keep an eye on the hole while the doc stitches to make sure no extra brains fall out. You can't afford to lose anymore."

"Not funny," I said. "Seriously. Why don't you go call Carolyn or something and tell her I'm going to be fine."

His hand tightened in response, and it didn't look like he was moving. It should have annoyed me... after all, who wanted Jack here anyways? It must be the blow to the head that was making his presence tolerable... and dare I say... comforting?

"Hey," Jack said unexpectedly, "what do you think about inviting Ryan up for dinner some night?"

"What?" I asked dumbly.

"He's never been inside Raspberry Hill and would love to explore. I thought maybe he could come for dinner and we'd give him a tour." His eyes twinkled a bit, "I told him he could bring Molly."

"Why would he bring Molly?"

Jack wiggled his eyebrows in what he probably thought was a suggestive manner. "Don't tell me you haven't noticed?" he sneered. "I noticed right away."

"You're crazy," I replied. "Maybe your brains fell out too. They're so small they probably fell out your ear..." I stopped to hiss a little as the doctor pulled something a little tight. Jack's hand got tighter too.

"My brains are fully functioning," he said. "And my eyes are too. Which is how I guessed that Ryan likes Molly." He leaned forward, "Actually," he confided, "I knew something was up the very first day I worked at the bakery. Molly came in to get a cinnamon roll (she comes in every day), and after she left, he was just standing there with a strange expression. That's how I knew."

I studied him carefully. "Well, aren't you just so observant," I said. "How long have they been dating?"

Jack shook his head, "They're not dating."

This was getting confusing again. Perhaps it was the concussion. "You just said that he..."

Jack sighed dramatically, "Ahhhh…. Love…. These kids nowadays just don't know how to express their feelings."

"You mean that he loves her and she doesn't know it?" I demanded. "That is crazy. She is right about her Crazy Knitter Theory. She's the craziest of the crazy."

"I don't even want to know what the Crazy Knitter Theory is," Jack drawled. "And how can she be the crazy one if he doesn't tell her how he feels?"

"True," I admitted. "They're both crazy. Go ahead."

"Go ahead with what?"

"Didn't you ask me if I thought it was a good idea to invite Ryan up for supper?"

"Yeah."

"Go ahead."

"Okay." He paused, "You'll join us for dinner, right?" I agreed. Jack's cooking was really quite tasty… far, far beyond my box-opening skills. "And do you mind if Celia…"

"All done," the doctor said, just at the right moment.

I turned my head to stare at him in shock, "All done already?"

He smiled, "Yep. Your friend there did a good job of distracting you, didn't he?"

I smiled cautiously back, "I guess he did."

The doctor sighed as he pulled off his gloves, "I only wish he could have been here to distract the little guy I had back here yesterday. He needed one stitch in his finger and it took me almost an hour."

I was home and tucked up in bed when it hit me. Jean had called Grandma Rose a murderer.

CHAPTER 13

Concussions were no fun. I didn't really expect them to be, but the reality was worse than the expectation. Headache, nausea, double vision, lethargy... all the while... on the inside... I longed to be up and going. I wanted to go back to work. I wanted to go track Jean down and demand an explanation. I wanted to be knitting. I wanted to go visit Sherriff Finn and get some answers. I wanted to be... I sighed and fluffed my pillow up a little higher... anywhere but in this bed.

Not even Abraham Lincoln was here to keep me company. Wasn't that rude? I mean, if ever there was a time for a little dog to lay down next to you and feel sorry for you – THIS was the time. Knowing him, he was waiting until I fell asleep to come in and make his presence known. Abraham Lincoln was quite possibly the most opposite little dog I had ever met. Well... I can't really say that, since he's really the only dog, little or small, that I've spent any extended time with.

Let's face it. I was bored. Even Jack had left me to go and start dinner. Blech. The thought of food turned my stomach inside out. If I ever ate again it would be too soon. A strange squeaking metal sound was coming down the hall. I perked my ears up interestedly. Maybe Abraham Lincoln had gotten stuck in a suit of armor.

There was a cautious knock on the door. "Come in," I called.

The minute Celia's blond head came into view, I instantly regretted my invitation.

She continued dragging what I soon realized was a TV cart into the room and then walked over to my bed. I felt strangely vulnerable.

Her face was creased in sympathy, "I'm so sorry, honey," she said. "Jack told me what happened. How are you feeling?"

"Fine," I replied warily.

"I brought you my TV," she said, stating the obvious, "because I thought, with the concussion and all, that you might not be up to anything else and you might be bored."

"Thanks."

She fluttered around the room, pulling the curtains more securely shut, arranging the TV cart, plugging it in until I had to close my eyes from all of the movement.

"There," she finally said, "it's all ready for you." She laughed somewhat nervously, "Of course there's no cable or anything, so I brought some movies that I thought you'd like." She held up a handful of VHS tapes for my inspection. I didn't realize anyone still had those. "Which one would you like first?"

I shrugged. I know. I wasn't being nice. I actually wasn't quite sure HOW to be nice to my mother anymore. And it was making me feel very guilty, which really made me mad.

"I'll just put one in then," she said, doing her best to smile... as I was obviously breaking her heart, "and we'll just go from there. How does that sound?"

When I woke again, nighttime had fluttered in on soft, dark wings and landed with the soft moonfall across my bed. Someone had been in to turn off the movie and open the curtains. I'm guessing it was Celia, as Jack probably did not remember my love of the moonlight. I was a bit shocked that Celia did. I sat up cautiously in bed and waited for the room to stop its impression of a boat at sea. I clearly did not have a bad concussion... otherwise... why had they let me sleep so long? Weren't you supposed to wake people up who when they had concussions every so often to make sure that they weren't dying, or something like that? How rude. Maybe they wanted me to die.

I crept cautiously out of bed and across the floor, instinctively knowing that any bright lights were not going to be pleasant and walked towards the bathroom.

Everything was fine. I purposely kept the lights off in the bathroom, too. I didn't want any images of what was sure to be an ugly bruise ruining the rest of whatever sleep I could get tonight. My head was starting to pound again. Some painkillers would have been nice, but there were none in the bathroom, and I really did not think I was capable of going all the way downstairs. I headed back towards the bed as soon as I was ready.

Sometimes, don't you think that beds are a little haven in a big, scary world? Isn't it so wonderful, after a rotten day, to crawl into a nice, warm bed with a big, fluffy blanket and pretend like nothing else existed? I longed, with every fiber of my being, to be back in bed right now. Instead, I was still halfway across the room, walking like a little old lady with shaking legs and blurry vision. I paused in my great pilgrimage to take a breather. A cold breath of air caught me by surprise, and goosebumps peppered my arms. I looked around for the cause, but was stopped by the... the...

And, for the second time today (if it still was today), I welcomed the blackness.

Something wet and rough was being rubbed up and down my face. I was wrapped in something warm and laying on something soft. Something smelled familiar. And, even though I couldn't remember...I knew that something was wrong. Really wrong.

"Natalie," someone was calling urgently. "Wake up. Look at me." Hands patted my shoulders and arms gently.

Bossy. Why should I when I was completely warm and comfortable? Well, except for the wetness on my face that wouldn't stop. A breathless little yip and snort suddenly made sense. Ugh. I was being licked by Abraham Lincoln. Dog breath.

"I just don't know, Jack" a voice wailed. "I don't see any listings for doctors in Rose's directory." I could hear pages flipping.

"Then find one in the phone book," he snapped, anger coloring his tone. "I don't think we should move…"

My face was going to be completely licked off by Abraham Lincoln. Why couldn't they do something about that instead of trying to call a doctor? Who needed a doctor anyway? Like everything else in life, I guess I was going to have to do something myself, so I pushed Abraham Lincoln feebly away with one hand.

"Natalie!" Jack exclaimed, grasping my other free hand just as he had done in the Emergency Room, "Are you awake?"

"No."

"Come on," he said, in the gentlest voice I had ever heard him use, "open your eyes and let us see you."

Summoning the strength, I peeked one eye open and was shocked to see his face so close to mine. Every freckle looked like an asteroid. "Blech," I said, ashamed of how weak my voice was, "I think I'll just keep them closed."

His face crumpled with, what looked to be, relief. "Thank God," he said fervently. "We were so worried."

I risked opening the second and looking around. I was back in bed. Hallelujah. Memory rushed back to me. I grabbed his other hand with mine and looked wildly around the room, "Do you see it?" I demanded, trying to get up. "Where is it?"

It was almost ridiculous how easily he pushed me back down, "What is your problem?" he demanded, "Settle down."

Celia came running from across the room, flinging a small spiral notebook down on my bed stand. It looked like she might have been crying, "Oh my dear," she said, her voice catching, "I can't tell you how glad we are to see you awake!"

But, I didn't have time for small talk. I was busy looking for the ghostly apparition that had been floating in front of the window. I couldn't see a thing, though, not with Jack's big head in the way.

Celia stroked back my hair fondly, but I wiggled away, "No," I said, ignoring the hurt look on her face, "there's a… a…."

"A what, sweetheart?" she crooned anyway, "Did you see something? Was it a mouse?"

"No!" I said, clutching Jack's hands tighter, "It was over there – by the window – it was – it was – a ghost!"

I really expected more of a reaction than what I got. Wouldn't you be a little bit upset if someone told you that there was a ghost in the room? Yep. Me too! These people were weird. And they didn't even have the excuse that they were crazy knitters. They were just plain crazy.

Celia's mouth fell open in a little "O" and she exchanged a meaningful glance with Jack, who looked a bit grim.

"There's no ghost, Natalie," he said quietly and firmly. "It's just your concussion. The doctor said that you might see things that aren't really there for a day or so."

I yanked my hands out of his and struggled to sit up- away from Celia's arm range. Okay. I could see their point. I might be inclined to think the same thing if Jack had hit his head and then said he saw a ghost. It was a completely logical assumption. I was just going to have to convince them otherwise with my slow and methodical reasoning.

"But I felt cold when it appeared. On TV, the ghost always comes when there's a blast of cold air."

From the looks on their faces, I don't think that was quite as logical as I would have liked it to be.

"You're probably cold because you're walking around in bare feet and …" Jack began.

I grabbed him by the front of his shirt, "You listen," I snarled. "I was coming out of the bathroom when I felt a blast of cold air. I looked around the room, thinking that something was causing it and I saw it. It was hovering just above the ground. A shadowy figure, transparent, yet solid… it was wearing some sort of long dress… and when it turned…" I paused to take a breath and keep my voice from trembling, "It didn't have a face. I could see right through it. It was horrible. And then the next thing I knew, I woke up here on the bed."

Both Celia and Jack sighed deeply. I was clearly a difficult patient. They exchanged meaningful glances once again. It was really quite annoying. Did they think I couldn't see them?

It appeared that Jack was the designated speaker. "We've been checking on you every two hours," he said. "It's just after midnight now. The last couple of times we checked, you were sleeping and only woke up enough to mumble and snore."

"I guess you're not trying to kill me then," I said sarcastically.

They generously chose to ignore the remark, "When I came to check on you this last time, you were laying in a heap on the floor. I tried to wake you up, but you wouldn't respond. I put you back in bed, yelled for Celia, and we both tried. It took almost ten minutes for you to rouse even just a little." His eyes dropped to study the duvet, "We were getting a little worried."

I was still trying to peek around Jack's big head, "I know what I saw," I said stubbornly.

"Normally, I would agree with you," he said, "but you've had a blow to the head and reality just isn't quite as real as it normally is for you right now." He smirked, "Although I'm not sure how normal your reality is normally."

I gave him my best stink eye. "I'm not seeing things," I argued. "I know that I saw a ghost."

They both humored me by making a big show of checking in all the closets, looking under the bed, opening and closing every door in their "ghost hunt." Which was really just ridiculous. Whoever heard of a ghost hiding under the bed? I decided that it was time for them to leave. The worst thing after a supernatural experience was to be around skeptics.

"If you're too scared, you can always sleep with me," Celia offered, as they were both preparing to leave and head back to their own nice, warm beds. Yeah. That was a really tempting offer, wasn't it? Not.

"We can move you to another room..." Jack had offered. That was pretty stupid, too, wasn't it? If the ghost could be here... then the ghost could be there. Right?

After they left, I did my best to stay awake and monitor for otherworldly activity. None came, but needless to say, I didn't get very much sleep the rest of the night. Although, when Celia and Jack came in to check on me, I was quick to give the impression that I had.

CHAPTER 14

I was a prisoner in my own room. Celia and Jack had decided that I was unfit for work today, and so I was exiled to my room. And, after seeing the impressive bruise and accompanying swelling... with the added beautiful touch of several stitches... I was inclined to agree with them. No amount of makeup was going to cover this monster up. There wasn't a polite way to say it. I looked ugly.

So, I moped in my room and watched movies until I couldn't stand to watch another one. I must have dozed off, because when I awoke, there was a strange presence in my room. I instinctively knew that it wasn't Jack or Celia. One look at her happy little face and the horribleness of the night felt just a little bit farther away. It was Molly.

"Jack's in the kitchen cooking up something that smells absolutely wonderful," she confided to me. "I hope I'm invited to stay for lunch."

I smiled my first smile since yesterday, "Consider yourself invited then," I said. "You're always welcome here."

Her smile faded a bit, as she studied my forehead.

"Looks ugly, doesn't it?" I asked. "I look like a freak."

She hesitated, "It doesn't really look that bad," she said. "In a day or two..."

"It will still look ugly," I interrupted her. "You are too nice, Molly."

She eyed me uncertainly, "No, I'm really not," she said, "and I do think that the swelling has gone down since yesterday. Keep ice on it and I really do think it will look a bit better tomorrow." She giggled, "And maybe you could part your hair the other way so that it hangs over your forehead and hides your ugly..."

I laughed, "So what are you really doing here?"

She sat down on the side of the bed, ignoring the chair next to it. Amazingly, I didn't seem to mind. "I was really worried about you," she admitted. "Jean confessed and told us what she said before you... um... fell."

My fingers became very interesting all of a sudden. "I'm sorry to have created such a scene in the store."

"Natalie!" She said, sounding shocked, "We couldn't care less about the scene in the store. What we care about is you." I looked back up at her and was amazed to see Molly, usually so gentle, looking quite fierce. "We're furious with Jean for spreading her lies, and especially for telling them to you." She looked around the room as if to make sure no one else was listening, "Jean can really be a big pain in the you-know-where," she admitted. "She seems to enjoy causing trouble."

It was time to talk.

"What did she mean by calling Grandma Rose a murderer?" I asked. "I need to know."

Molly shook her head, "I don't know." She held up a hand to still my protest, "I really, really don't know. I haven't lived here in Springgate for that long. Carolyn knows something, but she said that since all she knows is hearsay and second-hand opinions, she won't repeat it." She shrugged helplessly, "The only thing she would say is that your Grandma Rose was a sweet soul who wouldn't hurt anyone."

"Of course she wouldn't!" I exclaimed indignantly (even though I really had no idea). "My grandma might have been a bit of a recluse, but she would never...." I met Molly's sympathetic gaze and somehow felt forced to tell the truth. "Actually," I admitted, "I don't know what my Grandma Rose could have done. I never knew her." Molly's face folded up with sympathy. My denial and curiosity speech seemed like a million years ago, and grief was closing in on me. I put both hands over my eyes and swallowed the tears down hard.

Molly's little hand closed over my arm, "We'll go talk with the Sherriff tomorrow," she said. "I'll go with you. I'm sure he would know what happened. Or perhaps your Grandma's lawyer. We'll figure this out. Don't worry."

Just like that. Amazing. Just like that, I had an ally. Who knew that having someone to share a burden with could lighten the load so much? It had been my intention to talk to the Sherriff or Mr. Garvey anyways regarding the death of my grandmother... now I could add a few more questions to that conversation. Molly was a genius. Of course, had I been thinking clearly, I would have arrived at the same course of action myself. Which, also, made me a genius, I guess.

I couldn't talk about Grandma Rose any longer, so I decided to change the subject. In the bright light of day, my ghost seemed quite unlikely. Although I would never, ever, never admit it to either Jack or Celia, I had a sneaking suspicion that they might be correct. It was possible that the ghost had been a concussion-induced hallucination. Which I would be teased about for the rest of my life. Which meant that they would tell everyone I knew about it too. So, I might as well get a jump on them and tell Molly myself.

I made my eyes as big as they could go, "I saw a ghost last night."

Molly blinked. It took her a few seconds to realize that our conversation had just switched gears. "Oh really?" she asked politely, "What did it say?"

"It didn't say anything," I said. "It only hovered."

"It sounds like you have a dud," she said, a little dimple popping out as she smiled. "It should have at least moaned or clanked some chains or something ghoulish like that."

I sighed, "You're right. My ghost was a dud."

Molly jumped to her feet, "Where did you see it?" she asked.

I pointed to the window, "Over there. Between the window and the armoire."

Molly stood in the approximate spot, "Right here?" she asked, looking at me for confirmation. "Huh. That's pretty exciting. But, then again, I hear that Raspberry Hill is haunted, so it's only to be expected that there are ghosts."

"I guess so," I agreed. "And if it's going to be such a quiet ghost, I guess that I can share my space."

Molly spun experimentally on her heel in her most ghost-like manner, "Oooooohhhhhh."

I shook my head, "That's pathetic."

She stopped mid-spin to swivel her head to look at me, "Now that's just rude, Natalie. At least I…" and she stopped.

Tilting her head from side to side, she studied my old, sturdy armoire. "Weird," she said. "I could have sworn…" and she resumed the tilting of her head.

I didn't say anything. What? This was more fun than watching movies.

"There!" she exclaimed, running towards the armoire. "I see it now." She turned to look at me, "Do you have something on the top shelf of your closet that's shiny?"

"It's an armoire," I told her, in my most superior voice. "Not a closet."

Molly wrinkled her nose, "Well… la-di-da!" She stepped back to examine the area. "I need a chair," she determined. She ran across the room to get the pretty little chintz-covered chair and dragged it back to the "closet".

This was getting quite interesting, so I swung my covers back and walked very carefully (as I wasn't quite certain that my head was not going to fall off) over to where she was going to inspect the top of the armoire.

She opened the door, "See!" she said excitedly, "there's something in here. I could see it glinting in the sunshine."

I must admit that I had not gotten around to fully inspecting the armoire. What? You needed a chair to reach the top. I had better things to do than go around standing on chairs to peer onto the top shelf of all of the free-standing closets in this room. Then again, perhaps I should have made the time. "If it's a diamond," I said, "I suppose you get to keep it." As you can imagine, I really did not think it was a diamond.

"Deal!" she said, eagerly reaching up higher and pulling something forward. Rats. I couldn't see a thing. The door was in my way. I sidestepped it as best I could and was amazed to see the look of shock and indecision on Molly's face.

"What's the matter?" I cried in alarm. For pity's sake, I hope she hadn't found a body or something. My certainty of Grandma Rose's innocence might not hold up too well if a body was found on the top shelf of my closet. I wonder if Molly could be bribed into silence. Would that be right?

"Natalie," she said in a strange voice, "I'm not quite sure how to tell you this." We stared at each other for a few long moments. I wanted to hear. And I didn't want to hear. Molly was having no such internal battle…she clearly didn't want to tell me what she had found.

"It's a body," I said hoarsely. "Isn't it?" My knees were weebling again.

"No!" she answered quickly, "it's not a body." She choked back a laugh and rolled her eyes, "Honestly? Like a body would fit up here?"

"Well…." I began defensively. It wasn't the strangest idea that I have ever had.

"Besides…" she continued, "if it was a body, I think you would have smelled something."

I can't believe she just said that. It would have been funny if her expression hadn't been so worrisome.

"Good grief," I said. "Take pity on the poor, concussed patient and just tell me what it is before I die of frustration and you have to stuff ME up on the top shelf to hide my body."

She bit back half a smile, "There's just no nice way to say this," she said, pulling out something that looked decidedly new and quite mechanical. "It's a projector."

You can probably imagine what happened next. I almost think a body would have been nicer to find. Because… frankly… a projector meant one of two things… Jack or Celia. One of them tried to scare me. While I was weak and hurt… and vulnerable. And then, one (or both) of them pretended to feel shock and concern when they found me passed out in my room. It should have made me mad. But, really, it just made me incredibly tired. I felt old. And sad. I sank to the ground, feeling like a balloon that someone had popped a hole in.

Molly set the projector back in the armoire and closed the door quietly. She sank down on the carpet next to me and hesitantly put an arm around me. "I'm so sorry," she said. "I'm sure it was just a joke…"

Hope blossomed quickly. And then died a terrible death. It wasn't a joke. "While I had a concussion?" I asked skeptically. "Why would that be funny?"

I turned to Molly. I needed an ally, and I had to trust someone or I would go crazy. "Can you keep a secret?" I asked.

She nodded solemnly, her eyes wide. "Of course," she whispered. "What is it?"

I filled her in the best I could of how I had come to be here and what the terms of Grandma Rose's will were. She listened without interrupting (which confirmed my hunch that she was going to be a great ally).

"So what you're saying is that if anyone leaves and doesn't live here, they will forfeit their entire inheritance?" I nodded. "And so you think someone is trying to get you to leave?" I nodded again. She looked around the room calculatingly, "This house has got to be worth a fortune," she mused. "And I bet the property is worth a lot too. Seeing as it's technically on Main Street, it's probably even zoned commercial already. Someone could make a killing," she winced at the term, "sorry…. I mean a lot of money either by selling or leasing to any number of people or types of businesses."

I had never thought about the house being zoned for commercial use. But, it made sense. It's just possible that one of my darling little family members downstairs had had the acuity to ask Mr. Garvey when he was explaining the terms to them. They were obviously more than a little ahead of me.

"But the question remains… is it Celia or Jack… who wants to get rid of me?" I asked glumly. Either way, it was dreadful to contemplate. And depressing. Even though it's what I really expected…sometimes it's not so nice when you're always right.

Jack knocked on the door and entered without waiting for a reply. His eyes widened in alarm at seeing us on the floor and he came through the door quickly. "Is everything okay?" he asked.

"Just fine," I said, as normally as I could. "We're contemplating ways to redecorate." I must have sounded pretty good because I caught Molly's admiring gaze out of the corner of my eye.

Jack stopped in his tracks and looked around, "It looks ok in here to me" he said cautiously.

"That's because you're a man," Molly said, twinkling and dimpling at him. She was so cute. "You just don't know any better."

Wow. She was pretty good too.

He looked suspiciously from Molly to me and back again, "I have a feeling you two are up to something, but unfortunately, I don't have time to figure it out. I forgot to get noodles at the grocery store, so I'm going to go and grab some." He turned to Molly, "Would you mind staying here and keeping an eye on her until I get back?"

"Hey!" I spoke up indignantly, "You can't talk about me like that. I am perfectly capable of watching myself. However," I raised my voice to be heard over his, "it just so happens that I have invited Molly to lunch, so…"

"Perfect!" he declared and turned back towards the door. "You girls behave yourselves."

We smiled angelically after him, which only caused him to look more suspicious.

"Natalie!" Molly exclaimed, grabbing my arm, as soon as Jack was gone, "I just remembered something. My brother had a projector like this. It works by remote."

My gaze swung to hers. "So if we find the remote…"

She nodded, "We might figure out who's trying to scare you."

It was perfect. Celia was at work. Jack was gone.

The search of their rooms did not take long.

We found the remote tucked neatly in a sock drawer.

Jack's sock drawer.

I didn't expect it to hurt as much as it did. But, as I told myself gently, "You shouldn't be so surprised. You knew he couldn't be trusted. A leopard doesn't change its spots."

CHAPTER 14

Jack was in the kitchen, where he seemed to be most at home, washing up the dishes while I waved goodbye to Molly. I don't believe either of us could even tell you what we had eaten for lunch. The only thing I know was that it tasted like sawdust.

"It really doesn't prove anything," she whispered in my ear as she was getting into the car she had borrowed from her friend Helen. "It could have been planted there. For all we know, there could be a third party involved." Her brow furrowed for a moment and then lit up, "Maybe it's Mr. Garvey!"

I sputtered, "Mr. Garvey?" Somehow, I just could not picture Mr. Garvey having that much imagination. But, she was clearly in love with her new theory, "Yes, Mr. Garvey. Maybe if all of you leave before the time is up, he inherits or something!"

I didn't have the heart to tell her that she was wrong. It wasn't Mr. Garvey. If we all bailed, the house was going to the Society for Historical Preservation or some such nonsense, if I remembered correctly. But, I smiled kindly anyways, "We can find out," I said, "and then we'll see."

Molly, at least, was happier.

I, however, was once again all alone in a big house with two people who may or may not want me gone. I don't know why, but it really depressed me to find the remote in Jack's bedroom. Then again, Celia was smart and crafty. She could have easily planted it there herself. But, did it really make me feel better that my mother (albeit a mother that I wasn't currently talking to) did it? I don't know.

On the brighter side, my vision seemed to be clearing up, and my head no longer felt in danger of falling off.

I gave myself a stern pep talk as I headed back inside. He (or she) could try all they wanted. I was staying. Unless, of course, they tried to kill me. Which seemed very unlikely. Right? Hey. I said… right? Right. You could be a little quicker with your affirmations, you know. It would make me feel a lot better. Work on that, would you? Thanks.

I closed the front door behind me softly… when I heard it. Shouting coming from the ballroom. Again. My heart jumped and then settled. A trick. It was another trick. What a blessed relief – I wasn't losing it.

I stormed in, throwing the doors open, just as the voices ended. Empty. Quiet. Not even a swirl of dust to indicate that the villain had high-tailed it out in a hurry. No one was there. But, I was expecting that this time. Jack. Where was he? To my knowledge, Celia was at work. Or, at least, I thought she was. But, maybe she wasn't. Whoever had turned off the… speakers… or whatever they were… had to still be in the near vicinity. I walked as fast as I could to the other door, flinging it open. No one was there. I stalked to the kitchen. Jack was gone. Well, that was convenient. Of course, he wasn't in the kitchen. He was too busy operating his stupid remotes in the ballroom. Walking past the basement door, I heard something that made me pause. What was that? There was a funny little growl sound. Was that Abraham Lincoln? Had he somehow gotten shut into the basement? Or was there something more foul afoot?

I tested the handle. It was open. A wave of musty, stale air blew back at me and the dark hole yawned like an open mouth. I hesitated. Did I really, really want to go down there? I'm sure if it was Abraham Lincoln, he knew his way around well enough that he would be just fine. I eyed the rickety stairs with a practiced eye. I had seen worse… but I had certainly seen better too. Why is it that basements always get so neglected? Why can't they be just as bright and clean and happy as the rest of the house? I strained my ears and heard the distinctive sound of a foot hitting a hard object. There is just no disguising that particular sound, is there? First, it's the thud followed by the in-drawn breath and the slight hop on the other foot. That did it. If Jack (or Celia) were in the basement, there was absolutely no good reason they should be doing so in the dark. It could only mean one thing. He – or she – was up to something. And we were going to find out what that was.

I flipped the light switch and scurried down the steps as fast as my aching head would let me. There! I saw it! Flying right around the corner! It was either the ends of a dress (which, hopefully, would rule out Jack – if he was wearing a dress we had bigger problems to worry about) or I was still hallucinating. I followed the flapping piece of white through the twists and turns of the basement. It was really too bad that the bare bulbs hanging sadly from their sockets were not fulfilling their ultimate destiny of shining forth and fully illuminating their surroundings. If I stayed living here, that was going to change. If I ever got a job that I could keep and made enough money to change the bulbs, that is. So far, working in Springgate wasn't really going very well for me, was it?

Junk was piled high on both sides of me. This basement was huge. It must go the entire length and width of the house. I felt a bit like a rat in a maze, and for one panic-stricken moment, I felt a little lost. I looked anxiously around and was relieved beyond measure to see the reassuring gap of light at the door. Two quick steps to the right and I thought I had the figure cornered, but as I walked around a pile of Time magazines that were taller than my head, I stopped short. I was at a dead end. There was a wall in front of me and nowhere she could be hiding. She was gone. Just like that. Gone. There was a faint, sweet scent in the air. Great. If I was still hallucinating ghosts… now I was hallucinating ghosts that wore perfume. Just great. I don't think that's a step in the right direction, do you?

I sighed. Ghostbusters I was not. Turning slowly on my heel, I decided to go back upstairs to the land of the living. Walking past an old baby carriage with two wheels missing surrounded by stacks and stacks of what looked like plates… I saw her again. She was there. And she wasn't there. Her image wavered in and out of focus. A cold sweat broke out on my forehead. Oh. My. Goodness. I was looking at a ghost. And it was staring back at me. If I didn't know better, I would have said that it looked just as surprised to see me as I was to see it.

The stare down continued for several more long seconds. I grabbed the handle of the baby carriage to steady myself. Not that I was scared or anything.

"Are you a ghost?" I whispered. Duh. Someone, please nominate me for the 'stupidest question ever asked'.

The ghost froze. She was quite an elderly ghost. She wore a long dress that had lace at the throat and wrists. Her hair was done up in an elaborate up-do. She looked dainty and frail. And not at all fierce or frightening. The expression on her face was one of haunted grief. And just like that... I was not afraid. Please don't think this is weird, but I felt an intense emotional bond with the ghost. Her face reflected the feelings of my heart, and I wanted nothing more than to help her find her peace. Isn't that what one did with ghosts? I hadn't been to church in a while... I wasn't sure what God thought about ghosts... but I was pretty sure that they weren't supposed to be here. According to all of the Sunday School classes that I had attended... when someone died they either went to heaven or.... you-know-where (I'd have to check my Bible again tonight). But, then again, they might be wrong. The ghost flickered. Obviously, they were wrong. I was looking at one, wasn't I? Then again... maybe I wasn't. Maybe it was still a concussion-induced ghost. It couldn't be a fake ghost like the one in my room. There was no way you'd get a projector to zip through the basement, around objects and corners. At least, not to my knowledge there wasn't. Jack and Celia didn't strike me as being THAT technologically advanced. So, either I was staring at a ghost or I was having a psychological breakdown. Either way... there was no harm in being friendly, was there?

I realized that the ghost was shrugging her shoulders sadly at me. I nodded back, "You mean you don't know?" A shake of the head. I decided to help her out. "I think you are probably a ghost," I advised. "Although I heard you moving around down here." I paused to think, "So you must be able to become... what's the word... corporeal... is that the right word? .... whenever you want to because I thought I heard you hit your foot on something."

She nodded sadly, lifting her right foot for my inspection. My grip on the baby carriage was so tight I could feel the wood grain embedding itself into my palm.

A thought occurred to me. "Are you..." I took a fluttering breath. "Are you my Grandma Rose?"

What? It was a logical question.

She shook her little grey head again. I wasn't expecting the feeling of crushing disappointment. After all, it would have been great to get to know my grandma – even if I had to do it while she was a ghost.

"Then... who are you?" I whispered.

She floated backward. She was drifting away. "No, wait!" I called, taking a step forward. But, she was gone. From the deep depths of the basement, an ancient voice spoke one word in a voice that wavered and crackled like parchment paper. "Mildred." The name hung in the air on gossamer strands, tying me to the floor. Mildred. I had just met a ghost named Mildred. My heart hammered in time with the two syllables, barely uttered. Mil-dred. Mil-dred. Mil-dred.

It was like a beautiful, sad dream.

"Natalie! Are you down there?"

A beautiful, sad dream that ended with a nightmare. Jack. I had almost forgotten him. And Celia.

He called again, so I sighed and began my trek back to the shining rectangle of light in the distance. "Hold your horses," I called. "I'm coming."

But, he was already descending the stairs. "What are you doing down here?" he demanded. "The light is terrible. You shouldn't be moving around so much. What if you fell? It's just lucky for you that I came home and saw the door open. What if the door had swung shut and you had been trapped down here?"

Huh. That would have been a great idea for him to try, don't you think? If he had been trying to get rid of me, that is. I wonder why he didn't do it. It would have freaked me out just a bit. Not enough to get me to leave, though... remember? I was STAYING. They could scare me all they wanted, it's not like they were going to try to kill me. Right? Thank you. Your response rate was much better this time. Keep up the good work.

"Or, I could have tripped on any of this old junk and fallen and hit my head and opened my stitches back up," I supplied helpfully. "And the rest of my brains could have fallen out."

He was getting closer now, dodging an old fishing pole hanging from the ceiling quite neatly, "Exactly," he snapped, "but you obviously don't appear to have any left to fall out."

He grabbed my arm and started pulling me towards the stairs.

This conversation was getting old. "Well, I obviously have some brains left," I snapped, wriggling in his grasp, "otherwise I wouldn't have been smart enough to look in your sock drawer."

He paused in his manhandling to stare down at me, "DID you hit your head?" he asked, squinting at me in the dim light.

I shoved him back, suddenly angry. "No. But maybe you wished that I had. Then you wouldn't have to keep thinking up ways to scare me into leaving."

"What are you talking about?" he demanded, "I haven't done anything. And what were you doing in my sock drawer?"

"AH-HA!" I exclaimed. "You admit it. You didn't want me in your sock drawer. You knew exactly what I would find, didn't you?"

A spider spun on her little thread down from the ceiling right in front of Jack's nose. He batted it away irritably. Strange. Normally, Jack was a wee bit, shall we say.... squeamish... in front of spiders. He must be pretty wound up now. "SOCKS!" he bellowed. "I would expect you to find socks in my sock drawer. And maybe some dryer lint." We resumed our march towards the stairs, and he growled like a cranky bear, "What has gotten into you?"

I shook myself free of his hands and climbed the stairs on legs quivering with anger. On the top step, I turned around to look Jack in the face. It was kind of nice to be the taller one for a change. It definitely made me look more authoritative. I stuck my face in his. "Well then," I taunted, "why don't we just go and look at your sock drawer and see what we can find?"

Jack closed his eyes and took a deep breath. When he opened them again, he spoke as if to a child, "Since you have suddenly become so fascinated by my socks," he said, enunciating each word clearly, "I think it would be a great idea to go and look at them."

Our trip upstairs was silent and strained. We both tried entering Jack's door at the same time. He took a step back and gestured grandly, "By all means," he said. "Ladies first."

I glared at him, "I'm only going first because I don't want you destroying the evidence."

He looked genuinely baffled. Or, at least, he *looked* genuinely baffled. That's the problem when you have to deal with people who lie. You never know when they're telling the truth. "What evidence?"

"Stop acting so innocent," I said. "I figured it out, so you might as well come clean."

"The horror!" Jack said, slapping his face with mock despair, "You figured out that I don't sort my socks by color. I am so mortified."

"Shut up," I said, pulling open his sock drawer. I looked in and took a step back. "And how do you explain this?"

He took a cautious step forward to peer into his sock drawer. The way his expression changed from contempt to confusion was almost comical. "What is that?" he demanded.

"Ohhhhhh!" I said sarcastically, "Let me show you what THAT does." I snatched up the remote and walked out the door and down to my room, expecting him to follow. He did. "Here," I said. "Just take a seat over here by the bed." He eyed me strangely and stood by the bed, but did not sit.

"Now what?" he asked warily.

"Hold on," I said. "Since it's not dark I'd better shut the curtains first."

I made fast work of closing all the curtains. "Now," I said, addressing Jack, "pretend you just woke up. You have a concussion. You're tired and dizzy and nauseous. Your head is throbbing and you're cold."

He shrugged his wide shoulders, "I'm still totally confused."

I smiled grimly, flipping my hair back behind my shoulder and turning toward the armoire. "You won't be," I said. I clicked the remote.

Right on cue, the ghost girl appeared, floating mysteriously above the ground. She had her back to us, and her long hair blew gently in a non-existent breeze. Since Molly and I had watched the whole thing (more than once), I used the opportunity to, instead, study Jack. His face had turned its own shade of ghostly pale as the implications of what he saw sank in. Then, she turned slowly...her face a perfect void of blackness... and Jack flinched back. He cleared his throat in a very manly manner to cover the movement. "That's terrible," he said hoarsely. "Is this what you saw last night?"

I didn't answer. There was no need.

He sank down onto the bed. "I can't believe you think that I would do something like this." His shoulders were slumped with defeat.

"Didn't you?" I challenged. "To get rid of me? You always said you'd get even with me for ruining your life."

"I was eleven," he all but shouted, "and you were totally interrupting my summer plans."

"Like I wanted to stay with you and your dumb mom," I shouted back. "Do you think I liked being dumped with you every summer? Do you think that it was fun for me that my mom was glad to get rid of me so she could go do something 'more fun'? "

"Your mom was better than my mom," Jack said quietly.

I snorted, "How do you figure that?"

"She didn't marry total losers who took their anger out on kids."

I sank to the bed beside him. "You mean Jim?" I asked, studying his face carefully.

He wouldn't make eye contact. "Yep. It was just one year, but it was the worst year of my life."

"I'm sorry." And I really was. I sighed, "Believe it or not, I sort of know what you mean."

His head shot up, and I held up a hand to stop the next question, "No, no one ever hit me. But, it always scared me when Celia would hook up with a new guy. Suddenly there was another man living in our space. Some of them drank a lot… some of them smoked a lot… and some of them were kinda nice. It was confusing. And frightening. And sad, sometimes, because just when I would start getting attached, Celia would get bored, dump him and we'd take off again." I picked at the duvet with my fingers, "At least you had a home," I said softly. "Your mom loved you, and you knew where and what you were going to do next."

"Yeah," he said quietly. "You're right."

I swallowed, "Celia may not have been the best mother, but I never really held anything against her until now." I waved a hand in the general direction of the room, "If there was one thing I wanted in life – it was this. A home. And we never had that. Because that's just not who Celia is. But… all of this time… THIS was here! This was here, and a grandma was here. My grandma was here. And I never knew it. And I missed everything. I could have…" I couldn't go on. I covered my face and did the one thing that I promised myself I wasn't going to do. Denial and curiosity had strapped on their parachutes and jumped out of the plane. And the worst part was that I was crying in front of Jack. So humiliating. Which, infuriatingly, only made me cry harder.

It doesn't really matter what you tell yourself to think and feel or what you tell other people you are feeling… eventually, your real heart has to live and breathe and be itself. Mine just picked a really, really rotten time to do it. I don't cry very nicely either. Not pretty like they do in the movies. It's ugly. My shoulders shook, as I tried not to make any noise and get myself under control. But then, I felt a hesitant hand on my shoulder. It crossed my back and cupped my other shoulder, drawing me into a nice warm chest. He patted my arm softly, "That's it," he said softly into my hair. "Just let it all out." And, somehow, when he said it, it didn't sound like a cliché.

I don't know how long we sat there like that. But, by the time I could gather myself together, my face felt red and blotchy, my throat was scratchy and my nose was clogged. The chest under my face moved suddenly, and a box of tissues appeared from somewhere. Where he got them from, I have no idea. But, I made good use of them before I sat up to meet his eye. I cringed when I saw the state of his shirt. Soaked. Completely soaked. I should have been totally embarrassed. Instead, I felt rather numb and light. It felt... good.

"You look like a mess," he said, but his smile was kind. "Do you feel any better?"

I nodded, not quite sure I could trust my own voice yet.

"Good." He sat up straighter and looked me in the eyes, "Then you listen to me."

Bossy. But, I met his eyes anyways.

"I'm not going to be dumb like Ryan," he said softly. I tilted my head in confusion. He squirmed a little, then squared his shoulders and continued, "I'm not going to be dumb like Ryan and not tell you what I feel."

OH.

MY.

WORD.

What was he talking about now?

Awkward.

I put up my hand to stop him, but he grabbed it and continued talking, "I didn't come here because I wanted any inheritance," he said. "I came here because I thought you might be here. And I wanted to see you again."

My mouth dropped open. I'm sure it was a very attractive finishing touch to my overall beautiful appearance.

"What?" I croaked.

Jack took a fortifying deep breath, "I feel like an idiot for having to explain this," he admitted. "I was hoping you would figure it out for yourself. I like you."

"You *like* me?" I'm afraid disbelief was coloring my tone just a little. In retrospect, I realize that this was probably not the reaction he was hoping for.

"Yes. I like you." He ran a hand through his spiky hair, "Don't make me say it again. I feel like we're in middle school or something." His lips twisted into a smile. "Even when you slammed the door in my face I liked you. I came here to…." He hesitated, searching for the right words. "Neither of us had an easy childhood. Our mothers were not perfect. But, I suppose that no one is. When my stepdad died, I thought it was the end of the world. I was angry at everyone. Including you. I just wanted to be left alone and forget, but you look a lot like him, you know?" I nodded. It was true. I had seen it in pictures. We had the same wide eyes and light blond hair. "I'm sorry, now, for how I behaved. After mom dumped Jim and started seeing Steve, things got better for me. And I changed. But, then, you stopped coming for the summers. And I never got the chance to tell you how sorry I was for making your life miserable while you stayed with us."

"I think our mothers argued about something," I said, trying hard to think back to that time. "But I never knew what it was."

"It was about how she needed to settle down and stop moving," Jack admitted. He smiled at my astonished look. "I was listening through the ductwork." He grinned unrepentantly, making his freckles dance. But, then his face darkened. "My mom totally alienated your mom with her little speech, I think. She came across as superior and condescending. I know she didn't mean to, but she did. So your mom grabbed you and left and that was the end of that." He squeezed my hand, "I think," he said softly, changing subjects abruptly, "that you have a problem with trusting people."

I pulled my hand out of his, stung. "I do not," I replied indignantly, anger bubbling up. "How dare you…"

"Oh yeah?" He challenged, raising his chin, "Name me one person you trust, besides yourself, of course," he added quickly.

I opened my mouth to reply, heatedly, but no words came out. That was the problem. There were no words to come out. He was right. I didn't really know anyone that well. Maybe I was learning to trust Molly, possibly Carolyn… but I had only known them for a brief amount of time. I scooted back away from Jack on the bed. He was right. I had no one in my life. I was all alone. Even though I had not barricaded myself in a big house and become a recluse… I was Grandma Rose.

Wetness began seeping out of my eyes. Great. I was going to cry again.

Jack stood up abruptly and paced back and forth in front of the bed. He ran his hand through his hair again. His hair gel was never going to hold up if he kept doing that.

Jack said a bad word.

"Excuse me?" I blinked at him through another tear that was threatening to fall.

He looked frustrated, "Sorry," he apologized. "It just slipped out. Won't happen again." He turned back to me, "This is not going how I wanted it to go at all, Natalie," he said. "I'm sorry."

"Stop saying you're sorry," I mumbled, "you're giving me a headache."

Jack looked stricken. "I'm so sorry," he began, then stopped, flushing bright red. "I forgot about your concussion. I should never have yelled at you or talked to you like that. How do you feel now?"

He was coming at me like he was going to check my temperature and tuck me in bed. I batted his hands away and scooted quickly off the bed so that I was standing on the other side.

"I'm fine," I snapped irritably. "Stop feeling guilty. You're not responsible for me. I am."

Jack backed up, hand in the air placatingly, "Ok," he said, "how about I say what I want to say and then leave you alone?"

"Sounds good." The leaving part sounded even better. He was confusing me, and I really, really needed some time alone to think.

"This is what I know," Jack said firmly. "I like you. I came here to make amends and to make friends with you. I'm not here for the money or the inheritance. I'd move out right now except I don't think you'd ever see me again if I did. I wasn't expecting to like you, but it just happened." He took a breath to look around the room, "I don't know what is going on around here. Something is obviously going on. I don't know if it's Celia or if it's someone else. But we will find out," he said seriously. "This house is not haunted."

Obviously, he hadn't met Mildred yet.

"This is a beautiful old house that is being manipulated by someone. It's not me," he repeated firmly. "You need to start trusting someone. So trust me."

His eyes were boring into mine expectantly, but I... I couldn't find it in me to answer him. A flippant answer seemed very out of place, and I didn't know how to answer him seriously. Trust him? TRUST him? I didn't really even know him. And, for that matter, was it even possible to know someone that well? What if I was trusting the wrong person? What if all of this was just a really big scheme? How did I know? How could I ever know?

My emotions must have shown on my face, because he smiled crookedly, "It's okay, Natalie," he said gently, "you don't have to say anything. Just know that I'm here." He paused, as if considering what to say next, "And remember this too – we might not understand it or see it, but God always has a good plan for our lives."

He strode over to the armoire and ripped out the projector. "And I'm not here to hurt you. I want to be friends." He walked over to the door and pulled it open. Without turning around he said, "And I can wait. Get some rest. Dinner will be ready in an hour."

But there was one thing I still wanted to ask him. "Wait!" I croaked.

He turned expectantly to me.

"Just tell me now," I said, "did you install speakers in the ballroom?"

He rolled his eyes and stalked towards the door. "I can wait," he muttered. "I can wait."

CHAPTER 15

I met Mildred again later that night. I was lying in bed…trying to sleep. You will note the part where I said *trying*. It's possible that the blow to my head had opened a rift in the time/space continuum and I was now living in a world where I existed in a different time than everyone else. I think I saw a movie like that once, so I am sure it's possible. If my theory was correct, one second to everyone else was like an hour to me. Which would explain, of course, why this night was lasting so long. I was ready to go back to my denial and curiosity plan… and that involved me getting out of this house and going back to work.

Tick.

Tick.

Tick.

Abraham Lincoln was…very annoyingly…completely and totally asleep. He no longer kept to his word of staying at the foot of the bed and was now curled up on the 2nd pillow by my head. He was snoring. Again. And with every little whiffle and snort came the charming odor of dog breath. I was going to have to buy him some doggie mints or something. Did they have things like that? Perhaps I could use a toothbrush to brush his teeth? Not mine, of course. Maybe Celia's…

Life got a little more interesting when my closet door creaked slowly open. From the inside. Because I am so brave of heart, I didn't even flinch. At least it was something to watch besides the ceiling cracks. I did prop myself up on my elbows when a little fog began seeping its way out of the crack. Huh. Perhaps it wouldn't be too bad of an idea if I called for back up?

The fog snuck out of the closet door, crawling and groping its way across the floor towards me. It was thick and I could feel the coldness. I pulled the blankets up a little tighter. Abraham Lincoln wiggled his nose in his sleep.

The door pushed open a little farther, and, somehow, I wasn't surprised to see Mildred's face pop out from around it.

"Hello Mildred," I croaked. "How are you this evening?"

"Why don't you tell me?" she said with a small smile. "You would know since I'm the figment of your imagination."

Yep. That sounded like something a figment of mine would say.

"You are obviously a ghost with an identity crisis," I said, trying to look serious. "Maybe we could find you a ghost psychologist."

She was definitely more solid tonight than she had been down in the basement. Maybe ghosts were more in their "environment" at night than they were during the day. I guess that made sense. After all, every ghost-type movie I had ever seen involved ghosts and chains clanking at night, not during the day.

"That would be hard considering no one but you can see me," she said. "And I don't think anyone is going to be too interested in MY psychological problems if you tell them that you need counseling for a ghost that only you can see."

Huh. Perhaps she really *was* a figment of my imagination.

I eyed her uncertainly... what was I supposed to do? If she was a ghost, should I be talking to her? And, if she wasn't a ghost... should I be talking to her and encouraging my own delusional behavior?

She winked saucily at me. "Cat got your tongue?" she challenged.

I curled my lip, "I'm just trying to decide how crazy I really am," I said. "I'm not so sure you're not a ghost, and if you aren't a ghost, then I'm not so sure how sane I am."

Her eyebrows tilted in thought for a moment, "Why don't you just consider me a by-product of your unfortunate brain trauma?"

I eyed her skeptically.

She tried again, "After all, if I am just a figment of your imagination, then it really doesn't hurt to talk to me. I've seen you talking to yourself plenty of times."

I frowned. She had a good point. And… after all… if she was just a splintered portion of my own psyche, then, in a really strange way, I had finally found a soul I could talk to. And trust. I mentally stuck my tongue out at Jack.

I pulled myself to a sitting position in bed. "Ok," I said slowly, "I guess I can live with that." She grinned happily. "Why don't you come all the way out of there so I can see you better?"

She shook her head, "Sorry. No can do. I ran out of energy and only my head is visible right now. You'd probably be a little upset to see my head bobbing around in the air."

Now that was suspicious. "If you're a figment of MY imagination, then how come you are acting like a ghost?"

She shook her head again, looking quite helpless, "I have no idea," she admitted. "Maybe because you still have ghosts on the brain? Don't blame me because you're a complete mess."

"Hey!" I protested a bit too loudly. Poor little Abraham Lincoln jumped to all four feet, fur standing on end. Sharp little claws sank into my knee as he sprang into my lap. "Sorry Abe," I said absently. "I didn't mean to wake you up."

Abraham Lincoln, paused mid-yawn to look up at me and did a double-take. His nose twitched. Then an ear joined the twitching. I pulled back in alarm, when, within seconds, his head began shaking…. Then his front paws… then his back paws until his whole little body was quivering like Jell-O during an earthquake. Just when I was seriously afraid that he was having a seizure, he took a deep breath, threw his head back into the air and let out the most awful sounding howl (or maybe it was a wail) that you have ever heard. It was probably even more awful because, due to the shaking of his body, the howl (or wail) wavered in and out in time with the shaking.

"Abraham Lincoln!" I said a bit louder than I wanted to, "Stop that. Right now."

Isn't it funny that I thought he was going to listen to me?

He, of course, did just the opposite. Only louder this time. And then, as if he could no longer contain the fury that grew within him, he jumped off the bed with a flying leap and ran from one corner of the room to the other as fast as his four little paws would carry him. He took the turns in a skidding slide. The howling did not stop. Gracious heavens. It's a good thing we didn't have neighbors. They would think we had a werewolf loose in the house. The sheer volume of noise coming from one tiny thing was astounding... as was the fact that he could maintain it while he was running at top speed. Howling and yipping and whining with a note of hysteria that really worried me, like a little bullet, he ran. And howled. And ran. From one corner of the room to the other. Back and forth. I looked to Mildred for help, but as I expected, she had gone. My feeble brain probably could not maintain her illusion when it had other things to occupy it. I must not have a very powerful processor.

I stepped gingerly off the bed, not wanting to step on Abraham Lincoln in one of his zooming passes. I tried catching him. Which, of course, turned out to be one of my more stupid ideas. How did one catch the wind? He eluded me with ridiculous ease each time I came close enough to try to grab him.

The howling and running continued.

I tried sitting on the floor.

The howling and running continued with the exception of snapping teeth directed at me each time he passed... excuse me... tore by. This was terrible. My dog was broken.

Oh my goodness.

I just called him MY dog, didn't I?

It was official. I had gone crazy. Maybe crazier than my dog. And that was saying something.

There was a pounding at the door. Abraham Lincoln zipped over to it, running and pouncing at it, but since it did not open, he squealed his tires and ran the opposite direction. Hoping it was Jack, I ran over to the door and waited for Abraham Lincoln's next pass. Once he was safely on his trip back to the other side of the room, I seized the two-second opportunity to open the door, grab the shoulder of whoever was standing outside and pull him in, shutting the door securely behind him.

It was Jack.

He looked like he had just jumped out of bed… which, of course, he probably had. Sleep creases still lined his face, and he looked grumpy, startled and just a tad worried.

"What is he doing?" Jack yelled, to be heard over the din of Abraham Lincoln.

And then I realized what I had done.

I grabbed Jack's arm. "OH NO!" I yelled. "This is all my fault. I called him…" I stopped. No sense saying the word out loud again.

"You what?" Jack shouted back, stepping forward to allow the little furry beast to zoom by again.

"I didn't call him by his FULL name," I said loudly. "I forgot."

Jack raised his leg in the air to let the little bullet fly under it before he took a step closer. His breath was warm against my ear, but I guess it was better than shouting. "You mean to tell me that all of this is because you didn't call him 'Abraham Lincoln'?"

I wrung my hands together. I've never done that before in my life. I've read about it in books, but never, in a zillion years did I think that I would be the hand-wringing type. Don't judge. You have no idea what you would do in this situation… now, do you?

I nodded frantically and reached out to clutch Jack's arm. "What are we going to do?"

We both jumped back as Abraham Lincoln's teeth came dangerously near our feet. "I guess Mr. Garvey was serious," Jack said, eyes glinting with mischief. "Would now be a good time to see what he does in front of a mirror?"

How could he joke at a time like this?

Somehow, as we had been moving and talking, we had moved, instinctively, so that we were standing with our backs against the door. We were being terrorized by a tiny, 3-pound dog. This was ridiculous.

Abraham Lincoln rounded the corner and came barking and growling at us for another pass. I took a deep breath and stepped forward. "ABRAHAM LINCOLN!" I bellowed, "You are behaving very, very badly. STOP RIGHT NOW!"

He screeched to a stop, smoke coming up from beneath his paws. Silence. Blessed silence. His little mouth gaped open up at me in shock.

I turned to look at Jack. His mouth was gaping open too.

"Whoa," Jack said quietly. "That was…"

I gave him my best stink eye, "Watch it," I said.

He held up both hands in surrender, "I was going to say that was amazing," he protested.

"Good answer," I muttered. Abraham Lincoln twitched restlessly, "Stay!" I snapped.

He stayed.

I slid down the door to sit on the floor. Abraham Lincoln came over hesitantly and immediately put his little paws up on my leg. I leaned over, and he licked my nose.

"No," I said, patting his head, "it was my fault. I'm very sorry for not calling you by your full name."

He licked me again.

"I can't believe you're apologizing to that overgrown rat," Jack said, sliding down the door next to me. "I have never heard a noise like that. Ever."

I shuddered, "Me neither. I guess I learned my lesson."

I felt his shrug, "Maybe," he said. "But somehow I doubt it."

"Hey!" I elbowed him in the ribs.

I was about to, very calmly and carefully, explain to Jack the benefits of keeping his mouth shut, when we were rudely pushed forward from behind. Hard.

"Hey!" I said again. My vocabulary wasn't very large at the moment.

"Something is in front of the door!" Celia yelled, shoving the door harder. "And I can't find Jack! Let me in!"

"I'm right here," Jack called back. We both scooted away from the front of the door, and Celia burst in. She looked wildly around the room.

"What are you doing in here?" she demanded, scanning the room suspiciously.

We stared at her. She looked like a mess. Her blond hair was messy and disheveled. The white cardigan she was wearing was streaked with dirt and who knows what else.

"What have you been doing?" Jack asked back.

She crossed her arms in front of her chest, "You two will tell me what you are doing right now."

Jack stood up and offered me a hand. He winked at me, "Now I know where you get it from."

He's just lucky my elbow wasn't in his vicinity.

"We were plotting dastardly and devious ways to take over the world," I said sarcastically. "What have you been doing? A spot of gardening?"

She turned to survey the room, "I don't believe you." She looked oddly vulnerable. I almost felt a pang of something. But, of course, I quickly squashed that feeling. I reminded myself that she practiced her vulnerable look three times a day in front of a mirror.

Jack sighed. He, obviously, was not immune to Celia's wiles. "Abraham Lincoln was having a bit of a fit," he said. "I'm surprised you didn't hear it. I came in to see if I could help, but your daughter had things well in hand."

Celia's gaze slid to Abraham Lincoln who was sitting very calmly, licking his paw. He looked up very innocently as if to say, "Who me?"

The suspicion did not leave her expression. "He looks pretty good to me," she said. "Are you sure you weren't up here trying to find another way to get rid of me?"

I rolled my eyes, "You caught us," I said flatly. "Darn."

She rubbed her hands up and down her arms, "I just saw a ghost," she said, looking around my room nervously.

Somehow her confession did not startle me. "I saw a ghost last night," I reminded her. "And no one seemed to care then."

Her lips thinned, "You had a concussion. It wasn't a ghost," she said. "But it was supposed to look like one. I just spent the last 45 minutes trying to figure out how they did it."

"It's probably a projector up in your closet," I said with a shrug, "That's where mine was."

She stared at me. "You found a projector in your closet?"

She was doing a really good job of looking innocent and appalled. Why couldn't I have been born into a family of really bad liars? Or else born with the gift of lie detection? It would make situations like this so much easier to navigate. It was entirely possible that Celia had discovered that I had found the projector and was now making up a similar story so that I would not suspect her. It was also possible that Jack had put a projector in each of our rooms. It was also possible that Jack knew that I would think Celia was setting her own self up, so he put the projector in her room. It was also possible that Celia knew that I would know that Jack knew that I would think that Celia was setting her own self up so she put the projector in her room. See what I mean? This was just getting ridiculous. If only I could yell at them the way I had Abraham Lincoln. They might behave better, and I would have an obedient family. What a beautiful dream.

I realized that Celia was still staring at me expectantly. Oh. She was probably waiting for an answer to something, wasn't she? What was the last thing she had asked me? Something about the projector?

"There was a projector in my closet," I said. "It had a remote that, when clicked, a ghostly figure would appear to hover in the middle of my room. It was quite awful. And, last night, when I was sick and cold and tired, someone pushed that button and made me faint." Celia's face had gone a lovely shade of white, "Any thoughts as to who that person was?"

"I have no idea." she protested, "Who would do something so awful?" She held my gaze squarely. Two bright pink spots appeared on her cheeks. I knew those spots. They were the spots of great stress. She obviously knew more than she was saying.

"So did you find a projector?" Jack asked, interrupting our silent stare down.

Her gaze cut to him, "I did," she said curtly. "It was out on my porch hidden in the vines."

Well, that explained the dirt.

"I wonder why you haven't seen a ghost yet," she wondered aloud. Two suspicious pairs of eyes transferred their gaze to Jack.

"We only have your word that you saw a ghost," he shot back. "You could be making the whole thing up."

"Did I make up all of this dirt all over me too?" she demanded.

He fingered his chin thoughtfully, "Well," he said, "it does make for a very good cover story."

Celia stalked towards him. Alas, we would never know what her intent was, for as she approached, the sound of breaking glass shattered the silence in the hallway outside my door. Abraham Lincoln gave a little bark of surprise, and then, like the fearless and brave dog that he is, ran straight to my bed and jumped up on it. I can't say that I blamed him. It's just what I wanted to do too.

We all froze – our gazes going from person to person. There was another crash of splintering glass. I caught my breath. Someone was breaking in? Another large crash had us all ducking closer together.

"Someone's breaking in," I breathed only loud enough for the other two to hear me.

Celia grabbed my arm. "Should we hide?" she whispered.

Jack looked back and forth between us skeptically. "How can they be breaking in on the second floor?" he whispered. "That just doesn't make any sense."

I hadn't thought about that.

He was already moving as if to open the door. "Jack!" we both hissed. I glanced at Celia –she genuinely looked scared. I probably did too. The thud of my heart was echoing in my ears – and in my head. I really, really didn't feel up to this.

He put his fingers up to his lips, "I'm going to go check it out," he whispered. "You two stay here and lock yourselves in. Call the police."

"My cell phone is in my room." Celia looked around anxiously.

They both turned their heads expectantly.

"Don't look at me," I hissed back. "I don't have one."

Jack looked like he wanted to say something, but he just shook his head and opened the door cautiously, peeking each way down the hall. Another crash of glass echoed along the corridor. We moved to pull him back in the room, but he shrugged us off and began moving stealthily down the hallway.

So, we shut and locked the door.

Not.

I wonder if, in the course of history, anyone who was actually told to stay put ever stayed put? Jack gave us a look that spoke volumes but wisely remained silent. Our little group huddled together, venturing carefully down the hallway. Shadows danced gleefully in the dim recesses of each corner. I couldn't help it, I grabbed the back of Jack's shirt. He spared a glance down at me, trying his best to smile reassuringly.

We jumped as one person with the next crash. It sounded like someone was systematically destroying each and every pane of the window in Jack's room. He reached a slow hand out to push the door open further, and I totally understood his hesitation. If someone were on the other side launching rocks through a second story window, perhaps it would not be wise to enter the room. Then again, it might scare away the perpetrator – or at least cause them to stop. Or, maybe, the person was IN the room, throwing rocks out.

Jack pulled gently away from my grasp and held up a hand to Celia and me… trying to communicate with us that he was going to enter first. By himself. I exchanged a glance with Celia. We shook our heads grimly at him. This was not a good plan.

Jack looked over my shoulder, his eyes widening with alarm. Celia must have seen the expression too because we both spun to look. In the time it took for us to do this, he slipped away through his open door, turning the light on and shutting it firmly behind him all in one motion.

Celia and I were shocked into immobility. The next crash, though, had us banging and pushing on the door.

"Jack," I yelled, "Let us in, you big rat."

"It's okay," Jack's voice came from behind the door. "Everything is fine. Go ahead and come in."

He sounded funny. I exchanged an uneasy glance with Celia. Was it possible that someone was standing behind the door with Jack, forcing him to invite us in? Would Jack do that to save himself? Who was I kidding? Of course, he would. I would.

Celia's eyes were wide and her hands were shaking as she grabbed mine. Normally, there is nothing in this world that could entice me to hold Celia's hand, but our fear for Jack's safety obviously blurred the lines between us. Which, in itself, was also strange.

"What do we do?" she breathed in my ear.

My head was really starting to pound, and, to make matters worse, nausea was creeping up the back of my throat. I took a deep breath. "I'll go first," I said, "and if something is wrong, I'll give you the signal and you run and call the police."

She pulled back on me, "No," she said, "I'll go first. You call the police."

"You have a cellphone," I whispered back.

"We also have a house phone here," she whispered a bit louder.

"That is all the way downstairs."

"So?"

"So..."

"So what?"

"So... by the time I get all the way downstairs the axe murderer could have chopped both of you up into little pieces by then."

She gulped. "And you think I want the axe murderer to chop you up into little pieces?"

"When you two are quite done deciding who gets chopped up first..." a voice behind us said. We both squealed in terror, but it was only Jack.

"What are you doing?" Celia demanded. "Trying to give us a heart attack?"

I shoved his shoulder angrily, "That was mean!"

He frowned between us, "I wasn't trying to be mean. I just wanted you to come in and see this and when you didn't come in, I came back out to see what was wrong. It's amazing how quickly you guys can jump from vandalism to axe murderer."

The sound of glass breaking again had Celia and I instinctively ducking, but Jack just shook his head sadly, "Come in," he said again, throwing the door open wide. "You need to see this."

Not quite as brave as Jack, we poked our heads around the door frame. It was unbelievable.

CHAPTER 16

W hat? You need me to tell you what was in Jack's room? If you had any imagination whatsoever, you would have probably guessed the answer already.

No one.

Not a thing was out of place.

No glass broken.

No axe murderer hiding in the closet.

No troubled soul winging rocks through the window.

Nothing.

Just a lot of noise. That stopped, strangely enough, once all three of us were in the room.

We looked and looked for the speakers that we were certain had to be there somewhere, but none could be found. No one would say "ghost" out loud, so, therefore, there had to be hidden speakers. Well, to be fair – Jack and Celia looked. Abraham Lincoln (who had became a lot braver once the noise stopped) and I sat in an overstuffed armchair and offered wonderfully helpful advice to Jack and Celia as they turned Jack's room inside out. I was probably their greatest asset.

After twenty minutes of looking, we heard another noise that had us all freezing in place once again. Raised voices. It sounded like two men. And they sounded angry.

I looked from Jack to Celia again. If only I could be certain that one of them was not responsible. From the looks of the faces staring back at me, they were doing a good job of looking like they thought the same thing.

The voices were coming down the hallway. Jack, who happened to be standing, quite handily, near an ancient armoire, held up a finger in the universal sign for silence. He eased the door open and pulled out a wooden baseball bat. Oh dear.

We, somehow, ended up, once again, huddled together as a group and headed for the door. This time, I held Jack's shirt in a firmer grip, while my other hand maintained a firm grasp on Abraham Lincoln (who had absolutely no desire to be a hero).

"Can you understand what they're saying?" Celia whispered.

I shook my head, "It sounds like a different language." I tried to listen more carefully. "Maybe German?" I guessed.

Jack turned his head to scowl and gesture emphatically for our silence. Bossy.

If my, somewhat diminished, sense of hearing was correct, they would be passing in front of our door in the next several seconds. Jack waited for them to pass, which was actually a very good idea (I'm not sure I would have thought of that), and then cracked the door open, peering out. A second later, he flung the door open, stalking out quickly.

"Nothing!" he said in disgust. "This is ridiculous."

I put Abraham Lincoln down onto the floor. He gave me a glare and scratched at Celia's legs. I think she picked him up without even realizing what she was doing.

Jack looked angry. The voices, however, did not stop and continued their descent down the hallway towards the stairs.

"Should we follow them?" Celia asked. "Or maybe we should just call the police."

Jack tugged at his hair in exasperation. "And tell them what?" he challenged. "That we're hearing things? That ought to give the night shift something to laugh about. There will probably be a story in the newspaper tomorrow morning about the haunting of Raspberry Hill."

"Maybe we are haunted?" Celia ventured timidly. Abraham leaped out of Celia's arms into mine.

There.

She said it.

I didn't.

Jack snorted.

I stepped out into the hallway, clutching the little monster. "If someone is doing this," I said. "Then does that mean they're in the house right now or would it be something that's on a timer?"

Jack's freckles stood out a little more against his skin. "I hadn't thought about that," he admitted. "They would almost have to be here to get the timing just right. The glass crashing stopped when all of us were in my room. Could that be a coincidence?"

"Either that," I said slowly, "Or one of us has a remote in our pockets."

A muscle twitched in Jack's jaw, "I thought we talked about this," he growled.

Celia said nothing. She just emptied her pockets, which consisted of a tissue, a bookmark and a half-eaten chocolate bar. Strangely enough, the chocolate bar looked delicious.

I had no pockets. I was in my pajamas, remember?

Jack didn't say anything, other than what his expression was saying, as he, too, turned his pockets inside out. He had pajamas on, too, but his had pockets. Lucky guy. There was nothing in them. A complete waste of pockets.

"Well," Celia said gloomily, "That doesn't actually prove anything. Anyone of us could have hidden a remote very easily during the search for the speakers."

She was right. Rats.

I sighed. There was going to be very little sleep tonight. "Let's go," I said, "and see if anyone is downstairs." I began venturing down the hallway, feeling rather rubbery. "But we all stay together."

Jack nodded grimly, "Then we'll know where each other is at all times."

"Do you want to link arms?" Celia hissed sarcastically, "To make sure we all stay together?"

He glared at her, "No, thank you. Just stay within eyesight."

"You too," she glared back.

Despite his protestations, Jack very kindly offered me the use of his arm as we descended the stairs. I have to admit that despite the fact that it was obviously not a ghost (right?) and so far no one had been hurt during any of these "incidents", descending the steps into the inky darkness was a bit unnerving. Abraham Lincoln obviously thought so too, because he snuggled in even closer.

The "men" seemed to have traveled down into the ballroom. They were quite fast little ghosts… I mean invisible men… weren't they? I clutched tighter to Jack's arm as we approached the room while maintaining a watchful eye on Celia. "How do you think they're doing it?" I asked. "How do they get the sound to travel down the hallway like that?"

He shook his head, "I have no idea."

Celia huffed indignantly, "I have no idea either," she said.

Of course they didn't. Why did I even bother asking?

Celia opened the door and quickly flipped the light switches on, bathing the room in wonderful, beautiful, glorious light.

The men were really angry now… their shouting echoed off of the mirrored walls.

We stood in the middle of the room and looked helplessly between each other.

"That's it," Jack said, "I'm calling the police." He left us standing in the middle of the room and walked toward the opposite door.

The shouting stopped. I exchanged glances with Celia. Jack paused mid-stride and turned slowly around. That was no coincidence. There had to be someone here. In the room. With us. Probably watching us. The feeling was decidedly unpleasant.

"I don't know who you are," Celia said, addressing the empty room, "But we are calling the police. And we will press charges. Show yourself now and we can talk."

The silence was deafening.

Jack and Celia walked carefully around the perimeter of the room, knocking on the paneling, examining every knothole and corner, but nothing presented itself.

When they met back in the middle, Jack lifted an eyebrow at Celia who shrugged in return.

Abraham Lincoln shifted restlessly in my arms. "What's the matter, boy?" I asked, patting his head to quiet him.

There was a small scratching sound coming from behind the far door, and we turned as one towards it. The hinges creaked and, with a slight jerk, the door opened slowly.

"Leave," a voice whispered. It was impossible to tell where it came from. It fell like dew from the ceiling around us. "Leave. Leave. Leave. Leave. Leave. Leave." The word became a chant that rose and fell in volume in a manner that was surprisingly disturbing. It felt... evil. For the first time in a really long time, a quick prayer rose to my mind, and I prayed it. Selfishly, it was a prayer of protection, but I'm sure that God would not mind in a situation like this.

"Leave. Leave. Leave. Leave. Leave." The voice rose in volume and the words came faster and faster. A sudden wind whipped the door open so hard that it rattled in its frame. "Leave! Leave! Leave!" the voice screamed.

Celia covered her ears, "I can't stand it," she wailed. "How do we make it stop?" I didn't know how to answer her. I was frozen to my spot on the floor and couldn't move.

Jack was trying to shout something to us from across the room, but I couldn't understand what he was saying over the noise.

Then, without warning... it stopped. Everything stopped. The wind was gone. The screaming was gone. The room was filled with an eerie silence, and, as if we somehow knew that whatever it was that was tormenting us was not done with us yet, we did not move.

"Leave."

It was back to a whisper.

"Or you will all die."

CHAPTER 17

We were a ragged group of survivors. At least that's how I thought of us. Survivors. By unspoken agreement, we had barricaded ourselves into the brightly lit kitchen while waiting for the police to finish their investigation. They had arrived in a very reassuring rush of sound and color... and humanity. They zipped around so quickly that it was hard for my very tired brain to keep track of them, but I do believe that there were five of them in all. Quite a response considering the fact that we actually had no proof of any foul play. More than anything, it was probably the novelty of coming to Raspberry Hill that created such an eagerness of service. In the harsh lights of the fluorescent bulbs, the events of the evening seemed very far away and quite unreal. If it hadn't been for the last sentence swirling around and around in my ears, I would have felt a bit foolish for all of the kafuffle.

In an unconscious bid to look normal and not as if we were strange people who were either the victims of foul play or possibly being haunted by loud and potentially murderous ghosts, we were drinking tea and eating scones around the kitchen table. At least, I was eating scones. I don't know why. I've never had a scone in my life. I've never even thought about being the type of person that was a scone-eater. They sound so pretentious. Scones. Like something a grand duchess nibbles on during her elevensies. I had heard that they were rather dry and potentially nasty, however, these were absolutely delicious. Jack boasted that he had made them this morning. The accompanying jam was courtesy of Ryan, who, of course, made his own.

You would think that, after the events of the evening, my appetite would have been down in the basement, but I was surprisingly hungry. One more scone, I told myself, would just hit the spot. My hand went to the plate in the middle of the table. "Hey," I protested. "Who ate all the scones?"

Celia looked up from her tea rather grumpily. "You did," she said. "You grabbed the last one five minutes ago."

"I did?" That was strange. I certainly didn't remember doing so.

"You nearly knocked us both to the floor trying to get to it first," Jack said, one eyebrow raised in humor. "I was quite alarmed."

"Really?"

"Really." They both replied.   Huh. I looked to Abraham Lincoln for confirmation, but he was busy licking jam off of his whiskers. Maybe I had shared with him.

Sherriff Finn came into the kitchen, and Jack rose to his feet. Abraham Lincoln dove for the safety that lived under the table. "Please come in, Sherriff," he said, gesturing to the empty chair at the table. "I'd offer you a cup of tea and a scone, but Cousin Natalie seems to have eaten them all."

Well, that was just embarrassing.

Sherriff Finn smiled in a friendly fashion but shook his head. "No thank you," he said. "I don't usually eat anything as fancy as scones." I could tell he was trying very hard not to stare at the swelling on my forehead.

"But," I protested. "they're really very good."

"Obviously," Celia grumbled, "Or you wouldn't have eaten so many."

Sherriff Finn shuffled his feet, "We did a very thorough search," he began, "however we were unable to find any signs of an intruder."

Thorough search? In less than a half of an hour? I don't think so.

I looked up from my tea. Everyone was staring at me. Oops. I must have said that out loud. I shrugged, "What? It's a huge house."

Finn nodded, "You're right," he admitted. "It is a big house, but, like I said before, this isn't the first trouble we've had up here, so we know the place pretty well."

"Of course you do, Officer," Celia said soothingly. "No one was trying to say that you weren't doing a good job. We're all ever so grateful that all of you came up to help us so quickly." She fluttered her hands helplessly, "We were quite scared."

Finn looked a little flustered, "Old houses can make strange noises..." he offered.

"Do old houses break windows and yell in German?" I asked.

Jack choked on his tea. Celia patted him on the back, smiling charmingly at the handsome Sheriff.

"Not usually," Finn admitted. "That's a little hard to explain." He flipped his little notebook open thoughtfully. "So you say that, first, you heard the windows in Jack's room breaking?"

He sounded puzzled.

"It was just the sound," Celia reminded him. "No windows were actually broken."

"Rii-ght," he drawled out the word, "But then that stopped and then you heard the Germans."

"Well," Celia inserted timidly, with a pointed look at me. "We don't know that they were German. They were only speaking German. We think."

Finn nodded his head. "Right. I've got all that in the report."

Jack groaned. "Great. A report."

The grin was quick and wide, "No worries," Finn said, "the report is confidential."

"So what do we do now?" Celia asked.

"I'm sorry," the Sherriff said regretfully, "but we've done all that we can. If something else comes up, please don't hesitate to call again."

"Wow," I said. "That's really reassuring." Jack actually kicked me under the table. How rude. "But a very kind offer. I'm sure we'll all sleep better tonight."

Abraham Lincoln growled from under the table.

And, surprisingly, I did sleep well the rest of the night. That is, after I had fully convinced Celia that I did not need her sleeping in my room. She insisted. Then I insisted to the contrary. She insisted some more. I politely pointed out that, should anything happen, I only had to call the d-o-g (who was currently back to sleeping next to my pillow) by his shortened name and any intruder in his or her right mind would hightail it right out of there. She tried to guilt me into it by protesting that perhaps she was the scared one. I patted her on the shoulder and gave her my best pep talk. It must have worked because she left.

Morning dawned bright and sunny... as it usually does. A cheerful little bird was sitting on the railing of my porch singing a happy tune as I dressed for the day. Not really being a person who has spent a lot of time with birds, I could not tell you what type he was... but he was just adorable. I parted my hair carefully on the side in a vain effort to cover the pretty picture of my stitches. I'm not sure it helped much, but there was no way I was staying home again one more day. No way. I needed to get out and go to work. I didn't need to sit around the house talking to ghosts that I may or may not be hallucinating. Thankfully, there had been no sign of Mildred all morning. Perhaps since I was now fully recovered (well – almost... only the tiniest bit of a headache remained, however, there was absolutely no need to tell Jack or Celia that), my friendly ghost would disappear as well.

That would be fine with me.

Before I left the room, I walked to the closet where Mildred's head had appeared from last night. I knocked around the paneling and the flooring cautiously, but since I had no idea what I was looking for or even how to find it, I don't think it did much good. I think that everything seemed normal. Whatever normal was.

Jack was waiting for me in the kitchen. He smiled sheepishly at me, "You know," he said. "We work very close to each other."

Oh dear. I knew this would come up. I just thought it might be a little longer. My toast popped up and I grabbed it, slathering it liberally with the jam from last night.

"Really?" I exclaimed. "How amazing. Tell me, Cousin Jack, where do you work?"

Abraham Lincoln jumped up on the table and began licking the crumbs. Jack made a shooing gesture, "Get that dog off the table," he muttered, "or we'll all die of dog germs."

"Abraham Lincoln doesn't have doggie germs," I protested, patting his ugly little head affectionately. "He's just a little sweetie."

Jack sputtered and stared, "What the..."

"Uh-uh," I said quickly, holding up a finger in warning, "You weren't going to say bad words anymore, remember?"

"I'll say whatever I..." he stopped and stared at me suspiciously. "You're just trying to distract me, aren't you?"

I made my eyes very wide as I popped the last bite of toast in. "I don't know what you're talking about," I said... with my mouth full. I offered the plate to Abraham Lincoln, but he turned his little nose up. Obviously, it was much more fun scouting out your own crumbs than being offered them.

"Shut up," Jack said. "Here's the deal. I was going to be nice and let you think that this was your idea, but now I'm just going to tell you what's going to happen."

I stared at him, "LET me think it was my own idea?"

Jack shrugged his shoulders, "Wouldn't be the first time," he said casually.

I gave him a look that should have turned him into a stone and stalked over to the sink to rinse my dishes and put them in the dishwasher. Grandma Rose definitely enjoyed her modern conveniences – thank goodness.

"Well," I snapped over my shoulder, "spit it out. Tell me what my great idea is."

His sigh was one of a person who has suffered long. "Since we both work so close to each other, and we're working the same hours now..."

I snorted, "What a coincidence."

He kindly ignored me, "I thought it might make sense if we drove together."

"You mean you thought it might be nice if I gave you a ride every day," I corrected him.

"Actually," he said, tidying the table and not quite meeting my eyes, "I was thinking that I would drive."

"You?" There might have been some unladylike sputtering right there, but you don't need to hear about that, do you? "I don't think so. My car. I drive." I grabbed my purse and began striding for the door. "Besides, I might not want to go straight to work and back home every day. I might have more important things to do."

He scratched the back of his head thoughtfully, "Actually, the doctor said you weren't supposed to drive for at least a week," he admitted. "I didn't want to tell you... you being so persnickety and stubborn."

I frowned at him, "I like to think of myself as charmingly independent."

His response is really not fit to be reprinted.

CHAPTER 18

"You have to use the little lever at the…"

"I know what I'm doing."

"But you have to lift and push…"

"You may find this hard to believe," Jack growled, "but I have moved a car seat back and forth a time or two in my life."

"You've never moved this car seat," I pointed out sweetly. "And my car has some idiosyncrasies that can be difficult for other people to understand."

"Like owner, like car," Jack muttered, finally freeing the seat to scoot it backward.

"What was that, Cousin Jack?"

He started the car up instead of replying, and we lurched forward.

"Easy!" I cried. "Mr. Darcy isn't used to such rough handling."

He slammed on the brakes, throwing us both roughly against the dashboard. "You named your car 'Mr. Darcy?'" he demanded incredulously, "What does that make you? Elizabeth Bennett?"

I grinned, "Jack," I said, even sweeter than before, "you are just too easy." My grin widened, "And so literary. Who knew that you were a fan of the classics?"

Jack began muttering under his breath. It's a good thing I wasn't listening because I don't think it was anything good about me. We had gone a whole 10 feet when we stopped once again. Jack bent low over the steering wheel, peering intently at the gauges.

"There's a half tank of gas," I said patiently.

"I'm not looking at the gas tank," he said. "I certainly wasn't planning on buying you gas."

"Well that's not very nice," I said. "After you commandeer my car, the least you could do is fill it up."

He switched his attention to the side paneling of the door, running his hand along the side, "I am doing you a favor," he protested, not even bothering to look my way. "If it wasn't for me, you'd be stuck at home."

"If it wasn't for you," I said, "I would be driving my own car on the way to my own job."

"The doctor didn't want you driving," he was now inspecting the front control panel.

"I don't see the doctor in this car, and even if he was…" I began, but gave up. The suspense was killing me. "Alright. What are you looking for?"

"Nothing," Jack said, "Well. Almost nothing. I'm looking for the control that moves the side mirrors. The one on your side is in the wrong position for me."

I stared at him.

He stared back.

I stared harder.

He was not getting it.

"For pity's sake," I sighed dramatically. "Are you kidding me? How old does this car look to you? It's amazing that it even has an engine that doesn't need to be cranked before it's started." I rolled down the window, and yanked the mirror, "Is that better?"

"Huh." And that was all he said until we were safely in town and parked in the employee parking lot (aka the parking lot behind the building).

He got out, flexed his shoulders and slammed the car door, "And I suppose that there's no automatic locking system either?"

I pushed the button on my door and reached across the seat to push the button on his door too before getting out, "At least I have a car," I pointed out. "Where is yours?"

"I don't need a car where I live," he grumped. "But if I did, I would certainly take a little better care of it…"

"My car is completely clean!"

Jack rolled his eyes and started walking towards the back door of the building, "I wasn't talking about how clean it was," he called over his shoulder. "When was the last time you had the oil changed? The thing runs like a tractor."

Well now. What a thing to say. I had the oil changed. Once. Shouldn't the car tell me if it wanted its oil changed? This could explain a lot of things, though. Rats. Now, if I got an oil change, Jack would think that it was all his idea.

I turned to walk around the building and go in through the front door of my place of employment like a civilized person. (Actually, I wasn't too sure how Carolyn felt about people coming in the back door.) Actually, I also wasn't too sure how happy Carolyn was going to be with me. I have a feeling I had oozed a lot of blood over her nice clean floor.

"Hey." The voice by my shoulder had me practically jumping out of my skin. I spun wildly, swinging out with my purse.

"Hey!" the tone had changed to one of surprise and protest as my purse found its target with someone's ribs. The fear abated a bit as some of my other senses returned.

"Jack," I yelled, "for pity's sake, are you TRYING to give me a heart attack?"

He stepped back, rubbing his side, "No, actually I wasn't *trying* to give you a heart attack. I was trying to get your attention. I've been calling you for the last thirty seconds. You don't pay enough attention to your surroundings." This sounded like the beginning of a really good lecture, so I decided to nip it in the bud.

"I'm very sorry," I said formally. "I will be more careful in the future."

"Right," he was looking at me strangely, "I have a feeling that you have something up your sleeve today."

"Nothing but arms," I said saucily, wiggling the aforementioned appendages. "Is that all you wanted?"

"No," he said, "I wanted to know if you and Molly wanted to have lunch with me and Ryan today?" His eyes twinkled, "I think Ryan needs some help…"

Was he serious? Uh. No. I had plans already cooking that didn't involve Jack and Ryan. Maybe there was something up my sleeve. I thanked him nicely (because that's the kind of person I am) and refused. I told him I would meet him back in the parking lot at closing time.

We both turned to go our separate ways.

"Have a good day," Jack said with a crooked, warm smile. "Don't let any more of your brains fall out."

I scowled, "It's not in my plan," I said. "Don't burn any buns."

"It's not in my plan," he said. I watched a thought pop into this head. "One more question," he said. "Why don't you have a cell phone?"

"I don't really have anyone to call," I answered truthfully. Rats. He had caught me off guard. A lump formed in my throat. Why had I said that? "I mean," I quickly amended, "there's no one that I *want* to call. People rely too much on impersonal interaction and we're rapidly becoming a society that is losing its social skills…"

Jack snorted, "Yeah, yeah, yeah," he said, walking away and talking over his shoulder. "The truth is you probably can't figure out how to use one."

He really was an impossible person.

CHAPTER 19

I hesitated in front of the store door. It was such a sweet little yarn store. One glimpse into the big picture window showed Molly and Carolyn sitting at the big round table, knitting together. It was a poignantly sweet scene, and, for some reason, I felt an incredibly strong urge to duck and run the other way.

I briefly considered the route I would take. It would have to be back the same way I came, even though the movement would draw more attention to myself. If I went the other way, Jack or Ryan would probably see me, which would lead to some awkward questions.

Molly glanced up, ruining my escape plan. Her face lit up with a light that looked too real to be faked, and my heart lifted up briefly. I could see her saying something to Carolyn, and she looked up too. Before I knew it, they were both at the door.

"Natalie!" Carolyn was exclaiming as she shooed me gently inside, "What are you doing here? We didn't expect you back so soon. Are you sure that you should be working today?"

I laughed, "I'm totally sure I should be working today," I assured her. "If I stay home a minute longer I could turn into a crazy person."

"From what I heard," Molly said wickedly, "It wouldn't be a long trip."

Carolyn looked at Molly in astonishment before her face broke out into wrinkles of amusement, "That wasn't very nice, Molly," she scolded gently. "Especially on Natalie's first day back."

They acted like I was a long-lost employee back from her deathbed instead of someone who had been only working a day.

"Actually," I said slowly, "I did want to make sure you still wanted me…"

"Wanted you!" Carolyn exclaimed in astonishment, "Of course we want you. Why wouldn't we?"

I tugged my hair further over my forehead, "Well, I don't think I was the most stellar employee you've ever had," I said. "And I'm fairly sure I messed up your store pretty badly."

Her small little hands were surprisingly strong as they shoved me down into a chair, "You were perfect," she said. "I love how you handle the customers. We all have our own way, and your viewpoint on life is refreshing and fun." She pushed the spectacles back on her long nose, "And you are most certainly not to blame for having an accident."

Ah ha. What a perfect segue into what I was dying to know about. I took a deep breath, "Well, I did want to ask you about that," I said. "What did that lady mean about…"

Carolyn stood up abruptly and began backing away, "The best advice I can give you is to not listen to what other people say."

"That's funny," I said, "I've learned in life that even when someone is gossiping, there's an element of truth in there somewhere, and I'd like to know what that truth about Grandma Rose might be."

Carolyn eyed me strangely, but shook her white head, "No," she said. "What's done is done and what's in the past should stay in the past. There have always been rumors about your Grandma Rose, and I'm certainly not about to repeat hearsay. That's almost as bad as gossiping in the first place. Besides, I knew your Grandma Rose just a little bit, and I've never sensed anything other than love and kindness from her."

And no amount of begging, pleading or coercion from either me or Molly was going to change her mind. What a bummer. I was usually pretty good at begging, pleading and coercion.

We puttered around the store, re-fluffing the yarn on shelves and straightening the books until it was time to open. Molly spent a great deal of time at the sock yarn display, and I could hear her muttering about stupid sock knitters and what was up with stupid knitters who liked to knit socks.

Obviously, she had not embarked on the journey of sock knitting yet. I hadn't either. I still needed a new project... maybe she'd want to knit one with me?

I wandered as casually as I could over to the spot where the "incident" had occurred. I was half afraid to still see a blood stain on the floor, but everything had been scrubbed clean and it looked like nothing had ever happened. I wondered if I owed Carolyn some new kitchen towels or something? Surely there must be some kind of repayment or act of gratitude for spilling your blood all over someone's floor and then not even sticking around to clean it up.

About two minutes to opening time, Carolyn grabbed both of us by the hand and said a prayer. A quick glance at Molly's face told me that this was not a new experience. I guess I was fine with that.

The first two customers of the day came and went so smoothly that I was almost convinced my luck was changing. And then... SHE came back in. My forehead started throbbing as soon as I saw her. And I didn't feel guilty a bit about ducking behind the baby yarn and pretending to re-sort it by color. Her shoes were a bit squeaky, so I had no problem following her progress across the floor. She walked slowly past the counter, said a short good morning to Molly, and squeaked her way over to... oh dear... me.

I kept my eyes carefully on the shelf closest to the floor, making sure each skein of yarn was arranged just perfectly. She cleared her throat. I started working on the pink. She shuffled closer. I wasn't happy with the position of the pink on the bottom, so I started my little pink pile over.

"Excuse me?" she said softly.

I was obligated to look up, and it really didn't make me feel any better when her eyes focused on my ugly bruise and zig-zag of stitches. If guilt were a color, that's the color she would be.

"I just stopped by to apologize," she said, still staring at my forehead and avoiding my eyes. "I didn't mean to say anything that was upsetting to you."

"I haven't had much experience with the phrase, 'I don't do business with murderers,'" I said dryly, "but I'm pretty sure just about anybody would be upset by that."

Her narrow face flushed a bit, and I looked over her shoulder to see Molly standing a few feet away, not even pretending to have a reason for standing there, with her arms crossed over her chest. I didn't think it was possible for Molly to look intimidating, but she was almost doing a good job of it... and I was touched.

"I didn't mean to say that," she said in a rush. "You just caught me by surprise, and sometimes I blurt things out without even thinking about them."

I looked her carefully up and down. Her right hand was clenched so hard, her knuckles were turning white. I decided to take pity on her. She might have meant to be cruel, but she hadn't meant for me to fall. I could handle mean. "Don't worry about it," I said. "It's over and done." I paused. "Although, I would like to know what you meant."

She laughed nervously, her eyes shooting around the room and landing on Carolyn who now stood next to Molly looking even more threatening than a little old lady had any right to look. A little glow fired up somewhere inside of me. These people actually liked me. Even though they knew me. Amazing, wasn't it? "I didn't mean anything," she protested. "I just... I just... I've heard...." and, still mumbling... she made her way over to the brown yarn we had been looking at before she had decided I was unfit to help her. She grabbed four skeins and practically ran over to the counter.

Molly reluctantly followed her and began checking her out. Knitters were weird. Carolyn expertly negotiated the swinging rack of needles and came to stand beside me, "Are you sure you're all right, dear?" she asked. "You're looking a bit pale."

"You could tell me what's going on," I said with a forced smile. "I'd feel a lot better then."

Carolyn rolled her eyes and adjusted her headband (it had a large purple flower bursting off the side of it), "You never give up, do you?" she asked, patting my hand affectionately. "Just be sure not to overdo anything today. You're also going to take an extended lunch hour so you can get some rest."

She was a horrible boss, wasn't she?

As Molly was finishing up with Jean, the little doorbell over the door tinkled happily and two little old ladies entered. I had to hide a grin behind the acrylic blend of baby yarn. They looked like the perfect stereotype for what everyone thinks that knitters should look like. Little old grannies with more time than skill. And taste.

The first lady had on an old, worn cardigan that she had obviously knitted herself. It was frayed at the button band and elbows and hopelessly pilled. Her wild hair was wispy and white, and the wrinkles on her face were so deep I wondered if they had a bottom. I was glad to see her sensible support shoes. They were the only thing on her body that had some weight. At least she wouldn't blow away in the wind.

Her friend wasn't much better. She wore a crazy sweater that looked like it had been knitted with some especially gnarly mohair. Actually, to be honest, it looked like she was wearing a wild animal. A bright orange wild animal. Her hair was hidden beneath a headscarf that could have also helped direct traffic at night – a brilliant combination of orange and scarlet to compliment her sweater, no doubt. Her shoes were little pointed things with two-inch heels that had disaster written all over them.

"Have a nice day," Molly was saying to Jean, trying very hard to look like she meant it.

"You too," Jean replied, practically choking over the words. She nodded curtly at Carolyn and started making her way to the door.

"Enjoy your moebius, Jean," Carolyn said softly to her. "And you know where to come if you need any help."

Jean's face softened into a shy smile, "Thank you, Carolyn," she whispered.

Molly caught sight of the two little old ladies over Jean's shoulder, and her face lit up with delighted surprise, "Old Mrs. Harrison," she exclaimed, "how nice to see you."

I quickly turned my spurt of laughter into a cough, as the two old ladies turned to glare at me. Old Mrs. Harrison. Ha. Who knew that Molly had it in her?

The lady's face also lit up, "Molly, dear!" she called, "I've got someone here for you to meet." The other lady was looking dubiously around the yarn store. "Gertrude, honey," she said, pulling at her furry sleeve. "You're just going to love this place."

Gertrude did not look that impressed. "I'm sure I will," she said.

"Are you a knitter?" I inquired politely. Look at me. Making small talk with complete strangers. I was really getting to be good at this whole yarn store thing. I'm sure that no one would guess that it was only my second day on the job.

She studied me so carefully that I felt a bit self-conscious. Her eyes didn't miss a thing... from the top of my head to my cute little shoes. At least, I thought that they were cute. The way that she stared at them made me wonder. But, really, she was a granny wearing two-inch heels. She had no reason to judge.

"I'm sorry," she said, after her examination was complete, "What did you say?"

Oh. She was hard at hearing. Of course she was. She was an old lady. That explained a lot. "I asked if you were a knitter."

Her head nodded enthusiastically, and her face exploded into one of the prettiest old faces I have ever seen – complete with dimples. I couldn't help but smile back. "I've been knitting for a hundred years," she said. Now that was something I could believe.

"Me too," I said. "Well, not a hundred years like you…" which made her smile again. I decided that I liked her.

Old Mrs. Harrison was busy walking forward and grabbing Molly by the arm and pulling her along to where her friend and I stood. It's a good thing Molly went along willingly. If she hadn't, Old Mrs. Harrison might have lost her arm.

"Molly, dear," she repeated. "I have someone I would like for you to meet."

Obviously, Old Mrs. Harrison thought that Molly's name was 'Molly Dear'. Sigh. I wonder what it was like to be so sweet and have everyone love you. I shrugged to myself. Why waste time wondering? It wasn't likely that I was ever going to find out.

Molly Dear beamed at Old Mrs. Harrison and her friend, "How lovely," she said. "You didn't mention that you were having company."

"Well, Gertrude surprised me," she admitted. "And it was just the best surprise ever."

Gertrude gave a small snort.

"Molly, dear," she said formally, holding out one frail hand grandly. "I would like for you to meet my second cousin, Gertrude Dalyrmple. She lives in Oklahoma."

"Where the wind comes sweeping down the plain," Gertrude said solemnly, but with a twinkle in her eye.

Molly held out a hand, "It's so very nice to meet you, Gertrude," she said smiling. "We just love your cousin."

Gertrude grinned, "I sure hope you're not going to call me 'Old Gertrude.'"

We all laughed. Carolyn finally stepped forward from her silent survey of the scene in front of her to shake Gertrude's hand as well, "I do believe we've met before, Gertrude," she said quietly, shaking her hand and looking her in the eye, "But that was many years ago. Perhaps you don't remember me? I do believe we had a long discussion about the pros and cons of circular knitting needles the last time you were here."

Gertrude studied her seriously for a moment, "Yes, I do believe you're right," she said. "I didn't think you would recognize me. I've changed a lot since then, haven't I?" They stared at each other for a long moment, "Of course," Gertrude said cheerfully. "You've changed a lot too. Your hair used to be brown." Her eyes gleamed, "Tell me something...do they call you 'Old Carolyn' now?"

Carolyn finally cracked a smile, "The only reason we call Betty "Old Mrs. Harrison" is because we have two Mrs. Harrison's here and err..."

"Old Mrs. Harrison is way older than her?" I hazarded a guess.

Everyone laughed and Molly's hand went to her head in mock despair, "We really need to work on your people skills, Natalie," she said.

Old Mrs. Harrison whacked me affectionately (I hope) on the arm, "Shucks, girl," she said, "I think your people skills are just fine. You call it like you see it.

Nothing wrong with that." I smiled at her. I was starting to like her too. Although I doubt she was ever going to call me Natalie, Dear.

"Come on, Gertie," Old Mrs. Harrison said, shuffling her way to the little love seat, "I told you that this was a great store. Look at the comfy sitting area. I'll just park myself right here while you poke around."

"It shouldn't take me too long, Betty," Gertrude said, "I just need some new sock yarn. My fingers are just dying to knit me some socks."

"Me too!" I exclaimed. "I was just thinking about starting some socks as my next project while I think about the sweater that I want to knit."

"Socks are great for thinking," Gertrude said thoughtfully. "They keep your fingers busy, but only require brain power at certain times. There's certainly a lot of space in there for getting some good thinking done."

I found myself walking her to the sock yarn, "And do you find yourself in need of a lot of thinking time?" I inquired, as something in her demeanor had changed and sparked a sense of seriousness in her words.

My question seemed to startle her, and she turned her head to look at me, "Gracious," she said, smiling again, "please don't pay too much attention to me. I'm an old lady. I've got lots of things I want to think about. It's about all us old ladies can do."

I shook my head, "Now you know that's not true," I protested.

She grinned, "Darn. I can usually get away with my little old lady spiel with most youngsters," she said, "But you're too smart for me."

I rolled my eyes and began pointing out the various pros and cons of the sock yarn that Carolyn had on hand. It was a really good thing that this morning Carolyn had told me the pros and the cons of the sock yarn that she had on hand, wasn't it? Ha.

You know... sock knitters are really an interesting species. You can tell a lot about a person just by how they knit their socks... at least you can according to Molly and Carolyn. For example, did you know that some people turn their noses up at any sock yarn that isn't a solid color? They think that sock yarn that makes its own stripes and patterns is cheating. Also... did you know that some people will only knit natural colors because they don't want to call any attention to their feet? (Maybe you might get kicked out of the Whatever Club if your socks are too bright??) And... did you know that some people, when they knit with sock yarns that stripe, they HAVE to make sure that both socks match or they would die of embarrassment? The funny thing is... when was the last time you actually ever looked at someone else's socks? Yes, my friends. Knitters are crazy. And weird.

Apparently, Gertrude did not care if her feet were too loud (which, considering her sweater, was really not that surprising) and she also did not consider self-striping yarns to be cheating. She picked a skein of red, pink, orange and aqua that did a stripe and dot pattern as you knit them. The yarn was wool with just a touch of acrylic... in case you were wondering.

"Now," she said, turning to me, as I had been watching with abject fascination as she sorted through the yarns, "How about you?"

"Excuse me?" I asked, raising my eyebrows, which I instantly regretted, as my stitches pulled.

"I thought you wanted to knit socks?" I nodded. She sighed with the patience of one talking to someone who isn't very smart. "Well, then..." she said, "what sock yarn are you going to pick?" I hesitated. "Come on," she encouraged, "we don't have all day, pick one and be done with it." Ummm.... Excuse me? This? Coming from the old lady who had just spent the last 15 minutes trying to decide between red, pink, orange and aqua versus red, pink, orange and blue?

She poked her head around the sock yarn display, where Molly had been politely lurking. Molly was very protective of her sock yarn. "And what about you, Molly Dear?" she inquired with a touch of mischief. "I think it's time you knit some socks."

"How do you know she's never knitted socks?" I asked.

Gertrude put her nose up in the air and played with the ends of her scarf with a great air of self-superiority, "I can just tell."

Molly was not impressed. She grinned knowingly, "Old Mrs. Harrison told you, didn't she?"

Gertrude rolled her eyes and with more speed than I would have given her credit for (especially in those shoes), zipped around the display and had Molly standing in front of it looking slightly uncomfortable in a record amount of time.

"I'm really busy knitting other things right now," Molly began timidly. "I've got a lovely scarf that I'm finishing up right now." She eyed Gertrude desperately, "It has a ruffle on one side."

"Fiddlesticks," Old Mrs. Harrison had joined us at the sock yarn. "That's the great thing about knitting socks. They're small and portable, and you can have one going even if you have other projects going as well."

"But," Molly protested, "I'm not one of THOSE kind of knitters."

That's it. She lost me.

Gertrude and Old Mrs. Harrison burst out laughing. Apparently, they had followed just fine.

"Then it's about time you were," Gertrude said. "Unless you think you're better than us by only knitting one project at a time?"

Molly looked like a cornered fox at a fox hunt. She tried backing away, but the two little old ladies had a firm, albeit frail, grip on each of her arms.

And then Old Mrs. Harrison went in for the kill, "And besides," she said wickedly, "I happen to know you were knitting a scarf for a special male friend at the SAME time you were knitting your sweater."

Well now. That was interesting.

Sweat beaded on Molly's forehead, "But that was different," she protested, looking between her two hunters, "I needed to make a present and I had just started the sweater. I didn't have *time…*"

"Now don't you be making excuses," Old Mrs. Harrison said triumphantly. "Just pick out some yarn, Molly, dear, and then we can get started."

Poor Molly. I have a feeling that she did not want to knit socks. Ever. Strange. An idea popped into my head, "I'm very sorry, ladies," I said, "but we can't knit socks right now, anyway." They looked at me blankly. "We're supposed to be working."

Gertrude and Old Mrs. Harrison looked at each other and giggled.

"What?" I asked. Molly looked even more dejected.

"Oh, Carolyn..." they called out in a sing-song voice together.

Carolyn popped her little head around the sock yarn display – as there was no room for one more person to stand in front of it. From the look of her smile, she had been listening to everything. "Yes, ladies," she said smoothly, "how can I help you?"

Old Mrs. Harrison tilted her head to the side in such a fluid manner that I was becoming rapidly suspicious of her little old lady routine. She had obviously used this once or twice before. "Carolyn," she began, "what is your policy on your employee's knitting during working hours?"

Carolyn made her eyes wide, while Molly stifled a groan. "Why, they are more than welcome to knit," she exclaimed. "I like to think of it as perfecting your craft... something I strongly encourage all employees to do. That is, only if there are no customers that need help and all their other duties are attended to," she quickly amended.

"Because, really," Gertrude said, "if a customer comes in with a question about how to knit socks, your employees really should know how to help them, shouldn't they?"

Molly looked up and, catching Carolyn's encouraging eye, heaved a great sigh and grabbed a skein of sock yarn from the shelf. It had glitter flakes in it. Poor Molly. I don't think she even knew what she grabbed. She really didn't strike me as a glitter sock sort of girl.

As we all marched to the checkout counter, I heard Molly mutter to Carolyn, "I'll get you for this."

CHAPTER 20

I t was just Molly's rotten luck that there were very few customers today. I was actually feeling a bit guilty about working and getting paid for sitting on a chair and knitting. Not much. Just a little. Besides, Carolyn was sitting and knitting too, so that made it seem much more legitimate. Knitting socks was, apparently, very soothing to the soul.

I had chosen a black and white yarn striped with random streaks of bright color. They were going to be so adorable. At least for my first pair. My second pair was going to involve cables and lace and maybe something crazy like bobbles. I wasn't going to just knit plain socks the rest of my life.

Molly looked up from her "toothpicks" – a.k.a. her double pointed needles and frowned, "Isn't this strange? We should be busier than this. Don't knitters usually come out of the woodwork in the fall?"

Carolyn nodded to Molly over her own knitting… "Usually, Molly," she said. "Historically, the autumn season is one of our busiest times of the year. But knitters can be fickle."

Molly sighed. "Knitters are weird."

"And it probably doesn't hurt that Happy Knits is having a huge fall sale either," Old Mrs. Harrison said with a chuckle, peering over her glasses - fingers flying over her needles. Old Mrs. Harrison was so good, she did not even need a pattern to knit from.

Molly's jaw hit the ground. "How did I not know about this?" she demanded.

"Maybe they figured out your fake name on their email list and removed you," Carolyn suggested with a gentle smile.

Molly scowled, "That's impossible," she protested.

"Ah-ha!" Carolyn crowed, "So you admit it!" She turned to the rest of us, "You're all my witnesses."

Molly looked embarrassed. "Well," she admitted, "someone has to keep an eye on them. Especially since you won't."

"Who says I don't?" Carolyn protested. Who knew it was possible to look mischievous and innocent all at the same time?

The cheerful jingling of the doorbell alerted us to a red-haired man with an impressive grey beard. He walked in carrying a large white box, but stopped suddenly when he saw the crowd of ladies sitting by the window.

"Good morning, Mr. Morrie," Carolyn called out cheerfully. "Please come in."

He smiled shyly and shook his head, "I just came to deliver this box," he said, holding the box out higher as if the invisible person standing in front of him would take it out of his hands.

Molly rose to her feet, looking grateful for the interruption. "Now that looks like a box from Ryan's bakery," she exclaimed. "My favorite kind of box." She tossed her knitting aside, "Let's hope it's full of cinnamon rolls." Mr. Morrie handed her the box with a small smile that made Molly's smile bigger. "Thank you for bringing it over, Mr. Morrie," she said.

He blushed a little and handed her the box carefully, "My pleasure," he said.

Both Molly and Mr. Morrie studied the box for a moment, and then Molly's head shot up to meet Mr. Morrie's gaze. His right eye closed slightly in what could have been a wink.

"Well," Molly said, "I'm going to go start some coffee. Why don't you pull up a chair and stay and have some of the deliciousness that's in this box."

He scratched his head thoughtfully while backing away. "I've already had half a coffee cake," he said slowly. "I think I'll be just fine until lunch."

"No," Carolyn protested. "Please stay."

But, Mr. Morrie was already shuffling away, the door shutting softly behind him.

Molly glanced at the box again and giggled. "Ummm… Natalie," she called, "will you come help me start some coffee?"

I put my knitting down reluctantly. How many people did it take to start some coffee? I was just done with the ribbing and ready to start the leg. My fingers itched to keep going. But… I suppose that a job was a job… and technically this was a job. Even if was just making coffee.

Gertrude and Old Mrs. Harrison had finished their ribbing a while ago and were making great progress on the leg of their socks. I was a little envious. I was going to have to work on my speed if I wanted to knit all of the projects done that I had planned to do before I turned 80.

Molly was already back in the little kitchen area behind the store when I got there. She had made no attempt to start the coffee yet. Slacker.

She grabbed my arm as soon as she saw me, "You've got to see this," she whispered, pulling me towards the box.

"It's not like I've never seen pastry," I protested, allowing her to pull me along.

"Look at that," she hissed.

There was writing on top of the box. It said, "These pastries are but a paltry comparison to the sweetness that is you. Will you have dinner with me?"

Paltry comparison? Good grief.

Her face was pleasantly flushed, "What do you think it means?" she whispered.

I grinned at her, "I think it means that Ryan would like to have dinner with you."

Molly tugged at her hair self-consciously. "It doesn't say me," she protested. "It could be any of us. It could be for you." Her eyes lit up as a sudden thought occurred to her, "Maybe Jack wants to take you out to dinner." Obviously, her brain did not want to allow her to contemplate the idea of Ryan taking me out to dinner. Perhaps Jack was right. Maybe they did like each other.

173

I snorted and rolled my eyes, "I can assure you that there is no way that Jack would ever consider me as sweet as a pastry."

Her eyes were wide, and she looked a little panicked. "What do I do?" she whispered.

I tilted my head and tried to smile in my most motherly fashion, "Well," I said, "do you want to go to dinner with Ryan?"

"I don't know," her voice was soft and filled with doubt. "I've never thought about it."

"Liar!" I said a bit too loudly. She looked at me in astonishment. "I've seen how excited you are to go next door," I explained. "And I've seen your face when you talk about Ryan. You've thought about it, honey."

Her cheeks went even pinker, "Well," she amended, "perhaps I have thought about it. But I'm not really sure I want to get involved with someone right now. I really enjoy our relationship. What if it ends badly? We work so close together... it would be so awkward... and... and..."

I laughed, "It's just dinner," I said, "not a marriage proposal. Chill out. If you want to go, then go. If you don't want to go, then tell him you're not interested in him."

She stared at me, "You make things sound so easy." Molly sighed heavily and collapsed dramatically into a kitchen chair, "He's just gone and ruined everything," she said sadly. "We'll never have this back again."

I touched her shoulder, feeling old and wise, "No," I said, "you'll never have what you had before, but you could have something new and different. Something even better than what you have right now." I decided that now was the time to change the subject. "Well," I said cheerfully, "give it some thought. In the meantime, I know exactly what we should be doing."

Her head perked up, "What's that?"

I began opening the box, "Eating delicious pastries."

Her naturally sunny disposition took back over, "Now that's a good plan," she said, helping me to wrestle the top of the box off. We both gaped.

Inside the box was a beautiful assortment of pastries... donuts, coffee cake, pastries and scones... and, of course, cinnamon rolls... all perfectly beautiful...

but extremely miniature. The little cinnamon rolls couldn't have been bigger than an inch in diameter. The wee little coffee cakes were even drizzled with icing, and the tiny little donuts were frosted and filled flawlessly. Each little scone was topped with an equally small dollop of jam.

"What on earth," Molly said in wonder. "Why…"

I pointed to the little note that was tucked in the middle. She reached in gingerly and pulled it out from between a delicate apple turnover with flaky pastry and a powdered, jelly-filled donut. She shook it to scatter the powdered sugar from the paper, and I peered over her shoulder so that we could read it together.

"Ladies, please enjoy these treats as much as we enjoyed making them for you. We've made them small enough so that you can try everything we have to offer. We know you love our cinnamon rolls, but sometimes it's easy to get stuck on one thing and not realize that there are even more delicious options available to you. And, if you decide that cinnamon rolls are the only thing you ever want to eat, that will be fine too. P.S. Don't let Natalie eat all of the scones."

Molly sighed happily and clutched the note to her chest, "That is just the sweetest thing I have ever seen," she gushed. "I can't believe Ryan did this."

Well, the note certainly sounded like Cousin Jack's handiwork, but I had no desire to tell her so.

"They certainly are adorable, "I said. "They look like something that little fairies should eat." An idea popped into my head, "Wouldn't that be cute if there were little knitting fairies?"

Molly spun to face me, all gushiness gone from her face. She slapped a hand over my mouth, eyes wide and full of panic, "Don't you say that," she warned. "Don't ever say anything about knitting fairies."

Whoa.

I took a step back from her sticky little hand, "Sorry," I said cautiously, "I guess somebody doesn't believe in fairies?"

She shook her head, her eyes darting around the room in a rather paranoid fashion. "Oh no," she said seriously, "I believe. That's why I don't want to talk about them."

I tried to keep a straight face. I really did.

Yes, my friends, knitters are crazy.

We arranged our wee little delicacies on a tray and waited for the coffee to stop perking. I decided to seize my opportunity.

"Hey, Molly," I said casually, "what are you doing for lunch?"

She eyed me warily, "Why, do you want to double date or something?"

I re-arranged the packets of creamer nervously, "No," I said, "something much easier. You see, Jack said that the doctor said that I wasn't supposed to be driving. So he has my car keys. And I really need to go see the Sherriff about something."

Her face creased with sympathy, "You mean to ask about your grandmother…"

I sighed, "Well… that… and…" I paused, but the look on my face must have spoken more than I thought.

"What happened?" Molly exclaimed, "Is everything alright? Did you have a break-in?"

"No," I hissed. "Keep your voice down. It wasn't a break-in." I paused to consider, "Well, maybe it was a break-in. I don't know." I waved my hand impatiently, "I'll fill you in on everything later, but, you're right, I do have to go and ask the Sherriff how my grandma died."

She stared at me. "Whoa," was all she said. Obviously, she was finding it difficult to think of something appropriate to say. She surprised me with, "Did you ever figure out who was responsible for the projector in your room? Was it Jack? Was it Celia? Was it Mr. Garvey?"

I admired her ability to topic-hop. "I'll tell you all about that, too," I said, "if you'll take me to the Sherriff…"

She put a hand on my arm, "Of course I will, Natalie," she said sincerely. "I'll help you with whatever you need to do. You know that. We're friends now."

"Are you two coming with those rolls?" Carolyn called from the shop floor. "We're getting hungry out here."

Molly grabbed the coffee and the carousel of cups and coffee accessories and started marching back to the front, "We're coming right now," she called… leaving me to carry the tray of goodies.

I popped a chocolate-covered donut into my mouth – just to prove to Jack that I could eat whatever I wanted. It was absolutely delicious. And then, just to prove that he wasn't the boss of me… I ate a scone.

Lunchtime couldn't come soon enough. Carolyn had, not surprisingly, given her blessing to our lunch together. I felt a little bad about leaving her at the store by herself (after all, she was the boss), but since we hadn't had too many customers and Old Mrs. Harrison and Gertrude were still there knitting away on their socks, I figured she wouldn't get overwhelmed… or lonely.

Molly forgot to mention one little thing.

She didn't have a car.

We stood outside Crabapple Yarns and looked at each other. "You could have told me that you didn't have a car," I said a little grumpily.

"Then you might not have told me what was going on," Molly replied simply, brushing her long hair away from her face. The wind was picking up. I wished I had remembered to bring my coat. It was really turning into coat-weather.

"Do you even have a license?" I demanded.

She looked affronted, "Yes, I do," she said, putting her little nose up into the air. "Just because someone can't afford the luxury of an automobile doesn't mean she doesn't have the tools necessary to do so." I rolled my eyes. "Besides," she continued with a mischievous grin, "one doesn't need a car for most things in Springgate. One can just walk."

I stared at her in disbelief, "You mean to tell me that the Sherriff's office is within lunch-hour walking distance?"

She nodded happily.

"And you couldn't just tell me that?"

Her happy nodding continued, "Nope." Her grin widened. "Because," she clarified, "once again... I wanted you to tell me everything."

"Molly, Dear," I said severely, "you are terrible."

"I know," she sighed, "Don't worry. I'm working on it." She gestured towards Main Street, "Shall we?"

I sighed and went to walk next to her.

"And," she said, "as we walk, please feel free to share with me every juicy detail of life on Raspberry Hill."

Right about there, we passed the bakery and found Ryan just "happening" to come out the door. He even managed to look just the right amount of surprised. Obviously, Jack was coaching him. "Good afternoon, ladies," he said calmly, even though his cheeks were turning the exact color of his hair, "did you enjoy your treats this morning?"

I decided to let Molly answer, even though I could feel her twitching at my side. "We did," Molly answered truthfully. "They were so adorable."

Ryan nodded, "We're thinking about offering them as options here in the bakery. You know, for people who don't want to have a large donut... or for people who like to have a variety...or for people who want to try something new..."

I knew what Ryan was getting at. I poked Molly discretely in the side. "Sure," she said, somewhat breathlessly, "I think that's a great idea." She smiled at him shyly, "I tried all of them, and I thought that they were delicious."

His eyebrows rose up into his hairline, "You mean you didn't just stick with the cinnamon roll?" His smile was gentle and teasing... and the slightest bit hopeful.

"Nope," she said, "I decided that sometimes you just have to try something new."

They both stood there grinning at each other.

Oh brother. At this rate, they wouldn't get married until they were 97. And that was an optimistic estimate. Kids were going to be completely out of the question.

"Hey," Jack called from inside "is that Natalie and Molly?"

"Yeah," Ryan yelled back in. "They're leaving for lunch."

"Ask Molly if she wants to come over for supper," Jack yelled back out. "I'm making chicken fettuccine."

Good ol' Jack. He's just so subtle.

After agreeing to dinner, with a great deal of blushing and stammering, we were back on our way to the Sherriff's office.

CHAPTER 21

The Sherriff's office was a squat little place built with brick and minimal curb appeal. Some brave soul had tried to plant geraniums on the path up to the door, but had obviously decided that watering was a waste of money. Poor little things. They were scraggly and holding on to dear life through sheer willpower alone. I felt a wave of intense sympathy for them.

"I feel like we should do something," I whispered to Molly, as we strolled up the path. "It seems wrong to just walk by."

Molly was still deep in thought from everything that I had hastily told her. "What are you talking about?" she asked, looking around. "What's wrong?"

"Never mind," I said, pulling open the front door, "you're just not a multitasker."

She entered in front of me. "Now that's just rude," she said. "I'll have you know that just last week I helped three customers at one time."

"Oooohh," I said, trying my best to sound impressed, "well, now. I stand corrected."

"And one of them had a toddler," she added. But, I was done listening because I heard something. It sounded a lot like… I strained harder… yep. It sounded just like my mother.

"Shhhhhh," I hissed at Molly, who was, undoubtedly going to continue her tirade of how well she could multitask. "I hear something."

"What is it?" she whispered back. I put a finger to my lips. There was an open counter to our right. It didn't look like anyone was in the office behind the counter, but you never knew. Celia's voice was coming from deeper in the building. I ducked so that I was lower than the window and crawled my way past. I felt Molly gasp. I turned to look at her. She was making violent gestures with her arms. I could be wrong, but I think she wanted me to come back. Instead, I made my own violent gestures for her to follow me. She shook her head. I gestured again. She sighed. One more gesture had her dropping to her knees. I could see her mouth moving, and I assumed that whatever she was saying was nothing good about me.

We snuck down the hall to where the voices were coming from.

"Is this legal?" Molly hissed in my ear.

I zinged her the stink eye. Good grief. We were just standing in the hallway of a police station. What could possibly be illegal about that? I decided to ignore Molly and focus on... my mother. What was she doing here?

"...I'm sorry," Finn was saying.

"So you're telling me that my mother died in a fire in the guesthouse?" Celia was asking. She sounded quite suspicious. "I find that hard to believe."

So did I. I grabbed Molly's arm without even thinking about it. Her gaze was sympathetic and pained. I liked her for that.

"I'm sorry," Finn said again. "But yes, she did. There is definitely no doubt about that."

"But how did the fire start?" Celia demanded.

"The cause is still under investigation," Finn admitted. "We're not quite sure how it started. It didn't appear to be electrical or..." his voice trailed off.

Celia might like to play dumb and helpless, but she was as sharp as a tack. "You think it was set deliberately." It was a statement, not a question.

There was a creak of a chair and the rustle of fabric. I could picture Sherriff Finn scratching his head. "Well now..." he drawled, "like I said, the cause is still under investigation."

Celia did not miss a beat. "Are you saying that my mother started the fire herself?" Celia sounded outraged.

There was another creak and then a thud that sounded like elbows hitting the desk. "Like I said," Finn repeated through his teeth, "the cause is still under investigation." Celia was going to have to start backpedaling pretty soon, I thought…otherwise the good Sherriff was going to kick her out in the next 30 seconds.

I could hear Celia settle back in her chair. "You see, Sheriff," she said in such a pleasant voice that I knew Finn was in big trouble now, "I seem to remember that not everyone in this town liked my mother."

Molly's hand landed on my arm, squeezing tightly.

There were a full 10 seconds of silence in the room. "What exactly are you implying?" the Sheriff finally asked. "Because I don't think that I like the sound of it."

"I'm saying that, 30 years ago, she was accused of murder, and from what I've heard in this town, some people still remember that."

Finn cleared his throat, "We do not suspect foul play at this time," he said with an air of finality. There was a scraping sound of a chair being pushed back across the floor. Less than 30 seconds. Impressive.

Molly's grip on me tightened at the same time mine tightened on her. Our gazes locked. One thing I knew for certain. I did not want to be here when Celia and Sherriff Finn came out of that room. From the look on Molly's face, neither did she. I doubted our reasons were the same, but I was glad we were of the same mind. We ran past the window, not even caring whether or not it was occupied. We ran past the dying geraniums and all the way to the corner. I looked around wildly. Which way to go?

Molly was already pulling me into a little store. It turned out to be a women's clothing store, and we huddled together behind a rack of newly arrived woollen sweaters.

I sank to the floor in relief. "I'm sure Celia didn't see us," Molly offered helpfully.

"I don't think she did either," I replied, mind spinning with the revelation of what I had just heard. Grandma Rose was an accused murderer? That nasty little knitter, Jean, had been right? My beautiful dream of a sweet little old grandma morphed into a tiny soap bubble and burst into a million pieces all over the nice clean floors of the women's store.

"This is ridiculous," Molly exclaimed. "What a rip-off."

My head shot up. What in the world was that girl talking about now? She was holding the sleeve of one of the knitted sweaters and looking at the price tag in disgust.

"Can you believe that some people pay this much for a sweater? I could knit this myself for half – no – way less than half of this."

"Molly," I said.

"And it's just stockinette stitch," she continued to mumble, turning the sleeve over in her hand. "Nothing fancy. Not even ribbing at the bottom."

"Molly!" I snapped.

She looked up to glare at me. "Why can't everyone just learn how to knit so that they don't get…"

"Molly!" I snapped again. "Pay attention. Were you listening? My grandmother is a suspected murderer."

She sank down to the floor next to me, "But, Natalie," she said, her face turning sad, "it sounds like that was a long time ago."

"Murderer," I repeated. "I might be related to a murderer."

"Suspected is not the same thing as convicted," Molly pointed out. "If she really killed someone, then she would have been convicted."

I grinned half-heartedly at Molly, "You underestimate the women in my family," I said. "We're quite remarkably good at getting out of trouble."

She had no reply to that, but I could practically hear the gears in her brain turning. "The library!" she suddenly blurted.

The saleslady chose that unfortunate moment to check up on her "customers". We probably made quite the strange picture sitting on the floor behind the winter sweaters. She looked like the type that would never even consider sitting on a floor. She was dressed impeccably, with hair that a hurricane would be hard-pressed to disturb.

"Can I help you?" she asked coolly, one slim hand coming up to slide over her heart in a manner that suggested she was feeling slightly threatened by us. Nice touch.

Molly jumped to her feet, obviously self-conscious, dusting off her rear and trying not to make eye contact with the sales lady. "Actually, Irene," she said, "we're good. We were just… ah… going…"

I rose slowly to my feet, "Actually," I said, mimicking Molly, "my friend here was just wondering how you could, in all good conscience, charge such an arm and a leg for a simple stockinette sweater?"

The saleslady's jaw fell open. It was not a pretty sight.

Molly made a choking sound and started pulling me by the arm, "Ha!" she said with a chuckle that sounded as forced as it looked. "My friend here is such a joker."

I dug my heels in to keep Molly from pulling me any further, "Actually," I said again, "she thinks that she should convert all of your customers into knitters so that they don't have to buy your high-priced sweaters."

This time, I had mercy and allowed Molly to start pulling me out of the store. "I really didn't," Molly protested, hovering in the doorway… but her inherent truthfulness reared its ugly head, "Well, I might have said…" I laughed and pushed Molly out of the store to land back on the street. Much to the relief of the saleslady, I'm sure. I expect she was well into her smelling salts by now.

She gave me a good-natured shove, "How could you do that?" she demanded, only half serious. "I can never go back in there." She smacked both hands to her face in a beautiful demonstration of total and complete humiliation, "And why did Irene have to be working today?"

I shrugged, "You never went in there anyway."

She huffed impatiently, "No, but I might have wanted to someday."

"Why?" I demanded. "To buy an over-priced sweater that you could have knitted yourself?"

She rolled her eyes. "I can't believe you're even joking at a time like this," she protested, shoving my shoulder again. "Weren't you just…"

"Molly, Molly, Molly," I sighed, "when you get as old as me, you'll realize that you have to seize every opportunity that you have to enjoy the moment."

"Maybe when I get as warped as you," she muttered.

It was time to come back down to earth. "So what were you saying before we were so rudely interrupted by the saleslady?"

Molly had a bit of a harder time returning to the present, "I was saying," she said slowly, "That we should go check the library. We can go through the newspaper articles and see whose murder your grandma was accused of."

Molly was a genius.

I glanced at my watch and tried to keep pace with Molly. "Are you sure we have time to go all the way over to the library?" I huffed.

Molly shrugged, "We haven't really even been gone that long," she pointed out, "and Carolyn did tell us to take our time." She gave me a wry smile, "Although I really don't think that this is what she had in mind."

As we marched purposefully towards the library, I had a chance to admire, once again, the charming downtown area. One of these days I was going to have to come down here and do some serious exploring. Someday when my house wasn't haunted, there wasn't a mother I wasn't talking to and we had cleared my grandmother's name of murder. I hoped the town would still be here by the time I got all of that done.

"There it is," Molly said, love shining in her eyes. "The library."

I looked at the church building and then looked back at her. "That's a church," I corrected her. Poor thing. The stress must be getting to her already. She just wasn't cut out for sneakiness and…

She whacked me on the shoulder, "Shut up," she said good-naturedly. "It used to be a church. Now it's a library." She stuck her tongue out at me, "You don't know everything," she said.

"Well," I said with mock indignation, "I don't think…"

She laughed suddenly, an impish smile lighting up her face, "You're too funny," she said, "You should see your face." She sobered as I reached for the door of the library. "Actually," she whispered, "there's something you should know." She bit her lip and didn't quite meet my eye, "I was fired from here not too long ago. The librarian doesn't like me very much… so be prepared."

I gaped at her. Molly? Fired? Who would fire someone as sweet as Molly? Gracious heavens. If MOLLY couldn't even keep a job, what were MY chances?

"What for?" I finally managed to get out.

She smiled sheepishly, "Conduct unbecoming a librarian," she admitted, her cheeks heating up slightly.

My gape continued, "Really?" She looked so crestfallen, that I forced myself to pull it together. "Well," I said with my most wicked grin, "I'm so impressed."

That did it. She looked at me in astonishment a full 2 seconds before the laugh flew out of her mouth. Which was also enough time for us to enter the library and earn an A+ scowl from the curmudgeon sitting behind the desk. Whoa.

"Please keep your voices down," she said. As she spoke, frost fell and grew along the spines of every book, turning them white with fingers of iciness. "We don't disturb our serious studiers."

"Whoa," I said only loud enough for Molly to hear. "I now understand why you were fired."

"She still scares me," Molly admitted, her face twisting a little. "And… I'm also very sorry for her."

Molly was probably a better person than me. What did you just say? Never mind.

"Good afternoon, Mrs. Goldmyer," Molly said politely approaching the desk.

Mrs. Goldmyer slowly removed her eyes from the book in front of her, adjusted her spectacles and eyed Molly up and down. "Ah," she said, "Ms. Stevenson. I almost didn't recognize you."

Molly smiled bravely, "It's very nice to see you again," she said, pulling me along with one hand. "My friend and I were just going to look something up in the archives."

Thin lips parted into what could be considered a smile… you know, the kind of smile you'd see on a snake right before it bit you. Her little eyes gleamed with an unholy glee. "I know exactly who your friend is," she said coldly. "And I know what you're looking for."

"Excuse me?" I interrupted. "What do you mean?"

Her gaze flicked to me and then back to Molly again. "I set everything out for you," she continued smoothly, as if I had not spoken. "I knew you wouldn't have time to linger over your lunch hour."

"How – how kind of you," Molly stammered.

Again… the smile, this time accompanied by a bob of the head, "On the back table, Ms. Stevenson," Mrs. Goldmyer said, "And please remember to keep your voices down."

Molly all but dragged me to the back table, "What is going on here?" I hissed loudly. "Why does she know who I am and why I'm here?"

Molly shrugged, "I don't know," she whispered back, "But this is a small town. Everyone here knows everyone else. And… about half of them are related too."

"Do you think Mrs. Goldmyer is related to Renee?"

Molly looked at me strangely, "Who's Renee?"

I was going to tell her about Renee, the Mean Waitress, but then I realized I couldn't remember if Molly was from here or not. It could be that Renee was her 2nd cousin twice removed or something, so I just sighed and began sifting through the papers that were laid out on the small rectangular table, "Never mind. Let's get busy reading these."

The research Mrs. Goldmyer had laid out were all old newspaper clippings. Molly attacked one pile, while I attacked the second.

"Natalie," Molly said excitedly several minutes later, grabbing my arm. "Listen to this: 'This morning, Rose Whittman, widow of William Whittman, was named a person of interest in the disappearance of Abigail Jeffries. Abigail Jeffries was last seen leaving for Raspberry Hill on the evening of the 21st. Her disappearance was reported by, Mildred Whittman, close friend and sister of William Whittman. Her car was found the following morning on the road to

Raspberry Hill, the motor still running. The driver's side door was open. Copious amounts of blood were found at the scene. Anyone with information regarding this matter is asked to contact the Sherriff's office… blah blah blah…'" Molly's face was twisted with sympathy, "That's just terrible, isn't it?"

But my brain had gone fuzzy. *Mildred.*

Molly paused to give me another funny look. "What's the matter?" she asked.

"Did you just say… Mildred?" My mouth was suddenly very dry. Could it be a coincidence? It couldn't be. Could it? But it had to be. Right?

"That's what it says," Molly read it again. "'Mildred Whittman, close friend and sister of William Whittman.'" She looked up from her article, "Why? Is there something special about Mildred?"

"I don't know," I said slowly, "but there might be." I would have to think about this. Molly didn't need to know about Mildred just yet.

I showed her the clipping that I was reading. "This one has that plus it says…" I scanned the document to find the spot I was looking for. "'A reliable source has confirmed that earlier on the day of the 21st, Abigail and Rose had a violent quarrel at Raspberry Hill which resulted in Abigail leaving the house in a fit of anger. According to Mildred Whittman, Abigail planned to return to Raspberry Hill later that evening to make amends. It was Mildred who alerted the police to Abigail's disappearance.'"

"This one says that Raspberry Hill has been owned by the Whittman family for over a hundred years. Apparently, Mildred was William's sister."

"When did William die?" I asked out of curiosity. Strangely enough, I hadn't really considered the man that my grandmother had married.

Molly flipped through the clippings in her hand. "I thought I just read that somewhere," she muttered. She found the date in one of the newspaper accounts and read it out loud. We stared at each other. It was so quiet in the library that you could actually hear the gears in our heads spinning. Either that or the library had a heater that was making strange sounds.

"So," Molly said slowly, "William died two days before Abigail disappeared?"

"What does that mean?" I asked, "It has to mean something, right?" *And Mildred,* the little voice in my head whispered, *it has to all go together.*

Molly sank back into her chair next to me, "It has to mean something," she agreed.

"Listen to this," I said, holding up another paper, "According to the Sheriff's report, two sets of footprints were found outside of Abigail's car. Precise identification was impossible due to the heavy rains, however, it does appear that both sets of footprints were those of a woman."

"In this paper," Molly said sadly, "Mildred accuses Rose of murdering Abigail and hiding the body." She sighed, "Apparently everyone just loved Abigail. This article goes on and on about all of the charity work she was involved in."

Poor Grandma Rose. No wonder she had been a recluse. Everyone hated her for killing Abigail. No. Everyone hated her because they THOUGHT she had killed Abigail. But... did she? That was the big question, wasn't it? I found it very difficult to believe that a relative of mine was a murderer. But, then, I found it difficult to imagine anyone murdering another person.

A thought came to me, "Have you read anything that said what they were arguing about?"

"Who?" Molly asked, her eyes turning reluctantly from the newspaper in front of her to look at me. "Do you mean Rose and Abigail?" When I nodded, she shook her head, "Nope. No one said."

"When did Mildred die?" I asked suddenly.

Molly's eyebrows rose to the ceiling. "I get dizzy trying to follow your thinking." She looked around the little back room, her eyebrows rising even higher when she spotted the little computer in the corner, "This is new," she muttered. "We never could have a computer when I worked here. 'Laziness, Ms. Stevenson. Why would we need a computer when you can look it up? Are we not here to serve the people?'" Her impression of Mrs. Goldmyer was quite good. Her little fingers zipped over the keyboard until she sat and stared at the screen.

"Well?" I demanded. The suspense was killing me.

Molly's gaze met mine over the monitor, "She didn't," she said solemnly.

"She didn't what?"

"She didn't die," Molly explained patiently. "She's still alive. She lives in SunnySide Retirement Home."

Oh. My. Word.

"Let's go," I said standing up so quickly that the newspaper clippings went flying.

Poor Molly was understandably bewildered, but like a good little friend, she was already on her feet as well. "Where are we going now?"

I began a quick march out of the library with Molly jogging alongside, quietly lamenting the mess we had left the back room in. I felt bad about that too. Just a little. But it couldn't be helped. I had a ghost to confront. And there wasn't much lunch hour left to do it in.

CHAPTER 22

We took a taxi to SunnySide Retirement Home. It was getting late and Molly was getting tired. At least that's what she said. In reality, I think that she thought that I was getting tired. She was right. My head was starting to throb from all of the busyness, and I took full advantage of the short taxi ride to practice the breathing exercises I had once learned from a school psychologist who thought I needed a way to release stress. They didn't help anymore now than they did then. So, I did what I should have done in the first place. I said a quick prayer. I was starting to realize that life was way bigger and more complicated than I could ever imagine, and I that I wasn't capable of handling it by myself anymore. And, not so remarkably, I felt a lot more peace after that.

SunnySide Retirement Home was really not that sunny. The cracked paint and aging brick lent it an air of respectable untidiness. It was a long building with wings that went east and west with the central door directly in the middle. A tired looking nurse gave us Mildred's room number without any bothersome questions. I poked Molly, "Shouldn't she have asked us for some identification or something?" I whispered as we walked down the hallway in search of Room 25b.

Molly shrugged helplessly, "We could be anybody," she agreed. "It's certainly not very safe. Although I do think that mass murderers probably have more to do than visit nursing homes and murder little old people playing Parcheesi."

There were quite a few people playing Parcheesi on portable tables up and down the hallway. I sighed. Getting old really did stink.

We came to Room 25b. It sounded like someone was already visiting Mildred. The door was only partially shut, and we could hear their voices drifting out through the crack. I held up a finger to Molly in the universal language of silence. She nodded, her eyes wide.

"I don't care. You said you were going to take care of it." The voice was old and high-pitched but still carried well.

There was a deep rumbling answer that was obviously male. And was obviously someone who was concerned about keeping his voice down. Rats.

"No!" The reply was strong and angry, "That's not acceptable. It's really not that difficult. If you don't do something soon, I will."

The answering voice was pitched soft and soothing and was followed by the crashing of something loud and metal.

There was a flurry of activity from inside and a large form burst out of the room, shutting the door firmly behind him.

I couldn't believe my eyes. It was Sherriff Finn. Molly obviously could not believe her eyes either. She stared at him with her mouth slightly open. The Sheriff, one hand on the door handle and one hand mid-way to putting his hat on his head stared right back. He was the first one to regain his composure.

"Why," he said slowly, putting his hat on firmly, and releasing the door handle to extend a hand to me, "It's Natalie. How are you?"

"F-fine," I stammered, shaking his hand. "And yourself?" I asked stupidly.

He blinked. "Fine." The big smile came out then, but it looked all wrong somehow here in SunnySide. "What brings you here?"

I couldn't think. I tried. But, I couldn't. Molly's mouth opened and closed, but nothing came out. She was absolutely no help. I knew what she was thinking. Should we tell him that we were here to see Mildred? Or was it too much of a coincidence that he was in speaking with her? What was going on in Springgate? Was the whole town conspiring against me?

His smile grew a little forced, "Are you ladies alright?" he asked. "Do you need me to help with anything?"

I gave myself a good mental smack. "No, thank you," I said politely, "we're just here to visit someone."

He eyed me skeptically, "And who might that be? I didn't think you knew anyone here in town."

Ah. I was trapped. He was good.

Molly finally thought of something to contribute to the conversation. "Oh," she said, just a tad too brightly, "Natalie doesn't know anyone here of course. We're here to visit my friend Clarabelle."

I shot her a look. Clarabelle? Seriously? She could have thought up a better name than that.

His face relaxed a bit, "Well," he said, slipping back into a more friendly spirit, "how nice."

A few more pleasantries and he was gone. We pretended to walk farther down the hall until he was well out of sight before sneaking back to stand in front of Room 25b. I took a deep breath and put my hand on the handle. This was it. Mildred was in trouble now. Her days of haunting were so over.

Molly clung to my sleeve as I turned the handle as quietly as possible and entered the room. The silhouette of someone sitting in the chair by the window was the first thing we could see. The sun shining through the window obliterated her features.

"Can I help you?" she asked grumpily.

I blinked, willing my eyes to adjust and focus. I entered the room farther, clearing my throat. "Mildred?" I asked, not liking at all how weak my voice sounded.

"Yes," she said. "What do you want?" She leaned forward out of the light.

I gasped in astonishment.

It wasn't Mildred.

I hadn't been expecting that. I suddenly had no idea how to proceed.

"Mildred Whittman?" Molly asked timidly from behind my left shoulder.

Mildred gave a great sigh and pulled herself to her feet. "Yes," she said. "If the only thing you came here to ask me is my name, then I will be thanking you to leave right now..." but then our eyes met. Her face turned white and she stumbled blindly backward, "No!" she yelled, "Don't touch me! Get out! Nurse! Nurse!"

"WHAT is going on here?" a voice bellowed in my ear. The next thing I knew I was being dragged backward out of the room as two nurses entered. "What do you think you were doing in there?" the voice continued yelling, even as I heard the nurses speaking soothingly to Mildred inside the room. I looked up to see Finn staring down at me with such anger, that, for a moment, I was more than a little afraid. Molly stood bravely next to me, patting my shoulder awkwardly.

"You didn't have to push us," she scolded the Sherriff. "Natalie is still recovering from a concussion." It was really nice to have a friend like Molly. "And stop yelling," she said, her face turning bright red as she realized that she was speaking to the Sherriff. "It's not polite," she finished primly.

The Sherriff took a deep, cleansing breath, blowing it out through his mouth just like the counselor had tried to teach me. I wondered if it was working any better for him, but I seriously doubted it as the vein in the middle of his forehead was still throbbing rapidly.

Sometimes the best answer is no answer. So, I just stared him down coldly. I really did not appreciate being manhandled. Or being yelled at. Or feeling afraid.

He took another breath and swiped his hand through his hair. "I am very sorry, ladies," he said, in a controlled voice, "but Mildred is my grandmother. She is in a very fragile state of health right now." He eyed us up and down. "It's her heart," he admitted, his face falling. "Any little thing can set her off and trigger another attack. I should not have treated you that way. I was just concerned for her wellbeing and acted without thought. I apologize."

Molly's face folded up with sympathy. "No need to apologize," she said. "We're so sorry. We should have called first. You see, we just wanted to meet Mildred because…"

Oh dear. She was going to blab the whole thing, wasn't she? Guilt was a powerful motivator. Unfortunately, I wasn't buying his story quite so readily. She had looked pretty healthy to me. I had to do something. Now, normally, I don't believe in playing the part of the helpless female, but all of my living with Celia was finally going to pay off.

"Oooohhh," I said faintly, one hand going to my injured forehead as I sank unsteadily down the wall to land on the questionably clean floor. "I'm not really feeling so well."

Like I said. Guilt was a powerful motivator. But this time it was Finn who felt terrible. In the end, he stopped asking questions and we got a free ride back to Crabapple Yarns. That's what I call a double win.

Carolyn looked up as we entered Crabapple Yarns, "Gracious," she said with a faint smile, "how did you two end up coming back from lunch with a police escort?" She was sitting by the table with a paper in one hand and her glasses perched precariously on her long nose.

"It's a long story, Carolyn," Molly said, pushing me inside and shutting the door, "but we should probably get Natalie here to sit down…"

I stepped nimbly out of her reach, "No," I said with a grin, "I suddenly feel so much better."

Molly looked outraged. "I can't believe you were faking!" she exclaimed.

"And I can't believe you were going to tell him everything!" I responded. "You're way too easy."

Molly dropped her gaze to her shoes, "I know," she admitted. "It just slipped out." She looked back up at me, her embarrassment turning to admiration, "You were amazing."

That made me a little sad. The last thing in the world I had ever wanted was to be like Celia. And now look at me.

Carolyn looked back and forth between us. "Well," she said crisply, "I have no idea what you're talking about, but I'm glad you're back."

"Having trouble keeping up with all of the customers?" I joked half-heartedly, looking around the empty store.

Her little grey head shook slowly, "No, my dears," she said, "there is something we have to discuss. Molly, if you could please turn the sign to 'Closed' and lock the door?"

Molly looked at her in astonishment, "But, Carolyn," she protested, "we're not that late. It's only…"

Carolyn rolled her eyes, "This isn't about your lunch hour, dear," she said. "Just do as I say and turn off the front lights."

Two minutes later the door was locked, the front lights were off and the shop was closed for business. We sat around the table together.

"I just received this letter from my lawyer," she said slowly. "It says that our building has been condemned."

We waited for the punchline.

Apparently, there was none.

"Condemned?" Molly and I both said at once. We looked between each other. "That's ridiculous!" Molly protested. "There's absolutely nothing wrong with this building."

"I know that, my dear," Carolyn said. "But, according to this letter, this store has been condemned and we are to vacate immediately."

She handed us the letter to read for ourselves, and, holding the paper between us, we gobbled up the words that were our death sentence. Vacate. Criminal charges if procedure not followed. Demolition to begin.

"What does this mean here about water damage and corroded interior shelving?" I asked, pointing to the second paragraph.

"That was the Knitting Fairy," Molly exclaimed indignantly, "not the fault of this building."

"Knitting fairy?" I repeated blankly. "What is going on here?"

Carolyn patted my hand, "Never mind about the Knitting Fairy, dear," she said. "I've already called my lawyer, and they said that complaints have been filed. According to them, the building inspector has classified this building as a health hazard, and it's been condemned."

"All three shops?" I demanded, gesturing with my hand to encompass Mr. Morrie and Ryan's stores as well.

"No," she replied, shaking her head, "just this one. Which, of course, just shows you how silly of a letter this is. Now," she continued, "I called the building inspector, and he cannot remember inspecting this shop. And, I, of course, know that he's never been here. But, there is a report on file that he was, and that is what the public record will show."

I shrugged, "Doesn't sound like such a big deal," I said. "Just have him come do another inspection."

Carolyn rested an elbow on the table to hold up her chin, "If only it were that easy," she said with a tired sigh, "But, according to the building inspector, once a building has been condemned it takes a good six months to a year to get it uncondemned."

"Why?" Molly demanded, her eyes bright with tears.

Carolyn sighed again, looking, for the first time since I had known her, like an old lady. "There has to be tests and inspections and meetings. And, of course, all of the people that need to do these things are all booked up... and..."

Molly slapped her hand down on the table, "I can't believe this," she said. "Who would do this to us?"

"Well," Carolyn said, "I can think of a few people."

Molly wrapped both her hands around one of Carolyn's. "But what are we going to do Carolyn?" she asked softly. "If we don't have a store, how can we stay in business?"

Carolyn smiled bravely, "Molly," she said, "I don't know right now. I'm going to go home and give it all to the Lord. He will know what to do." She rose to her feet, "And I hope you'll both do the same. We have 48 hours to vacate the store," she said. "So let's pray that God sends the answer tonight."

A thought just occurred to Molly and her eyes grew wide, "But... but..." she said.

I had no idea what she was talking about, but Carolyn seemed to know right away. "You can come and live with me, dear," she said gently. "Don't worry. You won't have to live on the street."

Molly looked at Carolyn gratefully and rose to give her a hug, "I love you, Carolyn," she said softly. "I don't know what I'd do without you."

My own eyes were growing a little moist with the emotion filling up the yarn store. I blinked back the tears and forced myself to think realistically. Great.

Another job down the drain. It was really a bummer, too, since I was growing very fond of Carolyn and Molly. And, I loved working here. At least, I think I did. So far, I hadn't made it through a single day without a catastrophe. Do you think, maybe, it was me?

Carolyn sent us both home shortly thereafter. She said that there was no use talking about the same thing over and over. God was the only one who could help us, so why talk to each other when we should be talking to God? She had a good point, so, Molly and I found ourselves dismissed for the day. I reminded Molly that she was having dinner with us (no sense in changing those plans now), and she went upstairs to go and get ready for supper. Personally, I thought it was a bit early to do that, but hey – what did I know?

Carolyn's eyes were troubled as she walked me to the door, and she turned her attention to me. "Natalie," she said, frowning slightly, "I think maybe there's something I need to tell you…"

I shrugged and smiled as kindly as I could, "It's okay, Carolyn," I said, "don't worry about me. I know that you can't keep me on if you don't have a store. Don't worry about it."

Her expression didn't lighten despite my reassurances, and I left feeling a bit strange about the whole thing. I meandered my way back to the library. Amazingly, I made it past the bakery without being seen. At least I had that much luck.

Mrs. Goldmyer's expression told me exactly what she thought of the way we had left the back room. I shrugged to myself. I could explain, but really… I couldn't. I found my way to the back room again and sat down to read and re-read the articles over and over again. But, unfortunately, they yielded no more clues than they had this afternoon.

I plodded my way back to the parking lot to arrive at my car just before Jack got there. His arms were full of groceries. His eyes were sparkling, and he looked very smug with himself. "How's that for a day's work?" he gloated. "New products for the bakery and Ryan and Molly will be dating in no time."

I eyed him as he put the bags in the trunk, "You're feeling pretty good about yourself right now, aren't you?" I asked, amused despite myself.

"Yep," he answered, unlocking my door before he went around to unlock the driver's side door. "I am."

He started the car and turned to face me, "Are you feeling okay?" The look on my face gave him his answer, "Gracious," he muttered, "you don't have to bite my head off. I was just asking because I wanted to stop at the other grocery store before we go home. I need to get a few things that this one didn't have."

"That's fine with me," I replied, buckling my seat belt. "You're the driver, oh bossy one."

He rolled his eyes, "So, what did you do today?"

Ha. If he only knew. Well. I guess I would have to tell him a little. Molly would probably blurt everything out at dinner anyways.

"Well," I said casually, "Let's see... helped a little old lady buy sock yarn." Jack bobbed his head in understanding. "Went to the Sheriff's office. Went to the library. Found out that Grandma Rose died in a fire and, 30 years ago, she was accused of murder."

I had chosen my moment well. We were still in the parking lot. Which was fortunate because Jack slammed on his brakes with such force that my seat belt snapped into tightness and I heard the groceries tip over in the back. I hid a smirk. He turned to me, his eyes wide with shock. "What?" he demanded. "What are you talking about?"

I frowned at him, "You're not being a good listener, Jack," I scolded. "I haven't even got to the best part yet." He raised an eyebrow, silently allowing me to continue. "I also found out that Carolyn's store has been condemned and she has to be completely out in 48 hours."

I didn't think it was possible for Jack to be speechless. Apparently, it took a lot, but it was possible.

I waved a hand in front of his face, "Hello?" I said, snapping my fingers. "Anyone in there?"

He managed to close his mouth and swallow, "So which part of that did you make up?" he finally asked. "Because, I have to tell you, the shock value was amazing, the delivery was very good, and your facial expressions were perfect."

I rolled my eyes. "Thank you," I said. "But, I'm afraid all of it is true."

He shoved the gearshift into park with such violence that the car creaked in protest. "Hey!" I said, "be careful with Mr. Darcy."

"Mr. Darcy can jump in a lake," he said. "What I want to know is how someone who is supposed to be taking it easy because she has a concussion managed to get into so much trouble all in one day. What do you do? Put a sign around your neck?"

"Actually," I supplied helpfully, "this was all before the early afternoon. I spent the rest of my afternoon in the library re-reading the old newspaper clippings about Grandma Rose."

Jack scrubbed a hand over his face, "Alright," he said slowly, as if talking to a child, "start at the beginning and explain everything."

I pointed to the gearshift, "You'd better drive as I talk," I said, "otherwise we're going to be late for dinner - which would be kind of embarrassing since you've invited people over to eat."

He reluctantly threw the car into drive and we made the slowest turn that a man has ever made out of the parking lot. "I'm going to drive this slow for the rest of your life," he said through clenched teeth, "unless you tell me everything. I'll know if you're leaving anything out."

He drove a hard bargain. Ha. Ahem. Excuse me. Pardon the pun. I told him everything as we crawled our way to the grocery store. Well. Almost everything. I left out the part where we snuck into the Sherriff's office… and the part where Finn yanked us out of Mildred's room. I also did not tell him that the reason I wanted to see Mildred was to see if she was my ghost. I saw no reason for that. Do you?

"Poor Carolyn," Jack said thoughtfully. "This must be tough for her. I hear she's had that yarn store there since time began. There's no way she's going to be able to stay afloat until all of this gets fixed."

"Carolyn is tougher than you think," I told him. "She went home to pray and ask God for help. She's pretty confident that He will give her an answer tonight."

Jack nodded his head, "Good for her," he said. "I bet she's right too."

Huh. Excellent answer.

We pulled up in front of the largest grocery store in town. "What are we getting?" I asked as we climbed out of the car.

Jack consulted the list from his pocket, "Strawberries," he said, "whip cream, lemons… and some nice looking napkins. I'm not using those ugly old things that I found in the pantry." The produce section was right up front. "You stay here," Jack said, "and pick out a couple of quarts of strawberries. I'll get the other stuff and be right back. Try to stay out of trouble."

I stuck my tongue out at him. "As long as the strawberries don't give me any sass, we'll be fine."

The strawberries, as it turned out, were rather sorry looking. I was forced to sort through them case by case. Why Jack needed strawberries when it clearly wasn't strawberry season just showed you how strange of a person he was. To be more efficient, I started a little "maybe" pile of some of the less pathetic looking quarts of strawberries. It was challenging work. Most of the quarts had at least one berry that was beyond hope. I just couldn't buy something that was bad already. I think you'll agree with me on that. It would be a total waste of money. You might as well go to the garbage dump and buy a couple bags of garbage in the hopes that there was something worthwhile in there. I kept my little "maybe" stack to one side and waited, with amazingly sweet patience, when I was interrupted by other customers who thought that they also needed strawberries. I was completely and utterly flabbergasted when a gentleman of middling years came up and took a quart of strawberries from my "maybe" pile. Just as bold as anything. Right off MY pile. My pile. The pile that I had spent hours slaving over, picking and choosing.

"Excuse me," I said politely, "but those are my berries."

He looked at me in surprise and then looked down at the berries in his hand, "They weren't in your cart," he pointed out.

"I know," I said sweetly. "They were in my 'maybe' pile."

"You can't have a 'maybe' pile in this store." he said flatly. "If it's not in your cart, then it's fair game."

"I don't think so," I said in my friendliest voice. "I sorted through all of those rotten berries to find somewhat edible berries. That was a lot of work, and now you've stolen...."

"I didn't STEAL anything," he protested, face turning red. "I took a quart of strawberries off of the display." He examined the berries closely, "Hey," he said, "these berries do look good. Thank you for all of that hard work."

I growled low in my throat and was about to retrieve my berries myself when a hand on my arm stopped me. "What are you doing?" Jack hissed. "I can't leave you alone for five minutes. Good grief. Now you're fighting about strawberries."

"That was MY pile," I insisted. "He took the berries I was going to buy."

Jack rolled his eyes and then looked closely at the strawberry display, "You know," he said conversationally to the guy, "she's actually right. You can clearly see that she's got a little stack there. It really wasn't very nice of you to take the ones she had sorted out." For a minute, I thought that the little berry-stealing rat was going to make a run for it. Jack crossed his arms casually and adjusted his stance, "I think maybe you could give them back, don't you?"

The man looked around at the little crowd that had gathered. His beady eyes calculated everything, and with a smile that was both faked and forced, he handed me back the little quart of strawberries.

"Thank you," Jack said politely, "that's very nice of you." He swung his elbow to nudge me.

"Thank you," I parroted lamely. The man swiped another quart of strawberries from the pile at random and angrily stalked past to continue his shopping. I couldn't believe it. Jack had helped me. Helped me even though it was ridiculous to fight about stupid strawberries. Helped me even though, technically, the man had been right. Amazing. Strange. A little bit scary.

CHAPTER 23

Dinner was, as usual, delicious. Celia was working late at the diner, which made it even more tasty. We sat companionably around our dinner table, candles glowing on the oak table gently (that had been my idea). Ryan had brought fresh, homemade rolls to go with the chicken fettuccine, and I ate so much that I was beginning to think that I would need a new wardrobe if I actually managed to live here for the rest of my "term".

Molly was glowing too. She looked absolutely lovely tonight in a grey tweed sweater and dark pleated skirt. It suited her hair perfectly, which was pulled smoothly back into a charming little messy up-do. She had arrived looking nervous and slightly ill, but Ryan and Jack were so casual and charming, it was impossible for anyone to remain ill at ease. I only hoped that this was the way Ryan always would act toward Molly, and that he wasn't using this lovely behavior to lure her in and then turn into a real tyrant. I had seen it before. More than once as a matter of fact. Celia had been a great one for falling for charming men.

"So," Jack said, interrupting my somber train of thought, "I was thinking that after dinner we could give Ryan and Molly a tour of Raspberry Hill before we had dessert."

I nodded my agreement. "Sure," I said, trying to remember that I was also a host of this little dinner party and that I should be acting a little more in the mood, "and maybe we'll even get to meet a ghost or two."

Ryan smiled uneasily, "Jack told me about your little adventure last night," he said. "Aren't you two just a little bit concerned?"

"I don't believe in ghosts," Jack said stoutly, setting down his wine glass carefully, "and if someone is trying to scare us away, they're going to be disappointed." He met my eyes squarely.

"That's right," I said evenly, meeting his gaze. "It won't work."

Ryan and Molly looked between us and Molly laughed nervously. "I don't think anything would scare Natalie," she said. "You should have seen her sneak into the Sherriff's office."

Ryan and Jack both dropped their forks as if on cue. I rolled my eyes at Molly. "Way to keep that one a secret, Mol," I said with a reluctant grin. It was impossible to be mad at Molly. It would be like kicking a puppy. Speaking of puppies… or, rather, ugly old dogs… where was the Abraham Lincoln? He was missing a prime opportunity to terrorize some innocent newcomers.

"And why exactly were you sneaking into the Sherriff's office?" Ryan asked carefully, as Jack's face was turning a rather unbecoming shade of reddish purple.

"Well, we weren't really sneaking," I clarified. "We merely heard Celia and the Sherriff speaking down the hall, and in order to hear them just a tad better, we may have ducked a bit to walk under an open window and…"

"And snuck in," Jack finished, his eyes glinting. "I can't believe you. One day back. One day. Couldn't you wait at least two days before embarking on your latest scheme of mayhem? And to think you dragged poor Molly along too."

Ryan let out a bark of laughter that had me jumping. Jack and I stared at him incredulously as Molly's face turned just a shade redder. "Sorry," Ryan said, "but that just struck me as funny." He turned to Jack, "Trust me," he said. "You don't have to worry about 'poor little Molly', she's done her fair share of mayhem."

"I don't know what you mean," Molly muttered into her chicken.

Yeah. I was so going to hear the rest of this story later.

Abraham Lincoln chose just that moment to make his presence known. He meandered his way into the room. Stopped. Did a double take. Looked at me. Looked at Jack. Looked at Ryan and Molly again. The hair on the back of his neck rose slowly, even as the teeth began to shine brightly out from his black fur. A small growl was starting in the back of his throat.

I chanced a look at Molly, and she looked like she was getting ready to jump up onto the table herself. Like that would help at all. People can be so silly. I quickly stood and scooped up Abraham Lincoln with one arm. "Now, Abraham Lincoln," I said severely, "this is Molly and Ryan. They are our friends, and you will behave yourself." His tail went limp and his little pink tongue came out to loll happily. I walked him over so that I was standing between Molly and Ryan. "Don't be scared," I said. "He's really not a bad dog. He's just not used to company."

Ryan frowned at him, "No, I heard that your Grandma Rose never came out of her house. She even had her groceries delivered."

Molly smiled tentatively at him, "Hello," she said in her friendliest voice that trembled just a bit. "I think you're a very handsome dog." What a little liar. But, Abraham Lincoln sat up in my arms just a bit straighter and gave her the benefit of his full attention. Molly, encouraged by his positive reaction, put her hand out, palm up, "You have such pretty fur." She reached for him before I could warn her. I stepped back quickly, pulling Abraham Lincoln back with me out of her reach as he erupted with barking.

"He has to work on his people skills," Jack said with a scowl.

"Perhaps he's just cranky because he hasn't eaten yet," I said, feeling oddly protective of the monster. "I'll be right back."

I deposited Abraham Lincoln in the kitchen, scooped out his dog food, patted him on the head and went back to my hostess duties. I stepped back into the dining room and gasped. They were gone.

Gone. All of them. Their plates, mostly empty, sat quietly on the table, mocking me with the knowledge that they alone possessed. Ryan's fork still had a last bite of food on it. The chairs were exactly how I had last seen them... as if one minute they had been sitting around the table, and the next minute… they weren't. Vaporized into a pile of dust? I checked a chair just to be sure it was clean. Teleported up to the mothership?

"Don't be ridiculous," I told myself. "They just walked out of the room." But why wouldn't they have waited for me?

I yelped when something wet and cold touched me on the back of my bare leg. I spun in terror, but it was only Abraham Lincoln, still licking his lips from his doggie supper. "Where did they go, Abraham Lincoln?" I asked.

He gave a little bark and backed up, wiggling his rear end in excitement. I looked at him suspiciously. "Do you know where they are?"

"Arf," he barked, turning his little body around and looking behind him to make sure that I was following. Which, of course, I was.

He headed straight for the ballroom. And, he was right. Voices were coming out of the ballroom. Voices that, this time, I recognized. I flung the door open, "Here you are!" I exclaimed in relief. "I guess you weren't abducted by aliens then." Abraham Lincoln plopped to his little bottom just outside the door as if to say, *You're on your own in there.*

"Natalie!" Molly called in excitement. "Jack just had the best idea in the whole world." Her eyes were shining, and Ryan was beaming from ear to ear. They were standing in the middle of the ballroom and Jack was paused mid-gesture one arm flung out dramatically.

I was just a little annoyed with them. Just enough that I could not gather up the required energy to join in the happiness. "Oh really?" I asked skeptically. "What might that be?" I smirked at Jack, "Did you want to open a haunted house here? Scare the local kiddies?"

"No," Jack said, his freckles dancing as he smiled, "but you're on the right track." Molly and Ryan's heads bobbed in tandem with suppressed mirth.

I glanced around the ballroom rather irritably. Nothing good had happened to me yet in here. The memory of the ghostly whisper threatening to kill us all was still just a little too vivid. "Well?" I demanded impatiently. "Are you going to leave me in the dark all night? It was bad enough to come back and find everyone gone from dinner."

"Oh, Natalie," Molly cried, squeezing my arm warmly, "I'm sorry. We never even thought about it. You see, Jack said something about the size of the house and then Ryan said it was big enough to fit all three stores from Roberts Alley into it and then Jack said…" she turned to Jack. "But maybe you wanted to say it?"

But he didn't have to say it. I already knew what he was thinking. Molly was right. It was his best idea ever. The only question remained was… would Carolyn go for it?

"But dear," Carolyn said frowning slightly, "you've only just moved in. You surely don't want strangers coming in and out of your house."

I waved a hand magnanimously, "We sure don't care about that," I said. "We'll just have to figure out some way to keep the customers in the ballroom and out of the rest of the house."

"That would be easy," Molly piped up from my left. "There are two large doors that go out onto the front porch from the ballroom. We could keep the house doors locked and direct all the traffic in through those doors."

We had already figured that out last night, but there was no reason to tell Carolyn that. We were currently standing in the condemned Crabapple Yarn Shop. Molly and I were hiding behind the baby yarn display and Carolyn had propped herself up against the solid-looking bookcases filled with yarn behind her. We had been forced into hiding – and into keeping the lights off, as customers kept coming to the door and knocking. That sort of made me laugh. Seriously? Like the fact that the door is locked and the sign says "Closed" wasn't enough of a clue? Knitters were weird. Either that or they had spent too much time in yarn-land and forgot how to function in the real world. Either way – knitters were weird. Present company excluded, of course.

"But it's not just you, Natalie," Carolyn said, her brow knit with concern, "this could be upsetting to your cousin and your mother."

"It was Jack's idea," I pointed out, "and he thinks it's a great idea. And Celia doesn't care. Jack asked her last night." I decided I had better explain about Celia a bit, "She doesn't really understand about knitting," I said slowly, "so she's a little…"

Carolyn laughed suddenly and her warm hand was around my wrist with a comforting squeeze, "You don't have to say anymore," she said, still smiling. "I completely understand."

I guess after you've had a yarn store for about a million years, you've probably heard it all from everyone.

Molly smiled too, "And you don't have to tell me either," she said. "My whole family thinks I'm nuts for working at a yarn store."

Well, that was a relief. I could only hope that Celia would stay out of our hair. It was a beautiful dream.

There was another round of dreadful pounding from the front door. Molly and I made faces at each other as we waited for it to stop. Which it did. And then it started again.

"Well," I said, "they certainly are persistent. Maybe I better go tell them to scram."

Carolyn's eyebrows rose, "I think," she said carefully, "that maybe we'd better make sure it's not someone who really needs us and not just one of our crazy customers who refuses to read signs."

Carolyn walked to the door, peeked out and called back to Molly and myself, "It's Rachel and Helen," she said. "I'd better let them in before they beat down the door."

"Oh!" Molly exclaimed, "I didn't know they were back already."

Carolyn opened the door and a tidal wave of talking and giggling rolled through the door. I stood back and watched the embracing and animated talking. Rachel and Helen were obviously very fond of Carolyn and Molly – and the feeling was mutual.

"I can't wait to tell you about the show," Helen was saying to Molly and Carolyn. "Patrick and I took the most fabulous classes on knitting theory and…"

"Never mind that," Rachel interrupted, eyes wild with delight. "You wouldn't believe how the pipsqueaks sold! The orders came in like hotcakes."

Pipsqueaks? Were they selling children now?

They both stopped when they saw me, Helen brushing her hair back with one hand self-consciously. Carolyn was quick to introduce me as the "wonderful and brilliant new employee taking Louise's place for a little while."

Rachel eyed me, "Gracious," she said, "that's quite the forehead thing you've got going on there. Dr. Hanover's work, I do believe."

I stared at her. Helen laughed and smacked Rachel on the arm. "Rachel's a nurse, Natalie," she explained, "and such a know-it-all."

"They've just been to a large knitting conference," Carolyn said. "Rachel and I recently launched a new line of patterns for children called 'Pipsqueaks'. Helen and her husband, Patrick, went along to help Rachel and to also take some classes at the conference."

Over the next half hour, Carolyn explained why the store was closed and what Molly and I were proposing to do – that is – move the store to Raspberry Hill for as long as it took to "un-condemn" the building. It really only should have taken ten minutes, but Rachel and Helen interrupted every other sentence with exclamations and their own opinion, which was actually quite amusing to watch.

"So," Carolyn said, wrapping it all up, "I do believe that now was the time Natalie was going to say, 'Why don't you just come up to Raspberry Hill and see if you think it would work?'"

I grinned, "Yep," I said, "that's exactly right. You're a mind reader, Carolyn. So, who wants to go on a field trip?"

Both Rachel and Helen stuck their hands up in the air, turning pleading looks upon Carolyn. Molly laughed as Carolyn appeared to hesitate. "You might as well let them come, Carolyn," she said with a mock sigh. "They'll just follow us anyways."

There was one little problem, though. Between the five of us, no one had a car. Well, I had a car. I just wasn't allowed to drive it. Which wouldn't have stopped me had I had the keys. Which I did not.

We ended up sending Molly down to the bakery with a plea for the keys to my car. Five people in Mr. Darcy (what? I can't help it. The name just stuck.) would be pushing it, but it was less than a mile, and it beat walking. I did not want to walk up Raspberry Hill. Ever.

Unfortunately, she came back with Jack and Ryan. "Mr. Darcy isn't big enough to hold all of you," Jack explained with a smile.

Rachel was clearly taken with the freckles and broad shoulders. She smiled up at him from under her long eyelashes and introduced herself. She was a very pretty young lady, and I watched with more than a little curiosity to see what Jack's reaction would be. He smiled politely back at her, introduced himself as my cousin and then promptly arranged everyone into cars. Molly, Ryan and Helen would drive together, while the rest of us would go in Mr. Darcy.

Which is how I ended up in the backseat of my own car with Rachel as a companion. Gracious heavens. Did this girl ever stop talking?

"Oooohhh," she was saying, as we climbed Raspberry Hill, "I've always wondered what it would be like to live here. I just love the house. But these trees are really..." she paused in her soliloquy to study the road before us, "they're just a little bit spooky, aren't they?"

I couldn't answer her. My mind was caught in the past. According to the papers, it had been the night when Abigail had attempted her fateful overture of reconciliation. The papers had said it was raining and storming that night. She must have been so scared... climbing up Raspberry Hill alone in her little car... bravely driving through the forest that would have been just as happy to see her under its roots rather than driving over them. Was that where she was now? The police had never found her body. Was she deep in the ground... her lifeless body now just a skeleton... never to be found... never to give peace to those who loved her? How was it possible to be a living, breathing human being one minute and the next minute be... dead? Gone. Had she known her murderer? Had she had time to feel the terror of impending death?

Unfortunately, I could see the scene just a little too clearly. The night would have been dark and heavy with storms. The car pulled haphazardly off to the side of the road, headlights cutting through the rain to shine wetly on the trees… the motor puffing out great clouds of warm smoke for a driver that would never come back. The door would be flung open, like a mouth open in an endless howl of agony… unable to convey the horrors of what it had just seen. The overhead lights dimly illuminating the inside of the car with a flickering glow… just enough to catch the dark glint of blood on the steering wheel and down the side of the door… where it dripped soundlessly into a little puddle that was beginning to roll its way down into the ditch.

Had the murderer stood there…weapon in hand surveying the scene of death that he (or she – I reminded myself) had just created? Were they filled with remorse? Horror over the realization of what they had just done? Or was there a triumphant smile of victory upon their evil countenance? And then, ever so slowly, was the body moved with the wrenching and hauling of now motionless limbs? But where would they have taken the body? Deeper into the woods? Into another vehicle? Shoved off a ravine? Buried under a carpet of ancient leaves? Wouldn't the blood have left a trail?

A hand on my arm had me jumping, a cry escaping my throat before I had the sense to try and catch it. I pulled away, pressing myself against the door before reality returned.

Rachel was pressing her own self up against the door, as if to give me more room in the back seat. Carolyn's face was tight with worry – as was Jack's who had turned all the way around in his seat to see me. We were stopped in the middle of the road… in probably much the same spot Abigail had been. At least, that's what went through my somewhat tangled imagination. My breath was coming in shallow pants. I looked around outside a bit wildly but forced myself to relax when I saw we were alone on the road. Ryan, Molly and Helen must have been ahead of us. I took a deep breath and tried for nonchalance, "Something wrong?" I asked innocently. "Why are we stopped?"

Jack scowled at me, "We're stopped because you were freaking out in the backseat."

"Was not," I retorted immediately. I did not freak out. Especially not in front of strangers.

"Sorry," Rachel said, "I thought you were having a panic attack or something. You weren't hearing me, and you were breathing rapidly."

I took another deep breath and shoved my shaking hands under my legs, "No," I said, smiling brightly, "I'm sorry. I was just lost in thought. I do that sometimes. I didn't mean to worry anyone."

Carolyn's face relaxed. "I do that myself," she said with a small smile, "especially in the car. It's easy to get lost in your own thoughts."

Rachel smiled hesitantly, "So you're all right?" she asked.

I nodded quickly. "Of course I am. Sorry."

Jack's face did not lose its suspicious look, but he turned around and re-started the car to finish its trip up the hill to where Raspberry Hill awaited us. Raspberry Hill. Silent and solid. And filled with unspeakable secrets of love and hate.

CHAPTER 24

The ballroom was going to be perfect for the new home of Crabapple Yarns. Carolyn absolutely loved it.

"Ballrooms are meant to be filled with brightness and laughter and people," Carolyn said, twirling on one foot in the middle of the room, admiring herself in the reflection from the mirrors on the wall, "They're not supposed to sit silent and sulking for years on end. It's just wrong."

I could have told her that this ballroom had been anything but silent, but I didn't want to open THAT can of worms right now. I looked up at the big oval mirror on top of the gilt paneling on the far wall and was shocked to see Mildred's face smiling benignly down at us. I gaped at her. Oh dear. I had hoped that my figment would be gone by now. She stuck her tongue out and waggled her eyebrows. I made discrete shooing motions with one hand. Molly turned from her animated discussion with Rachel and Helen of where to put the seating area to eye me strangely.

"Something wrong, Natalie?" she asked. "Are you feeling okay?"

"Yeah," I said, and swiped the air again, "I thought maybe there was a bug."

"Oh!" Helen said, her eyes wide with apprehension, "It wasn't a moth, was it?" She giggled nervously, "Wouldn't that just be awful? Moths in a yarn store?"

I left the three of them giggling about the pros and cons of having store moths to walk over to Carolyn who was, now, standing next to Jack, talking quietly.

"Is there something the matter?" I asked.

"It's actually too big," Carolyn admitted, her fingers fluttering nervously in the fringe of her scarf, "My inventory is going to look pretty sparse in here if we try to fill up all this space."

"I was thinking we could save ourselves a lot of moving muscles by using seating and shelving from around here, Carolyn," I said. "Would that help? Some of our pieces are quite big, and we could add even more room for seating and teaching."

"It might be nice to have some additional seating and more room," she said, her eyes roaming the large room, "But we're still going to have a lot of extra space."

"Perhaps we could just move the shelves so that they were farther apart?" Molly suggested as the three of them came over to join us.

"Or," Jack said unexpectedly, "we could open a little café in the back of the ballroom."

I blinked at him. "Excuse me?"

Jack was at his most charming when he wanted to talk people into things. It practically oozed out of his freckles. "Well," he said, "I was talking to Ryan the other day, and he said that it would be great to expand his shop into things other than baked goods, but he doesn't have the time or the room to do anything like that in his current place. This would be the perfect place to give it a shot." He crossed his arms and looked every inch the serious businessman, "Of course, we have a lot of things to talk over, but I think it could work out."

"Seriously?" Rachel asked.

"Seriously?" I asked.

Despite the similarity in words, our tones could not have been more different. Her eyes were shining with admiration for the genius that she saw residing in Jack's head. I, on the other hand, was wondering if there was anything at all in Jack's head.

"I'm not so sure Carolyn is going to want you to be guilting her customers into buying food from you, Jack," I said somewhat severely. After all, I didn't need him hanging around here all the time scaring the knitters away.

His smile faltered just a bit. "I'd like to think that we'd be bringing in more potential customers to Carolyn," he said. "Of course, we'd put up some type of partition to keep the two businesses separate. I was even thinking of putting some tables and chairs out on the porch for as long as the weather holds out."

Carolyn patted him on the arm, and smiled sweetly, "I think it's a wonderful idea, Jack," she said, "and I wish you the best of luck with it." And, up in the mirror, Mildred nodded and smiled with enthusiasm.

He was so infuriating. I decided that was my cue to leave. "Come on, Molly," I said. "Let's go look for furniture that would work for Carolyn."

Abraham Lincoln growled good-naturedly at Molly as we passed, "Good doggie," Molly said hesitantly, bending down just a bit to study his little face. "But you're not going to fool me into trying to pet your head again." He trotted along happily after us.

"I was thinking we could use some of the bookcases from the library," I said, heading towards that room, "There's so many things in the basement... not to mention the bedrooms we don't use, and I think that there's an attic up there somewhere that's probably stacked with old stuff too."

"Ugh," Molly said with a groan, "my muscles hurt just thinking about it."

"Mine too," I said. "Now that I think about it. That's going to be a lot of hauling up and down stairs." I looked around to make sure we were alone. "You know, Molly," I said slowly, "There is something I wanted to say to you."

She met my gaze nervously, "That sounds ominous."

"Not at all," I said with a laugh. "It's just that I know you're going to be homeless soon, and I know that Carolyn offered to let you live with her, but I wanted you to know that you would be welcome to live here as well, if you would like. Especially since the yarn store will be here... it would almost be the same as living at Crabapple Yarns. The yarn would be downstairs and you would be upstairs. Just like home sweet home."

Molly was the type of person who showed her emotions easily, and it was fun to see her whole face light up with delight. "Do you mean it?" she asked excitedly. "I would love it. Not," she said hastily, "that I don't want to live with Carolyn, but..."

I laughed, "It's okay," I assured her, "you don't have to explain. I would love to have you here." Yes, my friends, I was being totally selfish. With Molly here, interactions with Jack and Celia could be kept to a minimum. My conscience kicked me. "I do have to offer a word of caution," I said, turning serious. Selfish was one thing... inconsiderate was another, "I've told you everything that's been happening. So far, it's been pretty low key, but I don't know what's going on, and there's a chance that things could get..."

She held up a hand, "I'm so glad you asked me here," she said, her own little face now serious, "and one of the reasons is because if I'm here you'll have someone to talk to about all of this."

I wished I could be half as nice as her.

Helen came running down the hall behind us, waving something in the air.

"What are you doing, Helen?" Molly teased. "Waving the flag of surrender already?"

"Death first!" she shouted with gusto, and then slapped something into Molly's palm.

"Sticky notes?" Molly asked in confusion, looking down at the little yellow squares in her hand.

Helen's head bobbed up and down, "You know," she said, "to mark what furniture you want to use for the store. That way you can mark it and we can move it later."

"You're a genius, Helen," I said with admiration. "That's very clever."

It's a good thing that we didn't have more than one stack of sticky notes. We might have gone a little bit overboard. As we sat in the "lived-in living room," collapsed in various stages of tiredness, Jack came in scratching the back of his head, "I'm not quite sure how it's going to work, ladies," he said.

"What's that?" Rachel asked, perking up and swinging her feet to the floor gracefully. "What do you think isn't going to work?"

Jack perched on the edge of the sofa next to me, which, for some reason, sent a warm glow of happiness spinning through my stomach. He smiled gently at Rachel, "I'm not sure how we're going to fit all of that furniture into the ballroom and still have room for the yarn."

She frowned at him, "I'm not sure what you mean," she said. "We only picked out a few sofas and some bookcases."

He tilted back so that he could bring one knee up to his chest. "You picked out nine sofas, 19 easy chairs, 32 bookcases, 12 tables, 28 end tables, 5 sideboards and I don't know how many dining room chairs and more odds and ends than you have half the shelf space for." He winked at me, "You do plan to put some yarn out, don't you? Or are you just going to have seating areas and cute things to look at?"

I rolled my eyes at him and didn't bother to answer. I thought about what he said, trying to remember what all we had stuck a sticky note on. Huh. When you heard it totaled up like that, it did sound a bit silly. This house did have a ton of furniture… and we hadn't even bothered going down into the basement or up to the attic.

Helen and Molly started giggling, "I told you we were getting carried away," Molly said to Helen, half-heartedly whacking her with a throw pillow, "but you said that one could never have too much seating."

Helen fluffed her brown hair and tried her best to look indignant, "Well," she said, "it's true. Knitting stores need lots of seating. We've got to have better and more seating than that stinkin' old Happy Knits."

I sat up a bit straighter, knocking Jack's legs aside, "I would really like to know what a Happy Knits is," I said. "Molly was talking about it with Old Mrs. Harrison…. and wasn't Jean talking about a Happy Knits before I…" the memory came back in a rush, and to my complete dismay, my voice cracked.

Jack's hand was suddenly warm on my shoulder. "Happy Knits is the other yarn shop in town," he said, his voice colored a bit with surprise, "I thought you knew that."

"I thought that might be it," I said, "but I wasn't all the way sure. Where are they located?"

"Right on Main Street," Molly said glumly. "With nice big windows and a huge sign. They have classes almost every night and a monster inventory of yarn."

That certainly did not sound good. I looked around carefully for Carolyn, but she was nowhere to be seen. "I'm sure that Carolyn's customers are extremely loyal, then, aren't they?"

Molly and Helen exchanged glances. "Well," Molly said slowly, "most of them are."

Rachel's head bobbed in agreement. "Anyone who comes to Crabapple Yarns and doesn't love it is just too ridiculous."

"There are a few traitors," Helen said darkly, "but I've got a few ideas about what to do about them."

Jack and I laughed, but judging from the looks of Molly and Rachel… she was serious.

CHAPTER 25

The next day brought nothing but work and then more work. It was a grand time. To start with, we had to go around the house and remove the extra sticky notes. This proved to be slightly difficult. There were many heated arguments. For example, Helen was positive that the bookcases from the bedroom upstairs were eminently more suitable for holding yarn than the ones that Molly had chosen from the drawing room. She was quite emphatic about it. I didn't think that there would be any talking to either of them until… Helen and I tried to move the aforementioned bookcases… then she was quick to concede the merits of giving first consideration to items on the main floor.

I don't think we could have done it without the help of Jack, Ryan and a few of Ryan's friends. They were quite helpful. And that's the understatement of the year. In the end, we used bookcases to create a charming little divider between the "café" and the yarn store. Jack and Ryan dragged mismatched tables and chairs into their area, and despite how terrible that should have looked – the effect was actually quite charming. Jack even found vintage tablecloths to drape over each table. To my astonishment, he actually even ironed them himself. Ryan provided the utensils and condiment and napkin holder thingies. Their little finishing touch included candle holders that dripped with pearls and fake diamonds. Like I said, it should have looked dreadful. But, it didn't.

The yarn store area was even better. Or, it would be even better once we got things organized. Bookcases, dressers, stacks of drawers, little pieces of furniture… whatever we could find (and drag)… were arranged in little groupings around the ballroom. We stole the long sideboard from the formal dining room for the checkout counter. Instead of one main seating area, we created little seating areas here and there. My favorite one was just one cozy armchair snuggled in between a bookcase and a chest of drawers. It was the perfect spot for one little knitter to sit and knit and think.

Poor Mr. Darcy made so many trips up and down Main Street to Carolyn's shop, dragging yarn and rugs and needles and assorted knittery-stuff back to Raspberry Hill that I felt quite sorry for him

I wish I could say that it was all nicely sorted and ready to open tomorrow, however, what it really looked like was that a yarn bomb went off in the ballroom. I had doubts as to whether it would ever get organized. But, at the end of our very long day, Carolyn had rubbed her hands together in glee and pronounced herself completely satisfied with our progress.

I was just glad that we had gotten everything out of Crabapple Yarns that we needed to move. I was pretty sure that Sherriff Finn would have come along and yanked us all out by our hair and put the biggest padlock that he could find on all the doors. And probably all the windows too. Not that I could have fit through a window. But perhaps we could have shoved Molly....

Speaking of Sherriff Finn... he was here. Standing in the ballroom, looking around with an annoyed expression. And he was accompanied by Nathaniel Goldmyer. I rose to my feet... this couldn't mean anything good.

Jack was already rising as well. Carolyn looked up from her slice of pizza and daintily wiped pizza sauce from the corner of her mouth. "Good evening, Finn," she said sweetly. "How are you this evening?"

"Fine, thank you," Sherriff Finn said stiffly.

"And how nice to see you, Nathaniel," she said, her smile widening. "How is your mother?"

Nathaniel's smile was a bit forced as well, "She's fine," he said, and then, as if he remembered his manners, added, "thank you."

Jack crossed his arms, "What can we do for you two?" he asked, his expression not as friendly as it could have been. I liked that.

Sherriff Finn cleared his throat, "Well," he said, "it has come to my attention that you folks are planning on opening a business here at Raspberry Hill."

"That's true," I piped up. "We are."

Nathaniel stepped forward, straightening his tie, "Unfortunately," he said, "you are not licensed to operate a store in Raspberry Hill. You're not zoned for commercial here."

Oh. No. My heart sank. The thought had never occurred to me. Why had it never occurred to me? I felt like crying. Carolyn and Molly were gaping openly. Thankfully, they were the last of the people here. Our other helpers had long since gone home to rest up for our next battle with organization tomorrow. I looked towards Jack in despair.

But Jack wasn't looking at me. He was staring at Nathaniel. And his smile was like a shark. He showed all of his teeth when he spoke. "No," he said clearly, "you must be mistaken. Raspberry Hill is zoned for all commercial uses."

Nathaniel took a step forward, "No," he said pleasantly, "it's you who are mistaken. You're not licensed for a … " he curled his lip, "yarn store, and you're most certainly not licensed for any type of food business."

Jack smiled again and took a step forward. If I had been Nathaniel, I would have taken a step back. Nathaniel did not step back.

"If you don't want to take my word for it," Nathaniel said, "I'm sure Sherriff Finn would be happy to explain it to you."

Jack laughed politely. "I don't need anyone to explain it," he said, pulling some papers out of his back pocket, "because I know how to read."

Sherriff Finn finally stepped forward, "I don't understand," he said. "What can you read?"

Jack flourished the papers so that they were open, "I can read this paper," he said, "and it clearly states that Raspberry Hill is licensed for any and all commercial uses including but not limited to a food establishment. It also states that the kitchen is already fully authorized to use as a commercial kitchen."

Wow. Genius.

Nathaniel made a noise in the back of his throat, "I highly doubt that the papers you are holding are legal."

Jack waved the papers negligently in the air, "Yeah," he said, "I think they are. They're notarized and everything."

Nathaniel took a step forward, looking like he was going to snatch the papers out of Jack's hands, but Sherriff Finn interceded, "May I please see this document?" he asked.

Jack handed them over with a friendly smile, "Sure," he said, "but don't go getting any funny ideas. Those are just the copies. I have an official copy in a safe place."

Sherriff Finn read the documents and then handed them to Nathaniel. "These look in order," he muttered. "Where did you obtain these?"

"My friend and I paid a visit to Township Hall a while ago," Jack said. "A few days after I moved here. I was curious as to the status of Raspberry Hill." His smile turned terribly charming as he looked between Nathaniel and Finn, "I was quite surprised to find such liberal zoning for Raspberry Hill. I was also surprised to find that it was such a recent development." Jack's eyebrows rose suggestively at the Sherriff. "But what I'm most surprised about right now is you, Nathaniel Goldmyer."

"I don't know what you mean," Nathaniel said stiffly, but a light flush began rising up from his collar.

"Well," Jack said, spreading his hand expressively, "it was you, Nathaniel, who set up the zoning for Raspberry Hill."

Finn shot Nathaniel an inscrutable look. "It appears that we have been mistaken," he said, handing the papers back. "I should have done more research before coming up here. Please forgive us for the interruption." He gestured sharply with his hand for Nathaniel to exit before him.

"But what I really don't understand," Jack said, as their backs were turning, "is why when I went back to check the records – all the documents relating to the zoning of Raspberry Hill were gone." The shark smile was back, "Wasn't it great luck that I had copies made?"

Nathaniel said nothing, but with head held high, strode from the room. The Sherriff turned to address us all. "I will look into the matter," he promised, looking apologetic. "Sorry again for the interruption."

"I'll see you to the door," Jack said.

I sank back down to the sofa, mind spinning. When Jack came back in, Carolyn was the first to speak. "We are so fortunate," she said to Jack, "to have you."

Molly murmured her agreement. Jack squeezed Carolyn's shoulder in a friendly fashion and inquired if anyone else would like something to drink. I caught up with him as he was striding towards the kitchen.

"Jack!" I called. "How... how did you..."

He smiled enigmatically. "I'm not just a pretty face, Natalie," he said, trying to look serious.

I rolled my eyes. He sure knew how to ruin a moment.

CHAPTER 26

C arolyn left shortly after those two characters slunk out. While Molly was upstairs putting her things away, I surveyed the room with a critical eye. Carolyn had way too much yarn. That was all I had to say about it. We had bags and bags and bags and bags of the stuff dripping and oozing out of every portion of the ballroom. It was ridiculous. There was no way it was ever going to get organized. Ever. Well. Now I was just being dramatic, I guess. Carolyn had assured me that she had a great game plan for tomorrow. That didn't really cheer me up. Somehow, I think she always had some sort of game plan.

Abraham Lincoln sat on the threshold of the doorway between the foyer and the ballroom, looking inquisitive. I guess it was a good thing that he did not enjoy being in the ballroom. It would make life a lot easier with the customers if we didn't have to have a sign on the door that said, "Welcome to Crabapple Yarns. Please do not attempt to pet the dog. Please do not speak to the dog. Please do not look at the dog. Please do not feed the dog." The list could possibly go on and on. It would not be particularly welcoming.

Molly, Helen and I had picked out almost all of the furniture except for one piece. A lovely old desk. I ran my hand over its smooth, polished wood appreciatively. Carolyn had absolutely fallen in love with it. "I just wish I could know," she said, with a wrinkly little smile, "all of the things that this little desk has seen. If only it could talk." She was thinking way too small. Forget the little desk – I wanted the whole house to talk and give up its secrets. At least I think I did. Celia always used to say that there was no life in secrets that got told. Yeah. I have no idea what she meant either.

I sat down at the little desk. It would be really cute if we could stack sock yarn on it. Or maybe we could keep extra needles in the drawers. I opened a drawer experimentally. No, it wasn't deep enough. I pushed it back in and stood up. I chanced a glance up at the mirror on the wall. Sure enough. She was back. Mildred looked down at me from the glass. She didn't look happy. I scowled at her. "Go away," I said. "My concussion is all gone. So you should be too."

She scowled back. Well. How rude. And strange. I shook my head and decided to ignore her.

I was halfway across the room and headed towards the door when it hit me.

"I'm an idiot," I whispered. Purposefully still not looking at Mildred, I went back to the little desk. The drawer wasn't nearly long enough. Not for the length of the desk anyways. "A secret compartment," I crowed to myself. "I love it." Carolyn was right. This desk had a story to tell. And I was going to find out what it was.

And I was right. There was a secret compartment. Right behind the drawer. My fingers shook with excitement as I scrambled to open it. Secret treasure? Old love letters? A will that didn't involve having to live here? This was really exciting. Except… it was empty. Well, now that was disappointing. Really disappointing. I sighed and shoved the drawer shut irritably. I should have known. This house was nothing but a big pain in the… wait a minute… there was a matching drawer on the other side. It also had a hidden compartment. My fingers trembled as I opened it. And this one was full. Of letters.

Jackpot. Love letters. I knew that Grandma Rose had married William very late in life. He was not, in fact, my grandfather. Have I ever mentioned that? No? Sorry about that. She had only been married to him for several years before he died.

I opened the first letter… and dropped it like I had been burned. Definitely not a love letter.

"I know what you did." The letters were spelled out with words from newspaper clippings. They looked oddly malevolent on the plain white paper.

Each subsequent letter was more of the same. I opened them quickly, stacking them up on the desk.

"Who do you think you are?"

"Tell them or I will."

"How do you sleep at night?"

"You have two days."

The letters were all still in their envelopes. That was handy. They weren't old letters. As a matter of fact, the last one, giving her two days, was dated, in fact, two days before Grandma Rose had died. A chill ran over me from head to toe, and I looked to see what Mildred was doing. She was gone.

I stared at the pile of letters. Was this proof that Grandma Rose was murdered? Who had sent them? Was she being blackmailed? Did someone send these letters because they believed Grandma Rose had murdered Abigail? But, maybe the most important question was... why now?

I have to say that I slept a bit better knowing that Molly was snoring (sorry, just a figure of speech. I'm sure she doesn't snore) in the next room. Mercifully, the rest of the night was free from the terrors of ghostly (or non-ghostly) visitors. As a matter of fact, the only disturbance I had was from Abraham Lincoln who decided to join me shortly after midnight. I was beginning to look forward to my little furry sleeping companion – which just shows you how warped I was becoming by living here.

I slept with the threatening letters under my pillow and re-read them again in the reassuring light of dawn. Upon further inspection, I saw that the letters had all been mailed from Springgate, which wasn't too much of a shock, really. My next step was trying to figure out who I should share the letters with. Celia? She would march them right over to Sherriff Finn as proof that Grandma Rose was murdered, wouldn't she? I'm not so sure that would be the best idea. Don't you think it would be better to try to figure out who sent the letters before we tipped our hand? Me too. I could show them to Jack, I suppose. But, then....

he had a habit of asking too many questions and getting bossy. Perhaps I would just show them to Molly and go from there.

Ah. Doesn't it feel good to have a plan in the morning? There's nothing worse than getting out of bed and being indecisive about what you are going to do with your day. I was going to show the letters to Molly, eat breakfast and organize a yarn store. Life was good.

Unfortunately, life had no intentions of cooperating.

Molly's shriek echoed from one end of the house to the other. At least, that's what it seemed like. I ran, like a streak of lightning, towards her room and I could hear Jack following me close behind.

"Molly!" I exclaimed. "What's wrong?"

Molly was pale and shaking. Her long hair was wild and disheveled. She had the look of someone who had just woken up. She lifted a hand to point at her bathroom.

"I…. I…." she said. "Head… head…"

Jack and I looked between each other. He shrugged. "Did you hit your head?" I asked cautiously.

She shook the aforementioned appendage vigorously. "Head…" she repeated, her finger still pointing towards the bathroom.

I felt a little sick. *Oh God*, I prayed, *please don't let there be a dismembered head…* The awfulness of it had me holding my breath.

Jack strode bravely towards the bathroom. I tried to follow, but Molly pulled me back, and the horror on her face had me patting her shoulder with what I hoped was comfort. We could hear Jack determinedly opening and closing all of the drawers and cupboards. A few minutes later, he came back out, "I'm sorry, ladies," he said, "I couldn't find anything out of place."

I let out a sigh of relief. *Thank you, God!* What would we have done if it had really been a…?

Molly wilted onto her bed. My heart sank. She was crying!

"Molly, please," I said, patting her arm awkwardly again, "don't cry. I'm sure there wasn't really a head rolling around your bathroom."

She looked up at me, and it was hard to tell if she was laughing or crying. A bit of both, I think. Jack looked like he wished the floor would open up and swallow him. Unfortunately, the way out the door was past us, so he remained where he was, fidgeting and looking at the carpet.

She half-giggled, "I'm such an idiot," she gasped. "I must have been dreaming, right?"

In another minute she would be having full-blown hysterics.

"Molly," I said in a very stern voice, "pull yourself together. You're going to be having hysterics in a minute. Do you want me to call Carolyn?"

That made her stop.

Sometimes, I really think I could be nicer. And, judging by the way Jack was looking at me, I could see that he thought so too.

"Sorry," she said, sucking in a shaky breath, "how silly of me. I'm so embarrassed."

I tried for a more gentle approach, "Why don't you tell us what happened?"

She nodded shakily, brushing the hair away from her face, "I- I... ummmm."

"Take your time," Jack said kindly, shooting me a look that wasn't kind. "Just tell us what happened."

She managed a small smile at Jack, "I was going in to take a shower and I was looking for the towels." Her eyes darted anxiously around the room, "I opened the big cupboard up... and... and..." She took another deep breath, "I opened the top door of the cupboard and it was sitting on the shelf."

Neither of us wanted to prompt her further, as she was still obviously teetering on the edge of crying again. She laughed in a rather high-pitched way, "It was sitting on the shelf. It was a head." She looked at me, and I could see the remains of the horror in her eyes. "It looked at me," she whispered. And, somehow, that whispered confession scared me too.

Then, common sense kicked in. "Let's go check for a projector," I said.

Molly blinked at me. Then, a warm smile blossomed and grew. A real smile of friendship. "Thank you," she said.

"For what?" I asked curiously.

"For not thinking I'm just a…"

"How can you say that?" I demanded, "After everything I told you about what is going on around here."

"Although," Jack said darkly, "I do think that someone is stepping up their game. I think if I had seen a head in my cupboard I would have been screaming too." He smiled at Molly, "No one could look at your face and think that you were making it all up," he said.

We searched and searched, but couldn't find an explanation for the head in the cupboard. In the end, we (that is, Molly & I) decided that perhaps there was safety in numbers, and we moved her bed (thankfully it was the type of bed that came apart easily) into a corner of my room, where, hopefully, we would both feel safer. I did warn her about Abraham Lincoln's nocturnal visits. No sense waking everyone up with her screaming again.

By the time that we moved the bed and all of her belongings, Carolyn and the rest of the Crabapple Yarns Pack were already busy rearranging the new yarn store downstairs. We worked all day long and far into the night before Carolyn deemed Crabapple Yarns in a fit state to be open. I collapsed gratefully into my bed that night, and I heard Molly do the same.

I was just about drifting off to slumberland, where I hoped a pleasant dream involving a beach awaited me when a horrible thought jumped into my poor little, tiny, exhausted brain. "Molly!" I exclaimed.

There was a pause and then a rustling of bedclothes. "What?" came the somewhat-justifiable irritable reply.

"No one is going to come."

"What?" The reply this time was more curious and less grumpy. "Come to what?"

"Come here," I said. "No one is going to come to Crabapple Yarns on Raspberry Hill." Man. I was so stupid. How could I not have seen this coming? All of our great ideas. I groaned internally. All of that work. Moving furniture. Cleaning. Rearranging. Cleaning. Moving. All of it for nothing. Carolyn was going to be so disappointed. She wouldn't make any money. Molly and I wouldn't get a paycheck, and…

"Why wouldn't they come here?" Molly sounded bewildered now.

"Because," I hissed. "Because of who Grandma Rose was. You saw how Jean acted. She said…"

"I know what Jean said," Molly said quickly. And then she giggled. What that girl thought was funny now was anyone's guess. I hoped she wasn't going into hysterics again. This time, I might have to slap her or something. "You are so, so wrong," she said, trying to hide another giggle. "They'll come."

"I don't think so," I said grimly. "How could I not have seen this coming? All of our great ideas…" Was I repeating myself? I do that sometimes when I get upset.

"They'll come," Molly said, sounding much older than her years. "Don't you worry about that. Everyone will come."

"How do you know?"

"Because," she said simply, "everyone wants to see what Raspberry Hill looks like. No one's been here for years. The town is practically dying of curiosity. Just you wait. We'll have more customers than we know what to do with."

Well now. Huh. That did kind of make sense in a completely warped, sort of way. Molly was going to have to change her theory. It wasn't just knitters who were weird. People were weird. I thought, for a moment, on the general character of people everywhere. It was just amazing, when you thought about it, that God still loves us after all of the horrible things that we do and the way that we act. Sorry. Just a little philosophizing there. I've been doing that a lot lately. Evidently, a huge change in your life forces you to look at things with a new perspective. It gets rather tiring, really.

"Do you know where the projector is?" Molly asked suddenly from across the room. She had been so quiet that I thought she had fallen asleep.

"Why?" I asked suspiciously. I could tell from her tone that she was plotting something.

"Because, if we could get people to believe that Raspberry Hill is haunted, we'd have people coming in from all over…"

"For pity's sake, just go to sleep!"

CHAPTER 27

I wasn't even supposed to be working for the Grand Opening. Can you believe it? Carolyn had patted me on the arm and given me the day off. Like that was going to happen. She claimed that I had been working much too hard and needed a day off to rest. Apparently, tomorrow was going to be Molly's day off. Paid, of course. Carolyn was unbelievably sweet.

But there was no way I was going to miss this.

Molly had been right. Although Grandma Rose was a terrible murderer that no one could speak of without spitting, Raspberry Hill was an irresistible magnet of horrible fascination. They came in droves. And, they almost all bought something... as their excuse for being there, of course, so that was good. Business was booming. I could tell that Carolyn was pleased. Her face was flushed quite prettily. Some of the knitters had already cozily helped themselves to the seating areas as well. I was very relieved. Despite Molly's words of encouragement last night, I had visions of us rattling around like little marbles in a lonely pinball machine.

Thankfully, Mr. Morrie had installed very secure locks on all of the ballroom doors. I caught more than one pesky little knitter trying to make a break for it. Of course, they all had an excuse. Their favorite one was that they were just "looking for the bathroom." They were all very, very disappointed to learn that the ballroom came complete with fancy bathrooms. I tried my best to tell them this civilly, but I might have offended one or two of them. One lady, in particular, really objected to being told to "hold it."

After Carolyn had shooed me away for the twelfth time, I decided to go check up on the café. Ryan had graciously closed his bakery for the day so that he could help Jack get things running at the "Raspberry Hill Café." The menus looked quite good. They should. After all, I created them. I was very surprised to see the line of people waiting for a table.

Ryan and Jack bustled back and forth between the café and the kitchen, both looking flustered and overwhelmed. This wasn't good. One of them was supposed to remain in the kitchen to do the cooking while the other one took orders. They were going to look into hiring someone later if it seemed like the café was busy enough to justify it. Ryan was trying to take an order from the table by the window, while the people who stood in line clamored unceremoniously for his attention. Jack was delivering food… to the wrong table, it seemed. They all laughed rather good-naturedly, but I could tell from the way a red blush was rising up Jack's temples, that things were about to get ugly. He quickly set the orders down (on the right table) and rushed back to the kitchen for more.

There was no way around it. I was going to have to step in. See? It's a good thing I have had so many different types of jobs. Perhaps, my whole life, up to this point, had been a training ground for living at Raspberry Hill. Oh brother. Let's hope not. In any case… remember this - lots of varied knowledge really helps you to be bossy in any situation.

"All right, Ryan," I said, coming up behind him, "you get to the kitchen and help Jack. I'll get the customers seated and take their orders. Either you or Jack can bring out the orders, but make sure someone stays in the kitchen so that the cooking keeps going. It's going to get real ugly around here if these people think that their food isn't coming. Once the customers start banding together and getting cranky – it's all over."

Ryan blinked at me in surprise. Obviously, he wasn't used to being bossed around. I raised an eyebrow experimentally. "Okay," he said, with a slow grin, "may I please finish getting the orders from that table over there?"

I sighed dramatically, "I suppose that will be fine."

When Jack re-entered the café bearing two more plates, he stopped in his tracks when he saw me seating an elderly lady and her daughter. His head swiveled to watch Ryan disappear through the door with his order pad. He set the plates down at their proper place with a friendly smile at the customers and then strode across the table to where I stood.

He walked with purpose and didn't stop until he stood right in front of me. He was looking at me so strangely that I took an involuntary step back. "What?" I asked. Was my hair sticking up or something?

"This," he said suddenly, and he took a hearty step forward, throwing his arms around me. One hand came up behind my head and I found myself staring at the front of Jack's checkered shirt. "Thank you," he whispered in my hair.

I pulled away from him, certain that I was blushing, "Stop that," I said. "What will your customers think?"

"We'll think that that young man is sweet on you," the elderly lady behind me said with a chuckle.

I shoved him away, "I was just trying to be helpful," I muttered. "Don't read anything into it."

He just smiled – an irritating, knowing smile, and headed back to the kitchen.

"Young lady," the elderly lady called from behind me when I would have walked away, "you should be careful with him."

"Why's that?" I asked curiously.

"Because," she said with a sigh, "men don't wait forever, no matter what they say. And hearts are funny things. Un-returned love can change into something else." She looked around the ballroom with sad eyes, "I bet your Grandma Rose, if she was here, would say the same thing."

"Do you think so?" I asked, trying not to sound too eager. "Did you know my Grandma Rose well?"

"Noooo," the lady said, shaking her grey head, "I did not. Not really. I thought I did at one time, but… you know how that goes." She sighed heavily. "People can change so much sometimes."

I stared at her for a moment, not really comprehending. In my experience, people did not change much at all. Their circumstances did. But they stayed the same. Then again, perhaps the death of Abigail had affected her to such a degree that she was no longer capable of being herself. The elderly lady was starting to squirm, so I decided that perhaps staring at the customers was not the best idea ever.

The café stayed busy until early afternoon. I was happy to see, glancing around the partition from time to time, that the same was true for Crabapple Yarns. Molly had been quite a good study of human character on this one. I was, in truth, still quite amazed by it. After all, I think it could have easily gone either way. But, for Carolyn and Jack... and, of course, myself, I was glad.

Once there were no people standing in line anymore, I decided that I had been nice enough for one day, and I grabbed my little bag of knitting to go and observe the goings-on of Crabapple Yarns. Surely Carolyn couldn't object to me sitting innocently and knitting?

Ducking around a bookcase and dresser with a large mirror, I headed straight for my favorite spot... the little spot designed for one knitter... and was dismayed to see that it was already taken. The nerve! The grey head (they were hard to tell apart from the top) was bowed over a pair of wildly colored socks. My irritation vanished instantly. It was Gertie.

"Good afternoon, Gertie," I said politely, with my warmest smile, "how are you today?"

She looked up with a smile of her own, "I'm great!" she said happily. "I'm almost ready to decrease for the foot."

It took me a few seconds to realize she was talking about her knitting. "Oh," I said, "errr... that's wonderful." I held up my own bag of knitting, "I'm almost to the tricky part of the heel," I admitted.

Her eyes brightened, "Can I help?" she asked. "I love turning the heel." (In case you don't know – turning the heel is knitter terminology for when you do some fancy-pants stuff that looks a lot harder than it really is... and then... all of a sudden... you have a heel... or at least that's what I've been told. I'll let you know how it goes.)

234

Before I knew it, I had stolen a chair from another corner and was tucked up with Gertie as she patiently explained the steps of turning the heel. She was a remarkably good teacher. Then again, I was certain that I was an above-average learner.

"How long have you been knitting?" I asked Gertie, as soon as I was confident enough to knit and talk at the same time without losing my place.

"Oh," she said with a vague shrug, "years and years and years. I learned when I was a young girl. I'll leave it to your imagination how long ago that was." She peered over her glasses at me, "And you?" she inquired. "How long have you been knitting?"

I thought about it for a moment. "About five or six years," I said slowly. "Yes, I think that's about it. The lady who lived next door asked me for tea one Sunday afternoon. She was a nice old thing." I looked at Gertie, "She kinda reminds me of you."

Gertie sputtered with laughter, "Thanks a lot," she said, "but I don't usually consider myself that old."

"No, no, no," I backtracked as fast as I could, "I meant that you are just as patient and kind as she was. I was just all thumbs at first, but she was so sweet." I smiled with the reminiscence. "I moved shortly after that, but I'll always be grateful to her for teaching me to knit."

Gertie patted my hand, "Knitting is contagious," she said. "Which you'll figure out soon enough. For some reason, knitters are never content with just knowing how to knit for themselves, and they soon develop an irresistible (and sometimes annoying) desire to teach everyone they know everything that they know too." She grinned, "Which is why it was so fun for me to show you how to turn your first heel."

I nodded thoughtfully, "I see what you mean," I admitted. "There is something satisfying about helping someone learn how to do something new."

Gertie nodded too, "Yep," she said, "although sometimes it's fun to watch someone try to learn themselves too." Her face crinkled up into a wicked little smile, which I could not help but return.

Gertie sighed suddenly and looked around the room. "If only these walls could talk," she said wistfully,. "I wonder what kinds of stories they'd tell." She looked at me carefully, "Oh, I'm sorry," she said her face filling with regret. "I hope you didn't think I was trying to talk about your Grandma in a bad way... or... "

Strangely enough, I didn't think that. Instead, I agreed with her. "I think that quite often," I said. "And then, sometimes, I think that these walls ARE talking."

Her head shot up, eyes gleaming, "So you've heard things, have you?" she asked, grinning foolishly. "I heard that Raspberry Hill was haunted. So, what was it?"

I shook my head, "What are you talking about?"

She leaned forward, "You know what I mean," she insisted. "Was it ghostly wailings down the corridor? Terrible moaning in the plumbing? Chains clanking..."

I stopped her. "No," I said, rolling my eyes, "it's nothing like that. I just mean that sometimes it's like I hear people talking... or yelling, but there's no one there."

She sat back in her chair, looking disappointed. "Oh," she said, "Is that all? Well, that's not very exciting, is it?"

Huh. She had no idea how exciting it could get around here. But I certainly wasn't going to tell her anything. We didn't need *that* kind of gossip getting around. Molly was still, crazily, hoping that some sort of ghostly occurrence would happen in the midst of all our customers. I was beginning to wonder if I shouldn't be locking up the bedsheets just in case she got the idea to put one over her head and do a little knitterly haunting herself.

"So, what do they say?" Gertie asked suddenly, her face oddly inscrutable.

"Excuse me?" I asked, still busy imagining Molly capering around the ballroom dressed as a ghost. "Who said what?"

"What do the voices say that you hear?"

I looked over my shoulder self-consciously, "Please don't say that so loud," I whispered. "What would people think if they heard that?"

She shrugged, "And here was me thinking that you didn't care about what people thought about you."

I considered her carefully, "Gracious heavens," I said. "Aren't you just the observant one?" I grinned suddenly, "But you're right. I really don't care. I just wouldn't want anyone to think poorly of Carolyn or the yarn store." I thought for a moment, "I'm not really sure what they say," I said. "I've never really listened."

"Well," she said matter-of-factly, "Maybe you should listen next time."

I made a face at her. "Maybe I will," I said. "But what if the one person is threatening to chop the other person to bits…"

"Now, Natalie!" The voice came from behind me and startled me so bad that I almost fell out of my chair.

"Gracious, Carolyn," I said, my hand holding my heart, "you almost scared the life out of me."

"Well at least I'm not threatening to chop you in half," she rolled her eyes and re-adjusted the ruffle on her scarf so that it framed her face prettily. The scarf was a gift from Molly, knit in lace and then edged, along one side, with an adorable ruffle. I had already squirreled some yarn away to knit one for myself. "Didn't I tell you that you had the day off today?"

I held my sock defensively, "I was just knitting," I protested. "I wasn't working. And Gertie was showing me how to turn my heel."

Gertie's eyes were big and round, yet hiding a glimmer of mischievousness, "That's right, Carolyn," she said solemnly, "she wasn't doing a lick of work."

I glared at them both and gathered up my knitting. "That's it," I said. "I'm leaving."

"Good," Carolyn said. "And don't come back until after closing. You need to rest up."

Why did everyone always seem to think that I needed resting up? Just because I had a lump on my head? Did lumps need lots of rest?

There was something niggling at the back of my brain, though. Something that had been bothering me since last night. But, what was it? As I approached the doors to the ballroom, key already in hand, it hit me. I walked quickly back to the counter where Molly sat, knitting discretely, her mouth set in a grim line as she plodded along with her sock.

"Molly," I hissed, getting her attention. "Nathaniel Goldmyer."

She put her knitting down quite willingly and approached me, "You'd better not let Carolyn catch you," she warned. "She already told me that you're not supposed to be here today."

I waved my hand dismissively, "Never mind that," I said impatiently. "The lawyer that was here last night. The one that works with Mr. Garvey."

She waited expectantly. I couldn't believe that she didn't know what I wanted.

"Well?" I asked. "Is he related to Mrs. Goldmyer, the Librarian?"

She nodded, not looking particularly impressed or excited, "Of course," she said simply. "He's her son."

"Ah-ha," I crowed triumphantly. "The plot thickens."

Molly raised her eyebrows, "What plot?"

"Never mind," I said, already walking towards the door. "I'll see you later."

For once, I knew exactly what I needed to do.

But alas, as almost all plans do, mine had a fatal flaw. Once I got outside I realized that I had a wee little problem. Mr. Darcy was still off limits for me. Then again... whose car was he anyway? Mine. So, who got to drive him? Me. That's who.

I snuck back inside and back to the kitchen pantry. I had seen Jack put Mr. Darcy's keys on the hook inside the door yesterday. It was no trouble at all to sneak the keys off their hook, backtrack my way to the front door and, in no time, find myself happily driving along back to town.

I know what you're thinking. I could have walked. But, what are you thinking? Walk down that scary road? Or, I know you're thinking that perhaps I could have asked someone for a ride. But... what fun would that have been? Sometimes, I think that you think too much.

I headed straight for the library. Didn't you think it was strange when we walked into the library and Mrs. Goldmyer had all of those newspaper clippings out and ready for us? I did too. What I really wonder is why you didn't say anything sooner, because it didn't make any sense at all at the time, but now that we had such a pleasant visit from her son, Mr. Nathaniel Goldmyer, who obviously did not want us either opening up business or staying at Raspberry Hill (I didn't know which it was yet), things were becoming a bit clearer. Perhaps it was time to do some research on my own.

Mrs. Goldmyer's beady little eyes widened fractionally when she saw me walking through the door. She recovered herself quite nicely, though. "Is there something I can help you with?" she asked, "Or have you come to put my back room in shambles again?"

I squashed the little feeling of guilt that popped up and promptly reminded myself that she was, quite likely, in cahoots against us. Somehow. Why? Now that remained to be seen.

"No thank you, Mrs. Goldmyer," I said coolly, "I think I'll just help myself today." I smiled, with what I hoped was a suitably mysterious smile and walked quickly toward the back room.

It was interesting what one can find when one looks for themselves.

I used the computer.

Poor Mrs. Goldmyer. Technology was going to be her undoing. It would have taken me much longer than the time I had to go through the hard copy files. As it was, I found what I was looking for very easily. Mrs. Goldmyer had provided us with all of the information available. All except one article. I'm not sure what I expected to find, but one piece of new information popped out. Instinctively, I knew that this is what she had been hiding.

Further searching proved useless, although there were several relatively recent articles detailing suspicious activities at Raspberry Hill. I assumed that this is what Sherriff Finn had been referring to when he had so kindly visited us with his business card.

Interesting. Very interesting.

I walked out of the library with a slow step, pondering this new information carefully.

Sherriff Finn had lied to me.

I didn't like liars.

CHAPTER 28

By the time I got home, the yarn store and the café were closed, and Carolyn was heading home. Everyone looked quite happy and sufficiently tired. I longed to share my find with Molly, but, annoyingly, Celia was home. And we had been so fortunate to be seeing so little of her.

"Oh my dears," she was saying, her feet flopped dramatically up on a footstool, "I am just exhausted. They simply have to hire someone new soon or I will just..."

They probably couldn't find anyone who could work with Celia.

"Have to quit?" I guessed, trying very hard not to sound too sarcastic. After all, that is exactly what Celia did when she got tired of something. Or, if she had to work too hard.

She shot me a look that was hard to read. "I was going to say, 'die of exhaustion.'"

Molly, clearly feeling the tension in the room, giggled rather nervously, "I'm sure they appreciate all of your hard work, Celia," she said.

Celia beamed at her. At last! Someone who appreciated her suffering. I groaned and pushed myself to my own feet. This was going to be a long, long night, but I didn't have to spend it with Celia.

I decided to go upstairs until supper time. Perhaps a wee spot of snooping was in order?

I passed the door to the inner room that was always locked. Snooping was going to have to wait. I needed to know what was behind that door. I tried hairpins. I tried a credit card. Where did I get the credit card? Well... I may have done a tiny bit of snooping to find my necessary cat burglar supplies. I was trying the hairpins one more time when Jack caught me.

He didn't look happy, and so I discretely slipped the credit card into my back pocket. No sense in adding any potential fuel to the fire.

"Hi, Jack," I said as cheerfully as I could in spite of the thundercloud that was on his face.

"What did you think you were doing?" he demanded.

"Well," I said calmly, "I was thinking about breaking into this room. We don't have a key, and I'm dying of curiosity about what's in here."

"That's not what I'm talking about," he replied. "Why did you steal Mr. Darcy's keys?"

Oopsies.

Gracious.

Can you believe he was actually still upset about that?

Which is exactly what I said to him.

Which led to quite the little heated argument about double vision and death by tree. He was really, really overreacting. I was completely fine. Which I told him. He didn't seem to care.

There was no arguing with him. Besides, he almost looked cute when his face was all red and his freckles jumped. I smacked myself upside the head (figuratively of course). Wait a minute. This train of thought needed to get derailed. Now.

"So are you going to help me or not?" I asked, stopping him in mid-sentence.

He paused. "Excuse me?"

"Are you going to help me open this door?"

He frowned, "I think not," he said. "Give me the keys back."

"They're in my purse," I protested, "and stop changing the subject. This could be important."

"I'm not sure what could be important about a room." Jack said. "I came up here to tell you that supper was almost ready."

"Did you tell Celia?" I asked curiously.

He paused again, a rueful smile briefly lighting his face. "I wasn't going to," he admitted, "but Molly was with her, so I did."

"You're nicer than me," I said.

He sighed, "I know." He studied me carefully. "Step aside."

"What?" I asked. "What are you talking about?"

He pulled me by my elbow away from the door. "Stand back," he said.

Before I had time to ask what he was talking about, he threw his shoulder against the door and it gave way, opening with a splintering of wood and a dreadful creaking.

I was impressed.

The room inside was dusty and dim. Sheet-covered mountains of furniture were quiet and still. There was a light switch on the wall, but flipping it only resulted in a dull, flickering glow from one of the lamps on the ceiling. The other lamp was out. We peered in cautiously.

"Look," Jack said with a whisper. "Someone has been here."

He was right. The wood floor was dusty except for a track of footprints leading to one corner of the room.

"They dragged something out," I whispered back, pointing to the marks in the dust. I looked at Jack over my shoulder, "Why are we whispering?"

"I don't know," Jack whispered back, "but somehow it just feels right."

I walked in and approached the first sheet covered object. I pulled at it cautiously. It came off smoothly in a small cloud of dust.

"What the…" Jack began, but I pinched his arm.

"Weird." We both said it at the same time. It was some sort of examination table.

Jack walked further into the room and pulled off another sheet. It was a table on wheels that was covered in horrible looking tools.

"It's a torture room," I gasped. "Grandma Rose was a spy or something and this is where…"

A noise from the doorway had us both jumping.

"Oh my dears," Celia said, her delicate body shaking with laughter. "You two are just too funny. Didn't you know? Rose's husband was a doctor. This was his examination room. He preferred to keep his business off of the first floor so that it didn't interfere with the daily life of his wife." She paused and reconsidered, "Well… wives, I should say," she said. "I gather that his first wife, in particular, didn't like to be reminded that her husband was a working man."

Celia took a disdainful step back. "I really wouldn't poke around in there, dears," she said, "Who knows what germs there could be."

Well now. That was just embarrassing. Jack and I didn't look at each other as we headed back towards the dining room, but he did whisper, "Torture room?" Like I said. Embarrassing.

The lady at the counter was driving me nuts. Completely nuts. Maybe I wasn't cut out for working at a yarn store. I seriously doubted that Carolyn would approve of me whacking her customer upside the head with her own knitting needles. But, it was tempting.

"So," I tried again, "what you're saying is that you are looking for a yarn that is off-white?"

She smiled serenely at me. She was not perturbed or frustrated at all. I rather think she was enjoying our little discussion. Knitters were weird.

"No," she said patiently, "I want a yarn that is the color of meringue."

Which was… off-white… right?

"I'm afraid I don't understand…"

She patted my hand, "I understand your confusion," she said, "but here's what you have to do. Take 4 egg whites, 1 cup of sugar and 1 tsp vanilla and beat them all together."

I blinked at her. "And?"

"And that's the color I need the yarn to be in. It's for my daughter's wedding. I know you don't have anything like that in stock, but I'm sure if you make the meringue you'll understand and know what to order."

Gracious heavens. Was this woman serious?

One more pat of the hand, "I'll be back tomorrow," she said firmly, leaving in a cloud of happy cluelessness.

I headed straight for Carolyn. "Carolyn," I said urgently, "I need your help. That lady…"

"Yes," Carolyn said, "I saw you helping Lucille. How was she?"

"She's…" I searched for words that I could use that wouldn't shock Carolyn. The list wasn't long.

"I know she can be a bit of a handful," Carolyn said, while I was still mulling over possible phrases, "but please do your best to help her out. She's such a good customer and a dear friend."

I rolled my eyes, "But, Carolyn," I protested, "she wants to knit a shawl."

Carolyn's eyes lit up, "How perfect," she said with excitement. "Most likely for her daughter's wedding." Her eyes turned slightly wistful, "Such a lovely girl."

How could you argue with that? So, when my lunch break approached, I marched myself straight to the kitchen and opened the refrigerator. I rummaged through the contents, oblivious to Jack's cry of dismay.

"Just be quiet," I said irritably. "Don't worry. I have no compelling desire to rearrange your shelving system."

Jack made sputtering noises while keeping a careful eye on the hot griddle. My mouth was watering. Grilled chicken salad with three kinds of cheese and Jack's own blend of mustard. So far, it was his biggest seller, and with good reason too.

He saw me eyeing the sandwich, "If you get out of the refrigerator," he said, frowning, "I will make you a sandwich."

Gracious. He was worse than a mother sending her little baby off to Kindergarten. It was just a refrigerator. But, the offer was tempting. Really tempting. Who cared what meringue lady wanted anyways? I wavered, hand on the door. But, then, sadly, Carolyn's wrinkled face came into my mind and I resumed my search. The second drawer from the bottom was filled with eggs.

"What are you doing?" Jack demanded incredulously, watching me pull four eggs out. "We need those eggs."

I scowled at him, "You've got a whole drawer full of eggs. I'll buy some more when I go into town later."

This made Jack's frown even deeper. "I thought we discussed yesterday that…"

"I will get a ride from someone," I said in between my teeth. "And now if you could just be quiet for a minute I have to do something."

He was shaking his head as he flipped the grilled chicken salad, "You'll never eat all of those eggs," he said wisely. "Why don't you just crack the ones you're going to eat and leave the rest?"

I rummaged through the cupboards looking for a bowl. Jack had the weirdest system of organization that I had ever seen. All I could find were pots and pans.

Jack flipped the sandwich onto a plate with a wedge of lettuce and tomato, sprinkled it liberally with chips and added a pickle. As if on cue, Ryan walked into the kitchen to take it from him. Good grief. Those two were worse than an old married couple. They were already reading each other's minds.

I started rummaging through the drawers.

"Now what are you looking for?" Jack demanded, reading the next order slip and starting another sandwich.

"I need the little beater thingie," I muttered, "Where do you hide those? And a big mixing bowl."

"The little beater thingie?" he asked in disbelief. "What are you up to now?"

I decided to take it easy on him before he had apoplexy or something. "I need to make meringue," I explained, still rummaging.

"For lunch?" he demanded incredulously. "That is ridiculously unhealthy."

"Technically," I said wisely, "there's hardly any calories or anything… well… except for the sugar."

"My point exactly," he said. "No nutritional value whatsoever."

"Not everything in life needs to be nutritious," I said. "Sometimes you just have to eat things you love to eat."

He abandoned the grill and stared at me, "I never knew you liked to eat meringue," he said, looking at me strangely.

"I don't," I admitted, sighing. "This crazy knitter who came this morning needs to make a shawl that's the color of meringue for her daughter's wedding."

Jack still look puzzled. "She told me to take 4 eggs, 1 cup of sugar and some vanilla and beat them all together and then I'd know exactly what color she was looking for."

Jack's mouth fell open, "You're joking," he said. "You're actually going to do that?"

I don't know why Jack continued to be shocked by everything I did. Really. Was making meringue to keep a customer happy so unheard of?

I shrugged helplessly, "What am I supposed to do?" I asked. "Apparently she's one of Carolyn's best customers." Jack's mouth was still open, which was a little annoying. "So where's the little beater thingie?" I paused and thought, "Or should I use the blender? Would that be faster?"

Jack's laugh had my temper flaring higher. Before I could gather the words to tell him what I thought, he pulled me by the elbow to the refrigerator again, reached onto the first shelf and pulled out a bowl. "Save yourself some trouble," he said. "I made meringue this morning."

"Oh," I said, peering at the meringue with a sinking heart. Off-white. Just like I knew it would be. How on earth was this going to help me?

"Oh?" he said. "Is that all you can say? How about 'Thank you, Jack' or 'I'm so glad I didn't crack the eggs yet.'... something like that?"

I sighed, "Thank you, Jack," I said automatically, "I'm so glad I didn't crack the eggs yet."

"Huh," he said, looking into the bowl with me, "You know, it does help to see it in person. It's off-white, but it's also iridescent and really almost has a hint of gold to it."

Good grief. He was in the wrong business. Either that... or I was.

CHAPTER 29

Thanks to Jack's beautiful insight into the true color and spirit of meringue, I was able to successfully find a perfect yarn for the crazy lady. Which was a good thing because we needed the extra time to start setting up for Knit Night.

What? Didn't you know? Check your calendar. Today was the biggest knitting day of the month. Well. Tonight was. Tonight was Knit Night. Which was the social event of the month for the knitters of Springgate. Carolyn also said that, due to the "unique location," we could probably expect record numbers.

Jack, very obligingly, offered the use of the café if we found ourselves short of seating. That was highly unlikely, as, in my opinion, we had enough seating for every knitter in Springgate - and its surrounding counties. Carolyn had also hired Ryan to cater the event. Normally, she said, she made her own snacks and goodies, but seeing as how everything was different now, she was going to save herself a lot of time and give Ryan some business at the same time. She was a very smart lady. Plus, I really didn't feel like baking cookies. After all, I had already come *this* close to making meringue. That was quite enough kitchen-time for one day, don't you think?

Between customers, I pondered the news I had gleaned from the library yesterday. Why had Sherriff Finn lied? He had specifically told Molly and me that Mildred was his grandmother. However, that was not true. Abigail was his second cousin. Mildred was Abigail's best friend, but they weren't related. So, why lie about it? What was there to gain? It was a very interesting question, don't you think?

It was making my brain hurt, so, in the meantime, I decided to accomplish something that was a bit easier. I was working on my people skills. It was my turn to man the cash register, and one thing that I had noticed about Molly was that she always had something nice to say to every person as they were leaving. It was an easy place to start.

The lady I was currently helping had said her name was Jennifer, and she seemed to know Carolyn and Molly quite well. I struggled to find just the right thing to say to her as I scanned her yarn into the computer. She was making a sweater for her friend's little girl. It was an adorable shade of lavender with a hint of sparkle every now and then. We had, unfortunately, already discussed the yarn to death, so there wasn't much left to compliment in there. I looked at her carefully. Ah ha! I had it.

"I love your shirt," I said, as warmly as I could. "It's so pretty." She smiled happily at me, which encouraged me into continuing. "It reminds me of the curtains I hung in my new apartment."

Her mouth fell open. Then shut with a snap... as her face turned a most unbecoming shade of purple. What had happened? She left in a cloud of indignation. My sad eyes watched her go.

Molly was standing at the end of the counter laughing at me.

"What did I do?" I asked helplessly. "I think I offended her or something."

"Just a little," Molly said, still grinning. "I don't think you should have compared her shirt to your curtains."

She could be right. I rolled my eyes. "I meant it as a compliment," I insisted. "I really love that pattern. After all, they were the first curtains that I ever bought."

People skills were not as easy as they looked.

"The Sherriff is here," Molly whispered, sidling up to me. "He says he wants to see you." She gestured with her head towards the front of the house, "He's in the front foyer. I thought it would be best if he didn't come back here. He says he has a few questions for you."

Really? Maybe I wanted to see him too. I just might have a few questions of my own. I made my way quickly to the front foyer, but Sherriff Finn stood waiting.

"Can I help you?" I asked sweetly. I figured that this would be my best plan of attack. Be sweet… and then zing him.

"Good afternoon, Natalie," he said friendily (I think he was using my plan too), "I was just checking in."

My eyebrows rose of their own accord, but I managed to smile up at him. "Checking in?" I questioned. "I didn't know you reported to me."

"Well," he said, standing just a bit closer, "regarding the events of a few nights ago."

Oh. Right.

"And what did you discover?"

"Nothing," he said regretfully. "I'm afraid we just didn't find anything suspicious here at the house… or around the house… we've done some other checking around and yours is the only house that has been bothered by any type of… disturbances here in Springgate."

"You came all the way up here to tell me that you didn't have any answers?" I asked, probably not quite as nicely as I should have.

"I thought it would be the polite thing to do," he said stiffly.

I stared at him for a moment, "Why did you lie to me, Sherriff?" I asked.

His expression didn't change. "I don't know what you mean," he said blankly.

"You told me that Mildred was your grandmother. But that's not the case, is it?"

He was good. Not a flicker of guilt…. Or a trace of evasion. He smiled broadly, "You must have misunderstood me," he said easily, "she's *like* a grandmother to me, but, of course, there's no blood relation there."

I shook my head, "I don't think so," I said slowly, "and I do believe Molly could corroborate…"

His smile was set firmly in place with super glue, "Well, then," he said, "I must have misspoke in the heat of the moment. I suppose I can be quite protective of the ones I love." He put his hat on his head, "But," he added, "I'm sure it really doesn't matter if we're related one way or the other does it?"

I watched him leave, knowing deep inside my heart that, yes, it did matter. It mattered a great deal. If only I knew why.

There really was only one thing to do. I was going to have to pay a social call. On Mildred. Which left me with one, small problem… how was I going to get there?

In the end, I ended up hitching a ride back to town with Helen. I wouldn't say that I *sneaked* out, however, the truth of the matter was that I didn't exactly alert anyone that I was leaving. What did you say? No. I couldn't find the keys to Mr. Darcy anywhere – that's why I had to hitch a ride with Helen. Gracious. Do I have to explain everything to you? I figured I could go to town and pop back "home" before anyone really even realized I was gone. How is that possible? Well… it is possible that Carolyn thought that I was going up to my room to rest. Just possible. I didn't tell her that, of course… as that would be lying. She drew her own conclusions. I can't help that, now can I? Let that be a lesson to you – jumping to conclusions is terrible exercise.

"Are you coming to Knit Night?" I asked Helen. After all, Knit Night started in less than 3 hours and I would have thought, given Helen's love of knitting, she would merely park herself somewhere and wait it out.

She sighed, "Of course," she said, "But first I've got to go home and get my husband." She grinned mischievously, "He is a great knitter too," she said with a twinkle, "and he certainly wouldn't want to miss Knit Night."

"Oh," I said, "that's right. You guys have just come back from a knitting seminar or something, haven't you?"

"Yes, indeed," she said, "Patrick is just dying to show off his new skills." She rolled her eyes, "He is such a ham sometimes."

I had her drop me off at the library. No sense in getting her all suspicious about what I was up to, now was there?

After I was sure that her taillights were well out of range, I walked as briskly as I could (without drawing any undue attention to myself, of course) to the SunnySide Retirement Home. As I walked, I gave myself a stern talking to about what I was going to say – and not say – to that old bat, Mildred. I seriously doubted that she had a heart condition, but just in case, I was going to be kind, but not *too* kind. I was going to get some answers. And she was going to give them. Today.

As I entered SunnySide, I was once more struck by the fact that SunnySide needed more sun. It was a gloomy place – plain and simple. That just goes to show you that names don't mean anything. It's what is inside that counts. Whoa. And that concludes your sermon for the day. Sorry about that.

I was nearly run over by a flood of little grey heads that barely came up to my chin. I struggled through to the front desk, "Where is everyone going?" I asked the lady behind the counter, pulling my foot out of the path of a formidable looking walker.

She looked at me in surprise, "Supper, of course," she said, looking flustered and irritable. "Can I help you?" She scanned me appraisingly, a frown growing slowly between her two bushy eyebrows.

Uh-oh. She was cranky. That meant she was going to be trouble unless I acted quickly. "No, thank you," I said sweetly, "I'm just here to say a quick hello to granny. Didn't I see you here yesterday when I visited?"

Her expression cleared, "That's possible," she said, my threat level obviously dissolving and turned to rummage through the papers on her desk. I seized my escape quickly and walked down the hall like I knew exactly where I was going. Which, of course, I did.

Supper time. Perfect. The old bat would be chowing down, and I could do just a bit of... my footsteps paused... *did I really want to be doing this? Was this right?*... cleaning up. Cleaning up. Ah. Yes. That was it. Her room did look a bit untidy. And how nice of me would it be to help a poor, old lady out in her time of need? I think, really, I could earn a badge or something for that, don't you?

I entered her room cautiously, but to my relief, she was gone. So I set to work... um... cleaning. Gracious. When was the last time that she had looked in the back of these drawers? Can you believe what I found in her... umm... undergarment drawer? Undergarments! The nerve! Did she not know that you were supposed to hide your deep dark secrets amongst your underthings? What were they teaching old people nowadays?

I checked the back of her closet. Under the bed. Everywhere that I could think of. I was standing on a chair going through the top shelf of her closet when it hit me. What little old lady was capable of standing on a chair to hide her deep dark secrets? Stupid! She would need to put it somewhere with easy access. But where would that be? I sat down on her bed to think like a little old lady. Then it hit me - under the mattress! Of course! I was not very good at this... cleaning business.

I checked one side at the end and then the other. And then... near the head of the bed... jackpot! There was a small leather journal. Strangely, or perhaps not so strangely, I felt no guilt as I slipped it under my shirt, tucked it into my pants and surveyed the room. It didn't look like a person had just been rummaging through Mildred's room – or, at least, I hoped that it didn't. Had that lamp been standing in the corner when I came in – or had I moved it when I looked under the bed? Oh dear. Oh well. I got out of there as fast as I could, deciding not to risk a chat with Mildred after all. She would probably only lie anyways.

As I walked back down Main Street, I realized something. Something just a little bit important. I had neglected to get a ride back to Raspberry Hill.

CHAPTER 30

Rats. Double rats. Triple rats. If only I had Helen's phone number. Or knew her last name. Or knew anyone's last name. Or… I had a phone that I could call someone with.

Yes, alright. I could probably find a pay phone and call Jack or Molly. But that would be just a bit humiliating, wouldn't it? Besides, more than one uncomfortable question would be asked regarding my whereabouts and doings. What do you think Jack would think about me stealing some poor little old lady's…. well… you get the idea.

"It's only a mile," the little voice in my head said. "Why don't you just walk?"

I stood at the end of town and looked up Main Street to where it climbed up to Raspberry Hill. And gulped. Such a short piece of road… yet so long. Only a mile, I reminded myself. Most people could walk that in less than 20 minutes. A person truly inspired by fear (like me) could most probably make it in less than half of that time. Speaking of which… I checked my watch. My walk and dastardly deeds had taken up much more time than I had thought that they would. Knit Night was due to begin in a very short time. My absence would not go unnoticed. Rats. Double rats. Triple rats.

Fear not. For I am with you. Whoa. Where did that come from? What? Yes, I know it's from the Bible. Thank you. I was just remarking about how it suddenly popped into my mind. It was exactly what I needed, though. I took a deep breath, said a very quick prayer of thanksgiving and protection and set off down the road. It was just a mile, after all. 5,280 feet. Which, I believe, was just about 2,000 steps. Easy.

It was getting dark. Which, really, was just the icing on the cake. The darkness, however, could be from the clouds that were rapidly gathering. I was definitely due to be wet before I got back to Raspberry Hill. Rats. Double rats. Enough of that. Sigh. I hated this part of the road. The trees were really quite horrible. I still wasn't sure what kind they were. The horrible kind, that's for sure. They were bent and gnarled and had terrible, abundant thorns that stuck out at least three inches. Anyone running through these trees was sure to meet a prickly fate.

Fate. I shivered. Abigail had met her fate on this very road. "Stop thinking about that," I told myself sternly. There was an ominous rumbling in the distance which made it really hard to stop thinking about things like fate and... fear.

Behind me, a twig cracked. It was exactly the same sound a foot would make stepping on a small stick. Without realizing what I was doing, I scampered to the side of the road, huddling in the shadow of one of the ugly trees. I decided that another prayer of protection was in order... along with a quick word of thanks that I had chosen to wear dark clothes this morning. I held my breath and waited. There was no possible reason that anyone else would be walking up this road. Not on foot. Any knitters coming would be arriving by car. The wind blew past my ear, ruffling my hair with cold fingers. There was absolutely no logical explanation for why I was so scared. But I was. Fear had gripped my heart with a fist that wouldn't be shaken. Someone was out there. In the twilight, where darkness was just beginning to gather itself... someone was out there who did not like me. I backed off the road a bit more, bending to avoid the prickery thorns of the tree. One snagged my sweater, and I could hear it tear as I pulled away. The bark of the tree was rough under my palms as I gripped its trunk, circling around to hide even further behind it.

Molly had confided to me that she was once followed down Main Street by a van and was scared half out of her mind. I had thought she was being a bit over-dramatic, but now I thought that, just possibly, I could empathize a little bit more. The unknown could be much more frightening than reality.

The sweep of headlights coming up the road had me ducking, but the car roared past without stopping. I wonder if, possibly, they had seen anyone on the road behind me? If I had been a bit braver, I could have stepped out onto the road and asked for a ride up to Raspberry Hill. Instead, I was hiding behind a tree that was possibly going to scratch me to death.

I waited.

This was just silly.

Of course there was no one else coming up the road. I probably heard an animal... or the wind blowing through the trees. Like there was really a "bad guy" lurking up the hill to... what?... Kill me? Throw me down the hill? I snorted.

Silliness.

I hesitantly stepped back around the tree, towards the road. "Give me back my sweater," I hissed to the tree, as it crooked its fingers out to snag me once more.

Thunder was cracking above me as I began my trek back up the road, and the first few drops of rain gifted me with their presence. My quick walk up the hill was taking entirely too long. I bolstered my resolution and began walking briskly... for another few feet... pausing when I heard something behind me. Again.

It was hard to hear anything over the wind through the trees. I decided that, really, a brief rest on the side of the road was not such a bad idea. Just to catch my breath, of course. I wasn't hiding.

I picked a nicer tree this time. Its branches were a bit higher off the ground, which allowed me to duck and sneak around it without any further damage to my favorite sweater. Rain pattered on my head... although... I have to admit... there was more rain on the road than on my head at the moment, thanks in no small part to the canvas of leaves over my head. Any further into the fall season and I would not have that benefit.

I shivered again, wishing, for the first time in my life, that I was at Raspberry Hill. Even if Celia was there. That just goes to show you how desperate I was. Anything would be better than huddling on the side of the road, scared to go forward and scared to go back. Perhaps if I just waited here, the person would pass by, and then I could either go on or go back. That was a good plan, don't you think? I think so too.

As I stood there, in the growing darkness and cold... I started getting the strangest feeling. I felt as if I was not standing behind the tree... instead, I was watching myself from outside of myself. Have you ever felt that way? Like the world is passing you by without you... and you have no control over it? Like you were in a trance... or a dream.

The shriek from up the hill had me jumping and clutching my heart. A woman was running down the hill, her hair streaming behind her and mud splattered on her dress. She was waving her arms wildly and yelling. *What was going on?* Another set of headlights cut through the gloom. My breath caught in my throat with horror. The car was headed straight for the lady running down the hill. I stepped out from behind my tree, calling out a warning... She was going to be hit! There was a great squealing of brakes, and, at the last moment, the car swerved, coming to a stop in a puff of smoke and the smell of burning rubber. I blinked the rain out of my eyes. The screaming woman was gone. I looked back towards the car... and as I watched, the driver's side door creaked open... and in the glow of the overhead light I could see a woman, her head against the steering wheel... a dark red stain already spreading down the side of her face, which was turned towards the door. Even from here, I could see that she was dead. I stared at her in horror. And then... and then... the most horrible thing happened... her eyes popped open. They were blank and staring.

I think I screamed. Giving up any pretense of hiding, I ran as fast and as hard as I could up towards the safety of Raspberry Hill. I turned back, despite my own volition... but the car was gone. No smoke. No lights. Nothing. A sob caught in my throat. I was going crazy. That must be the answer. I ran faster, but the wind seemed intent on pushing me back down the hill.

There was a dreadful cracking behind me... like someone else had come out from the woods and was also running up the road. The fear returned, and I did not know what to do. I ran forward, looking over my shoulder, and then, the terror getting the best of me, dove again for the theoretical safety of the side of the road. The feeling of safety was short-lived. My breathing was sure to give me away. I tried to stifle my ragged sobs with the palms of my hand, when I heard it - someone was calling my name. Not in a way that someone would call someone that they were looking for, but in a soft, sinister way. The way that a hunter calls to its prey, knowing that it can hear... and mocking it for its weakness.

I wish I could say that knowing this strengthened my resolve and bolstered my courage, but that wasn't exactly true. It did help to bring me back my senses and think a bit more clearly. The adrenaline still pounding through my veins had me wanting to run... run... run... but I had the distinctly uncomfortable feeling that my hunter would be faster and stronger than me.

"Natalie..." it was a male voice... "Natalie"... maybe not. It was too hard to tell. And, at this point, I didn't really care. He was getting closer. The rain fell harder. Thunder crashed, and the wind whipping through the trees had me jumping at every movement. I sank down to my knees, covering my face with my hands... figuring that it would be harder for someone to find me if I was a smaller package. The theory made sense at the time.

"I see you," the voice said through the rain, branches cracking not more than two feet away, "you're not hiding very well."

It took every last ounce of willpower that I had not to move. What to do? On one hand, if they did see me, I should definitely be running. If, on the other hand, they were trying to trick me, then I should stay where I was. I stifled another sob. *Please, God,* I prayed, *please save me.*

Another set of headlights flared through the darkness, filling me with the light of their hope. I surged to my feet and flung myself straight into the path of the oncoming car.

The tires shrieked as the driver obviously slammed on its brakes to avoid hitting me... the scene playing out so closely to the one I had just seen, that I felt stunned, not knowing what was real and what was still in my imagination.

With numb feet, I took faltering steps towards the driver's side door, not knowing what I would do if I saw the horror of a lifeless body behind the wheel. Instead, the door burst open and a living, breathing and very much alive body burst out of it.

"Natalie," the most perfect voice in the universe exclaimed, "what are you doing?"

Sobbing with relief, I threw myself at the warm body that was reaching for me. "Jack," I cried, "he's out there."

His arms were warm and solid, and I've never felt so safe in my life. "Who's out there?" he asked sharply, pulling me away from him despite my attempts otherwise. "What's going on?"

To my utter embarrassment, I cried even harder, my body shaking with relief and cold and the ebbing flow of adrenaline. "Shhhhh," he soothed. "Let's get you back to Mr. Darcy."

He helped me into the passenger seat and, when he stepped away, I reached out to grab him, "No," I said, quite irrationally, "don't leave me."

His hands rubbed against mine briefly, "I'm just going to the other side of the car," he said. "I'll be right back."

I reluctantly released his hands and held my breath until he was safely in the driver's seat. I heard him take a deep breath, "Now," he said, "tell me what's going on."

I mimicked his example, taking a deep breath of my own. "There was someone chasing me," I stammered, wiping the rain and tears out of my eyes with a shaking hand. "I don't know what he wanted, but he – or maybe it was a she – was following me and..." I faltered, not quite sure how to communicate my feelings... "and I was scared. " Jack's face was angry, and he looked ready to go back out into the dark, so I grabbed his sleeve, "Please don't," I begged. "Please just stay with me."

I could see the internal debate in his eyes and was remarkably relieved when I saw it come to an end. He put his hand on the gear shift but did not make any further move to go forward. Instead, he reached into the backseat and produced his coat, offering it to me without a word. The beautiful warmth that flooded me was partially due to his nice wool coat. The rest was all because of Jack. Because, with the sudden clarity that a shock can sometimes bring... I realized something. Something terrible. I was in love with Jack.

I clutched his coat closer to myself and turned in my seat, "Jack," I began... and then stopped. What I wanted to say was, "I'm so sorry. I love you." But somehow, the words just couldn't come out. I wanted them to. But I didn't want them to. They were stuck in my throat and I think a pick-axe would have had a hard time dislodging them. Instead, I said, "I think I'm going crazy."

Despite the circumstances, his eyes crinkled in amusement, "I've known that for years."

I sputtered a laugh that only sounded a bit hysterical. "I mean it this time," I insisted. "I think I just saw Abigail's murder." I scratched my head, "Well, maybe not the murder, but the events leading up to the murder. Or, at least, the car accident before the murder. Well. Maybe there wasn't a murder. Maybe she died of her wounds and..."

Jack's lips very effectively cut off the rest of my sentence. His kiss was as warm as I would have expected it to be... had I ever taken the time to contemplate what kissing Jack would feel like. And then, for the next few blissful minutes, I forgot everything else other than... Jack.

When he pulled back, he gently pushed the wet hair back from my face, "I think I love you," he whispered, "even if you are crazy."

"That's good," I whispered back, "because I am beginning to think that perhaps I just might love you too." Huh. It didn't even take a pick-axe.

His kiss was even better that time.

It was sometime later when he said, "Let's get you back to the house, and then you can tell me everything that happened."

"But, Jack," I clutched at his sleeve.

He patted my hand and put poor Mr. Darcy into drive. "We'll talk at the house," he said, "after you are warm and dry."

"Thank you," I said gratefully, hoping that he understood my full meaning.

He shot me a crooked smile as we drove the last half mile to Raspberry Hill. "You're welcome," he said softly.

CHAPTER 31

B ut we didn't talk. There wasn't time. As soon as I walked through the door, I was overwhelmed by Carolyn and Molly. Despite Jack's protests, they exclaimed over my appearance, scolded me for leaving and being late… and reminded me that Knit Night was beginning in less than a half an hour. I was sent upstairs to change, and Jack enlisted Ryan's help in making sure the doors were securely locked – the exception, of course, being the French doors that went into the yarn shop.

Standing in the bathroom, I looked at myself in the mirror. Did I look different? They say that love can change your appearance, but, if you asked me, I looked the same as always. Bummer. And then… I remembered his smile and the way that I felt when he was… and I smiled… and as I smiled, I caught another glimpse of myself in the mirror. There it was. Yes, there it was. A new spark. A new light. In me. How wonderful. And exciting.

I changed my sweater and went down the stairs with a happier heart than I had, quite possibly ever had. Maybe I was going crazy, but Jack didn't seem to care. Isn't that amazing? He loved me. And the doors were locked. Life was good.

Molly sidled up next to me, "Maybe you should have changed your pants too," she muttered. "You're just a little…" she wrinkled her nose, "dirty."

"Fiddlesticks," I said happily, "what's a little dirt?"

She waved a friendly greeting at an entering knitter, "Don't forget your nametag," she called to her, and then turned to me. "What happened to you anyway?"

"I think someone may have tried to kill me on the road up to Raspberry Hill," I said with a smile, enjoying her shocked look. "But everything is fine now."

Molly seemed to be having trouble getting her mouth to close, "And what is sticking out of the back of your pants?" she asked. Which was the last question I had expected to hear from her.

I spun, trying to see what was behind me. Oh! Mildred's diary. It seemed like a hundred years ago that I had stolen it.

I grinned unrepentantly at her, "That's just Mildred's diary," I said causally. "I stole it from her room this afternoon."

Her eyes were like saucers. "You stole Mildred's diary?" she demanded, incredulous. "I can't believe it."

I reached back and pulled out the leather-bound book. "Believe it," I said. "I just can't wait to open it."

Molly grabbed my arm and pulled me behind a very convenient bookcase full of yarn and we cracked open the book together.

How disappointing. There were no deep dark secrets. Just a bunch of old drawings all folded up together. We both sighed.

"Oops," I said.

She whacked me on the arm, "Oops?" she hissed. "Oops!? Is that all you have to say? You just stole some poor old lady's book of drawings for nothing and all you can say is… ooops?"

But, what else was there to say? I guess the question now was… how was I going to get them back to her? Well… upon consideration… that was really no problem, was it? I would just wait until dinnertime tomorrow. Ha. Easy! Which is exactly what I told Molly. From the look on her face, though, I don't think she was very impressed with me right now. Or, I could just mail them back to her. Anonymously, of course. Or maybe not. Maybe with a nicely worded note.

The ladies were having a great time at Knit Night. They filled all the seats that we had, which surprised me, but not Carolyn. Her eyes were gleaming with happy contentedness. And the ballroom never felt so beautiful. It was fairly glowing with life and happiness. Jack and Ryan were in the corner, to the great delight of Gertie and Old Mrs. Harrison. Carolyn was twirling in her knitted skirt for a group of ladies to admire. Yes, that's right. Carolyn had knitted her own skirt. Can you believe that? And it was adorable. She was quite proud of it, twirling it for everyone who would watch. It was hard to remember, sometimes, that she was a little old lady.

I sat behind the counter, enjoying the noise and bustle, embracing the safety of the room and the people in it. The events of an hour ago seemed so unreal now. If the memory of the voice did not haunt me still, I would think, sitting here, surrounded by friends (well – potential friends) that I had imagined the whole thing. Clearly, I had imagined the ill-fated last trip of Abigail Jeffries. It had felt so real, though. Was it possible that I had imagined the other as well? You know what? Before I moved here, I never ever realized that I had such a vivid imagination. I sighed and pulled out Mildred's book again.

I set the drawings out one by one. There were three of them. They seemed to be architectural drawings... like blueprints. I wondered about that. Why would the old bat be hiding ancient blueprints under her mattress? Had they been the blueprints to her cherished house? I studied them closely. Hey. What was that? That looked like... Whoa. I about fell off my chair. They were blueprints of Raspberry Hill.

I decided that this was more important than Knit Night, so I pulled the patterns off the counter and sank down to the floor behind it to study them further. Not only were they blueprints to the house... but there was something else too... there were shaded areas that I could not quite understand.

"What are you doing?" the voice came from over the counter, causing me to jump.

"Stop it," I hissed. "I've had enough scares for one night."

"It's just..." Molly's brow furrowed in concern, "I'm not quite sure what to do. Or who to tell."

I stared at her, "What are you talking about now?" I asked, annoyed. I wanted to go back to studying my plans.

"It's just..." she said again, "It's just... Gertie is missing."

CHAPTER 32

I gathered up the leather binding and the drawings and dragged Molly out through the café doors into the hallway by the kitchen. "What are you talking about?" I hissed. "How can she be missing?"

She shrugged helplessly, "I don't know," she insisted, "One minute she was here and the next minute she was just... gone."

"Well, she must have left," I said. "Gone out the door."

"No," Molly said, "Carolyn was by the door. She would have seen her leave."

"Not if she was busy twirling her skirt," I muttered.

Molly wisely ignored me. "The point is," Molly said, "She's gone. She came with Old Mrs. Harrison - and she's still here. None of the other knitters have left, so she must still be here somewhere." Her gaze turned puzzled, "Do you think that she's off exploring the house?"

"Could be," I said slowly. "But how did she get through the locked doors?"

Molly shrugged, "They were locked when I checked them. Maybe she picked the locks with a hairpin." Her gaze turned wistful, "I've always wanted to know how to do that."

"Well, we'd better go look for her," I said with a sigh, "before the others start suspecting something. Heaven knows that we don't need all those knitters in a panic looking for a lost little old lady."

"I'll start on this floor, if you do the second floor," Molly said, her lips twisting together. "Let's hope that we find her pottering about somewhere."

I tried stuffing the diagrams back into the journal, fumbling with the binding, and in my haste, it fell out of my hands and hit the floor. Molly scrambled to pick it up, "It would not do," she said, "to get caught with this." But this time, her expression was more amused than appalled. I was obviously corrupting her.

As she handed it back to me, I saw with dismay that the leather binding was coming undone. "Rats," I said, "now we've done it."

"Now *you've* done it," Molly pointed out wickedly. "She's going to notice that, for sure."

"She's an old lady," I argued. "Maybe she won't notice. We'll smear her glasses or something." I examined the cover, fingering the break. "Hey," I said, "what's this?"

"What is it?"

I pulled at the edging a little further, "Why, it's an old photograph, stuck in the lining. How strange"

Forgetting poor Gertie, we examined it eagerly.

It was three ladies, and judging by their clothes, it was about 30-some years ago. The lady in the middle was wearing a wedding dress. I flipped the photograph over, "A, R & M"

This must be a picture of Grandma Rose! Now, finally – I would know what my grandmother looked like! I was so excited. I studied the picture, trying to calm my shaking hands.

Time stopped. And I was frozen with it.

I sank to my rear in the middle of the hallway. The happy faces swam before my eyes. It was all so clear now. Well, clear and muddy. But, mostly clear.

Sorrow washed over me, and I have never felt such a wave of remorse and regret in my life. My heart felt like it was dying. I pressed the heels of my hands to my eyes to try to stem the tears that I knew were coming anyway.

Molly had yet to see. She pulled the photograph from my hand to study the smiling faces more closely. "Why!" she exclaimed. "That must be your Grandma Rose." She studied it a bit longer. "Strange," she muttered, tilting her head slightly, "your Grandma Rose looks a lot like…" her face rose from the photo in confused wonder.

A ragged sob tore from my throat, "It is," I said, through the tears running down my face. "Grandma Rose is…"

Molly sank down next to me, her arm coming around my shoulders. "Gertie," she whispered. "But how?"

"I don't know," I admitted, trying, for the second time tonight, to get control of my emotions. "But I know what it means. My Grandma Rose is alive. And she… never told…she pretended…" I cried harder. "I can't believe…"

"I'm so sorry," Molly whispered. "I don't know what to say…"

I took pity on her and, with an enormous effort of will, took my feelings about Gertie, wrapped them up and stuffed them down. Deep down. "That explains how she got out, then," I whispered, "she has the keys. This is her house." I wiped my eyes again… this time, for the last time… and looked at the picture with as much objectiveness as I could, "That's clearly Mildred, although time didn't improve her any, did it?"

Molly's laugh was a bit forced. "Be nice," she said without any conviction. She pointed to the third person, "So that's Abigail?"

Poor Molly. She still had no idea. "Yes," I said with a sigh that came from my soul, "It is. And it's Mildred."

"Mildred?" Molly exclaimed, "No it's not. We saw Mildred at SunnySide, remember?"

"Not that Mildred," I said. "That's my Mildred. She's my ghost." I thought for a moment, "But I think she was really pretending to be Grandma Rose… living here at Raspberry Hill all these years."

Molly stared at me hard without blinking, "Abigail was pretending to be Mildred, pretending to be Rose?" she asked. She studied me carefully. "I think I had better go get Jack," she said slowly.

"You just stay where you are," I hissed. "We'll get Jack later." I pulled the drawings out to study them again. "What do you think these dark spots are?"

Her eyes brightened, "Wow," she said. "These are drawings of Raspberry Hill, aren't they?"

I was feeling a bit impatient with her, "What I think is that these dark areas are secret passageways," I said. "What do you think?"

She looked surprised but bent her head to study the drawings again. "Yes," she muttered, "I would have to agree with you on that." She turned her still-astonished gaze to me, "But how did you guess that?"

"Well," I said, "how else do you think Mildred... or Abigail... or whatever her name is... how do you think that her head got into your bathroom closet?"

Her mouth made the perfect little "O" shape.

"I'm going to go find Gertie," I said grimly. "You go back and pretend everything is all right so that Carolyn doesn't start to worry." Molly, unfortunately, looked a bit too frayed. "Try to act normal, will you?" I said, with a smile that I didn't feel. "I have a feeling Gertie has just gone to have a reunion with her old friend."

"Abigail?" Molly asked, obviously still confused. "I mean Mildred? Err... Rose?"

"At this point, it's too confusing to explain," I said. "We'll discuss it later."

She scurried away, and I studied the plans. If I was reading these drawings right (which I hoped I was), then there was a passageway that ran alongside the ballroom. Another one ran from my bedroom (and probably had at least one exit in my closet – which I now knew), it looked like it came out in the closet in Molly's bathroom (which explains the head Molly saw... she probably caught Mildred coming out of the secret passageway – an experience quite startling to both of them, I'm sure. But where would Mildred (or Abigail... or Grandma Rose... whatever...) go to meet Gertie (or Grandma Rose.... whatever)? My fingers traced the shadowed areas. It looked like there was even a tunnel that connected the basement of Raspberry Hill to the basement of the guest house. Perhaps there was some poetic justice to that? If it wasn't falling down in ruins, then maybe... just maybe... the scene of the crime would also be the scene of the reunion?

I took a deep breath and made my way as quickly as I could to the basement, running down the rickety stairs much faster than was safe. Next to the furnace... there was an old coal bin... which wasn't a coal bin. Once you knew that, it was easy enough to find the door and pop it open. The tunnel was quite low, and even though I could fit without bending over, there was an overwhelming feeling of claustrophobia. Because I am a forward thinker, I had grabbed a flashlight... without it... I don't think I would have had the courage to continue my journey.

The smell was quite awful. Dank and stuffy, reeking of things that we won't speak of. I just hoped that nothing either furry or slithery would happen upon me. I'm not quite sure what I would do if that happened. I think I walked forever. Just when I thought I would die of the smell and the stuffiness and the despair that seemed to accompany this cursed tunnel, I reached the other end. A door loomed up in front of me. A wooden door. I wondered what was on the other side. And what would I say to them? To her? Just as I was turning the handle, the thing that I dreaded happening – happened.

Something furry attacked my leg.

Shrieking, I dropped my flashlight... and I fell backward, trying to get away from... good grief... Abraham Lincoln!

I don't think I was ever so happy to see a dog in my whole life. I picked him up and actually kissed his little ugly head. "What are you doing down here, huh?" I asked, stroking his fur. "You crazy..."

He wiggled to be put down, so I obliged him. Perhaps he did not like doggie kisses. He gave a little snuffly-sound and ran back the way he came. Well. That was a short visit. Somehow, though, he had lifted my spirits, and I felt a little more prepared for what I knew was going to happen.

I scooped up the flashlight again, gritted my teeth and stepped through the door.

The door creaked open with a great, sinister groan. Great. So much for sneaking in. Although, with the way that my teeth were chattering... and my hands were shaking... and my mind was whirring... I doubted that too much sneaking would have been possible anyways. I felt sick. And furious. But mostly sick. I don't know why. I mean... obviously Grandma Rose had no desire to keep in contact with me. I knew that. But somehow, I had been okay with that when I thought she was a poor old recluse, unjustly accused of murder, rattling around like a sad little pea in this great big monstrosity of a house. The fact that she was alive, robust and clearly not homebound, rather changed things, don't you agree?

The basement of the guest house was relatively clutter-free compared to that of Raspberry Hill. It must not have been used a great deal. Personally, I would have used the guest house as storage (if no one was living there) and kept the big house nice and clean. You're right. I'm stalling.

There was a strong smell of smoke down here. It was rather... cloying. After the dark and dank of the tunnel, and the smell of this old basement... I longed for a breath of fresh air. So far, there was no sign of Gertie – or Mildred... or... you know what I mean. I was sure they wouldn't be upstairs... that just wouldn't be safe for two little old ladies (or me).

Then, I saw it. There was a glow coming from the far end of the basement along the floor. There must be a separate room. I walked with purpose, not even bothering to be quiet anymore and shoved the door open. It was almost worth it – seeing the looks on their faces.

They jumped apart, shrieking just a little... Abigail clutching her heart dramatically.

"Alright, ladies," I said in my most pleasant voice, "the game is over."

They looked between each other nervously. I sighed, feeling old. "I know who you are," I said, looking at my *ghost*, "and I know who you are too," I said, facing Gertie. "And I want some answers."

"Gracious," Abigail said, her gaze wavering between me and Rose, "You look a little bit..."

"Mad?" I supplied helpfully, "Angry? Sad? Disappointed?" I scowled at the two of them, "Pick one."

"I'm sorry..." Rose began.

I held up my hand, "You know what?" I said. "I've heard that from Celia all my life. I'm sick of it. I don't think this family even knows what the word means. You're sorry?" I sneered, "Sorry for what? Sorry for pretending to be dead? Sorry for..."

Rose put a hand on my arm, and I pulled back, "I'm sorry for everything I've done," she said, with tears in her eyes. "I'm so sorry for all of the pain that I've caused."

"Yeah," I said in the hardest voice that I could find, "I'm sorry too. I'm really sorry for all of those tears that I cried for you."

"But..." Rose began, stepping forward once more.

"Awwwww.... Isn't this sweet?" the voice came from behind and had the three of us jumping. I spun. I saw the gun – and the gleam in his eye. Somehow, I had felt all along it was him. And then I knew. I knew we were in big, big trouble.

CHAPTER 33

"I should have known it was you," Abigail spat. "You were a rotten as a little boy too."

Gracious. We sounded like an outdated version of *Scooby Doo*.

"Now, now," Finn said with fake politeness, pulling the rope that bound us all together tight, "that's not very nice."

"What do you want?" I asked, trying to catch my breath... as unfortunately, the rope ran right over my chest. "Why did you chase me up Raspberry Hill tonight? What do you want?"

He pulled the rope tighter to finish the knot. "What do I want?" he hissed. "What do I want?" His eyes glittered in the lantern light. "I want you and your miserable little family to leave Raspberry Hill. I want Rose to sign the deed over to me."

I snorted. "You don't want much, do you?"

Abigail narrowed her eyes, "So it *was* you," she said. "Trying to scare me to death." She tilted her head a bit, "It must have been quite a blow for you when I died." Her smile was just a little bit terrible, "I bet you didn't care a thing for my new will, did you?"

"We had a deal," he said through his teeth, "and you backed out."

She shook her head, "We had no deal. Your father and I had an understanding. That's all."

"You were supposed to leave Raspberry Hill to me," he hissed. "To our family. You got what you wanted, and then it was our chance."

"You knew?" I demanded. "You knew that Abigail was pretending to be Grandma Rose?"

"Well," he said, rocking back on his heels, "not at first. Not until my father was dying. And then he passed on his 'big secret' to me."

"So whose body did they find?" I asked, curious, despite myself. I squirmed a little... being tied up in between two old ladies was not very comfortable. Too bad they weren't just a bit "fluffier". Grannies were supposed to be soft and...Abigail's' skinny elbow was really starting to hurt.

"I bet she used my father-in-law's old skeleton," Rose said, "I do believe that back then they were real skeletons."

Abigail sounded a little putout, "I thought it was quite clever," she said.

"And then you stayed around so that you could play the ghost?" I demanded. "Why?"

"It was never my intent to be a ghost," she said indignantly. "I don't believe in ghosts." She tried to wiggle so that she could see me, "Why do you think I changed my will and tried to make you live here?"

"It boggles my mind," I said dully. "I have no idea."

She sighed deeply, "The regrets of the old are crippling," she said softly. "I knew Finn was planning something. I kept getting those letters and then the vandalism... and the other things... I knew my masquerade was going to be cut short. I wanted to tell the truth. To be honest, I've wanted to tell the truth for years and years now. But I didn't know how. And I didn't know what kind of people you were. So, I thought I could watch you. And then, somehow, I could confess and...."

"And what?" I said sarcastically. "We would forgive you? We'd all live happily ever after?"

Out of the corner of my eye, I saw Abigail flinch. I desperately squashed the little sprout of guilt. Turning my head, I looked to see what Rose was doing, and I was surprised to see two tears rolling down her cheeks. The sprout grew about two inches bigger.

"So what are you going to do now?" I asked Finn.

Before he could open his mouth to speak, his radio went off. It sounded like the deputies were wondering where he was. He muttered an expletive under his breath and then looked at us, smiling in a way that gave me serious doubts about his current state of mind. "Now don't you ladies go anywhere," he said smoothly. "I have a few things to take care of and then I'll be right back." He disappeared swiftly, and we heard the door to the tunnel open and close.

We spent the next few minutes wiggling and twisting and turning, but it was to no avail. Finn obviously knew how to tie knots. Plus, we were tied to some type of pipe. I huffed. "I don't think we're getting out of this," I said quietly.

"Me either," Rose admitted.

"You always were a quitter," Abigail said, sneering slightly.

"So," I said quickly to keep the two old ladies from starting a fight, "since I don't have a good feeling about what's going to happen when Finn gets back, I'd like to know what happened all those years ago." I thought they, at least, owed me that.

"The day of the..." Rose faltered.

"Accident?" I supplied helpfully.

Her voice brightened a bit, "Yes, accident. The day of the accident, Abigail and I had a dreadful fight. I do remember throwing a vase at her, as a matter of fact."

"You missed," Abigail said. She sounded a bit smug.

"Only because I wasn't trying to hit you," Rose continued. "I got a call later that night from Mildred saying Abigail was coming back up to continue the fight, so I ran down the road to stop her. It was raining and thundering, and I shouldn't have been out on the road. Abigail came up the hill too fast. She swerved, to avoid hitting me. I... I..." Rose's voice faltered momentarily, "I thought she was dead. So I ran."

Abigail sighed. "Don't you think that we owe her the truth?" she asked.

"That is the truth," Rose said simply.

"The truth with the whole truth left out," Abigail replied. She leaned forward to see me more clearly. "I believe," she said slowly, holding my eye, "that Rose ran because she saw you."

I felt like I had been kicked. I certainly could not breathe. "What are you talking about?"

"You didn't know, did you?" Abigail asked, so gently that tears sprang to my eyes. "You were here. You saw the whole thing happen."

I gasped, the room spinning. Here. I was here. I blinked my eyes rapidly, willing myself not to cry. Strangely enough, it made sense. The voices in the ballroom. The scene on the driveway. They were so real to me... because they were real to me.

"So," I said in a shaky voice, "I ran out after my grandma, and I saw what happened." The horror of it overwhelmed me, and I stared straight ahead. "I can't believe it," I said. "You left me out there. I was all by myself and you left me." Somehow, this was the worst.

"Of course not," Rose said, sounding outraged. "Your mother was there. She had followed you out. She took you back in." Unbelievable. "I told her that I would take care of things and for you to go back inside. You were..." she paused, "quite upset. But when you and your mother left, I found that I didn't have the courage I needed to face you again. I was a murderer. I ran. I've been running ever since." I turned to look at her, and she looked down in shame.

"But I don't understand," I protested. "There's no way Celia would have believed that Abigail was you."

"Ha!" Abigail said. "That's where you are wrong. After all, we were the same size and shape..."

"I," Rose said primly, "of course, was a shade slimmer."

Abigail snorted, "Celia saw your mother slip and fall and hit the front of the car. So, she knew her face was bruised. Mine was bruised by the steering wheel. The bleeding was quite terrible too. It was, really, all too easy... a few scarves... dim lighting..." she sighed sadly. "All too easy."

"That explains everything except why you pretended to be Grandma Rose," I said, my mind fluttering.

"I don't know," Abigail said slowly. "I didn't really *mean* to. It just happened that way. I woke up, in my car, feeling quite disoriented and lost. I remembered hitting Rose with my car. I thought, for a few horrible moments, that I had killed her. I stumbled up to Raspberry Hill, but she wasn't there. Your mother called out to me, thinking that I was your grandmother." Abigail shook her head helplessly, "I've always wanted to live at Raspberry Hill," she said softly. "I'm so ashamed of the things I've done. I tried to get George to marry me, but no – he married Rose. Rose! He didn't even know the slightest thing about her. I was so angry. And then, when he died – I accused Rose of…"

"Let's not speak of it," Rose said softly. "Things said in anger should only be forgotten."

"And Finn's father…"

"Was my cousin. He eventually figured it out and confronted me. But, at that point… it would have been, shall we say *awkward* for everyone involved if the truth came out. So, he let it go… and I promised to will the house to the family."

"But then Finn started sending you letters?" That made no sense.

Rose cleared her throat delicately. I craned my neck to stare at her. "YOU?"

"Well," she said, "I like to keep up on life here in Springgate. It was such a happy time of my life. They started putting their newspaper online a few years ago, and I started reading them. When I saw the "incidents" happening at Raspberry Hill, I had a moment of clarity. I realized, then, what had happened. I was so angry."

"Angry?" we both asked.

"Angry at myself. Angry at Abigail. Even angry at George for dying and starting all this in the first place."

I didn't want to think about that right now. Instead, I said, "So Finn started thinking you weren't serious about leaving the house to the family, so he starts trying to scare you into it…and, at the same time, you're receiving letters that threaten to reveal your true identity."

Abigail nodded. "I started feeling very… trapped. So, I had a new will made and then faked my death." For one moment, her eyes sparkled, "It was all very exciting."

"Only you would think to set a skeleton on fire," Rose jeered.

"Oh yeah?" Abigail said belligerently, "It worked, didn't it?" She lowered her voice conspiratorially, "I even put one of my rings on its finger." She looked around the basement wistfully, "It did seem such a shame to set this darling little house on fire, but I couldn't set Raspberry Hill on fire… and it was the only way I could think of to make people really think that I was dead."

There was an abrupt movement at the door, and for one glistening, beautiful moment, my heart dared to believe it was… but it wasn't. It was Finn.

"I really hate to interrupt this touching scene," he said, "but we have a few things we need to do…"

I blinked. Was that?? Abraham Lincoln trotted into the room behind Finn with all of the happy nonchalance of a dog that didn't have a care in the world. He plunked down in front of me and looked at the three of us quite seriously.

"I can't believe that mutt followed me," Finn exclaimed, making a movement with his foot. We all screamed, "Noooooo," and his foot stopped short of kicking the little fur ball, who now sprang to all fours, showing his teeth.

"Go home, Abraham Lincoln," I said urgently. "Go home." He tipped his head at me thoughtfully.

"That's right, Abraham Lincoln," Abigail said softly, fear still shining in her eyes. "Go home. Go back home."

There was a movement by the door. Just the slightest flickering of… something.

"I don't know what you're all so upset about," Finn said with a laugh. "It's not like you're going to be around much longer to care about what happens to some dumb dog."

I took a deep breath and prayed like I had never prayed before. I didn't see Finn's gun anywhere. So, I felt pretty safe with my new plan. "That's all right, Abe," I said deliberately and slowly. "We love you even if you are an ugly little dog."

I felt Abigail's breath catch and she stiffened… just as Abraham Lincoln stiffened. His little hairs began standing up on the back of his neck… and then… just as Finn was about to take a step closer… he erupted.

I knew what was going to happen. Finn, unfortunately, did not. "What the…!" he yelled as Abraham Lincoln startled everyone with his explosive barking and frantic running. Finn actually did a double step to instinctively avoid Abraham Lincoln's sharp little teeth as he rounded the little room for the second time. Finn's head swiveled to follow his progress… and Jack burst through the door, neatly knocking Finn to the ground in one blow. And, despite the fact that I was still tied up to two old ladies that I was more than a little bit angry at, Abraham Lincoln was on a rampage, and the Sherriff of Springgate was knocked out cold on the ground… I sighed happily.

CHAPTER 34

The deputies put former-Sherriff Finn into the squad car, still yelling and swearing. I was glad to see him go. What a total and complete rat. But... would he be a rat that got sent to jail? I wondered. After all, it's not like we had any proof... did we? I would have to talk it over with Jack later on. Speaking of Jack, it felt amazingly good to be standing next to him, his fingers tangled in mine. I peeked up at him, and he only half-smiled. He was still just a little... shall we say... miffed... that I had entered the tunnel alone.

"Let's go inside," I whispered. "It's cold out here."

Not that it was going to be that pleasant inside either. There were still two, no, make that three, other rats to deal with.

We found our little rats in the living room, huddled together on the couch. Celia was leaning over her mother, and Rose was talking urgently. I suddenly felt no need to speak to them right now, so I pulled on Jack's hand, and he followed me back to the ballroom.

Carolyn met us at the door, her eyes wide and worried. Molly hovered over her shoulder. "Is everything alright?" Carolyn asked, scanning my face.

"Everything is fine," I assured her, "We found *Gertie*... and a few other things, too."

From the look in Carolyn's eyes, I knew that she knew. "I'm sorry," she whispered, reaching forward and squeezing my hand.

"You knew." It wasn't an accusation. Just a simple statement. She nodded her head sadly. I remembered something. "You were going to tell me, weren't you? That afternoon."

"I'm so sorry, Natalie," she said, her eyes conveying the depth of her anguish. "I knew as soon as I saw Gertie. But, I didn't think it was my place, and…"

I shrugged, "It's fine, Carolyn," I said. It was amazing how sad and tired you could feel at the same time.

"I saw the Sherriff being taken away," Molly said in a low voice, "What was he…"

Great. Just what I needed. All the knitters in town knowing what had happened…I craned my neck to see what they were doing. Huh. Strange. They were just sitting and knitting and… talking… just as they had been the last time I had been in here. It seemed like hours ago, but I guess it wasn't even that long ago. "Weren't the other knitters upset?" I asked. "Or curious about why the Sherriff…"

Carolyn snorted in a very unladylike way. "They didn't even notice," she assured me. "They wouldn't notice if a semi-truck drove through the center of the room."

Knitters were crazy.

CHAPTER 35

I wish I could say that everything looked better in the morning. Jack had assured me that it would. Molly had too. But, I had lain awake all night and now that it was morning, I wasn't so sure. I dressed mechanically, brushing my teeth and combing my hair and went down the stairs with a strange feeling of trepidation.

Celia, Rose and Abigail sat around the table, eating breakfast, as Jack cracked another egg at the stove. Molly was nowhere to be seen. His smile was quick and welcoming, but his eyes were cautious. I knew what he was scared of. I had a feeling that the next few minutes were going to change all of our lives. One way or the other.

I sat down quietly, looking each one in the eye. In the bright morning sun, Rose and Abigail looked old. Celia had not bothered with any makeup this morning either, and the effect was rather refreshing. She looked open... and strangely... happy? I frowned as she reached out a hand to touch my arm. You would be very proud of me to know that I did not pull away. No sense in drama at this point. We had had enough of that to last ten lifetimes.

"I think you should know, Natalie," Abigail said timidly, not meeting my eyes, "that I said terrible things to your mother that night." Her voice choked slightly, "Terrible things that I can't even remember without wanting to die. I was mean. And vicious. And I threatened you. I think I was a bit... out of my mind... that night. I wanted you guys out of the house. I know that sorry isn't enough, and I can't..."

"It's my fault," Rose broke in. "I ran away. I ran away instead of facing what I had done. How could I have just left? I didn't even check to see if you were alive or dead. You looked dead. I could see one eye open and staring." I shuddered suddenly, knowing that we shared the same memory. "I ruined my life. I ruined my daughter's life. And I ruined my granddaughter's life." Tears ran down her face.

"No," Celia said fiercely, "I did that. I ran too. I thought Abigail was dead, and I left you to deal with it. I didn't even call the police. I didn't do anything." She turned to Abigail, "I had our bags packed even before you...before we... spoke."

I looked around at their faces. Each one was a picture of misery. And rightly so. I searched my soul for the anger I knew I should feel, and the words that I longed to say to each of them. And... I couldn't find them. Something deep in my heart splintered and broke. It felt good.

Rose pushed herself away from the table suddenly, "Well," she said, "I just stayed so that I could explain, but I can't explain. I was wrong and I wish I could take away all the pain that I caused, but I can't." Her eyes landed on Celia and then myself, wistfully, "I wish you two all the best." She began standing up.

"So you're just going to run away again?" someone asked.

Three (no - make that four – Jack had turned away from the stove) faces gaped at me in surprise. Oh dear. I think I just said that. I thought for a moment. I was right.

"I don't understand," Rose said slowly, "I thought you would want...."

"You thought I would want you to go away so that we'd never have to see you again?" I finished for her, keeping my face as blank as I could.

She nodded slowly, "Yes."

Celia's face crumpled, and she put a hand to her head. And, for the first time in my life, I thought that just maybe... Celia was being real. Another piece of ice fell away from my soul and melted deep inside of me.

I looked at my Grandma Rose seriously. "I think you're wrong," I said slowly. "I think you need to stay." I moved my gaze to Abigail, "I think you need to stay." I let my gaze drift slowly to my mother, "And I think you need to stay," I said softly.

"I don't want to stay if you leave," Celia sobbed. "I can't believe how I've behaved all your life… and I want…"

"You don't understand," I said gently. "I'm staying too." Celia's head shot up, tears still streaming down her cheeks.

"Why?" she whispered, "Why would you want to do that?"

"Because," I said, tears spilling down my own cheeks, "I think that we've all lived through the worst days of our lives. We've seen what it's like to live without each other and what it's like to hate each other. It hasn't done any of us any good. We can't live like that anymore. God doesn't want us to live like that. We've all hurt each other. It's over. And done. Now I think it's time for us to see what it's like to live if we all love ourselves and each other."

Rose put both hands over her face, "But how can I ever make up for what I've done?" she cried.

Abigail was crying too, "No," she sobbed, "It was me. I can never…"

I stood up and put an arm around each of them. "We're moving forward," I said firmly, "and not looking back. This is a big house, and I've got great plans for it. I'm going to need all of your help." I chanced a glance back at Jack, who undoubtedly had a piece of dirt or something in his eye, "Besides," I said, feeling inexplicably happy and light (I guess that is what love and forgiveness do to a person), "we've got a lot of work to do before the wedding."

And, with Jack sputtering and grinning behind me, I was enveloped, at last, in a hug with my grandmother. And then Abigail. And then Celia. And when Jack put his arms around the four of us, I don't think I've ever felt so content.

It was much, much later, after we had all had breakfast and were sprawled in different chairs and couches in the living room, that it occurred to me. Something that had been niggling at my brain for a while now.

"How did you do it?" I asked Abigail. She looked up at me, and I smiled so that she would know I was being friendly, "How did you become such a good ghost?"

"Well," she said, a mischievous smile spreading across her wrinkles, "it wasn't really that hard. The first time you saw me... you didn't even realize that you were looking at my reflection in a mirror. I was actually standing across the room. The mirror was dirty, I guess, and old, which gave it a more realistic effect."

"You used the secret passageways to visit me in my room," I said. "I've figured that out."

"Gracious," Abigail said, "that Molly sure did give me a turn when she found me in the closet."

I giggled despite myself. "She only saw your head," I said. "You scared her half to death."

Abigail looked serious, "I'll have to apologize to her later," she said softly.

"Well," I said, still smiling, "I don't know. A little ghost now and then does us all good." I thought for a moment, "But what about the breaking glass and the doorbell and the voices?"

She shook her head, "That wasn't me," she said darkly. "That was the Sherriff. He knew all the passageways too," she reminded me, "because he had Mildred's help. At first, I think he came to look for me to see if I was still alive. And then, I think, he saw the benefits of trying to scare you out of here too."

I sighed. If we had been a "normal" family, that might have worked. One more thought hit me, "But how did you get your face up in the mirror in the ballroom?"

Her face brightened, "That was pretty tricky, wasn't it?" she crowed. "I had to Google that one."

I had no words for that, so I turned my attention to Grandma Rose. "Something else is bothering me," I said. "Is there anything you want to tell me, Grandma Rose?"

She squirmed uncomfortably and shot a quick, guilty look at my mother. "What?" she asked.

I took a good, hard look at her, "When I met you at Crabapple Yarns, I liked you right away. Then, later, when we were talking about knitting… I said that you reminded me of the person who had taught me how to knit." A flush was creeping up her neck, "What do you think about that, Grandma Rose?"

She rolled her eyes, "Old ladies all look the same," she began, but then she sighed. "No. I'm done with lying and pretending…" She fluttered her hands helplessly as if she didn't know how to continue.

"You taught me how to knit," I said softly, "didn't you?"

She nodded her head miserably, "I did. And I also was your lunch lady in the 5th grade, and I baked you cookies when you lived in that apartment in Ohio… and…"

Celia and I stared at her in wonderment, "That's right," I said slowly, "you were there. I don't know how you did it, but you were there…" I thought for a moment, "You were there for me so many times."

I didn't think I was capable of crying anymore, but, obviously, I was wrong.

"I got very good at disguises," she admitted. "I followed the two of you almost everywhere. I lost you a couple of times, but I always found you again. I had to. I had to see you…" her voice broke, and before I knew it… Celia and I and Grandma Rose were hugging again. And it wasn't awful. Not even a little.

Later that night, as Jack and I sat cuddled together on the sofa, listening to Abigail and Rose argue cheerfully about who Abraham Lincoln should sleep with, I realized something. I was happy. It was such a strange emotion, that I almost didn't even recognize it. But I was. I was happy. Happy like I had never been before. Ever. I was happy living in a house that could be haunted – but wasn't. I was happy living here with my *family* – the strangest thing ever. And even though we didn't know what was going to happen with Sherriff Finn, or if the yarn shop would be able to move back downtown, or… how things were going to work out… I was feeling very content with life at the moment.

"You were right, Jack," I said suddenly, speaking into his shirt, too comfortable to move.

"About what?" he asked lazily.

"God does always have a good plan."

"Of course I was right," he replied, sounding just a bit indignant.

Then I realized something else.

"Celia never lied to me about that, either, Jack," I said suddenly. "She was totally right too."

He ran a hand down my hair, "Right about what?"

"Grandma Rose *was* a corker."

COMING IN 2019!

THE KNITPICKER

A Crabapple Yarns Mystery
Jaime Marsman

"Nothing can wait like an untold secret. And it's possible that the secrets themselves know the most terrible secret… that just because you are invisible doesn't mean that you're not there. It doesn't mean that someone can't by sheer coincidence, stumble upon you. And, with each year that passes, they grow just a little bit bigger. Just a little bit deadlier. And, still, they wait."
– Molly Stevenson, Amelia Tartan Contest Entry

Amelia Tartan is coming to town. Never before has the little town of Springgate hosted such a celebrated author, and, in honor of her coming, a book contest has been announced. Molly and Natalie are in hot competition to write a mystery story worthy of the skills of Amelia Tartan, when Molly gets the regrettable curse of…writer's block.

To her horror and dismay, her self-admittedly brilliant opening, detailing the lives of secrets and theorizing that the goal of every secret is to be heard, is now languishing and withering in the hot sun of her own self-doubt and criticism… and, worse, she now sees secrets everywhere…Carolyn. Ryan. Natalie.

Even Mrs. Goldmyer. Is it possible that Mrs. Goldmyer has been hiding a deep and terrible secret for years and years? Is it possible that Mrs. Goldmyer is an… axe murderer? What started as a humorous hypothesis, soon becomes all too frighteningly real. Deadly real. Because, somehow, Molly has stumbled upon an invisible secret with feet sunk deep in the past and rotten, gnarled fingers firmly gripping the present. Some secrets, it seems, should stay buried.

PSSSSSTT...

Hey, friend... did you find the secret code somewhere in this book that gets you a free knitting pattern? Better check it out! Hint: It's not on this page!

JAIME MARSMAN

Writer. Knitter. Daydreamer.
It's amazing, isn't it? Twenty-six humble letters in the alphabet.
By themselves... not very impressive. And yet, those tiny things
are put together in endless combinations and change the world.
Every day... every day... they change your world. That's a lot of
power. The same is true with knitting. One single (really, really
long) strand of yarn could be anything... a sweater, a scarf... a
turtleneck for a flag pole... and it's this endless combination of
words and fiber that inspire Jaime both as a writer and as a
knitwear designer for Live.Knit.Love. Her biggest wish for you
is that you, too, would use your powers for good, realize the joy of
creating, and follow your own dream and become who you are
supposed to be... YOU.
And no one else.

Made in the USA
Columbia, SC
30 December 2018